VALHALLA

ARI BACH

Published by
Harmony Ink Press
5032 Capital Circle SW
Suite 2, PMB# 279
Tallahassee, FL 32305-7886
USA
publisher@harmonyinkpress.com
http://harmonyinkpress.com

This is a work of fiction. Names, characters, places, and incidents either are the product of author imagination or are used fictitiously, and any resemblance to actual persons, living or dead, business establishments, events, or locales is entirely coincidental.

ISBN: 978-1-62798-718-9
Library ISBN: 978-1-62798-720-2
Digital ISBN: 978-1-62798-719-6

Printed in the United States of America
Second Edition
February 2014
First Edition published by Ari Bach: August 2010, March 2012.

Library Edition
May 2014

Chapter I: Kyle

OF THE million people in Kyle City, there was none so aimless as Violet MacRae. That's not to say she walked into walls or spoke in tangents, only that she lacked a purpose in life. Every night since she could speak, her parents asked her the same question: "What do you want to be when you grow up?" They would have asked even earlier, but this was the civilized world and children didn't get their vocal cords until they proved they knew when not to use them. Violet didn't get hers until she was three. At seventeen and a half, she had just passed her adulthood tests, and that old question was more pressing.

On the night of January 3, 2230, Violet and her parents stood on the deck of their apartment in Arcolochalsh, her native arcology. They watched the demolition of Skye Bridge 193 floors below. The decaying concrete monstrosity that had linked the Isle of Skye to mainland Scotland for the last 235 years was finally obsolete: Any vehicle that could jump its way past the wall of skyscrapers to the sea could easily jump the water itself. The bridge's destruction by explosives was marked by great celebration and pageantry, though it could have been accomplished at less cost by hiring a four-year-old to kick the thing. Not a minute after the bridge fell, June, Violet's mother, used the impressive spectacle to push Violet toward a career.

"How about demolitions?"

It wasn't bad compared to her usual suggestions. Violet's mom had recommended careers in everything from xenobiology to cosmetology, somehow managing to avoid the mention of a single job Violet could stand considering. Demolitions seemed almost tolerable until the stink of sulfur and concrete dust made its way past the filter pumps up to their nostrils. Violet didn't need to say no; the toxic cloud said it for her.

The trio walked indoors to escape the air and eat dinner. As her father closed the door, he was already planning a new tactic.

"Is there any place you want to visit?" he asked, "Any sights you want to see?"

Violet knew the question for what it was but appreciated the subtlety. She tried to think.

"The aurora borealis," she said. "Maybe the corona from orbit. Oh, and I want to see snow."

Having grown up in northwestern Scotland, Violet had never seen snow in person, only online. There it lacked the sparkle, the painful cold, and the underfoot crunch of the genuine article. She had learned in class that it was once a common sight all over Scotland. And she'd spent some of her free time looking at simulations of the far north, where snow still fell and people had to wear clothes all year round just to stay warm.

"Maybe you should get into solar science," suggested her mom.

Tracking photons was dull enough, but science meant working online. Violet had spent most of her life online, logged in to school. She wanted to live her life in the real world, doing something more physical.

"I'd rather fix zoo robots or fly trucks through the desert," she joked.

Her mom laughed. "How about sports?"

Now there was an idea, but Violet's interest was short-lived. Violet didn't care who could jump highest or run fastest. All the best sports were online anyway. Boxing and bullfighting and death-match wrestling had all been reduced to online versions that dared not let any real harm come to their champions, or animals. Even synthetic beasts with advanced enough artificial intelligence were gaining protective legislation. Sports had no real stakes, nothing to be ventured or gained. She wanted something meaningful but feared to say so. If she admitted she wanted a meaningful job, her dad would push his own choice yet again.

Nelson MacRae was a police officer and proud of it. When Violet was very young, that meant she heard tales of yakuza wars and Orange

Gang massacres, and even some stories about the mysterious Cetacean Divisionists and the dreaded Hall of the Slain. Of course she grew out of believing in such monsters. Her father's stories lost their mystery when pirates were revealed to be common net thieves and monsters turned out to be no more than ordinary humans who had engineered and modified their bodies beyond recognition.

Violet liked how her dad was respected by people around the arcology. He looked impressive in uniform, though he rarely wore it. She might have wanted to be a cop herself but to her shame, she couldn't apply. When she'd taken the maturity tests she ranked a twenty-nine on the VVPS (Verhoeven Violent Predilection Scale). Police specs demanded ranks under twenty-five. If she were one point higher, that would have meant neurorecalibration. Luckily, after years of having her test scores reported to her parents, the maturity test offered adult citizens their first private results. Violet didn't want her parents to know the real reason she couldn't be a cop, so she feigned disinterest in the job.

Her VVPS score was no surprise to her. Kids used to mock her angry demeanor often in the arcology playgrounds. The mockery made her want to rip the lips off their laughing faces. Such violent thoughts were relayed to the supervision programs through the net link antenna behind her ear, resulting in a lecture about violence from the nanny programs. She'd heard lecture 12D so often she knew it by heart: "Good kids don't think that way," it concluded. "Only bad little girls want to hurt people." She let every lecture go in one ear and out the other without a word of dissent. Dissent just triggered lecture 14B. Ignoring the words did no harm, she thought. But after so many lectures, something eroded its way into her subconscious. Not that she decided to be a good kid. She just came to think she was no more than a bad little girl.

So from time to time, she acted like one. More than once she had been logged out of class early with a note of bad conduct. Sometimes she would get into fights with other students. A fight between two children's avatars in a virtual classroom wasn't much to see, but it was enough to get them punished. They were punished by (what else?) a lecture from the teaching program. It was a gentle AI for kids, so they were never harsh, just horribly demeaning. Then after class she'd get the same lecture from her mom, in a voice even softer yet somehow more insulting. Sometimes it seemed to her that every adult and program in the world existed to talk down to her, except one. Her dad never gave her the lectures. He would just ask what happened, and sometimes she caught a hint of amusement hidden behind his eyes. He never even reprimanded her for playing games in class; he just thought it was funny she played Othello during a lesson on Shakespeare.

Violet was also plagued by the Lecture's elder sibling, the Apology. Whenever an incident involved another kid, she had to cough up a few apologetic words. When it involved an adult, the words were doubled and often dictated by her mother, thus resembling one of her lectures. To apologize was the ultimate insult, a lecture forced into her own mouth. But at long last, the days of lectures and apologies were at an end. She was an adult now. She was allowed all the privileges, rights, and responsibilities of a citizen. She could vote, work, hire, receive pay, pay taxes, own property, apply to own a company, fornicate, marry, adopt, apply to give birth, apply for military service, apply for apprentice education, file a lawsuit, enter adult zones online and off, commit suicide, drink, smoke, caffeinate, use adult-rated drugs, and best of all, if she did something wrong, she could go to jail for it instead of hearing another damn lecture. And she had to find a job.

"I've got it! How about carpet pattern design?" said her mom.

At times like this Violet envied programs and robots. Sometimes she wished she were just an AI. They had no choices before them, no field of a million options, no questions about their future. They had a purpose. They were designed for it. To Violet, it seemed a flaw that humans were made with none in mind.

Her dad appeared ready to suggest another line of work when she smelled something strange. It wasn't the debris cloud outside but a hot metallic smell. It was coming from the front door. Violet turned her head and looked across the apartment to see that there was no door. It had been melted off its hinges. Her dad saw it too and cursed loudly.

"Get Violet out of here! Get out now!"

Where the door had been, there were three men in orange hats and orange business suits coming in. There were two tall, tough men and one fat, ugly thug with a slack jaw. Her mom took her by the arm but had no chance to escape with her. One of the men already had a microwave pistol aimed at them.

"Do not move, not any of you," said the thug in a Dansk accent.

"Herr Kray," demanded her father, "what is this?"

"You know exactly what this is, Nelson. We know who you are, Officer MacRae."

"Hrothgar, I don't know what you think you—"

Then her father was dead. Violet had never seen a microwave go off, but she knew it when she saw it. A black burn mark just appeared on his chest, over his heart. She knew that a beam had just burnt through his ribs, and in an instant he was gone. She knew it happened. She didn't go into denial. She would deal with it all when she was safe. The microwave was pointing at her and her mom.

"Do not move or speak," said Kray. Violet stayed frozen. She could feel her mom behind her shaking, holding her tightly. The thug waved to the third man, who took a small pack from his belt. From it he produced a nail gun. Then Violet realized what was coming. Her dad had told her once how the Orange Gang crucified its enemies. She'd never believed it before, but it didn't surprise or scare her now. She simply knew the likely course of events. She was keenly aware of every move the men made and aware that her mom was growing frightened and enraged. It occurred to Violet as strange that she was not scared too.

She watched Hrothgar Kray and the other man take hold of her father, preparing to nail him to the wall. Her mom couldn't stand it. She shouted out. Violet didn't hear what she meant to shout; the gunman was too quick. As soon as sound waves passed her lips, he shot her. Violet felt the hot air pass over her head. She smelled her mother's skin burn, and she did not move. It wasn't fear that held her still: She stood knowing that if she moved, she would be shot as well. She heard her mom's body flop back to the floor, then all was silent. Herr Kray looked to Violet. She stood still and expressionless. She knew he was deciding if she should live or die. The gunman waited for the order. Violet gave him nothing to inspire her demise. Kray quietly turned his back, leaving the gunman to keep an eye on her as he knelt down to her father's body.

The second man came to his side and helped him with the corpse. They tried to prop him up to the wall, but Kray was too short, and he let the arm slip. Her dad's corpse fell halfway to the floor. The gunman turned to see if they needed help. For a fraction of a second, he took his eyes from Violet and let his microwave drift a few centimeters off target. In that instant Violet showed an extraordinary skill she never knew she had.

Through the entire episode she had remained oddly, totally detached. The emotional impact of her family's death didn't register so much as the acute awareness of how it had happened. She saw how the gunman had unlocked his weapon and how he pushed a key on its side while pulling the trigger to fire. She saw how they were struggling with her father's body. She knew that behind her, her mother had fallen in a position that could trip one of the men if he were not careful. She knew with utter clarity that for the moment all three men had their eyes off her. This was all a defense mechanism, one that separated the hysterical, panicked fool from the calm and able. Her dad had told her ages ago how some victims wept and shook during a traumatic event and how others became strong enough to lift a car and focused sharply to fight at their best. That focus was now introducing itself to Violet.

She knew as soon as the man's eyes were turned that they might not turn again. She knew that though all of them were likely armed, only one had his microwave ready, and that if she were shot by the small nail gun, at this distance it wouldn't be fatal, not immediately. She knew that there was no way they could let her live after this, and only briefly did she wonder why Kray hadn't ordered her death a second ago. It only took her another instant to decide what to do. The gunman was standing within a meter of her. His finger was off the trigger. His grip looked loose. She put that to a test and grabbed it. She was wrong; his grip was quite firm. Now that he knew what she was doing, her element of surprise was at an end. She thought it best to surprise him further by twisting the weapon away from herself and toward the man with the nail gun. That proved a good idea when the microwave went off and fried the man's eyes out.

7

Violet saw that Kray was slow in recognizing the threat. The gunman was putting all he had into wresting the microwave away from her, so she kicked him very hard in the shin. As she expected he shouted in pain, but he did not let go. So she kicked him in the other shin. He still didn't let go, but he did fall to his knees, and that put his testicles so close to her foot that she kicked without thinking. That loosened his grip. She pulled the weapon from him and moved it to her other hand, letting go of the barrel and gripping the handle firmly, finger on the trigger. She was new at gunplay, so she tested what she had seen by pressing the same key he had and pulling the trigger. She was careful to test it in the safest possible direction, in this case at the gunman's forehead. A black burn mark erupted on his skin, and he fell limp and silent. Violet was content with this test and used her newfound skill on the blind man, who fell onto Kray.

She shot at the thug. Using his former companion as a shield against the beam, he managed to stand up and throw the remains at her, knocking her down and sending the microwave sliding far from her hand. She wasn't scared when she hit the ground. It registered only as a change of advantage, and that change didn't favor her, so she scrambled to her feet and ran, considering where best to regain control of the situation.

Knowing she had a better idea of the apartment's layout than the intruder, she ran through the kitchen and around the corner, down a hall and into the bathroom. She looked for anything that might be used as a weapon. In the instant before he came in, she ripped the safety controls from the molecular dispersion toilet. It was easier to break than she expected. She hid behind the door.

She expected him to have taken the microwave as she ran, so she was prepared for it. When he pushed the door open, she slammed it on his hand. It would have made him drop the weapon had he held it, but he wasn't holding it. A glimpse of his other hand revealed that he didn't have it at all. He must have felt she was no threat without the microwave. He would come in fast with brute force. She let him come. He burst in with such strength she had no problem pushing him farther, forcing his head down into the toilet's bare dispersion field. There was a harsh smell of ozone, a loud crackle, and Hrothgar Kray fell limp from her hands, his head absent, leaving only a cauterized neck stump.

8

She didn't let down her guard. It seemed possible that in her haste she hadn't killed the two others, merely stunned them. There could be more men outside. She left the bathroom with great caution, looking around for anyone else who might have entered. She found the two men on the dining room floor, one twitching, one not. She considered leaning in to take pulses but decided against it. She found the microwave under the table where it had slid. She ensured their deaths by firing point blank into their heads. She held the beam on the first until he stopped twitching, and on the other until his body began to heat and bloat, then burst. She watched the tissues blister, burn, and peel until the weapon began to overheat. Only when her hyperactive attention reminded her that overheating weapons can explode did she release the controls.

After glancing outside the melted door, she was satisfied that the immediate danger was over. It took her some time to figure out what "over" meant. While the event sorted itself through axons and dendrites and filed its elements into their proper lobes, she stood still. She became aware of the beeping sounds of microwave detectors and door alarms and of approaching sirens. The sirens echoed as noise in the air and over her link antenna. The link siren carried warnings and instructions: "We have detected microwave fire in your residence. Drop your weapons. Remain still."

She set the microwave down where she could reach it quickly. She was no doubt expected to collapse and sob, to lean over her family's bodies and lose all control, but she had no real desire to do so. Instead she stood there with the odd feeling that she had forgotten to do something important. She went over the events. The bad guys were dead. Her parents were dead. Authorities were en route and didn't need to be called. The air was thick with the smells of ozone and debris and metal and microwaved flesh, but this was no concern.

Soon a flood of police officers came in through the melted door. More landed on the deck. They all scurried about and took stock of the situation. They told her to sit down. One pulled up a chair. He asked her what had happened, so she told him calmly and clearly, giving every detail she thought might be important. She watched as a parade of medics, coroners, and detectives came and went. They prodded the bodies, scanned her, scanned the room, linking back and forth through their antennae and talking in whispers. She saw neighbors, the Frasers, through the doorway, demanding to come in and see her. As the police explained what happened, Mrs. Fraser broke into tears and held her husband. Violet felt nothing.

She felt nothing as they loaded her parents' bodies into body bag pods. She felt nothing as the pods took off and headed for the morgue. As she watched them fly away, there was a fraction of a second where she thought she felt something: a deep stab of fear—at least she thought it was fear—but then it was gone and forgotten, a drop of feeling lost in an ocean of numbness.

IN THE next few days, Violet learned just how little she knew about her father. She knew he was a cop. She had heard the stories. But now she heard the other stories, stories that fathers don't tell their daughters. Officer Nelson MacRae was the secret weapon in a war that had gone on for almost thirty years.

Everyone had thought the late Hrothgar Kray and his twin brother were the heads of the near mythic Orange Gang, raised together in Danmark, where they don't restructure their problem kids' brains.

Nelson was the one who'd discovered that Hrothgar was a mere lackey, in fact the gang's weakness. Wulfgar Kray was a genius, rarely seen and never vulnerable. Hrothgar was only in the gang because his brother didn't have the heart to kick him out. Hrothgar liked to nail people to walls and drench his hands with blood. Wulfgar knew that in criminal enterprises such panache was a liability. But it was his twin. He couldn't tell him to stop.

"So when the time came," explained Officer Lochroch, "Nelson volunteered to lure Hrothgar into a trap."

"Why my dad? What was the trap?" asked Violet, eager to hear more details.

"Well, he was very brave, the bravest—"

"How was it supposed to work?"

"Well, you see, Violet, he didn't think Hrothgar would ever find you, his family—"

"Obviously. What was supposed to happen? Where did it go wrong?"

"Well, we—Your father was a great—"

"You told me what he discovered about the gang. You didn't spare a gory detail, but you won't tell me what my father did to take them down? Or how they caught him?"

"It's classified."

"The rest wasn't? It wasn't classified that he was a cop. Everyone on our floor knew it. Did one of them blow his cover? And I want to know why he… why we weren't guarded, how the gang found his home, his family, why he didn't expect it, why—"

"Violet," he interrupted, "all of that is classified. There are good reasons we can't explain it."

She'd thought such treatment would end when she'd passed the maturity tests. She understood that police didn't give out such information, but she didn't want to know in order to tell the media or to post it online. She tried to explain herself clearly.

"I want to know the details because my parents are gone and this is all I have left of them. I want to know because the more I know, the more I might be able to help."

She thought it was a good logical plea, one that should push the right buttons. It had the opposite effect. The officer didn't want or expect cold logic; he expected tears. He and all who heard the girl's resolute statement were disturbed by her lack of emotion.

"It's okay to cry," said Lochroch, leaning close. He spoke to her as if she were still a child.

"I don't need to cry," she explained. She spoke to him with the same insulting tone. "I need you to stop talking down to me, stop trying to protect me, and tell me what the fuck went wrong."

That bit of honest clarity got her a ticket to the police psychiatrist office. They linked her in to post-traumatic programs that tried to bring out the tears, release the emotional pressure, and begin the typical human grieving process. They couldn't diagnose that in this one oddity of humankind, the process had been over the second her parents died. In such an enlightened era of psychological empathy, nobody recognized what a warrior a thousand years prior would have known and praised as incredible strength of mind.

Violet didn't recognize it either. She was vaguely worried that she wasn't all tears and sobs. She was also at a loss for why, with Wulfgar Kray on the loose, she was not getting rushed into protective custody. That part they were willing to explain.

"Hrothgar was so fast to… to uncover your father that he didn't fall into our live trap. He's useless to us dead. We need a new trap. We think Wulfgar will come to avenge his brother's death in person. And so we need you, well, see, we need you to—"

She was amazed at their shortsightedness. They were trying to use her as bait. She spoke quickly so as not to hear another pathetic euphemism. "You're ignoring the most important thing Dad discovered—Wulfgar is the brains. His brother was the one going out in person. Wulfgar wouldn't do anything so stupid."

As the police coddled her, lied to her, and tried to convince her to play along, she realized her father must have been an anomaly among cops. The rest were idiots.

They never guessed that Violet had her father's skills. The deductive abilities and razor-sharp wits that cut into the Orange Gang for her dad were the same that saved her life and the same that let her kill three very dangerous men. She knew more about the gang than the cops had told her, gleaning a multitude of useful knowledge from every scrap they gave her. Violet had always thought so efficiently and had always been hushed by her elders. As a result she didn't try very hard to explain it. She was unsure she even knew what she knew, and she'd never learned to have faith in her deductive abilities. Instead she learned in the company of officers to keep quiet about important things.

One thing she couldn't keep quiet about was the state of her parents' bodies. Though her mother's brain had been destroyed, her father had only been shot in the heart. If they'd had enough money, that wouldn't have ended his life: Within a few hours of death, anyone with a healthy brain could be salvaged by the skills of a good doctor. The police pussyfooted for hours before admitting they couldn't afford those doctors. Neither could her family accounts.

The cops left out one fact entirely. They didn't tell her that even if she somehow collected the millions needed, they still wouldn't have been able to save him, because her father's body never made it to the morgue. Nobody even considered telling Violet what the entire local force now believed: that the Orange Gang had hijacked the body to be desecrated. They expected the corpse to show up crucified publicly within the day. They were prepared to hide its discovery from Violet's eyes. They kept silent and let the horrible notion affirm their cause. "For Nelson," they said, "we must do anything to bring Wulfgar down! It's what he would have wanted!"

So they cast his daughter out as bait. The bait was far smarter than the fishermen, but without a scrap of real meaningful information about herself or the situation, she felt only a brick wall of ignorance. Amid math and science and language and history, students were not taught the difference between intelligence and knowledge. The tests themselves no longer knew the difference. Though Violet was smart enough to outwit the thugs and cops, she had no clue that she had any wits at all. Her educational tests came out below average because she couldn't care less about what company owned what country in what year. They could load information directly into children's minds but could not make them care. The police didn't tell her the facts that would have made her as sharp a weapon as her father, so she felt terribly stupid and considered herself useful only as a worm on a hook.

She knew Wulfgar wouldn't come for her, certainly not at home. Lacking the confidence to tell the police again, she resigned to let them try. She didn't really mind being bait. She didn't fully understand why she didn't mind it. If she were inclined to introspection, she would have decided that it was not for shock or depression but that old childhood bloodlust. If there was a man out there who wanted her dead, she wanted to confront him herself. She wanted him to come and try. She'd killed the last trio, and she felt deep down against all logic that she could take him too. The cops would have to fight her for the kill.

But he never came. Wulfgar, in mourning in Danmark, was as patient as Violet expected. He predicted the trap, the police, and

Violet's danger to him. After all, his brother had killed her family, and she would want revenge. Wulfgar knew that if this little girl had killed his brother, then there was more to her than was apparent. Hrothgar had always been quick to the punch. He kept the company of sycophantic friends instead of skilled workers. Now his poor judgment and poor company had gotten him killed. Wulfgar also knew of his brother's lust for all females young and blonde. He wouldn't have killed the girl when he should have because—Wulfgar couldn't finish that thought. Hrothgar was dead, so he didn't shame his brother's memory by thinking it.

Wulfgar was not subject to such obvious hubris and overconfidence. If Wulfgar did have a weakness, it was brotherly love. Hrothgar had been a liability, but he'd given him high rank and power in the Orange Gang. Hrothgar was a rapist, but Wulfgar turned a blind eye. Hrothgar got himself killed, so Wulfgar assumed that meant his own weakness had died as well. With his brother gone, the gang was stronger than ever. Strong enough to indulge in terrible vengeance.

It didn't strike Wulfgar that his need for revenge was the last vestige of love for his brother. This revenge couldn't be a weakness, he thought, because he was going to do it cautiously. He would let the girl find new friends and new parental figures for him to murder as she watched. Then he would keep her where he could hack her mind apart with great safety and solitude, and when her mind was broken, he would destroy her body as painfully as he could. He would do it all correctly, without any possibility of failure, and after so long his prey would taste like the nectar of the gods.

Violet waited. The cops waited. The Fraser family next door offered her their company and spare room along with an abundance of pity and hugs. Violet saw no reason to leave her own apartment or indulge in common emotional onanism. As an adult she was now sole owner of her family's quarters and belongings. Same with the money her parents had in the bank, now accessible through the monetary implant in her hand. Her mom had taken Violet to have it installed the day before she was killed. *That should make me sad*, she thought. *I could piss away all they ever earned with one handshake*. She tried to think the worst, to dwell on it. It struck her only as bad ideas and useless actions. No tears.

Before long she gave up trying to get herself to feel bad and cry. It was a waste of time. When she ate at the table by herself, she could stare at the places where the bodies fell, yet she felt only a slight concern that she should probably be feeling more. Soon that concern faded away too, and she found herself living a plain and aimless life.

Weeks passed. By day she shopped and paid bills, ate and exercised. In lucid sleep she wandered the nets in search of a job. Her inheritance alone would not keep her alive forever. She floated around the search sites, surrounded by the avatars of other job hunters. They came and went, but for hours she remained. Her intelligence scores were too low for the best business work, so again she lamented herself an idiot. Her VVPS scores were too violent for police work, so she lamented her temperament. She wondered where stupid, violent young adults went when they had no life, no ambition, and their only skill was killing people. She ran a search and found her answer.

Having decided to pursue a military career, she sent her test scores, status, and brain/body scans into the recruiting sites. She informed the police forces watching her, and they were happy with the idea. The trap wasn't working, and she would be safe. Violet realized shortly after applying that she was hopeful about the prospect of life in the armed forces. Had her parents lived, she'd probably have ended up there anyway.

Chapter II: Achnacarry

MILITARY RECRUITERS were a desperate lot. Applications came in by the gig from depressed idiots, drug addicts, deranged maniacs, and trick programs selling dead names. The typical live applicant could be sold to an army for a modest commission, but many a recruiter kept watch with hope that one day they'd find the diamond in the dung heap.

Wally Akercocke found her: MacRae, Violet T. A seventeen-and-a-half-year-old female in prime physical condition with a solid predilection toward violence and three confirmed legal kills. Good marks in all applicable fields and low marks in all others. She was the best profile to apply in years. Private armies couldn't afford an applicant like Violet. She wasn't in their budgets. Only the top company militias, and of course her native governing company (who had right of first refusal) would be able to pay the recruiter for this sort of find. Wally would get to retire.

Her rights were sold in a preempt to Scotland Military, owned by the company and country of Scotland, owned by UK Inc., owned by the megaconglomerate B&L, owned by GAUNE itself, which owned most of the western hemisphere. Violet was given a ticket to Achnacarry, only fifty kilometers south. She was surprised when the ticket loaded into her head. She had heard of Achnacarry Academy. The name carried a certain prestige. It was the commando factory whose graduates had won GAUNE the Jebel Sahaba Conflict—the last genuine war, over a century ago. She wasn't just joining the military; she was going to get elite training.

She left her accounts frozen and the apartment in the care of the Frasers, who walked her to the GET station. She was happy to travel by Highland Public GET. The ground-effect train was more of an amusement ride than transport. It was slower than flying in a pogo and offered the passenger a closer view of the countryside. If someone needed to get somewhere fast, they flew. If someone wanted time to think, or was traveling on the dime of the notoriously thrifty governing company, they got to take the train.

As she settled in the cushy seat and linked it to recline, the last boarding calls sounded and the train rose slowly up to its track and departed. Violet watched the city fall away, watched the Frasers turn into miniscule dots far behind. She hadn't traveled by GET for years and looked forward to watching the highlands fly past. But her attention would be elsewhere. Just after the train took off, she got a link from Achnacarry.

After a brief spoken intro, the signal made a new partition in her brain and began to fill it with rules, regulations, manuals, schedules, and a ton of information she couldn't unlock until ordered to know it. There was so much information she couldn't even begin to sort through it. By the time she was able to take stock of the forty-eight new memory sections, the GET had arrived. She regretted very briefly that she hadn't looked out the windows and enjoyed the trip. She kicked the thought from her head. She was an adult now, a soldier. Soldiers don't enjoy the scenery.

"Did you enjoy the scenery on your way in?" asked the gate office receptionist.

"No, Sir," she replied. She tried to stand up straight and tall. She was determined to make as good an impression as she could.

"Save it for the drill sergeants, kid. Okay, have you brought any luggage?"

"No, the recruiter said—"

"Not to. Good, you can follow directions. You'd be amazed how many can't. Do you have any implants?"

"One monetary, one ID, one link—"

"Not that, I mean unnecessary implants. Fashion mods, hair-color gags, foot fields? We don't let recruits skate around on foot fields. We march here."

"No, nothing like that."

It went on as Violet answered several questions she had answered in the application and several questions that seemed beneath an accepted adult. She began to understand what manner of recruit came in and wasn't surprised to hear that nine out of ten recruits wouldn't pass basic training. She was sure they told her the stats to scare her, to impress on her the difficulty of the course. She could handle difficult. She could handle a loud, angry drill sergeant. That was nothing compared to a kind, soft talk from her mother.

Achnacarry was a strange-looking place. Few of the buildings were connected; few had windows. Some appeared to be temporary, like tents. Everything was painted a drab olive-green color. The grounds were almost empty. In Kyle, every open spot of street was covered by a crowd. Here, there were only thirty people she could see, half of them marching in a line and others walking across the turf or cement. Two were riding a noisy contraption with six wheels. Violet followed a sergeant with the other new recruits to a building near the gate.

She was issued a uniform. It wasn't a snazzy blue formal uniform like her father's but a spartan tan coverall. It looked like it would be hot to wear in daytime—no doubt the intent. Soldiers, she imagined, would need to wear armor and therefore get used to wearing clothes in the highland heat. It also had dozens of pockets, latches, and other features. She looked forward to learning the purpose of every one of them. She threw her old shirt and shorts into the provided bin, then peeled off her footpads and threw them in too. Now she had boots: the funniest, bulkiest, biggest footwear she had ever seen. She could probably walk over a pile of nails in them. They were tight and let little air in. Her feet would sweat.

After being issued twenty pairs of socks and a locker of training paraphernalia, she was sent to the medical ward. She got a brief physical that confirmed the scans she had sent in. Then they sat her down to do something shocking and bizarre.

"Don't be afraid now," said the medic. "We're going to turn off your link."

"What?"

"Standard training. We do it dry, links turned off."

"Are you just going to dim it, you mean? So it's not active?" she asked. She heard her own voice waver.

"Off, completely. It will come back on after training, on the military net, but we can't just dim it. We have to remove you from the common world."

They were really going to turn off her link. All the way off. Bravery had its limits, and this was a troubling prospect. Violet, like every other human she knew of, had been linked as far back as she could remember. The first step into preschool was getting wired in and learning the interface. She wasn't even sure what life would be like without it.

"Don't worry, don't be afraid," he told her. "We lived this way for millions of years. You'll fall back into it. You'll also be sleeping unlinked. Dreams won't be lucid anymore. They may be bizarre and out of control. Sometimes they're kind of fun, sometimes you don't remember them at all."

"What about memory?"

"Your programming is still there. You'll still have partitions and direct access to whatever you file away. Trust me—every recruit in history has trained offline. You'll do fine."

Trust them, she told herself. *Let them do what they have to do.* She managed a nod and watched him put a device up to her antenna. He pushed a button, and the adverts disappeared from her peripheral vision. The net wasn't just ignorable and distant likc it was when dimmed. It was gone completely. Even the time and date were gone. She hadn't realized they were from her link. She instinctively tried to call up a diagnostic but nothing happened. She thought around toward the arcology net, toward the city net, even blindly outward for an Achnacarry net. Nothing. She felt queasy, as if her feet had disappeared. But that was all. It got no worse, and in seconds she knew the extent of what was gone and what was still there. She was somewhat ashamed that she'd been so scared by it. The medic must have sensed her shame.

"Don't feel bad, MacRae. You're the first one today who didn't faint."

Immediately after delinking, she was lined up with the rest of the new recruits to be sworn in. The oath had been loaded into her memory with the pre-enlistment link, but not as raw knowledge. It was a speech she would have to recite. With the others, she swore allegiance to his majesty, King Ethelred IV, and to Charles Lynton, his employer and CEO of the UKI, to defend her native company and country against all threats both financial and tactical, to follow all orders and various other things that seemed far too important to rest on the strength of a spoken oath. She'd have willingly let them put blocks and bonds in her brain to ensure her loyalty and found the concept of making her swear an oath rather crude. It would have been far more meaningful to Violet had they told her why the king and CEO were worth following, and why the country and company were worth defending. She assumed being born there was reason enough in the minds of her superiors and wasn't inclined to suggest otherwise on her first day. She had to wonder how weak their hold was on soldiers that it had to be constantly affirmed by archaic salutes and honorifics.

Soon she was adjusting to the quirks and traditions of military life. She knew from hours of entertainment that training would be brutal, and the instructors were to be cruel and even comically hostile. That was more appealing than worrisome, as conflict was so rare in the common world. Though some said the military was obsolete, that it was a waste of time or funds, Violet knew that beyond training was the slim possibility of action. The connotation of ancient warfare was split between those who claimed that "war was hell," and those who claimed it was an honorable, noble pursuit that should not have been forgotten. Violet didn't care about the debate but saw how it affected the demeanor of everyone she saw.

"If winning is no longer the goal, then perfection has to be," said Sergeant Cameron, their huge, buff drill sergeant, in a powerful brogue. He was one of many Camerons on the base. There was also Sergeant Cameron, his brother; Sergeant Cameron (unrelated); and Sergeant Cameron (also unrelated) who had been off the base when Violet arrived. There were also a variety of Lieutenant Camerons and even a General Cameron, CO of Achnacarry. The general was spoken of highly and given absolute authority, but Violet quickly learned that no Cameron truly ruled Achnacarry—the flies were in charge. A full hour of orientation was devoted to bug repellents and netting, along with the solemn notion that if an insect torments you while at attention, you may not swat it, you may not shoo it.

"You will stand still and silently thank the fly for teaching you how to stand still under torment! Someday you will come under fire, and if you buckle to swat a bug, you will get zapped. Love the fly, recruit—someday you'll find it saved your life!"

Flies were not the only method of torment. There were also giant geese to coat the grounds and remind the recruits to wear their awkward boots. One tall, strong cadet ran afoul of them during orientation and had to go to the medic. The cadets-to-be were treated much like livestock at first, and then exactly like livestock later. They didn't know what they were being treated like, having all been born a century after livestock was banned, so none protested. Still, only Violet was genuinely amused.

Another little misery for the troops involved the showers. There weren't any. Where sonic showers were standard to gently hum the grime off skin without the least bit of discomfort, the army needed something tougher and, for immodesty's sake, more painful. As soon as they gathered the recruits in a basement room, each was given a can of viscous orange dimethyl ammonium chlorides—army slang "napalm." They were told to dilute the goop in water and to apply it liberally to their bodies. A few recruits looked concerned; others began cautiously diluting and applying the substance to their bare skin.

Violet, assuming the army would do no permanent harm to their recruits, started with a 5 percent solution and gave herself a generous helping of the thinned goo. Just as she had covered most of her arms, she heard the screams. Then she felt the tingling, and then the itching, and then a sensation she later heard a recruit describe inadequately as being bitten by a billion burning bullet ants. She kept going, reasoning that the sooner it was all over her, the sooner it could all burn off. By the time she finished her feet, her arms felt cool and clean. She also couldn't help but notice that she smelled fresh and crisp.

"Smells like victory," laughed a colonel, who proceeded to slap the itchiest recruit on his itchiest cheek.

Such trifles were all in good fun to Violet and part of the atmosphere. It was the first time in her life that nobody assaulted her with constant "Pleases" and "Thank-yous," or the vulgar "You're welcome." The sergeants were very clear about what the recruits would do and where, though less than forthcoming about anything else. There was a clear need-to-know basis for questions, and conversations between recruits were forbidden at first. Everything was inflexible, hard, and rigid, especially the mattresses.

VIOLET AWOKE the next day to find she had no memory of any dream and no memory of falling asleep at all. She also felt more rested than she had ever been. At first her new life in the military seemed well suited to her needs and wants. She got to exercise almost nonstop. There was nothing to break her focus during straightforward tasks given to her in clear military language. The instructors yelled a lot and spoke in good strong voices, not like school programs, not like her parents, not that sweet, soft, calm fluff that had done nothing to save their lives. People here worked in a tough, resilient frame of mind, the kind that survives. These were the kinds of voices she wanted to follow, that gave an order worth giving and worth doing well. There was no surplus food to grow fat on or time to grow lazy. They threw everyone in the same napalming room and everyone used the same latrine. The toilets were positioned across from each other with no stalls, so they had to eschew their inhibitions. They took away individuality, and they took away humanity, which Violet liked very much, having never seen the appeal of being human. They stopped short of turning trainees into robots. The army didn't want robots. They already had enough of those—Achnacarry alone had almost a hundred.

Within a week she was marked proficient at cleaning, operating, and repairing those robots. She was proficient in all the skills she was taught. She could lift heavy things and run long distances while carrying them. She could hit targets with target-hitting implements and enjoyed the hard thunk of an arrow or round or beam squarely annihilating some scrap of plastic. She was ordered to open sealed parts of her memory, and she learned about the innards and physics of the microwave she had already used, and learned names for the tactics she had employed out of necessity. She began to understand just how exceptional her improvised defense and assault had been.

She finally got to fist-fight in the real world, like the old sparring programs but with people in person. Knuckles hitting meat instead of lighting up point zones. One student proudly informed the instructor that he had already downloaded every fighting style there was. The instructor immediately kicked him in the stomach, and the boy completely failed to block the man's foot.

"You can download all you want but your body has to learn it, not your head. You can't download experience."

So he gave them experience. Violet discovered the smacking sound and feel of a real hit. She had never been punched before. People simply didn't get punched back home, and she saw the fear in the faces of others going into their first hardening exercise. She was eager, curious, and deep inside, very excited. She let the first fist come, and then after all the anticipation, when it bruised her side, she could only wonder if that was all there was to it. For how much the other trainees had talked about it and bragged that they had done it first or long ago, Violet found it oddly unsatisfying.

One recruit threw a fit when the instructor drew blood.

"What the hell is this? You could have broken my nose, man. My nose is bleeding!" shouted the recruit. The instructor had clearly been waiting for such a complaint.

"People bleed. Get used to it," he said. "You get hurt in training. You get hurt because you need to learn to get hurt. If you complain to a mortal enemy that he has broken your nose, he won't back down because you sprang a leak. So you ask, what the hell is this?" He pushed the recruit's wounded nose harshly and held up his bloody hand. "This is nothing to you. This isn't enough blood to call a medic. This isn't reason for fear or pity. This is a stain on your uniform. Draw this from your enemy, and it's liquid demoralization. Spill it and show it off, because if it stays in their veins, it doesn't do you any damn good."

Sparring was fun, she learned very fast. She got bruises galore and admired her new spotty complexion. Her opponents got more bruises and a lot of broken bones. The medics liked her because they were no longer lonely. She sent them three injured recruits a day. They patched them up in minutes and sent them back out for more. She sent

Sergeant Cameron in for broken ribs twice and a broken arm once, but he was her worthiest opponent, and there came to be an understanding between them. As others tried to stay out of their way, Violet and Cameron were in a contest for who could break the most parts. Only eyes and balls were off limits.

With personal combat came courses in strategy, theory of defense, and weapon training, where they even taught swordplay. Blades began when the sparring instructor's brother, Sergeant Cameron, got back from leave. He was a short but dexterous man, covered in scars. One scar on his cheek was the exact shape and size as the edge of one of the knives he kept on his dojo wall. He wasted no time in putting wooden swords in their hands. He didn't tell them how to hold them properly; he made them feel it out. If anyone's grip was weak, he demonstrated their weakness by knocking the sword from their hand. If someone made the same mistake twice, he'd give them a scratch to remember it. Violet saw other trainees still taken aback at the prospect of real damage, but she adored the notion of a scar to remember every mistake. But she learned too fast to earn a keloid diploma. Her education remained purely hypertrophic.

She knew that every mistake she made became an advantage when made by her opponent. For her comrades the brutality of education seemed a regrettable necessity, but for Violet the process went past masochism into a philosophy. Learning was the process by which pain became a pleasure, a companion, a partner she could trust. Perhaps the emotional pains of childhood would be folded into the same steel. Violet was having too much fun to think about that sort of thing consciously. Nobody else thought about it either. They were all on their way home. Half were gone in two weeks.

She felt her time there was worth something more than the utter waste of school. Knowing how to survive a concussive explosion seemed far more important than knowing so many cheerful facts about the square of the hypotenuse or memorizing long-winded speeches about where milk came from (vats at Protein-Lactose Synth Factory B-45 South). This was a place devoted to her real interests, where she heard stories praising not science or philosophy but tales of warriors who would rape and pillage the weak or protect them for a price. Sometimes it was like hearing her dad's bedtime stories again. Idols here were not the kindest or smartest, not the peacemakers but the fighters, the Vikings and samurai, relics of a gladiatorial age when strength was not obsolete but the only trait that mattered. She never knew how much like a relic she'd felt outside until she knew what it was like to be the ideal.

The verbal lessons went on to redefine how they thought of the outside world. Violet was amazed at how often the world used to be at war. What little history she cared to remember from school was always mentioning a conflict or power struggle, but she never knew those were names for the slaughter of millions and for battles of fire and projectiles and bombs. For something rarely mentioned to the common citizen, violence was truly the way of life for the species, and she learned, all species. It wasn't always a cause for punishment. It was just the way things were. She felt vindicated.

They also taught the recruits about threats they might face and stripped bare the illusions that kept civilians feeling safe.

"The world is, for the moment, at peace, but peace isn't the natural state of humanity. Most of the planet might have forgotten war, but we cannot forget that such a thing existed and can exist again. You're still at risk if you bury your head in the ground and tell yourself it ain't happening. That's why ostriches went extinct. The fact is we are in a cold war. Those in the know call it the second world cold war. The first was a quarrel between Muslim and Christian countries. No, you don't need to know what the names mean. They were just ideas, god worship. The only violence in that war was the takeover of the countries involved by citizens who didn't want to fight over whose god was bigger.

"The second world cold war will not come to so quick an end. This time it's a fight for money, and the almighty never had so strong a grasp on nations as the almighty euro. You all know that Scotland is owned by the General Assembly of the United Nations of Earth, GAUNE. GAUNE owns most of the western hemisphere. The United Nations of Earth General Assembly, UNEGA, owns just about everything else. Have no illusions. Everything is owned by one company or the other under the guise of their subsidiary countries. 'Independent Unions' are run by UNEGA. The 'Unbuyable

Consortium' is really a joint venture of 'Consortium Buyers, LLC' and 'Unocal,' owned by UKI, owned by GAUNE.

"In ancient times, if a company merged or collapsed, it meant layoffs of employees or shifting of funds. Some of the media wants you to think that's all it means now, but I am here to tell you, that's not the half of it. When UNEGA corners one of our markets, when they take one of our subsidiary countries, the entire populace will become indentured servants. Mass slavery. Some unpatriotic bastards will claim we do the same. They're right. When you joined up, you gave up your right to care. You serve Scotland now, and you will make damn sure our homeland doesn't get sold to Asda.

"The world is so much more fragile than they tell you as kids. If the wrong company gets sold, if the wrong country gets subdivided, if the wrong corporation gets spied on, if the wrong base gets bought, then I assure you all, we will be at war, and world war doesn't mean Deutschland GmbH getting out of line again. It means mass nuclear annihilation, which we'll discuss next week. Until then, we have other problems. There are criminal enterprises to be quashed. The Orange Gang has menaced the UKI and mainland UNEGA for decades, despite having been commissioned and owned by the latter. The UKI police hope to end that fight soon. One of the Gang's top men was just killed. When the time comes to take their headquarters, you can bet we'll get the call."

He didn't even wink at her. She was very happy he didn't. He gave them a sizable heap of information about the Orange Gang. Violet knew most of it already, though her dad and the cops had only told her half. She wondered how she knew the rest, never suspecting that she had figured it out on her own. Soon the lieutenant moved on to other gangs like the yakuza, and then on to groups more bizarre than gangs.

"Cetaceans. Ownership unknown. A ferrofluid curtain has descended between oceanic colonists and land companies. Most Cetacean Divisionists want nothing to do with their land ancestors. There are rumors of a navy called the Valkohai but none are reliable. No legitimate Cetacean organization has ever attacked a human company. Nonetheless, we're to give you a rundown. The typical Cetacean has one lung and one gill, modified in youth and controlled by a second epiglottis. Vulnerabilities include…."

Lt. Cameron gave them solid briefings on the Cetaceans, but as the list of enemies grew more obscure, the information grew more sparse. The last two were the stuff of nightmares.

"'The Unspeakable Darkness'—I'm speaking about them, so they are in fact a speakable yet still very mysterious darkness. Owned by Zaibatsu, just like the yakuza. We know they have an air force. We know they are heavily modified, genetically and surgically. They bear no resemblance to humans, and descriptions vary to the point where they may not bear any resemblance to each other. More intel when you need it. Pray you never need it.

"We saved the worst for last. 'Hall of the Slain'—Ownership unknown. Every villain, every monster, every army, mob, gang, and powerful underground force fears them, fears them greatly. They're the monsters waiting under the beds of the monsters in your closet. They are known to be real, and they are known to be extremely powerful. And that is all we know."

Something in Cameron's voice suggested he did know something more because he feared them too. He would not be telling them why. That made the biggest impression. Violet had learned from the police that silence can teach more than sporadic facts.

Being linkless taught her how people can function without the nets. For her whole life, whenever she'd needed to know something, she'd just linked it out. When she found what she was looking for, it got dumped into her brain. This was the best way to learn information, of course. That's why they'd loaded her up with manuals before she arrived. But for ages, people didn't have it so easy. They had to learn from talk or text. Violet had assumed the ancient hieroglyphics all around her were decoration, but they were in fact the English language "written" on walls and floors and maps and pages of pictures. Sgt. Cameron claimed he could read the stuff but he didn't defend the claim when everyone laughed. It was an odd breakdown of order, and not the last. As weeks passed and the platoon thinned, the strictness relaxed.

One day in the dojo, Sergeant Cameron asked if there were any questions. It was more surprising than a hit from his favorite whacking stick. Violet welcomed the opportunity and used it first.

"What gave you that scar?"

He was amused.

"This did," he said, grabbing the like-shaped knife from the wall. "This is called a Bowie knife. It has a long, noble history that you don't need to know. But the shape is pure genius. It was the basis for blades for three hundred and fifty years, the best we had until the Carlin knife. I got this scar when I claimed to an American that the Carlin knife had made it obsolete. Take my word, MacRae, this thing ain't obsolete."

He passed it to her. It was weighted strangely compared to the usual Carlin bent dagger, but it had an antiquarian appeal. She handed it back but remembered the way it felt. He put it on the wall was quiet for some time. Then he said thoughtfully, "Another thing I learned from that American—strength ain't muscles, it's nerves. That's why he's dead."

He said no more about it, but the instructors grew more and more approachable. Then they let recruits speak to each other, and the order Violet had come to love was crippled. Private Static even had the chutzpah to let his hair grow beyond regulation and was not punished. It was a little longer than Violet's, but hers was keratin-welded down when she arrived. His flowed past his shoulders.

The first breakfast in which they were allowed to talk seemed more heavy a burden than the heavy-burden run or double-gravity PT. Violet alone remained silent for the first meal. She just listened to the others, so much like the kids from school. Days of pure silent order had done nothing to them. They reverted back to their old typical selves and they were even so vulgar as to discuss popular music idols and complain about their superiors. Violet did not say a word until dinner that evening, and only then when she was cornered.

"Violet MacRae?" asked a girl her age, one from her barracks. Brown hair, brown eyes, cute round face, and a voice that said she was tired of training but couldn't drop out. Violet assumed she was from one of those military families who joined out of tradition. But she said "Violet." They never used first names.

"Yes, how did you know that?"

"You're the girl who killed the Orange Gang men, yes?"

"Yes."

"Your face was on the news."

"Oh."

"My name is Heather. Sorry, Private Lyle. My uncle was killed by Hrothgar Kray."

"My parents too."

"Yeah, we all know. Thanks for helping me off that obstacle, by the way."

"Which?"

"On the course with the wood obstacles, you caught me and pulled me off the giant triangular thing."

"Oh, sorry, I didn't recognize you."

"Was covered in goosemud, wasn't I? That's all right."

Violet was suddenly aware this was the most she had said to anyone since the police. It felt awkward, unnecessary, disjointed. She was sure this person meant well and was trying to befriend her. All Violet could think of was the merit and quality of friendship among troops, and whether it would make them more or less efficient in battle, and other such practical nonsense. She concluded that interaction must have been approved or they would not allow it.

"What do you think this grainy stuff is?" Private Lyle asked.

"Corn bread." *Wait,* Violet thought, *this is small talk. Be funny.* "Or rubber, possibly," she added.

"Heh, yeah. I bet it bounces."

Enough small talk. "What did you hear about me on the news?"

Violet learned that her reputation had preceded her. She was not surprised to hear that she had been in the news logs for a few days, announced between the latest mergers and the latest kitten to climb a tree. The police had asked that her name and picture never be shown to the public, but freedom of the press had long ago conquered its last frontiers. Nobody asked her to recount her tale, not out of politeness but because they had simply heard it all before they came. So Violet humored the social goings-on and got to know her comrades. She gained a solid reputation as a model trainee and a frigid bitch.

DAYS BEFORE the end of basic training, order was in fast decline. The Sergeants Cameron began to treat recruits like people. They began to squander the respect they had earned by speaking casually. Violet didn't like the idea but understood that at some point the shouting had to end, or the drill instructors would go mute. One day the obscure Sergeant Bilby substituted for an injured Cameron and wanted to show the man's sparring class that they were still subject to flinching. He didn't know that Violet was not the flinching type, and he didn't explain his intent for the false punch. Seeing the fist coming at her, she assumed she was meant to fight back. She grabbed the arm and broke it, happy to have anticipated a test of fortitude.

The reactions of all concerned revealed her faux pas. She was not kicked out for it. The instructor had not told her specifically not to break his arm, so she had not really broken any orders, just an ulna. She was yelled at for a solid half hour, then thrown in a stockade cell for a few peaceful nights. She found the experience too remarkable for boredom or shame. By day there was an absolute quiet like nothing she had ever heard before. It was as though she could hear her own thoughts spoken aloud. At night she began to remember her dreams, and they were wild and unpredictable, sometimes scary or utterly surreal. She couldn't think of the time as punishment. Sensory deprivation and relaxation were the most generous of gifts.

When she came out, the other trainees treated her awkwardly, to say the least. The instructor whose arm she had snapped also looked at her differently, but not with disdain or contempt, rather, with a grudging respect—the unspoken pride in a student who had outdone her master. Sergeant Cameron counted the ulna on their running contest. She was treated well for a criminal among the ranks, slightly too well for the comfort of some.

She kept winning the contests and running ahead of the crowd. She didn't slow down for the weak, and why should she? It was their job to keep up. Her first true failure in training was that she didn't understand teamwork. The instructors' failure was in allowing themselves to be impressed by Violet's skills. They didn't explain teamwork to her, they didn't make her slow down, and they didn't force her to work with the others. Any officer who had lived in a time of war or even for three generations after would have known teamwork to be one of the most, if not the most important parts of training. But, however unforgivable, there were some lessons that a world without war forgets to teach. The romantic notion of a single soldier capable of great feats was no longer kept in check by the reality of battle, and even the highest officers now believed that a soldier alone could be more than useless. So they believed they were seeing the dawn of a great lone heroine and they treated Violet like she was special.

This infuriated the other recruits. They didn't handle anger well. Shades of her youth's social problems darkened the barracks. They didn't speak to her much after a while, and though she considered this silence pleasant, it began to manifest as a gap in morale, and the officials didn't seem to help. She tried to ignore the rumblings and throw herself into training, so she did even better, and the other trainees resented her more.

One morning they woke the recruits with loud simulated projectile fire and drove them into a muddy, filthy course without the benefit of breakfast or clothing. The course was made of sandbags, and though it was only three kilometers long, it was a cycle, and they were to run it again and again. If they slipped, which was a common matter with bare feet in the mud, they did fifty push-ups. Everyone slipped on the first circuit. Except Violet, of course. She traversed the course perfectly, and in an attempt to boost that decaying morale, when she came upon struggling soldiers she helped them up. Every time she helped someone, she felt good and thought they might finally forgive her. Sadly, they didn't think that way. When she offered them her muddy hand, they thought she was showing off, rubbing their failure in their faces, and they grew so sick of her on the course that the mud had a better name.

Then, finally, she slipped up. Literally, on a wet sandbag. She fell to the ground, hit hard, and felt mud attack every orifice on her head. For the first time she tasted why Private Lyle called it "goosemud." Horrible as it was, she was okay with it. *Everyone slips sometimes*, she thought. A few push-ups and she could get back up and let the rain wash her clean. But the worst possible thing happened. She was overlooked. Not because of her other accomplishments, but because Sergeant Cameron was picking his crooked nose and didn't see her. That would have been enough to earn the eternal hatred of her platoon, but she reacted terribly. She diligently, in a tone so soldier-perfect as to rub her team just the wrong way, informed the instructor that she had fallen. Cameron was impressed with her honesty and complimented her on bringing her fall to his attention, so she was not forced into the mud to do push-ups.

"What's the point of making this girl do push-ups?" he remarked. "When she hits the ground, it's the ground that weeps. On your way, MacRae."

Half the platoon heard it as they ran. The other half heard it as they did their push-ups and dipped their noses again and again in goose shit, slime, and sludge. She could tell as they grunted their pains and sorrows that this was the straw to break many a frustrated back.

She'd guessed the military code: Fuck up, get punished. Don't get what you deserve, get beaten by those who did. It was obvious. But to Violet, perhaps from a lack of tact or common honor, or even out of a shortage of social intelligence, it did not occur to her that she had to take it lying down, literally or figuratively. It was simply not in her nature to be a victim.

They came after sunset call with undiluted bathing napalm and a few ideas of where on Violet to smear it. She lay there, not asleep, and heard when they whispered the call to attack. She slipped into defensive mode, as she had months earlier in her apartment, but now with the added benefit of knowing what she was doing.

They would surely try to restrain her, so she drew in her arms and arched her back, causing them to bring a tightly rolled mosquito net down a full decimeter looser than they should have. From there it was a simple matter to grab the headboard bar and pull herself out of their clutches. She knew her advantage being on the top of a triple bunk bed and wasted no time in using it. On her way down, she counted twelve barracksmates, recognized their makeshift armament, and assessed their positions. Then she hit the floor by way of tackling the three closest bodies.

Violet rarely thought of any recruit by name, but looking up at the closest adversaries standing, she matched every face to a full name and a list of weaknesses she had subconsciously assembled and updated daily. She recognized Pvt. Till "Flake" Kruspe, left leg weak from a recent training accident. A good starting point. She grabbed the leg and sent him tumbling into the balance-lacking Pvt. Agatha O'Daimon, who crashed as Violet designed into Private Windir. Violet and two of those she'd downed made it to their feet at the same time. She was now on the same floor without any benefit over the others. Violet was, tactically speaking, screwed. Or she would have been, if not for the collective lack of understanding. As it had not occurred to her to take the punishment, it had not occurred to them that she wouldn't. They didn't know they were being attacked until she had pounded two more into the bedposts. Even as understanding moved through the ranks, hesitance followed. Violet took advantage of it as she'd learned to on day nineteen and noted how they failed to exercise the form and stances that they'd all been taught together on day four. Only Private Therion managed to uncap her napalm and raise it only to see Violet grab it, pull it from her, and elbow her in the back as she fell from the force of the pull. Violet's fellow trainees having failed in all aspects of their attack, she was overcome by a feeling of disgust. Had these people learned nothing? She almost told them aloud that they should be retreating, regrouping, and considering a flank or rear assault. Even Private Keenan, who had once expressed his desire to assault her rear, remained silent in surprise. Violet was not in the mood to advise these traitorous morons. More than half the attackers, including Private Suzuki, who she had always considered a friend in the making until this debacle, were on the floor in too much pain or with too little breath to get back up. Finally the remaining five figured out they were in a fight.

Private Static got in a well-formed side kick directly to her vulnerable ribs, breaking two of them. That only made her angry. Having now classified him as a genuine threat, she responded, after only an instant to regain her breath and form, by grabbing his nonregulation hair and driving his face into the floor, by pure chance into the puddle of spilled napalm. He screamed a sound no human should ever make. In her state that did not mean it was time to let up; it meant a demoralized enemy. She remained so precisely aware of her actions that she weighed in her mind the likelihood that she had gone too far in her mind as she picked up the howling fool to choke him into unconsciousness.

By now the last assailants were running away. Only Pvt. Heather Lyle remained and only then out of disbelief. Violet had once smiled when she helped Heather over an obstacle. Her expression now scared

Heather to the depths of her heart. Private Lyle had dropped her can early, having wondered if she should participate at all when the troops insisted she did.

Now they stood face-to-face. Violet was bleeding, broken, and more akin in appearance to a homicidal maniac than the girl she'd befriended. Heather was between saddened and afraid. Violet surveyed the threat posed by her conquered adversaries and slowly allowed herself to calm down slightly. Heather knew that her old pal would kill her if she made the wrong move, so she slowly raised a hand in surrender, meant to calm the beast. Violet only saw a hand moving toward her. She gave a front kick that sent Heather's four front teeth into the air and knocked her unconscious. Violet considered how Sergeant Cameron was never satisfied with her front kick. She was quite sure he would have found the ball of her foot oriented correctly at last. All was quiet.

As she stood atop the pile of defeated recruits, most either still and staring daggers at her or unconscious, she began to recognize that the establishment would find her to be in error for the fight, however successful she was. She wondered if they'd be right, if some irrational lust for violence had taken her over, some need to avenge her parents' deaths by beating up her comrades. Was she really in so dismal a state, or was it right after all to defend one's self?

In the eyes of the military, it was quite wrong indeed, and she was out of the academy as soon as word reached superior ears. Not without punishment, of course, and this time it was excruciating. They took hours talking to her, in patronizing tones so grotesque that they could be called cruel and unusual. They went on first about why they were there, why she was there, why they were in the office together. It was like grade school all over again. Watching her parents die had been easier, because at least she could kill the fuckers who did it. This, this was just sickening.

They spoke so softly, those strong voices she had once admired. They spoke as if they were trying to ease her out of her short-lived home. So damn softly. Were they afraid of her? The thought was repugnant, but no, that wasn't it. They were just revealing their true pathetic impotence. They were, in the end, no different than the nanny programs. When she did something wrong, sure, they yelled at her. But when she did something really bad, they just treated her like a kid again. *Odd*, she thought, *that when things go as badly as they can go, when her parents died and she killed three men, nobody yelled, nobody lectured her once. If things go bad enough*, she thought, *nobody says anything at all*. She should have just murdered everyone in the barracks.

But her thoughts distracted her only so long from the damned speech. They declared at length how disappointed they were. They'd had such hopes for her, how they'd paid so much for her. They seemed most horrified that a girl would so readily select good people as her enemies, that she would attack with equal ferocity one who intended to kill her and one who intended to haze her gently into military life with a mild beating. Violet knew that this at least was true. She didn't care if an opponent was going to slit her throat or spank her arse; an attacker was an attacker, and she saw no reason to allow herself to be attacked.

That's what she told herself as she spent another few nights in the brig. She slept late the morning they all graduated without her before going on to advanced specific training, the real commando crap she'd wanted most to learn. She couldn't tell how long she was in the brig. Light levels never changed there. She estimated a week. They let her out two hours before she'd have lost her appreciation for the room. Then they stood her before the military population. They berated her and stripped her of the patches she had earned. They ceremoniously took away her uniform and finally-broken-in boots. Through the ceremony, she felt only resolve. She hadn't let them attack her and that was that. She wasn't a victim, not in any degree. She'd always fight back, no matter what the cost.

The cost thus far was a military career, the one career she thought she might have enjoyed. That notion leaked away as she walked down the same path as the other training failures. She couldn't have enjoyed a life amid hypocrites. She couldn't have enjoyed fighting alongside the idiots she'd beaten down that night. She knew she was lying to herself, so she stopped. She would have loved every second of it. She had just lost the only hope she had for a future. She was too cruel and stupid for the Scottish army. She wouldn't even be able to face the Frasers after this. But she had to face worse before then.

At the end of the walk were her victims, all taking a break from training to hear her apology. The Apology had returned to her life, back like a drunken husband ready to beat her down. It was to be the crowning shame of her every low moment, but something was different this time. General Cameron himself wrote the apology she was to recite, but she thought of one loophole. She was a civilian already and didn't have to follow his orders anymore. She wasn't a victim to violence. She sure as hell wasn't going to stay victim to this. It was time for the Apology to die.

"You were uncoordinated and weak," she told them. "I should have killed you all."

And she walked past them to the gate office. For a moment she thought she saw, amid the gaping mouths and shocked faces, Pvt. Heather Lyle smiling a proud, toothless grin. At the gate desk where Violet had checked in, they returned her thin civilian shorts, shirt, and shoe pads. They hardwired into her brain and deleted every protected file they had given her. Though they destroyed files for all she had yet to learn, what had been opened and used was now part of her natural memory. Her training thus far was hers and not legally removable.

They turned her link back on and adverts piled quietly into the bottom of her vision. A ticket to Kyle loaded in front of them. They put her on the same Highland Public GET that had brought her there. The cabin was filled with civilians who didn't give her a second thought. She tried to realign her identity to consider herself one of them. But she was not one of them, nor was she a soldier. She was no longer a daughter, a child, or any categorizable sort of human being. She was absolutely nothing. She would let that soak in when she got to Kyle. For now she'd just relax. In her cushy reclining chair, the first civilian luxury she'd had in a month. She dimmed her link and looked out the window. This time she wouldn't miss the view.

Chapter III: Kvitøya

ACHNACARRY ACADEMY and its peripheral buildings fell away into the distance. The GET slowly traversed the mountains and rivers, which were sometimes far below but no less majestic in scale. She had seen the region up close when she was very young. Her dad had once taken her around the lochs and ruins to put her in touch with her native land. She'd have preferred a couple hours of games online back then, but now nothing seemed more beautiful. She didn't understand how she could have missed it up close. Everything was so green, so organic and serene.

Her dad had told her then how the soil and rock they walked on were the real meat of the world. It wasn't all concrete through to the core, but she didn't care. He'd pointed out grass and trees, but she didn't even remember what he'd said about them. Now it seemed to her nothing had been so important as what she must have missed. The terrain below was alive and ancient, and all she had done in her life was nothing to the thousand-year-old plants and million-year-old rocks. Then she saw the ruins.

That's what her dad had been taking her to see: the ruins of Eilean Donan Castle. She saw the island below, and on it the stones of an old castle. Her dad had told her everything about it when they were there. She remembered only fragments now. Back when families were clans, the castle was in their charge. It was a site of battles or escapes or something important to history. It had inscriptions about… someone. It was destroyed in… some year and built again, and destroyed and rebuilt again, and then finally, only recently, it was left in ruin. She cursed herself for not paying attention. What the hell had she been thinking? How could she have squandered so critical a moment with her own father? How much life had she wasted in apathy? Were Violet ever to cry, it would have been then.

She didn't. She watched the ruins fade into the distance and pushed her sentimentality with them. What was sentimentality but another way of avoiding the world at hand? Her father and that day were gone. Move on. Two minutes to Kyle. She turned her link back up and skimmed a short news log. She looked at the "top stories" icon and a few thoughts loaded. "WYCo. buys NWS." "Unocal litigation begins." She kept looking for anything like what she'd learned from Lieutenant Cameron, but there was no sign of the breakdown of world peace, no stories about Cetacean Divisionists. The train docked over Arcolochalsh before she could do a real search.

She couldn't stay onboard, but she didn't want to go back to the apartment. There was no reason to. The sky was only just going dark, and it wasn't like she had a bedtime anymore. She wanted to get back online and see just what the civilian world knew about itself, so she headed to the cyberlounge on the arcology's ground floor. She passed ten new construction zones on the way down and caught a glimpse of the 193rd floor. It had been repainted since she'd been away. The atrium and ground floor were also different—plants rearranged, walls moved, new kiosks and stores replacing ones she'd left so recently.

The cyberlounge was still there, unchanged except that it now let her inside without parental permission. She found the lounge full of civilians in civilian clothes. The sight amused her. She had become so used to full body uniforms that the men in naught but thin kilts and the women in saris and drapes were silly to behold. Even on the train there had been folks in skin-thin clothes or less, aside from one tall massive man in a suit, but here en masse the bodies were a joke.

She took a seat on a bean blob near the edge of the crowd and gave the room a last glance before immersing herself online. Civilians in every direction, ignorant soft civilians without cover. Except one man, a big guy in a suit. She thought it might have been the same one from the train, but his suit was a different color. Violet laid back and set her link to immersion. She watched the lounge go dark and let bright, opaque graphics assemble around her, forming her old home silo where she fell back into the net.

The tall man watching her tapped his hat and turned his suit bright orange. He linked to his team to tell them Violet had gone online and grasped the handle of his dagger.

THE COLORS of the Internet seemed doubly vibrant after Violet's long desaturated time offline. She couldn't decide if it all looked pretty or garish. She floated around the turf of Kyle's net, tapping her toes gently on the floor graphic to stay afloat, enjoying the near weightless preference set she'd adopted so long ago. The netscape was so perfectly, plastically clean. The loss of her senses of touch, taste, and smell was refreshing. Symbol menus stretched out beneath her, glowing, changing to predict her thoughts. The avatars of four hundred thousand people from Kyle City walked, floated, or blinked in and out around her.

She didn't recognize anyone in the short lists; no names popped into her head, none of her old games or haunts called out with recognizable tags. In fact, in the time she was gone, the whole of every net had been rewritten a hundred times. The construction that was busily making her arcology unrecognizable was faster and more irreverent online. There was nothing familiar. If one missed a day on the net, let alone months, they would not likely find anything where they left it. Nor did friends stick around, but Violet didn't have any to begin with. There was no one, nothing online to comfort her, but this was the Internet, so there was a whole lot of that comfortable nothing to be found.

She hadn't linked in to waste time and didn't feel like sifting through news logs anymore. She felt a great need to move on, so it was a job board she floated to, where she looked over the available fates. The listings were past her capabilities or terribly unappealing: architect, bookseller, creature designer, entertainment writer, photographer, illustrator, advertising—so on ad infinitum, ad nauseam. Nothing worth doing or paying enough to ignore that it wasn't worth doing. She was ready to sign out and head to the apartment when she heard a contact protocol.

"Violet MacRae?"

At a loss for who it might be, she accepted the contact. Two avatars, black from head to toe, floated up to her. They were featureless, androgynous, somehow more plain than the blanks of people who hadn't bothered to create a profile, which was what she was using. She had not posted her name or used her childhood purple squid avatar or a scanned likeness.

"Who are you? How did you know—?"

"We can discuss that in a private room," said one of the identical black figures in a generic voice. It offered its hand. The first thing any responsible parent teaches their child is not to follow strange avatars into private rooms. They could be hack traps, mind thieves, pirate programs, any one of a thousand malevolent creatures that lurked on public nets. Though Violet had proven herself quite tough in reality, she knew nothing about net defense beyond the one inviolate rule: nobody can harm you unless you give them your hand.

"Why should I trust you?" she asked.

"You shouldn't," said the other black figure. "You will because your hopes exceed your fears."

It was as true as it was concise. She touched the black avatars and followed them into a private room. The room was strange. Most rooms had a layer to show the conversation was private, but this one had shells of security and hack armor that showed it to be as impenetrable and exclusive as an executive board.

"So who are you?" Violet asked.

"We represent a possible employer. We offer training and residence," replied one.

"The life is high responsibility and heavily demanding," added the other.

"It does not pay but provides everything you could ever need," said the first.

She stared at them for a moment, then asked, "Police work? Military?"

"This is neither, though there are elements of both."

"This offer is available to you and you alone," said the other. "It will not appear on any general boards."

"Why are you offering it to me, then?"

"You are capable of the rare abilities we require. You also have nothing better to do."

Again, they were absolutely correct.

"So what is it?" she asked.

"Espionage and counterintelligence."

She called up a definition search and loaded the words to be sure. The definitions came in as raw knowledge with icon options for related entertainment, equipment sales, news items, history files, and every advert ever posted with the words. She ignored all but the implication. They were spies.

"Who would I be working for, and who against?"

They explained again with sharp, fast responses. "For the general good of society and against those who would undermine peace, freedom, and the balance of power with violent means," said one.

"Threats vary in purpose and urgency," added the other.

"And the gangs?" asked Violet.

"We monitor them and intervene often. Had the Orange Gang come back for you, we would have stopped them. You will have the opportunity for revenge, if you wish."

Violet didn't even know that she wanted petty revenge, and they were offering it like a dental plan. She was nearly offended at the suggestion. Nearly.

"You know I got kicked out of military training," she admitted.

"Yes, we do. You showed great mental discipline during the attack on your parents and proficiency in all activities at the training camp. The actions that ended your military career prematurely were more a result of their inflexibility than your own eccentricity."

"You want vicious crazy people?"

"We want people capable of original thought beyond ordinary limits and violence at corresponding levels. Our enemies often exhibit such levels and demand it in return."

The avatars spoke like programs; humans were never so eloquent, not online. What they said was appealing, but she was not one to let artificial intelligences determine the rest of her life.

"Everything I say is a lie—" she started. One of them interrupted. Programs rarely interrupt.

"Don't start, Violet. We're not programs. She just talks like one sometimes."

"The hell I do!"

Programs never bicker.

"You do. Yesterday you told—"

"Stop! No names!"

"I wasn't gonna say it, you twit!"

"Twit my ass. You said 'she.'"

"You are a 'she.' It's not classified. She's female, Violet—tell the news!"

Programs never ever got the hang of sarcasm. Violet was convinced. "Fine, fine, humans. I get it. So you want violent nutters working for you?"

The avatars dropped their feud. "We want those who can protect themselves and others," said the female.

"I didn't protect my parents," responded Violet.

"Detectors show you had no chance to. Instead you waited for an opportunity."

"Our analysis showed your actions that night were 94.2 percent of the ideal tactics. Your counterattack in the barracks was 99.1 percent."

"Gee, thanks."

"You are welcome. Your mind is a rare one. That it should exist in a strong, unaltered body is even more unusual. Your capacity to kill when necessary and to deal logically with the repercussions is most admirable. Your actions in training suggest personality traits that may be incompatible with military service but critical for our organization."

The other avatar floated gently closer. "With our training you could enhance your abilities to lengths you cannot yet imagine and put them to uses more important than anything the militaries offer."

"What company do you work for?" she asked.

"We are not owned."

She suppressed a laugh out loud. “You have to be owned by something.”

“We are not. We are the only body on earth or off that is totally independent.”

“You’re pirates? Rogue bureaus? Another gang?”

“They’re all owned as well. We are none of those. We simply are, and are alone.”

“How long do I have to think about it?” Violet asked.

“Our analysis suggests you have already decided to join us.”

Their analysis was 100 percent psychoprogram-quality correct. Violet remarked, “You sure you’re not robots?”

THEY TOLD her to log out and wait at home, so she left the private room, left the net, and returned to the real world. The lounge was still full of bodies, so full she had to step over numerous limp figures to make her way to the atrium. She looked up to the window at the top of the atrium wall. The sky was getting dark blue. The halls of Arcolochalsh were bustling with residents returning home after sunset. Violet’s head was busier. Possibilities were racing with concerns, colliding and crashing into derailed trains of thought. She was so withdrawn into her thoughts as she walked that she didn’t notice the orange suit following her out.

She was being offered what could be the perfect life for her, or the perfect life for who she had been. She might have lost her taste for violence after what she did to Heather and her fellow recruits. She might not be what they were looking for anymore. A pedestrian bumped into her shoulder, and she restrained the urge to break his neck with all eight ways Cameron had taught her. Still the same Violet. One problem down.

But the person they thought she was—she was taken aback at the suggestion that she would seek revenge against the gang, but she didn’t know why. On reflection she decided that she did indeed want revenge, and if these people weren’t asking her to regret it, they wanted it. They needed it. They needed her. But she had been a vicious brat as a kid, and she was a dangerous brat as an adult. But they wanted dangerous. Violet got sick of the loop of thought and gave it up at the lifts. The man in orange watched her enter and waited for the next car.

The pneumatic matrix picked up her car and sent it upward. Layers of atrium fell past, levels and levels of apartments, people living their lives. She felt certain now that none of their lives was so surreal as what hers was becoming. Windows lit up across the arcology, but those lights felt unfamiliar. She arrived on floor 193, where the walls were now ecru instead of the old pale tan. That might have been all that changed, but the place she grew up in felt as alien as Achnacarry had on arrival. This was not her home. Whatever it might have been in the past, the doors she approached were not home. She hesitated at the door. She checked the number to make sure it was the right one. She looked to the right, shortly down the round hall. The Frasers' door was black; they were out somewhere. She put her hand to her own door, half expecting it not to recognize her. It lit up and let her in.

She couldn't think why the black avatars would want her to head to the apartment. There was nothing there but useless memories and useless police detectors, the remains of their trap. The lights came up as she walked into the living room. They revealed autocleaned walls and dusted, vacuumed floors. They reflected off the screen wall and chairs and threw light into the corners, ending the darkness that hid the two people waiting for her. She'd expected people, the human versions of the avatars she had spoken to. She was not expecting them to be wearing orange suits or holding sinister double-ended daggers. She turned around to see the door, still open, and filling its frame stood the man from the train, tall and thick and dressed in orange.

Well, shit, she thought. *All those ups and downs and twists and turns, and it ends like this, with an old thread we never tied down*. The police, though.... They had the detectors on. But detectors detect projectiles and microwaves, not daggers. *They'll take video, but the cops won't watch it until they find me dead. Such incompetence*.

Her thought process struck her as strange. Why was she not jumping into battle mode again? There was more awry. The Orange Gang had never been known to use such daggers. The Orange Gang men could have taken her on the train, in the atrium, in the hall, or anywhere but here—where they must have known there would be detectors. Then the avatars online, where were they? They'd wanted her to head home, so surely they were part of this new Orange Gang trap, but why trap her with the promise of such a peculiar job? And how could the Orange Gang have known what they knew, and why, if they were the Orange Gang, didn't they fry her online when she touched them? None of it added up.

As if to add another curious integer to the crooked adding pile, the huge man who had followed her from the train was holding his dagger in the worst possible way. And that detail solved it all. She was not switching into battle mode because she was not in danger. They wanted her in her apartment so the detectors could see her. They weren't acting like the Orange Gang because they were not the Orange Gang. They merely had to look like it. To fake her death. She was not joining a company that recruited common people in common ways. This was an underground so deep it would need its denizens relieved of not only their earthly families and duties but their lives. They needed her dead to the world and alive in their hands. They needed to put on a show for the detectors and net monitors that would remove her from the living world.

Clever, she thought, without any concept of how she recognized it or any faith that her death was about to be faked. She hunted for anything to suggest it would be. Dagger aside, the fact they weren't attacking was a solid step. But why would he be holding his weapon so poorly, exactly how she had failed the first time in blade training? Because he wanted her to take it. She suddenly felt a flicker of gratitude toward her new recruiters. They were going to let her go out fighting. She didn't have to die fainted or failed. She'd get to die with a blade in her hand. He must have seen the realization cross her face. He moved to attack.

She took his invitation and his weapon and fenced lightly toward the other man. Had he backed off, she might have been disappointed, but like a good drill sergeant, he was not going to overlook a weak move. He struck back with such force that she questioned whether it was all fake. And so she gave it all she had, not to kill the man but to make the Sergeants Cameron proud when they saw how their old failure went out. So they fought, but they fought like her former teachers—to hit the knife, not the wielder. She fought in kind, and when she felt him push her ever so subtly toward the outdoor deck, she made her mock retreat.

When she made it to the deck, she saw a landed orange pogo. They wanted her on that transport, to appear to be taking her to Wulfgar, but secretly to take her… she knew not where. She did not care. Violet was delighted when they bested her, disarmed her, and forced her savagely inside the door, like a lioness taking a cub in her jaws. To the police it would appear to be the vicious capture of a girl fated to die, and to the cub, her mother was gently taking her home. One of the men pulled her into the back of the cabin.

She was set down in the seats and not restrained. The huge man boarded after her and spoke quickly. "Do you have any pets, any irreplaceable valuables in the apartment?"

"No, nothing."

She knew exactly why he asked. The third orange figure jumped in and removed her hat, revealing her gender and long hair, neither of which would have been found in the Orange Gang. She threw a device into the apartment and slammed the deck door. The pogo took off, and below, a flash annihilated the place Violet had grown up.

"Don't worry about the Frasers," the woman told her. "It's a containment grenade. Won't singe a hair beyond the set radius."

They began to take off their orange charades, revealing armored uniforms with gray camouflage coloration. They made no attempt to hide pride in a show well performed. The two men applauded, and another woman beamed back from the controls. Beyond comfort, Violet felt a blush coming on.

"Were you the two online?" she asked.

"No, we work with them. You'll meet them soon." The large man pulled a familiar device from under his seat, one she had been somewhat afraid of the last time she'd seen it. "We need to turn off your link again."

She wasn't nervous this time. She turned her head to let him at the antenna. He disconnected her, and she felt the net disappear again. He handed her a notarization pad. This was unusual. With her link off, the pad shouldn't work. Such pads functioned by linking through the user's own antenna to confirm that they were who they claimed. Without considering what a linkless procedure would mean, she touched the pad and it went black.

"You have been logged dead at 1912 hours, March 24, 2230. Your net accounts have all been deleted, so you won't be able to link until we reset you. Don't worry about any loose ends. We've handled everything." He smiled. "You put up a damn good fight, Violet."

"Thanks. Is that how everyone joins?"

"You join how you like. You could have given up."

"Has anyone?" she asked.

"Never. Our kind tend to prefer to go out fighting. I hope you don't mind being killed off."

"Not at all."

She realized immediately after she said it that she really didn't mind. She tried to think of how her friends would react. She realized it was okay because she had no friends. She couldn't think of anyone who would be surprised or hurt, except for the neighboring Fraser couple. She felt a vague regret that they would be further depressed by the now total destruction of the family next door. She was more taken by the idea she could be utterly erased in a day. Was her life so thin before? She knew it to be so, and again she didn't mind.

Considerations of her past ended when she saw the huge man slide his dagger into a gap in his chest plate. It looked like he had slid it deep into his own chest. She was about to ask about it when he introduced himself.

"My name is Ragnar. You met Ruger and Rebecca in the apartment. The lady piloting is Ripple. We're Reid team." When he said "Reid," he pointed to a shape on his belt. "Teams have runic letters. We'll explain it all soon. But we're the rescue team. We also pick up new recruits."

Violet was starting to detect an accent in his voice. Language across the globe had long since degenerated into a nearly homogenous yogurt of English, but there were still many local flavors. Ragnar's sounded gentle and faintly whimsical, reminding her of a net guide who'd once shown her some simulations of the far north. She looked out the window and saw a sort of confirmation.

They were headed northeast. They had jumped over the remains of her apartment, away from the arcology and over the remains of the old Skye Bridge. Soon she was beyond all vestiges of her former life. They passed out of the city and over the lochs, where the lights of civilization dwindled, and they passed into the darkness of the oceans. Without her link the darkness was near absolute, no ads, no icons, only stars above and the dim undulations of the sea below. It was as soothing to her eyes as solitary confinement, but infinite and empty and beautiful.

She thought about asking one of the men where they were going but decided against it. Though the people to whom she had just signed her life away had answered all her questions clearly, and though the team around her seemed kind and open, she suspected there were to be a great deal of things that one did not ask. Military policy had meant absolutely no questions. She suspected her new situation would be quite different, but she didn't want to pester them with a barrage of questions. She had so many that they wouldn't even form a proper queue behind her tongue, so she remained silent for much of the trip.

Some questions, though, stood out in her own mind. She didn't know why she trusted these people. It only occurred to her now that she probably shouldn't. Hadn't they just complimented her on the sort of character that would never trust strangers? Hadn't the strangers just put her in a flying crate and nuked her last possessions? Why, then, was she so wholly at ease? Perhaps the trauma was finally starting to affect her, making her reckless. Perhaps that was part of why they wanted her. She felt almost ashamed to be thinking such things. Her thoughts felt idiotic in the face of such an ingenious departure, but that was okay. Like her dad once said, "If you worry that people may think you inadequate, you need only stay silent to rob them of confirmation."

Soon they were traveling at extremely high altitude and the pogo cabin was still open. It was cold and windy. Suppression fields on the windows and doors only softened the effect of the raw elements. The vehicle was clearly meant for tough use by tough people. She was suddenly quite concerned about what would happen if she failed training when they'd already annihilated her former home and declared her dead. Would such people have any qualms about annihilating their failures as well? They flew north at high speed, so far and so fast Violet wondered if they were headed to the pole. She looked down and saw faint white patches in the darkness below. They were tiny. There wasn't much, but she thought she knew what it was. She had to ask.

"Is that stuff snow?"

"Snow and ice," said Ragnar.

"Can you fly closer? Can I see it?"

"Not now," he laughed. "You'll be seeing plenty soon enough."

And so she did. It was deepest night when they landed. They set down in a field of glacier-sculpted rock, and snow was all around, draped over rocks and floating down through the sky, just as the simulations had shown. Ragnar and Rebecca stepped out, and she rushed after them to see the flakes up close.

As soon as she stepped out of the pogo, the cold hit her like a wall. It was well below freezing, and windy, and she was still wearing the thin, scant cover of tropical Scotland. Now she was in air that felt like the inside of a freezer, that felt like skinny-dipping in ice cream. The cold hit the sticky pads that held her shoes on, and they fell off. She tried to get one to stick again, but it wouldn't stay on. Her feet were on bare freezing rock. She had absolutely no more desire to touch the snow. *Fuck snow*, she thought. *Snow is fucking cold.*

What kind of place had they taken her to? She felt betrayed by what she had learned online. Supposedly the global climate had warmed over the last three hundred years, enough to melt most of the world's polar ice, rendering the arctic like the subarctic, the subarctic like the temperate zones, the temperate zones like the subtropics, the subtropics like the tropics, and the tropics only habitable by Centaurian gremlins, who would still only live there in a time-share. But the poles were supposed to be like Scotland had been before. Scotland could never have been like this. People would have died. Only the wooly cows could have survived, the things that always looked overheated in all that hair. What she wouldn't have given for wool like that now. As if someone had heard her thoughts, a furry, warm cloak hit her from behind, and she pulled it around herself.

"Welcome to Kvitøya!"

She turned. There were people in fur coats. She quickly realized these were the same four, and they were in the same attire, but their armor had grown fur. She wanted armor like that.

"We're in the Svalbarð Archipelago," said Ragnar, "at the top of the world. Let's get inside!"

She shivered and nodded her agreement and followed the men to a spot indistinguishable from the rest of the unlit field.

Ragnar warned her, "Hold on!"

There was nothing to grip, so she held on to the nearest furry armor. The rock beneath them began to descend. Violet caught a last glimpse of her shoes as she dropped under the surface. Once they were below ground level, a ceiling moved into place. The air heated rapidly, the rocky ground heated too, and the team's coats rescinded their fur.

"Be glad this isn't midwinter. It's a lot worse."

She couldn't imagine any worse. "How far underground are we going?"

"It's not underground, just secluded," said Ragnar. "The ice that used to cover this island carved out a nice ravine for us."

"Actually," added Rebecca, "it's not technically a ravine, just a crevice. But we call it the ravine."

"And it wasn't technically for us. The whole thing used to be a terraforming lab," said Ripple.

Ruger started, "But about half a kilometer down is—" He stopped. The banded-gneiss walls of the shaft ended, and she could see where they were going. They were level with twisted crags that hid the sky, heading down fast into a deep pit of ice and stone. Small structures hung from the ceiling and clung to the rock walls. As they descended farther, she could see the lights of stalactite towers and communication arrays, all gold. What should have been darkness, hidden even from the starlight, was lit from deep in the pit by pure gold light. The light revealed walkways spiraling down across the outcroppings and glacial forms and a honeycomb of small caves cut into the walls, some with hangars or buildings, and others that seemed to extend deeper into the rock. Into every cell and up to every building were thin strands of something, all glowing with gold light. Violet thought she could see people walking on the shimmering lines.

Deeper still were towers and landing pads not unlike Achnacarry's, full of vehicles and strange craft she didn't recognize. For an instant she thought she saw the pogo they'd arrived in traveling down a larger lift across the great chasm, but then a network of glowing strands became sharply thicker and the source of the gold light came into view. The strands were all branches of one central trunk, a gargantuan glowing tree, twisted like an ancient ash. Its limbs stretched out to every section of the place, bringing light to every corner. At the base of its trunk, a city sprawled across the ravine floor, extending up the walls and into several massive caves that plunged yet farther into the earth. Every building was plated in gold, all reflecting the gold light of the core.

As they neared the ground floor, she could see people. Hundreds of them walking on the branches or walkways, standing atop the buildings, or on decks on the sides of stalagmites. Those on the branches had faint halos, as if the light was crawling up their sides. But there was something even more peculiar about the people. It was how she felt seeing them. She didn't instantly dislike them as she tended to with the nameless masses of Kyle City. They weren't a cold foreign crowd, but somehow inviting, like people she might someday know. The place felt alive yet calm, serene, and above all, bright. What light the world of her youth had was all false, projected into their minds by the links. All the colors and signs and busy glowing icons disappeared the moment she dimmed her link. But this light was real, and unlike the bright and garish Internet, it was warm. After that moment outside, this pit was the warmest place she had ever felt. What shells she had spent her life erecting began to crack at the experience.

The lift fell into darkness again behind a rock face. The tunnel illumination took over, and she could see the armored uniforms of the team changing color, losing their camouflaged gray tones in favor of different colors. She was about to ask about the phenomena when she was caught off guard by an intercom. It took her a second to remember that it was sound, not a link.

"Second report, 2115 hours. Arrival: Violet/Reid Team. Calling: Alföðr, Balder, Veikko, Vibeke to lift three."

Ragnar explained, "No ranks, no titles, no family names. For the most part, new team members choose new names after they arrive. They always start with the letter of the team you're in—R for Reid team. It lets you know who you're dealing with quite efficiently. You however, arrived in the middle of Valknut team's assembly. Violet would fit."

Ripple gave Violet a poke and cut in, "Vibs, that's Vibeke, kept her name too. She and Veikko are going to be your flatmates and soon teammates. You'll get a fourth someday to complete V team. Then W—Wunjo team—starts up."

"And those names are… you said runic?"

"Right. We used to use Futhark but ran out of letters." Without her link she didn't know half the terms they used. She was suddenly quite worried she might not be smart enough for the place. Ragnar continued, "So the alphabetical order got a bit deranged. Reid is nearly a senior team, but Mannaz, Othala, Perth, and Tiwaz are your immediate elders. Actually, Mannaz will be a middle team once yours is complete, and R will become senior, finally. The real elders are still A, B, and C."

"Then D, E, F?"

"No. Then K—Kaunan—the weapons team. Best not to worry about it yet."

She remembered two names from the intercom. "So Balder and Al, uh, Alfootir are—"

"'Alf' if you can't pronounce it. Yes. He wasn't the first here but he designed the rune system, so he's at the top of it."

"What happens when you run out of letters again?"

"A matter of intense mess hall debate. We've already had to improvise a few runes like Valknut. Other bases use Cyrillic, Latin, and Greek."

"Other bases?"

Before he could answer, the floor came to rest in a cozy lounge, a room that looked far too comfortable to be in a spy base at the outer reaches of the north. Every surface was curved and smooth; the colors were still based in gold but subdued by oranges and browns. The rock walls were left as bare rock, and some of the room was made of wood. Real wood. Wood seemed at odds with a fire in the middle of the room, one brighter and hotter than any she had seen before. It smelled strange. She gathered it must be a real fire, and it was only contained by a fireplace. It seemed unsafe. She almost said something until she pictured the result of the new kid telling the grown-ups to mind their fire. *Stupid*, she thought. *Keep quiet*.

They stepped out into the room, and Violet was suddenly glad her shoes had fallen off. The floor was shag grass—the softest, warmest pleasure a human foot could ever know. This place was definitely not like Achnacarry. Once her feet stopped hogging her attention, she saw the four who had come to greet them.

She took the eldest to be Alf. He couldn't have been more than fifty, but he was weathered, covered in scars that accented his eastern features. One of his eyes was not an eye, but a cosmetically incongruous implant with several irises. Once she got over the obvious, she was surprised again by his expression. It was less like the expression of a man and more like that of a marble bust, the inhuman stoicism of an ancient face sculpted from a heroic ideal instead of a real, flawed being. He might have been Buddha if he'd reincarnated as a Hell's Angel.

Balder, by contrast, had no scars at all and not a hair on his deep-ebony skin. He was tall and muscular and could have been forty or could have been twenty-five and handsome for any age. He was surely as tough and savvy as the best of the Camerons but was smiling, which the Camerons had never mastered. Unlike those drill instructors who demanded their respect, Balder earned it without asking. The gold light from above made him glow as if perfected in every way, past human and past superhuman, past Atlas in strength and Narcissus in looks. All the men she'd seen before who were overtly proud to be men had been something of a joke. This one made machismo look good for the first time.

They both wore armor like Ragnar's team, which she could now see in the brighter light to be more than plain metal, but a heavily mechanized assembly of materials. Everyone's armor was a different color, Alf's a rich wooden brown, and Balder's gold. R team's members each had their own color. And there were two others present, people her age who looked eager to be introduced. After a life of introversion, for the first time she was eager to meet people.

"I'm Veikko," said the boy in a thick Suomi accent. He had a warm complexion with fiery red hair tied back in a tail. He had a most mischievous smile that suggested a quick wit and cunning mind, which was quite an impression when all he had said was his name. He shook her hand with a palm that, after her brief time outdoors, felt very hot. His suit of red and yellow picked up the firelight to complete her sense of a flame living behind a human mask.

Next to him was a girl who embodied the opposite.

"Vibeke," she said. "Call me Vibs." Her voice was Norsk, something from the most northern reaches of civilization. She must have been at home in the cold. Her uniform was patterned like Veikko's but in blue and green, cool colors under her icy-white face. She even let the platinum roots of her hair show under the false black. *A hint of honesty*, Violet thought, *beyond fashion*. Her face was youthful, cute, so subtly round and soft in the way her lips moved, pronouncing the hard letter C like a whisper, and her Vs like Fs. Violet realized how much she must have liked Norsk accents. If her new surroundings were full of such people, then surely she'd died and gone to—

"*Velkommen til Valhalla*," said Alf.

She had no link, so she couldn't look up the words. The last sounded vaguely familiar, but she didn't know why.

"Valhalla?" she asked.

"Norse heaven," he said. "It means 'Hall of the Slain.'"

Hall of the Slain. Violet suddenly felt very cold, as if the surface air had followed her down. Her new friends were the monsters in her bedtime stories. Her dad had said the name once like it was forbidden. Lieutenant Cameron put it at the top of the feared list. It was the terror of the terrorists. And it was her new family.

Alf picked up on her shock immediately. "I see you've heard of it before."

She swallowed.

"Consider whatever you heard and weigh it with what you know. We are feared by the worst. What do the worst fear? More evil? Certainly. But what they fear most is us, the untouchable opposition. Those owned by the cruelest corporations fear those owned by none because we are the only thing they cannot buy out, intimidate, or send running away. Rest assured, Violet, we are the good guys," said Alf.

"But don't worry," Veikko added, "we still get to kill people."

VALHALLA, THEY told her, was where the dead warriors went to fight in the battles of the gods. They called the men there "*Einherjer*" in antiquity, but time dropped the genders and kept the more sonorous terms. These warriors took the name of the gods' daughters who brought warriors to the golden hall. They called themselves Valkyries.

Chapter IV: Tikari

VIOLET HADN'T eaten since she'd been in the military stockade, where, at 1300 hours, she'd feasted on half a bagel, two nutrient-enriched crackers, and a cup of water. At 2120 hours her stomach gave so loud a roar that Veikko asked if she wanted food or an IV. She chose food.

"This way to the cafeteria," Veikko began. "Watch out for the minotaur. We got one new girl here a week ago, tried to walk three meters in the labyrinth by herself. Never turned up again. Found a severed ear, though."

"Ignore everything Veikko says," added Vibeke. "The whole place looks like a mess at first, but you'll get used to it fast. It has a strange sort of logic to it. If you ever get lost in the ravine, just look up. Those lines all branch off from the central power system. They'll lead you to the center trunk. You won't get lost on the walls. It's all one long spiral to the top."

Veikko continued, "Yeah, yeah, seriously, the caverns are the hard part. The network of caves and cutouts goes about a kilometer into the rock in some directions. You can call up maps as soon as you're hooked into the local network. They'll do that tomorrow. But that's not important. This is." He stopped, turned to Violet, and spoke with the utmost sincerity. "Showers are sonic, sinks are still water, so don't bring glass into the shower or use potassium soap in the sinks. Especially the soap thing. I learned that the hard way. The really, really hard way."

He stared at her and nodded, and then his face broke back into a grin, and he led them deeper into the complex. Soon they were cutting through a variety of rooms and bays: a storage room full of small packets; a hangar holding what looked like giant mechanical legs; tunnels lined with steam pipes; and a rusty round vault that smelled strongly of organic oil. Near the trunk of the giant tree were three massive but apparently empty water tanks. The architecture showed a variety of styles, from parts that were carved into ice, to old stainless steel, to shiny plastic walls that appeared brand new. There were no crowds, but there was a substantial population. Mostly older people, in their twenties and thirties. There were a couple of groups of young men and women, but all looked over seventeen and under fifty.

"Is everyone in a team like us?" Violet asked.

"Not everyone," explained Vibeke. "It's a city and has a small population who, for one reason or another, didn't complete training or came on as specialists, a few locals who found the place and never felt like leaving. Some people like Snorri and Valfar have been here since the terraforming experiments. This place used to be a big science lab."

"Are people allowed to leave?" asked Violet.

"We do a full soul wipe," Veikko admitted gravely.

"No, we don't." Vibeke scowled.

"Not just the memories of us, but all memories," Veikko continued, "They have a programming bay set up for it. I've only heard of one instance. The girl they found turned out to work poorly with her team, so they rewrote her as a happy, well-adjusted lady, gave her a good job, and checked on her from time to time. She's the CEO of a publishing company now. Of course, if you don't work out, Vibs and I will have to stick you in south Indian sewage disposal. They use plumbing, you know."

"Here's the trick with Veikko," whispered Vibeke, "if he says something horrible, it's real. If he says something really horrible, it's real. But if he says something so horrible it would be funny to a psycho with the worst possible sense of humor—"

"Then it's still real. I am not a psycho. I'm just not an artificial intelligence like Vibs. She lost her brain on our last mission, had to replace it with an old calculator program."

"I'm not an AI, and we can do an easy shallow memory trick or two if you want to drop out."

"Isn't that illegal?" Violet asked. She felt stupid for saying it the moment Veikko laughed.

"Everything we do is illegal. If you want legal, join the cops."

"I can't," she admitted. She realized as she said it that she had just told these two more about herself than she'd told her parents.

"Neither can we," said Veikko. "Bad VVPS scores. I'm a twenty-eight and Vibs is a thirty."

Violet was immediately at ease. She wasn't afraid to ask Vibeke, "They didn't make you get recalibrated?"

"Well, they tried," she said, "but I kept hitting them till they gave up."

Violet laughed. She was laughing with friends, and the oddity of such a situation was both frightening and alluring. She had just met them. A thousand kilometers from Scotland and a world away from the familiar, she had friends, two more than she'd ever had before.

"Anyway," Veikko said, "barely anyone wants to leave. This place is like heaven without all the rules."

They came to the cafeteria, which was housed in a large dome. The interior was shaded with the same dark, warm colors as the first lounge. A massive fireplace stood in the center of the room with a tan chimney two meters thick. The whole area had a casual tone, more like a beer hall than a secret arctic installation. The chairs were bean blobs like those in her old cyberlounge, but the decor wasn't what made it feel so unlike the military. Everyone spoke casually, lightly. There was no formality, no strict rules or structure. It was the exact antithesis of the military yet held none of the shame Violet saw when Achnacarry began to allow talking at meals. Something told her that these people had earned the right to relax, and relaxed they were. Only the occasional announcement over the intercom and the colorful armor reminded her that this wasn't a civilian locale.

"C team departing pogo pad four," it said. "Good luck in Lucerne."

Violet wondered what they were going to do in Lucerne. She was going to ask when a more general version of the question occurred to her.

"So can either of you tell me exactly who or what we are training to fight against?"

Veikko considered what to say. Vibeke spoke first so as not to send Violet running.

"It's not the Cetaceans or the West, if that's what you mean. Not specifically. They'll teach you all about it, but the basics are whoever threatens the status quo. Not people who want legitimate change, not political rivalry, but people willing to use extraordinary means to get their way. If the divisionists want independence, fine. If they would go to war for it or kill for it, then we stop them. But some fights we allow and some peaceful problems we fix. Mostly we just do what we wish, within limits.... And not everyone here completely agrees. But most of it's pretty straightforward. Valhalla had a small war with the Orange Gang a couple years before we arrived. Now D team keeps an eye on them."

Violet was going to ask why they didn't end the gang, but Veikko spoke before she could ask. "Still, there's more to it than that. No, no, honestly, there have always been rebels, but now rebels are obsolete. They're a nuisance, not a threat. We're the ones to keep 'em that way. The real threat is from groups like this one. People who operate outside the laws. This isn't the only group of its kind. There are others that aren't so...."

"Benevolent," said Vibeke.

"Some are downright evil," said a voice behind her. Violet turned to see four people, all in flat gray armor.

"I'm Tahir," said one of them.

"I'm Violet," she said.

"We know who you are, came to introduce ourselves," said a woman beside him. "I'm Tasha, this fellow is Toshiro, and the huge guy behind him is Trygve."

"Hi," said Trygve in a soft, high-pitched voice.

"Just remember," said Tasha, "Tahir's Asian, looks like a Toshiro, Toshiro's Dutch, looks like a Trygve, and Trygve sounds like a girl. I'm the only girl in the team."

"T team is our immediate predecessor," said Vibeke.

"Yeah, I came in about a week before Veikko," said Trygve.

"We'll leave you three alone. See you around the pit," said Tahir, and they left. Their absence only revealed another man waiting to say hello.

"Uh, I'm Kabar. Kaunan team. Hi," he said, and then he bowed, turned, and ran away.

"K team are the weapons experts: Kabar, Kalashnikov, Katyusha, and Katana," said Vibeke. "They'll do some of your training."

Violet watched Kabar run away, then returned to her questions. "And you said we have no owner," she asked. "No company to answer to? Who pays for all this?"

"Our enemies," boasted Veikko. "We have plenty of 'em and no qualms about growing fat off their losses."

"You'll pick up the exact nature of why we do what we do once you do it." Vibeke reassured her, "They'll give you an assignment, and once you've done it, you'll recognize why, if it were not done, there could be problems."

"What kind of problems?"

"Hard to explain to someone who hasn't seen what's out there. But our first year or two won't be dangerous material, especially not before we receive and train a fourth team member."

She considered the implications of such things. The obvious question was how to know that these were the good guys, if there were good guys at all outside the boundaries of plain society. But that wasn't nearly as important as the buffet ahead.

Violet recognized the food as all synthetic, which was no surprise in this climate. She was sure if there was any real food to be found, it would be fish, an animal she had tried to eat once on one horrible day and never again.

Veikko leaned in close as she perused the options and whispered, "There are fish eyes in the tapioca, and that green stuff… an awfully soylent shade of green, if you ask me. I think he was named Richard." There were labels over each to disprove Veikko's claims, but they were text. Without her link Violet was left to guess at what they said, so she gathered a colorful selection of substances and hoped one would prove edible.

After the trio had loaded their trays, they sat down at a table near the fire. Violet gave up the slow decorum she kept in the army mess and eagerly tucked in to the synthetic meal. The green cubes were okay, the red and brown cubes weren't bad, but the yellow cubes were the best yellow cubes she had ever eaten. The pink cylinders and gray putty were also good, as was the tan lactose goo and orange juice.

"How's Richard?" asked Veikko.

"Tastes more like a John," Violet said, discarding the green stuff.

"That's too bad. It might have made a good Stu," he said, laughing and spraying a few bits of yellow her way. "You can get real food over at Pyramiden. It's a ten-minute trip by pogo, but the schmoo-food here is the best I've ever had, and I've spent a lot of time under water, so I know."

"Can we just leave any time we want?" Violet asked.

"You'll need to wait for the link," explained Vibeke, "so it can sign you in and out, and the lifts can recognize you, but yes, if you know how to fly. You don't, so we'll teach you next week."

A man behind Veikko waved to Violet. "Hi, I'm Mortiis, Mannaz team. Welcome aboard. Don't let me stop you eating. I remember how hungry I was when I came in. I had about fifty of the brown cylinder things. I love those. I think they're supposed to taste like some sorta meat, but they don't, but I mean they're really good. You can even mash 'em up and mix them in with the fruit paste. That's real fruit. I think they grow it in—uh, you eat, I'll go. Hi, Violet!" He walked away backward, still waving, tripping over a chair before he turned around and left.

Veikko smiled and went on. "So, local travel, you can come and go, but there's not much to do on this island, and less on Spitzbergen. Vadsø is the nearest metropolis, and that's a ways south." Veikko stopped eating for a moment to talk clearly. "Everything's south except the North Pole, about five hundred kilometers of ice water from here."

Violet tried some of the purple spheres. They tried to taste like grapes but failed miserably. She had more yellow cubes.

"There really is absolutely nothing to do on Kvitøya," he continued. "There's Andréeneset point, bit south of the ravine. It's a slab of rock with a smaller slab of rock sitting on it. And then Ostrov Viktoriya to the east, which is less interesting. The North Pole isn't too far by pogo, but all they have is a McDonald's."

"I haven't left for anything but off-site training since I got here," said Vibeke.

"How long have you two been here?"

"Vibs arrived two months ago. I came a month before that."

"Where are you from?"

Vibeke spoke first. "I grew up in Stavanger, then my mother left, and I went to Tromsø with my stepfather, who was not a good stepfather. I ended up killing him, and they took me in shortly after."

"Oh, I'm sorry—"

"Well, we know your family history, so it's only fair."

"I'm from south of Espoo, Suomi," Veikko added quickly, "one of the Itämeri colonies."

Violet was surprised. "You're a Cetacean?"

"My family was. My brother was all out, but I never got the gills or eyes. They all did, and I left for the surface."

"Were they divisionists?" Violet realized that whatever Lieutenant Cameron had talked about, these people probably knew more. "Valkohai?"

"Honestly, I never heard of such a thing until I turned landlubber. If there are fish armies, they weren't talking about it where I came from. Plenty of pirates and gangs. It's like America down there. A degenerate, dank world. One time I made noodles and—"

"For the love of Odin, Veikko, not that story on her first night here." Vibeke stared daggers at him. He stayed quiet long enough for another man to clear his throat and approach their table.

"Hi, Violet, I'm Øystein. I'll be helping with your training."

"Pleased to meet you," she said, and he waved and departed.

"Othala team," Vibeke thought aloud, "… Ozzy, Orchid, and…. Shoot, who else?"

"Opeth," said Veikko. "She's from the Israeli craters, like Gehenna from Gebo team. They're both covered in tribal scars and tattoos. You won't find anyone in this pit that fit into the outside world, over or under water. A good deal of us have had military careers as short and distinguished as your own. Balder even fought in the paroxysmal holocaust and the Catholic uprisings."

Violet had never heard of either event. There was so much she didn't know. She feared she would take ages to learn enough just to converse with her new friends. Veikko caught her worried expression.

"You'll catch up," he said. "As soon as you start orientation tomorrow, you'll be butter in the porridge."

"How many people are there exactly?"

"There are seventy-two people across nineteen teams. Alf doesn't have anyone else in A, only three of us in Valknut. Then there are just under three hundred people in the ravine: civilians and doctors and specialists."

"Where will I start out?"

"Individual training begins the first day," said Vibeke. "They start out with the tailor. You'll get your Thaco armor tomorrow."

Violet looked around. Everyone was clothed neck to foot, all in the same skintight armored jumpsuits of varying colors.

"It's very comfortable," Vibeke continued. "Keeps you cool in heat and warm in cold. If you go outdoors now, it'll grow fur. If it's hot out, it goes thin. Changes color for camouflage, or style, deflects most projectiles and beams. And much, much more. It's like a second skin." She looked at Veikko again. "Just don't think you can go without bathing."

Veikko hid his face.

"Is it powered for lifting, jumping?"

"No," said Veikko. "We prefer to grow our own muscles."

"But they do hook into specialty gear," added Vibeke. "Vacuum gear, water gear, gravity suit, varia suit, acid suit, sticky suit, powered suit if you really need one. Anything."

"Sticky suit?" Violet felt lost again.

Veikko grinned.

"It's a sex aid for—"

"It's for air travel and scaling," Vibs interrupted. "Sticks to things, like the outside of pogos or flat walls. But before armor you'll do the medical stuff, not too different from your army checkup."

Violet remembered the army routine. "Then the oath?"

Veikko laughed. "No, none of that old crap. There is a sort of treaty. You have to memorize it, but that's not hard because it's four words long: 'Don't Fuck Shit Up.'"

"He's actually telling the truth on that one," Vibeke said. "It's meant to be vague and subject to interpretation, but its nature is altogether serious: No party, whether they work for selfish gains or altruistic causes, is allowed to set the outside world into chaos. Underground individuals and organizations alike are all subject absolutely to it."

"Robot," Veikko whispered. He threw one of Violet's uneaten "grapes" into the fire and watched it pop.

"Makes sense," said Violet, "but who enforces it?"

"We don't know much about them," she said, "only that they scare the hell out of everyone here, even Alf. I've never seen them, but the description is black cloaks, always in pairs. Or one pair. See, we don't know if it's all the same duo or if there are thousands of them. In theory, they never come out, never have anything to do. But when they do, it's final. They're judges, jury, and mass executioner when they need to be. From what I've heard, they seem omnipresent and near omnipotent. They're called the Geki."

"And they control fire as a weapon, which probably looks really cool if it's true," said Veikko. "Now you know as much as anyone here."

Violet was as happy to be told every detail as she was intimidated by the meaning of it. They were letting her in on the secrets as if she were trusted. *She was trusted*, she reminded herself. For the first time, she was included at the deepest level, and it made her feel worthy of hearing it all. She wanted to thank them for it, subtly. "Not a lot of 'need to know basis' here, is there?" she asked.

Vibeke seemed to understand her gratitude and answered, "No, no oaths, no salutes, no secrets from friends. If you're loyal, you're loyal because we're worth your loyalty. If you turn on us, there would be a reason, either our fault for warranting it or our fault for selecting you. Either way we'd deserve it and have to fix the problem one way or another."

She said "or another" with the clear meaning that they would kill her. Violet wasn't offended by the idea. It made perfect sense. Vibeke was honest in the exact way the cops weren't.

"You actually tell people the truth here," Violet said with admiration.

"Well, *she* does," chuckled Veikko.

"Secrets only make things inefficient. If you tell the elders that someone's a traitor, they don't ignore you. If someone discovers something, they don't hide it from the juniors. If you're in, you're in. Alf knows what Balder knows what I know what Veikko knows and you're about to learn."

"And there's gonna be a lot, tons of mind-rotting crap," added Veikko, "But really, the guys in G team checked you out when they recruited you. They know how much your brain can hold, and they wouldn't have taken you in if you couldn't handle it."

Despite Violet's worries to the contrary, Veikko saying so didn't feel like patronizing compliments. She wasn't sure why, after a childhood of nothing but euphemism and white lies, she trusted them to do what nobody else had and treat her as an adult. It was what she had waited for her whole life. Now she had it, and it felt so good that she expected it to disappear by the next morning. Nothing so good could possibly last. She stopped the line of thought when a crowd of seven approached their table.

"I am Hellhammer!" shouted a giant, imposing man in black armor.

"And I'm Heckmallet," said a petite woman with a squeaky voice.

"Hetfield," called another man who appeared to be covered in burn scars. "Hammet's in the medical bay, recovering from a slight bout of Descolada. We're Haglaz, research and development specialists. *Enchanté,* Violet."

She nodded kindly, forgetting every name as she heard the next. Another spoke. "I'm Necrosis—we're Naudiz team." He pointed to his companions. "Neurosis, Narcolepsy, and Nail Fungus. Goes by 'Nails.'"

Nails nodded.

"Hi. Hi, pleased to meet you."

The seven left her to continue talking with her team. She tried to remember where the conversation had left off. "What's after the medical checkup and armor?"

"Then we link you up," answered Vibs, "after we install a second Tikari link."

"Tikari?"

Violet heard a gentle buzz and felt a gentle weight on her shoulder. She looked over to see the least gentle thing she had ever seen. If a dagger and a ladybug had a child, this would be the result, and that's very nearly what it was.

"Tikari," said Vibeke as the creature fluttered onto her arm. "They link in to a second antenna you'll have installed and act like a new body part. You can see through their eyes, listen through their tympana. They work as spies or tools or…."

The thing tucked in its legs to form a handle, its shell becoming a hilt, and the wings extending to become a Carlin dagger.

"…weapons."

Veikko chimed in with great pride in the technology. "They can fight on their own, have a link range just over a kilometer. It can record stuff, relay stuff, run simple missions, anything you think into it. An AI takes over as soon as you take your mind off it or send it out of range, so it'll just act like a pet unless you give it a standing order. The AI is like Vibeke-level smart so expect some personality after a while, mostly based on yours. But never forget, it's a weapon. Those wings are part of a blade, and they're made from permarazor steel. Do not ever, under any circumstances, try to pet it." He held up his hand to show the scar from a very deep cut.

Veikko took a deep breath and explained more. "A Tikari can do damn near anything. It's durable. You could bury it in Ganymede mud for ten years, and it will jump out ready for action. It can handle objects with great care with its legs. It can fly, walk, climb, and kill. It can send any sensory impulse and act as your eyes, ears, nose, tongue, and fingertips. It can fight in twenty-four styles, including berserker mode, where it'll kill everyone but you, so, um, please don't use that one around me. You can even set it as a mine, kamikaze mode. In knife form it can fly by gyroscope and rocket power, cut down an entire tree and still stay sharp enough to perform delicate surgery, which it can do in bug form, knowing how to perform over six hundred operations, none of them cosmetic. It can cut through bone, even sever a limb in one stroke. It can hide itself from M-scans, C-scans, X-scans, and P-scans. Same with the port—even the metal in it can pass for your real sternum. The AI can manifest online as its own avatar and set up a Roth IRA and protect its owner with tons of crazy hacks and viruses. Unlinked, it can find and return to its owner from across the solar system and stay in orbit indefinitely. It can heat its blade to eight hundred kelvins, trim your toenails, weave a basket underwater, and play back ten thousand songs."

"What can't it do?" Violet asked.

"It's not very good as a towel," Vibeke said as her Tikari wandered off.

"Where's yours?" she asked Veikko.

It crawled out of a vent in his armor over his chest—a green-and bone-colored creature, more like a praying mantis. As the Tikari crawled onto the table, Veikko explained, "They make it out of your sternum and rib cartilage, and it goes back to sleep there. They replace your bones with a plasticized port for it. Doesn't hurt. Your skin also gets a slight mod to open and close seamlessly. The organic materials make it impossible to fool or forge, and the devoted link is unhackable. That's why it's so short range. Most teams all have the same sort, the same insect and same blade. You saw R team's double-dagger beetles. We enjoyed your double-dagger beetle battle. But there are all sorts of bugs around here. I got a mantis spade, but Vibs went with a ladybug Carlin knife, so the line is broken. You can get whatever you want."

It sounded like an extraordinarily useful thing to have, but the enormity and insectity of it was hard to get past. Violet didn't particularly want a bug living in her chest, nor did she want to have surgery or spend time learning to use such a complex thing. "Do I have to get one?"

"You kidding? They're the greatest things in the world. You'll love it like a pet, body part, and trusty Swiss army knife all in one."

"And if I don't?" she asked, figuring they had to have more conventional weaponry around.

"Well, we have a couple lightsabers if you prefer, but they're the most annoying, impractical things to handle. They burn everything they touch or cut it in half and cauterize it. You can find both in the ice-gear closet if you want to play with them, but bring a mask. They stink up the place with ozone. And they don't repel each other if they clash. They just stick together and smell worse."

"Trust us, you'll love yours," said Vibeke.

Violet felt trepidation at the thought but had no will to avoid the inevitable. When in Rome she would do as the Romans, and when in Kvitøya she would get a second link installed for a robotic knife insect made from her sternum, which would be replaced by a docking port for it to live in while seeing and hearing for her or flying from her hand to kill someone.

"Any other mods?" she asked, afraid of the response.

"Intraskull armor," Veikko said. "But we know you got that as a kid."

"Of course, everyone does. I mean, are there any more living bug robots or weirder stuff?"

"No, we stay pretty human. Unless you die."

Vibeke nodded. "Yeah, if you die, you can count on med team to fill you with their latest gizmos. They're phenomenal, and they're not limited by a budget. If you die and you still have a brain, they wake you up again. Always. Almost everyone on a team has died. You're not even called a junior team till one of you has been killed. Tahir—the guy you just met—he only died last week. Got torn in half in a Skuzz factory. Big celebration. The doctor gave him some great robotic legs."

Violet looked to Vibeke to ask if he was kidding. She only continued on the same line. "Balder's the only guy in the elder teams who's never been killed. His whole team's died many times, even irreparably. They keep the same names as their predecessors, but most of them aren't much older than us. G team, the recruiters, they keep having to replace them. The latest new guy to take the name Bathory might have been in V team if not for the last Bathory getting blown up. Borknagar died too, but not badly, just lost his heart and lungs. Dr. Niide gave him all sorts of new stuff, gills and vacuum inhalers."

A woman waved from the buffet line. Violet waved back.

"That's Svetlana, Sveta for short—her real name from before she got here, I think. She's in S team with Skadi, Sigvald, and Snot," said Vibeke, "Anyhow, you exercised a lot before you came here. That will help, as will the bit in the Royal Armed Forces. It's good you know how to go linkless. You'd be surprised at how much we work offline."

Suddenly the intercom sounded: "Veikko, Vibeke, Violet, Sector 5B. Walrus detail."

"Oh fuck." Veikko stood up. "We have enough people now."

"What? What for?" Violet asked as she and Vibeke stood. The trio left the table following Veikko's lead. He walked as if he was following something invisible to their destination.

"Three people is enough for walrus detail," explained Vibs. "They get in sometimes."

"Walruses? How secure is this place if a bunch of blubber heaps can wander in?"

"That's the thing. Nobody's seen them get in, so we don't know what to seal off."

"How many live here?"

"Tons of 'em. Though each is about three tons, so it doesn't take many. Kvitøya used to have polar bears before they went extinct. Once the bears were gone, the walruses took over and got fatter. This island used to be bigger too, before the melt, and covered in ice."

"So we have to round them up?"

"We do now."

Violet had been there an hour, and already there was work to be done, work she didn't know how to do. "I haven't been trained in that."

"There's not much to learn," Veikko assured her. They walked a short way to sector 5B, and he showed them to a locker full of sonic equipment.

"It will run from the sticks. We want to move it toward the cages."

He pointed to a cluster of giant metal cages nearby. They followed Veikko to an alcove of rock where a massive frightened animal sat. It was nearly amorphous, just fat and tusks. Violet had never seen any living thing so gargantuan and grotesque, but it was clearly scared and alone. She waited for Veikko's lead.

He headed to the ridge behind it and set his sonic emitter to encourage the creature out of the nook. Vibeke and Violet had no trouble using their own sticks to keep it on course. With three wands directing it, the walrus predictably moved for the open direction, and without question right into the cage. Veikko linked a message to the cage system and automated cranes took over, hauling the beast up to the surface, where it was released. The three headed back to the cafeteria to finish eating.

"How often does that happen?" she asked as they walked back.

"Not very," said Vibeke.

"Yes, very," retorted Veikko. "Tahir said he lost count after a week."

"It's not that much."

"It's that much, and when one team has three people, they get all the calls. Until we find a fourth, we're screwed. You were the harbinger of doom, Violet."

"Don't let him pester you about being a third. Every team has full walrus detail for a while."

"When we get a fourth, it goes back to rotating around teams. But with just Vibs and I, we didn't have enough members to do it at all." He called melodramatically, "How I dreaded this day…."

"Shush. They don't come in all that often." Violet knew Veikko would keep arguing, so, as they took their seats, she started a new thread of conversation. "How long does training last?" She turned off the warmth field on her plate and dug in again.

"Till you're dead," said Veikko. "You don't graduate from anything, you just progress. And most training isn't simulated; it's all done for real. You just start out with the light work and get deeper and heavier. We're just starting on some of the important stuff, surveillance, communication."

"Like what, specifically?"

"We had to observe the vomitorium at a coprophagiac colony by smell alone," Veikko said solemnly.

"Har har. Our last assignment was a month of net surveillance and research. G team found a potential recruit, so we had to study their background and personality and online activity. Then data analysis: can we trust this person; will they be capable of our kind of work? We made a positive recommendation and asked to make contact."

"So what happened?"

"You thought Vibs was a program," Veikko snorted with a broad smile.

"We liked you anyway, and Reid team brought you in."

As they explained the thorough research involved in approaching new recruits, Violet began to understand more of why she'd been selected. Her entire life was recited to her in terms that seemed not like a biography but a resume. Her problems in the past were not a sad time in school but a prerequisite for a necessary psychological landscape. Her capacity for violence was a positive now; even her compulsive tendencies (which she did not know she had until Vibeke told her) made her a good candidate for their kind of work.

As they elaborated on her persona in terms so personal she felt terribly exposed, she gained comfort from the fact that these new partners not only knew her this well and still seemed to like her, but they were clearly selected for sharing every trait. She had never met people so like herself. She listened to stories of Valhalla accomplishments and of the lives of her new comrades, but she would remember little. Somewhere around 0445 she drifted off to sleep, landing facedown in her sugary gray putty.

VIOLET AWOKE in her own bed. It was the same size, shape, and firmness as her bed in Arcolochalsh, which she hadn't slept in for months. It had the same kind of purple blanket that she had left to be incinerated back in the arcology. There was also a new thick purple quilt. The rest was duplicated in every detail, except that it was in a small four-bunk room in a rocky pit in the far north. Violet remembered a fragment of conversation from the night before, something about how they'd researched every detail of her life before they brought her in. If the bed was any indication, they weren't exaggerating.

Her link was off, but a small display on the wall noticed her looking at it and stated the time as 1349. They had let her sleep in later than she ever allowed herself. She was alone in the room. Across from her bed were two made beds, one above the other. Above her own was an empty slab to hold a fourth. The only other object in the room was on the bed with blue covers, a small leathery block with text on its side. She assumed it to be Vibeke's. Somehow she could picture Vibs and Veikko at home in the room, sleeping, waking, adjusting the light of the fake window. She could as easily picture them working somewhere in the ravine, right then, letting her sleep in late after her busy yesterday. When she opened the blinds on that fake window and saw a terrible fiery hellscape, she knew which of them had programmed it last.

She found the bathroom and medicine cabinet stocked with the objects and brands she kept at home. Upon seeing them she realized that she must have missed them in the military barracks. The shower was set loud and scourging, which she preferred to the arcology's gentle, high-pitched showers. These were preferences she had not told anyone, online or off. Had they broken into her mind directly before she came in? She had never been hacked into and didn't know if she would recognize it if they did.

After a very long and loud shower, she checked the drawer under her bed and found a drape like those commonly worn in Scotland. She threw it on and walked to the door. She half expected to be locked in, but the door opened with a touch and let her into the barracks halls and atria. It felt like a luxury hotel, with sofas and fires, rock and wooden architecture. She saw people milling about at ease. One man in a hot-pink uniform waved to her. She waved back. In some ways the casual tone still offended her military expectations, but she got the impression that when the time came, these people would be far more reliable than her old comrades. There was no need for strict Achnacarry order here—the people were organized on their own. Something in their eyes reminded her of the scarred Sergeant Cameron, something that said their training must have been every bit as brutal as what she had enjoyed.

She stepped outside the building to find Alföðr waiting for her.

"*God ettermiddag*," he said. She didn't need her link to hear "Good afternoon." "I hope you found everything to your tastes?"

"Eerily," she said. "How did you, uh—"

"Vibeke demanded up front to know if we hacked into her brain," he said. "Veikko was downright frightened at the prospect. I am happy to say we did not. We merely do our research well. You'll learn to do the same shortly and will exercise the ability once we have another prospect for your team."

"You really check our shower settings, mattress firmness? Has it always been like that?"

"Not at all," he bragged gutturally. "When they brought me in, they only had mint toothpaste, to which I have the utmost animosity," he said with a snarl. "I prefer orange flavor and implemented the reforms that demanded attention to such details. Shall we start the tour?"

"Please."

"Then first, let me introduce you to Governor Quorthon."

After a short walk, they came to a cylindrical building with a lit dome and several triangular buttresses.

"This is city hall. The civilian population, two hundred and ninety people, enjoys a company structure, though they share our independence and the spoils of our wars. Governor Quorthon was a company representative for the Ares Corporation, who first built the labs here about sixty years ago. He's one hundred and twenty-eight years old, and has been reelected every year by the populace. He treats us all most kindly, keeps the residents out of our way in times of emergency, and has never failed to keep the cafeteria full of food or the specialists happy. From time to time he gives us a project, little things mostly. He also settles any disputes between the teams and the residents, but we haven't had any in, oh, at least ten years. Did Veikko and Vibs tell you about the treaty?"

"Don't Fuck Shit Up?"

"Exactly. It applies to the ravine as much as the rest of the world, as I'm sure the governor will tell you at least seven times. Humoring his remarks is a full 20 percent of my duties. It's best you have a go at it now in case you have to take over someday."

The governor was a tall man with long white hair. Beside him stood a short man in no fewer than three thick winter coats.

"Valfar!" said Alf. "I'm glad you could make it. Violet, this is Valfar, another man from the Ares company and our groundskeeper. He'll be showing you around today. Governor, this is Violet."

"Pleased to meet you Violet," said Quorthon softly. "I assume you have been told the treaty?" Quorthon went on to repeat it anyway, several times. It seemed like a lecture to kids but she didn't object this time, partly because he was seven times her age and partly because he was clearly just concerned for his people, admirably so. After a brief boilerplate introduction, he expounded on the treaty and pretended not to notice Alf's yawn. Violet was impressed at how long Quorthon could talk without actually saying anything. A skill she assumed kept him in office. After he and Alf said their good-byes, the trio left his office. Once in open air, Alf laughed.

"Was it the same?" he asked Valfar.

"Exactly," he responded with a thick accent. "Not a word different from when Vibs came in. Exactly thirteen minutes and four seconds."

"I'll have H team make sure his brain hasn't been stolen again." He turned to Violet. "Some of the younger civilians hack into it from time to time—an old tradition. Last time they left it on a loop, and we didn't notice for two years."

The two men gave each other a complex fist jab, and Alf headed away.

"I'll see you tomorrow, Violet, for training. Enjoy your tour!"

"Thanks," she responded and looked to Valfar. "Where do we begin?"

"At the core," he said. She thought he said "car" at first, his voice was so different from what she was used to. With her link on, the word would have come with knowledge of its intended meaning. But without the available footnotes and terminology options at her disposal, his accent obscured it. Veikko and Vibeke sounded only slightly strange, but Valfar reminded her just how alien the English language could sound around the world. Millennia of linguistic diversity had left their mark.

She figured out he meant "core" as they headed to the trunk of the giant glowing tree. The branches extended over her head in all directions, bringing power to every structure. She could see more clearly that people were walking on them; the Branches' apparent frailty was an illusion. When they reached the central trunk, Valfar rubbed his hands over it and nodded for her to do the same. The surface was warm but not hot. It was as hard as the hardest stone, and the glow seemed softer up close than from afar. She was about to ask what it was made of when Valfar spoke.

"YGDR S/L power system and distribution lattice, built to power the Ares project but repurposed with eighty-eight new S/L nodes to power Valhalla." His accent seemed to grow thicker as he went on. "Ya note the rainbow effect it has on the ice in the walls. Pretty, neh? Neh. Nah, the energy harnessed by splitting atoms can't compare to that earned more safely by flipping quarks. Sadly, thanks to old man Heisenberg, we can't really see the damn quark without moving it, so his theory was compensated for by having yer friends watch instead while you do the work. Then ya provoke disputes between muons and their massless partners. That's another orientation trick. See, when an overzealous muon can be convinced to leave its aging life partner for a young exotic atom, that releases the old electron from his duties, leaving his hot young neutrino home alone and desperate for attention!" She thought he'd just made a joke, but between his demented vocabulary, personification of subatomic particles, and accent, she couldn't be sure. He gave her no chance to ask what he meant. "I tell ya, when we started the first generator, someone got between a tau lepton and her young, got a furious outburst of third generation antineutrinos, and blew up an automated lab. Made an ugly, sticky lake of spare gluons and other particles that were rumored to be pentaquarks, if you believe in such nonsense. In any case there was no resulting radiation, so the resulting sludge lake was surrounded by a stone-and-turf barrier that we called Hadron's Wall."

He leered at her as if waiting for her to laugh. She was sure he had just said something that Vibeke might have understood and found amusing, but she was utterly lost, worried he had just told her something she might one day need to know. All she got was the word "atom" and a good sense that the thing powering Valhalla was way beyond her comprehension. Even if he'd not had an accent, the very first thing he showed her was so far past her understanding that she didn't even know what to ask about to clear it up.

"Ha?" she said to let him move on.

"Nch! Yar from Scatlin after all!" He laughed heartily and continued. "Ol' Alf spent days up there, wandering the branches to come up with the rune system. Clever guy, yah know. Yeh, yah can walk on the branches. Just watch out for nidhoggs an' be sure to get yer feet defuzzed on a defuzz pad."

He showed her a black pad on the ground, of which there were many around the ravine. She understood that she'd have to touch one to get rid of the static charge if she touched the power grid. He showed her how and spoke slowly to ensure she knew how much repair work he'd have to do if she forgot. He moved on to the doors of the nearest building and began to tell her how the doors worked and how to open them in an emergency. She understood less and less of what he said but more and more of what he showed her. Before long she gave up on the words and just watched.

She had expected to see only the parts of the city meant for the youngest of its residents, but the tour continued with the heaviest machinery and the depths of the place. She was shown the functional core of the heating and electrical systems, which had always been off-limits in the outside world. He gave her an overview of each machine, letting her know how to turn it off in an emergency, where to find the people or net files who knew how to repair it, and even the basics of how to do so herself. He took great pride in every system and gadget and didn't mind slowing down or repeating a critical bit of explanation when she really needed it. The rest of his remarks, most of which she assumed were humorous, were lost in his accent, speed, and esoteric terminology. She saw him demonstrate the emergency fireplace foamer system and learned how to use it herself, but she knew she would never know what he meant by "Farghplatz fough-marsissymn."

When they passed a closed door, he would open it, and if he didn't, he explained honestly why. She was never told that she wouldn't understand, never told that a section was not her business or something she did not need to worry about. The city gradually became familiar and lost its mystery in favor of a moderate understanding. Valfar even showed her the arsenals, special arsenals, and secret caches that housed weapons beyond her most sadistic imagination. He did not explain them only because she would be briefed on them later in a devoted session by K team. As they came to the pogo landing pads along the walls, he showed her a few things she never knew about how she had been traveling all her life.

"They're ground effect vehicles, like the old Caspian Sea Monster, but with field wings that extend out forever, allowing any height, so long as the craft is in motion. Early generations of the craft had to depart and land on a rather lengthy runway, but that was abandoned upon invention of inertial suppression systems, allowing the craft to just kick off hard into the sky and hit the ground just as fast. That hard liftoff and equally amusing landing earned the craft its name and inspired a sport in which the dampening effect was turned off to prove one's machismo, leading to the pride of dozens and deaths of hundreds."

He showed her a plethora of other vehicles she had never seen before. She would in time learn to fix, drive, tactically crash, and peel every one of them to the basic parts. He said little about each on that first tour, but Violet saw one contraption she had to ask about. She had seen a skiff before in a school video. The school wanted her to see it so she would never try to use one, ever. They were by far the most dangerous vehicle ever invented, and like their ancient relative the "skateboard," they were banned in all GAUNE companies and countries. Valfar confirmed what it was and that they used them from time to time.

"Just start its field and stand on its tiny frame as it floats over the ground, and try to keep balance as it flies one hundred and fifty kph over any terrain, but not now. Live a few more days," he said. Violet looked forward to training on it.

They finished the tour at the top of the spiral walkways near the surface, in the communications building, which hung like a bat from rocks that overhung the ravine. Valfar's voice was going hoarse and getting even less comprehensible.

"Com tower. Has the heaviest magnetic shield in the pit. Best place to broadcast, worst place for a magnetic system. The shield is so thick it'll render most magnets useless. They won't even show up on a mag scan. Makes for crystal-clear link signals. Also the com tower houses the HMDLR, the defense system, so accurate it can hear the grass grow, sounds the alarms if it hears anythin' we don't expect. Then we got the rampart."

He pointed out where the rampart ("Raghpurtht." She assumed he meant rampart) would rise up. In an era of repulsion fields and automated targeting beams, Valhalla had a new twist on an ancient safeguard. It had walls. Actual, physical walls. Nobody flying or even walking over Kvitøya would notice the glacial rock at the island's edge. It was just rock. But on short notice, seventy thousand tons of that rock was mechanized to lift up and close off the ravine entirely, to make an outer shell around the entire island complete with what was jokingly referred to as a "drawbridge" at the southmost point—a photonically selective gateway that could let vessels and personnel in and out through solid rock if they were tuned to the right rotating spectrum. The rainbow capabilities of Valhalla jumpsuits were not just for camouflage and décor. They were the only outfits that could pass in and out of the fortress when it was sealed up. Anything that tried with any single color would get halfway in, but then the spectrum would shift, and they would be trapped in solid rock.

"The rocks are very loud," he explained. "Haven't used it in years. Won't use it short of an all-out attack."

She could see over the ravine's jagged edge that the sun was going down.

"Ahh, night. Ya remember where med bay was?" he asked.

"Yes, north end of the floor, by the gymnasium."

"Yah, stuck in yer head, all right! Go there, they're expectin' ya. Great stuff in the med bay—phospholipid polarity drives that can back up fifty brains. They used to use neural nets, but the things kept changing their minds, ha! Ya have a nice night, Vielaht!"

"Thonks—Thanks. You too."

She walked down the path around the sides of the ravine. She was relieved to be heading to the med bay. Valfar's accent had given her a tremendous headache. But the man was kind, clearly brilliant, and constantly assured her that once her link was up, everything he said could be reinforced by maps and manuals. Despite the complexity of it all, she felt that she might not need them for some of the simpler elements of the city. She might never comprehend quark inversion, but she knew how to walk the branches. She could function the same way she'd worked through school—with the bare minimum. But would that be enough here?

The medical bay had a clear front wall, which let her see every patient inside. It seemed a cruel architectural blunder, but it let her find the doctor quickly. She could also see the tons and tons of machinery that allowed Valhalla's medical team to work at an exceptional speed. The doctor would program the machines to perform the surgery at hand, and then they would perform it with inhuman swiftness, removing and replacing a heart between beats or attaching a new limb before a drop of blood could spill out.

Dr. Niide was from the Nippon Company islands. His mumbles were easy to decode compared to Valfar's accent. He had a thick red beard and eyes that seemed to X-ray her as they looked. She realized quickly that that's probably what they were doing. They had silver irises and were clearly implants.

"Valfar.... Hmmm, show you everything?" he muttered.

"Yes."

"Here.... For the headache." He applied something directly to her forehead, and the pounding of her brain ceased immediately.

"Thank you," she said most genuinely.

"Mm.... Valfarism, everyone gets it.... I myself cause drowsiness.... Let's take a look at you."

He guided her to a table, where she began to disrobe. The table was in full view of the clear wall, but there was nobody outside, and years of traditional Scottish nudism had rid her of any such inhibitions. "No need," said Niide. He tapped his eye with the end of his stethoscope. "These can see... right through you...."

She pulled her drape back up while he looked her over, and his eyes adjusted to look at her internal organs and skeleton. He continued to mumble. "Hmmm, very severe.... Poor condition, heavy infection.... Disarticulation.... Oh no, no.... Clearly broken.... Mm-hmmm.... All right, then, all's well, perfect health, clear to go...."

She waited to hear what his mumbles might have meant, but he had no idea what she was waiting for.

"Go on, head to, mmm.... Ah, Eric. Armor.... Yes, will see you again.... Soon for the Tikari. Mmm, terribly painful.... Terribly.... Have a nice evening...."

He wandered away into his office. Eager to clear her head of the latest encounter, she headed to a small building in the back of a cavern near the north end of the complex, where Valfar had mentioned the "Targhlair." There she found Eric, who ran the tailor and armor plant. Much to her relief, he spoke like a human being. Mostly.

"We haves your jumpsuits ready. What colors you want? I'll programs it in for ya. Gotsta pick some features too. Most is standards—ammo pockets, armor plating, breathing mechanism, vacuums protection, heating, cooling, drying, damping, all that jazz. You like jazz?"

"Um, I don't really like band music," she admitted as she pulled on the jumpsuit.

"Modern girl, huh? Nothing wrongs with that," he lisped.

He tapped the collarpiece of her suit as he handed it to her. It gave a tinny sound, "Metal suit, the suit is metal, even the jumpsuits are metal based. Never never never never enter a magnetic zone without turnings on the damping fields! Remember that. Top button, back of your collar, just over the breathing gear. Never enter a magnetic zone undampened! Will freeze up on yas."

"What are these cuts in the arms?"

"For clingers. Attachments—you'll see when they gives you a microwave. Hooks right on."

He went on to show her the Thaco armor shell and jumpsuit capabilities, often repeating his warning about magnets. He had crammed the suits full of every field discriminator (like the one in the com tower) and mag plating known to humankind, but the suit was still metal, and still magnetic. Raw fields and magnetic tractoring waves could affect it if she didn't turn on the dampener. He explained that the systems used her body as a generator, so if she left the field on all the time, it would tire her out. The armor was tough. It could repel most small projectiles and common microwave beams, but it wasn't invulnerable.

"Best nots to get shot. When in doubts about the suit's defenses, don't get shot."

Next he took her deeper into the tailory and demonstrated a variety of specialty suits, heavy microwave and laser-proof features, gravity suits and vacuum-capable suits, and showed her a sticky suit, which bonded selectively to whatever the wearer wanted, using what Eric called "gecko hair." She tried on just a glove of the suit and found she was unable to let go of anything she handled.

"Just don't thinks about your hand. It will release."

But of course, she could only think about her hand being stuck. She decided not to wear the full suit until she had much more practice.

Eric suggested she get lunch, and she found her way to the cafeteria, where Vibeke was waiting. They sat down to eat. Violet kept to yellow cubes and orange fluids.

"Good color for your suit," said Vibeke, "in case anyone forgets your name."

"It seemed appropriate. Always been my favorite color."

"Just watch in case it changes. If it does, you're on duty. So can you find your way around?"

"More or less. The cavern complex is still confusing."

"It is. I try to think of it as two rectangles stuck to a triangle."

"That sounds about right. So Alf is going to give us our orders, handle everything we do?"

"Not always. The organizational structure is nearly chaotic. This isn't a military, nor was it founded from one big bang into a hierarchy. It just filtered into place from nothingness, bodies attracting and gravitating into masses like the rest of the universe. They'll give you the history if you ask for it."

"Yah, Ahlm Shaghr."

Vibs laughed. "Valfar starts to make sense as soon as you're linked in. Alopex has a special program just to translate for him. Snorri is the ravine historian, though. He's older than Quorthon."

"Who's Alopex?"

"That's right, they haven't plugged you in yet. We have a devoted network. You can get out to the web in one of those black avatars you saw us using when we met. When you plug in here, the first thing you see is Alopex, the local server broadbrain. She can tell you anything."

"I guess that will wait till tomorrow?"

"No, not at all. We're half nocturnal. Dr. Niide is still on duty."

"Why do I need him to link me in?"

"Because we can't turn it on until you have your Tikari link, and we can't give you that till you have a Tikari."

Violet was less than eager.

"Don't worry," said Vibs, "they can assemble a new Tikari in under half an hour."

But that wasn't what Violet was worried about.

TO HER relief it was fast and mostly painless. In theory it could have been completely painless, but a hazing mentality had lingered in the Valhalla clan that suggested giving birth to one's new body part should not be entirely without feeling. Her choices for weaponry and color and type were taken down for a Bowie knife / robber fly Tikari.

Dr. Niide programmed the machines, set them to her body scans, and activated a sterile analgia field overhead. He told her to lie still for at least two seconds. In those two seconds, the machinery came out of the ceiling, dug out her chest, put most of it back in, drilled a new antenna into her brain, applied healing systems, and then disappeared back into the ceiling. She continued to lay in place, motionless.

"Yes, Violet?" mumbled the doctor. "Are you waiting… for something?"

She got up and headed for the "nursery" to be briefed by the specialists. They explained the basics of the double-link system with a caveat about link damage. In order that a Tikari not be hacked or commandeered by the enemy, should the link be damaged or compromised, the Tikari would turn to weapon form and weld itself dead. It would be just a knife. Another could be made, but the few who had lost theirs didn't want another for a long time, if at all. It was like trying to replace a sibling.

Once finished, they left her alone in the operating room. A gel case came out of the Tikari lab wall and opened. Then she saw it. The body was the same color as her suit, name, and eyes, and unlike the first scary insect she had seen, this was simply the most beautiful creature in the world. It stood lifeless, but she felt at that moment as close to a parent as she ever would, in awe of the little bug that was made from her own ribs.

Then they hit the link, and she heard herself breathing from its sensory interface. Cold words for the warmest connection. She opened its eyes for the first time, and it was like opening her own, though she saw herself—not like a mirror, but like a child seeing her mother. But she recognized herself. There was such sensation seeping into her brain from its AI, she was nearly overcome. She felt from within it like one can feel their own heart when they lay perfectly still. It was eager to move. She stretched its legs for the first time. It felt like stretching her own. She wanted to fly, and so she—it—they could. It hovered, and she knew what it was like to take to the air, to beat her wings a hundred times a second. It was tremendously loud; the metal wings made a terrible buzz.

As soon as she wondered why hers was so loud, the Tikari link automatically told her what system to activate to make the wings soft as a whisper. She thought the system on, and the buzzing went silent. The Tikari was very user-friendly for a brain-linked insect robot. And it was easy to fly. She swooped close across the floor, the clarity of her new eyes still shockingly vibrant. They landed. In the next minutes all the confusion of the new sensations fell away, and she walked from the medical bay beaming. Somehow, the Tikari was happy too.

Once in the med bay lobby, she set the AI loose and told it to return home. The visuals and sounds faded away, and the critter happily snuck into the vent in her suit and tucked itself into her chest. And then she was Violet again, but not alone. The rest of her remained as close as close gets. The Tikari's internal chronometer reminded her that if she didn't continue on with Vibeke, she might spend eternity playing with her new knife.

Back in their barracks, Vibs logged in and gave the commands to start Violet's account. Violet restarted the conventional link behind her ear and saw Alopex. Alopex, unlike the typical home system, appeared to be a fully developed AI, represented by a white fox.

"Hello, Violet," said the fox, "I'm Alopex. I also answer to APX for raw interface. What can I do for you?"

"System immersion."

Reality blacked out, and she was alone in the darkness with Alopex.

"Where's the home silo?"

"Alopex system is not designed for immersion. Specific menus and imagery can be called up individually. Immersion in public nets is accessible by calling up any log-in point."

She snapped back out to the real world. She looked around, but there were no ads or wall graphics.

"Call up local titles."

Nothing appeared.

"Alopex system does not have local titles."

"Call up local directory?"

"Alopex system has no directory."

Violet could feel maps and menus ready to pop up if called, but it was true, there was no directory. It was almost like being unlinked. She dimmed Alopex and spoke to Vibeke.

"What kind of system is this?"

"It does anything you need. You can call up any information and get to the outside, but there are no local features, no wandering avatars or lobbies, just Aloe."

She had expected Valhalla to lose its mystery and sense of awe when the link returned. If she intentionally called up a map or label, she could see what building was what. She could call up a manual and comprehend some of Valfar's more mispronounced instructions. The link even read text for her like she was used to, but unless she asked for something, the link gave nothing. It was a net that she could control—the best of both worlds. She considered what other questions to ask the wise fox and her human companion, but the multitude of unknowns formed a logjam, and no single curiosity came forward.

"It's very quiet," Vibs explained. "No ads, no incoming labels, no interruptions at all."

The fox spoke. "Veikko, Vibeke, Violet, Sector 12A. Walrus detail."

Vibeke blew a stray hair from her face. They grabbed the equipment and followed Alopex, who trotted to sector 12A. As the fox moved, she left a lit path on the ground for them to follow. At the end of the lit path, they met Veikko on a section of the walkway that spiraled up the wall.

"This is our life now," he greeted them. "Ignore your dreams and aspirations. This giant blubber monster is your future."

"God, Veikko, give it up. We've only done it twice."

So continued their argument all the way to the cages, where Veikko left them to return to his own training.

"It's really not all that often," Vibs said. "Now, where were we?"

"Alopex. I have so many questions, and I can't think of a single one."

"Ask her the rest in your sleep. As for what the computer can't tell you, people tend to congregate in the elevator lounges and cafeteria, but the games in the gym are most popular. Did Valfar show you the gym?"

"He showed me where it was, but we didn't go in."

"You need to get hard as ice and stay that way. There's always human-instructed training in weapons and martial arts, all the usual exercise machines, but nothing compares to På Täppan."

Aside from the expansive and lush complex of the gym, with its soft shag grass floors and an immense artificial moonlit sky, the exercise facility had a full indoor field devoted to the ancient and noble art of civil warfare called "På Täppan," which Violet had learned under the Scottish name "King of the Hill." The rules were the same, but the stakes here were raised. Firstly, the "Hill" appeared to be composed mostly of losing players, team people in armor and civilian residents in whatever else. Second, it was played under an analgia generator, rendering players unaware of pain. This resulted in the most brutal sport ever conceived. In the massive throbbing pile of shouting bodies were acts of hedonistic cruelty that the playground version could never approach. People were thrown as weapons. People were stepped on, trampled, beaten, pulled on, everything short of bitten, and then they were savagely bitten. Winning was short-lived. One man was tackled as he bellowed his victory cry only to tumble down with his usurper. There seemed no real care for remaining on top, only for indulging in the horrible trial of it all.

Violet was still in peak military shape, and lasted exactly fifty-three seconds, making it one-eighth up the heap before she was thrown to the ground, out of breath. Vibeke, having a month more practice, lasted an impressive three minutes but climbed little higher. Violet couldn't help but notice the exceptional form Vibs showed as she climbed, how she was so strong, muscular like the strongest of climbers, yet still kept a most feminine figure. Her interest was half in the hopes that she too would look the same after as much exercise, and half something else. The short time spent in the venture proved it to be an ideal form of exercise, at least for the extraordinarily fit and somewhat devilish.

"Vibs," shouted a deep female voice with a Russian accent, "you are better suited to sparring, one on one, not this spectacle of twisted limbs and tumbling."

Vibeke, still out of breath, introduced the caller. "Hi. Mishka, Violet; Violet, Mishka, Mannaz team."

Mishka was buff and tall, with very long red hair. Her Thaco armor was blood red.

"Hi," said Violet.

"Hello, you must be the new meat."

"Must be," she replied, suddenly bashful.

"Mishka's been my partner for some time," said Vibeke. "Sparring, sparring partner. She's a monster."

"Pleased to meet you," Mishka laughed, though her smile never reached her eyes.

"You too. How long have you been here?" Violet asked.

"Two years. Forty-three major missions. But not a good deal of this mountain-climbing sort of thing. There are more dignified ways to stay in shape."

"When have you ever cared for dignity, Mishka?"

Mishka just grinned, bit her lip, and walked away, brushing against Vibeke as she left.

"*Do svidaniya*," Vibs whispered. Then she turned to Violet. "Sparring is important, but this anarchist equivalent has its charms. I think she's just annoyed I have a new teammate. She won't get to beat the crap out me anymore."

The two headed back to the barracks. Vibeke explained a few more bits and pieces of the new link system on the way. "Quantum cryptography. All automatic. The closer you are to Valhalla or whoever you're talking to, the thicker the encryption. If you linked to me right now, it would be the most private conversation two humans ever had. If you link to me from Mars, you'll be yelling so loud half the planet can butt in. You can also send Alopex along with the message if you can't locate the recipient."

As the analgia wore off, the pain caused by Violet's brief time on the hill began to manifest. She had worked herself even harder than she thought and began to limp. She was relieved that Vibeke wasn't immune to the same. They stumbled into the barracks to find Veikko waiting.

"På Täppan?" he asked.

"Yeah, she lasted almost a minute."

"Not bad," said Veikko. "I spent ten seconds in the pile my first time and left with broken feet. There's a reason the medical bay's next to the gym."

"Anything new?" asked Vibeke.

"Yeah, a problem. Detectors on special arsenal seven's gate have malfunctioned twice in as many days."

"An accident?"

"We don't know. Sowilo team is on it. Skadi told me earlier. But two separate failures suggests something wants them to fail."

"What's in the special arsenal? Valfar only gave me the short version."

"Special weapons, systems capable of unique attacks and so on," Veikko explained, "Nothing horrifically dangerous. We don't carry atomic or wave bombs here."

"But it's S team's job?"

"For now," said Veikko.

"What is V team supposed to be doing?" Violet asked.

"Training you and awaiting a fourth member."

"Tired, Veikko, no jokes?" asked Vibs. "You didn't tell her we had to go nuke Tunisia or something?"

Veikko laughed and explained, "That's Cato, the elder from Calc team. Ends every meeting with 'Nuke Tunisia.' You'll meet them all in time. I'm just starting to remember all the names without asking Aloe. Call the computer 'Aloe' if you don't want her to hear her name and barge in."

"He also knows Skadi pretty well," suggested Vibs with a raised eyebrow.

"Yeah, very smart, very cute, very tall. Still can't make her laugh. Nothing can make that girl laugh. As soon as we start our own missions, that's one of 'em—make her laugh. She did tell me her old name, though. Karrie."

"Does anyone forget their old names?"

He rubbed his eyes. "I'm sure trying to. My real name was, well, it didn't start with a V."

Before he could divulge his former nomenclature, the intercom intruded.

"Veikko, Vibeke, Violet, Sector 33B. Walrus detail." Veikko smirked.

"Okay fine," said Vibeke, "it's really damn often."

And so they dealt with another walrus. Later Violet learned a couple more ropes. She played with her Tikari and her new closest friends, then fell asleep to converse with Veikko and Vibs in her dreams. They didn't address any important matters while asleep and didn't teach her too much new material. They just talked and rested up for the next day.

Chapter V: Vadsø

AMID THE duties of her new life as a walrus tamer, Violet started her real training. She awoke when Alopex came to her team's dreamscape, fully rested after her first lucid dream in ages. Veikko rushed out the barracks door first to see Skadi and hear the latest news on the malfunctioning detectors. Vibeke headed to one of the arsenals, where she was learning new weapons with names like the "Talley Buffalo Cannon" and the "Cerebral Bore," which made Violet eager to dig quickly into her education. Alopex led her from the barracks to the caves and left her in the company of Snorri, a small and ancient man of 141 with an accent thicker than Valfar's. With her link back on, the meaning of every word loaded into her head as it was spoken, to Violet's great pleasure.

"Call me Snorri," he began. "I forgot my last name sometime in the nineties, but I know more about the history of this hole than we ever programmed into Alopex, who I programmed, by the way. Her voice came from my seventh wife. Her looks came from a fox my fourth wife ran over on our way here. We traveled in a vehicle with treads and wheels. I won't be boring you with any epic tales you don't want to hear. They just wanted me to meet you so you knew who to ask. You can't find me online—I don't have antennae. Find me in my hut if you want me. It's the hut made of bricks, little square things, over that way. You can always recognize me because I'm the only man here with glasses. Glasses are these things on my head. They help me see without resorting to Niide's eye surgery. Niide graduated 133rd in his class. Come anytime, ask anything. I know everything. Today I'm just taking you to Balder's office. He's given the last fifty-three recruits their first lessons. This way, ask what you will."

He turned and walked into the caves. Violet followed and a couple of questions came naturally.

“How many were in Dr. Niide’s class?”

“About 14,440 men, women, and various other genders. He’s improved since then, but these glasses have served me well for just under a hundred years, and I have no need for him to stick things in my eyes or anywhere else. I like to see, hear, and copulate manually, thank you very much. You can trust him, of course. He’ll save your life twice before the month is out.”

She didn’t want to ask how he knew that.

“Thanks,” she said. “So tell me about Balder. The short version, please.”

“Balder is so named because he’s nearly invincible. You might have noticed that most members his age bear the scars of reassembly, having been killed at least once or lost various parts. Balder has never been killed, resuscitated, or even bionically repaired. Before he came here, his name was Justin Robertson. He was from the Rocky Mountains in America, where as a child he survived the third Catholic uprising, in which his family was burned alive. He survived the following gang wars and the paroxysmal holocaust of 2199 and survived the crossing of the Atlantic on nothing but a cargo skiff with four pirates he met in Tortuga.” Snorri kept speaking without seeming to stop for a breath. “Only to arrive,” he continued, “in Iceland during the fires of 2204, where he stayed through 2205, whence came the genetic abominations of Høtherus, whom he fought off to earn his entry to our cadre. Valhalla was quite different then, only just reformed by Alföðr. Since then he has done his name honor by accomplishing over two hundred and seventy-five top-level missions, including our intervention with the Phobosian separatists—yes, that was us—and halting the rampage of the Greenwich Antipacifists through the London Underground.”

Violet called up a few specifics from Alopex as she listened. Every battle and disaster Snorri listed was described as the most terrible event of its time. The Rocky Mountains were as wild as the west got, the third Catholic Uprising was the most violent of the four, and the paroxysmal holocaust was the worst chemical war ever fought on Earth. The Greenwich Antipacifist rampage was closer to home and recent enough to have been taught to Violet in school. They rarely killed people anymore but the GAP punks were still active in parts of London, and every traveler of the underground was warned to be mindful of them.

"What's Alf been through?" She had to know.

"Quite a contrast. Old 'Alf' has been killed at least seven times and retains only his original heart, head, and a few other assorted parts. Though nobody here will agree, he calls it a careless streak from his youth. The fact is, he has only been injured at all in less than half a percent of his missions, the sheer volume of which have made him the experienced cyborg he is today. Bit by bit he's become laden with diverse machinery in his chassis, a body which he can fundamentally rearrange for any situation, even to the point that last year he managed to disguise himself as an industrial food blender to avoid detection during a recent raid."

Violet eyed him in disbelief, but he showed no sign of having a sense of humor. She tried to imagine just what modifications could make a human being so malleable and mechanical. Snorri went on. "Despite all that, Alföðr did not lose his eye in battle. Rather, he had it modified with an MMR five-lens system that can record and play back imagery from any point of view. It can also extrapolate impending motion. His Tikari, his fifth, is a tarantulesque little fellow with six eyes to correspond. Though he was never officially named the head of Valhalla, his word is respected above all and rarely disputed. When he arrived he was already a poet warrior, of sorts," Snorri laughed, "with training in more arts of war than most people could even name."

"Where did he come from?"

"From the far east. Nobody knows his given name, but his original surname was Gyatso."

"What happened to his team?"

"A tale you would have to ask him. Suffice it to say, they were all killed not two days after he arrived, and in their absence he set to work changing many a thing here. Valhalla was not always so peaceful a valley nor so noble or heterogeneous an organization. He's to blame for this place, for the good and the bad, and for the library on your left, in which he keeps hundreds of ancient paper volumes, some of which have never been scanned up."

Violet looked as they passed a clear vault door. The room was full of clothbound or leathery blocks like the one she'd seen on Vibeke's bed. As the books she knew had all been loaded into her mind within a few seconds, the notion of trying to learn a whole room's worth by text struck her as impossible, if not a waste of time and a cause of terrible eyestrain.

"Alföðr has also, since the first year of his arrival, written a monthly log called *Håvamål*, which is known for a dry sense of humor and words so sesquipedalian that they make 'obfuscate' look downright paucisyllabic."

Even the link didn't have a definition for the last word. Before she could ask, they came to Balder's office, with Balder waiting outside the door.

"Violet! Welcome and welcome again! Come in, come in. Thank you, Snorri!"

"Gogs, Balder," said the old man, and he turned and left. Violet followed Balder into his office, a cluttered room with bare rock walls. Most of the clutter appeared to be weapons and polishing instruments. Some of the blades and wooden contraptions were highly ornate, decorative beyond what she imagined a weapon would have use for. One of the walls held a Bowie knife not unlike Sergeant Cameron's, but this one had a handle of bone and a blade of uneven metal with small ridges. Unconsciously, her Tikari peeked out of her chest to take a look. It caught Violet off guard that it had such a mind of its own, but she could hardly blame it for peeking at its ancestor.

"Well, Violet, my first duty is to destroy your concept of reality, your ideas of how the world works, and give you at least some idea of what this place is all about. First: who do you think runs the world?"

"The CEOs," she replied without hesitation.

"Good! Yes, there are kings and queens and presidents and all manner of titles. They all mean the same thing: poster boys, poster girls. Chief Executive Management is the only title that means a thing, and it means the richest 0.00000333 percent of the world's living humans, all twenty billion on earth and off. What they do not control: they do not control us, and they do not control everything under the seas."

"What about space?"

"Everything in spacc. Even the PRA is owned by an earthbound company under UNEGA. All the Oort planetoids, Centauris, and everything on them are owned by Zaibatsu, UNEGA's cruelest subsidiary. But space is a near dead zone for our interests. There have been twelve manned expeditions and uncountable probes, and little of interest has been found outside the solar system. The most advanced extraterrestrial life-form that human exploration has found is the Centaurian 'Gremlin.' I've seen them myself. They look like two-centimeter tall albino penguins and taste like vulcanized rubber. Aside from a dull and decaying tourist industry, space is empty. But the seas—what do you know about Cetaceans?"

She knew a good deal, she thought, but didn't venture a word. She wanted to hear it all as he had to tell it. She shook her head.

"That's what most of us know. The fact is, aside from gills, cartilaginous skeletons, and some damn big eyes, they're human at heart. A good bunch. There has never been an attack on a human from their governments. More than they can say about us. Companies have assaulted them from time to time in a manner that should have provoked terrible retribution, but nothing came. One Suomi president massacred a sizable gathering of them, an act that cost the title of president its last powers. The Valkohai, if you have heard of them, are a myth to justify action. Rumors of their takeovers online are also false. There is nothing to suggest any Cetacean has ever even had a link. Veikko can tell you a good deal about their customs and culture, but I want to make clear exactly how their politics work.

"They are monastic, and not company based. Should a Cetacean wish to control a sea city or sea in general, they have to forfeit their life as a citizen. They give up family, money, and most contact with the world in order to become a sequestered monk. The sea state keeps them alive and more or less comfortable and gives them the power to fulfill the wishes of their subjects and no chance for anything more. Such people are not seen by the school, lest their appearance sway voters.

They're known as beings of pure policy and title, made scrupulously detailed to anyone concerned, and answerable, along with the enforcers of those laws, by death for any hint of stepping out of line. As the only appeal in their politics is wholly altruistic, only the most noble of fish folk apply, and it seems to me they can be trusted. All eighteen of them. Similarly, citizens only pay tax if they want to vote. As only those willing to pay for the greater good may participate, greed has no place in their democracy.

"That logic pervades the great majority of the benthic world. But there are pirates. We deal with pirates from time to time, and they range from petty thieves to villains of absurd proportions. Some even have a Robin Hood mentality and have done more for charity than Charity Co., which is, in truth, a division of the Vagrant Eradication Militia, GAUNE's bullies. The pirate varieties will get their own day of briefing in your training. All that is important now is that you not mistake them for the general ocean body."

"Got it," she answered. There was something else she wanted to know knocking at the back of her mind, but Balder moved on.

"Religious sects. You know, I am sure, from your army history class, that the last great cold war was a religious one. But they don't tell you just what that means. As I have fought them myself, I can tell you. Religion is a disease, a social cancer. It is the afterbirth of intelligence, of thought itself. Superstition has overgrown into belief, and some of those beliefs mean genocide, or war, or the severe delay of progress. It's hard to imagine now, but the planet was once so consumed that people would kill each other over these idiocies. Now, it is true that they have been tamed to some extent. When the great rebellions broke out over the nations, religions were banned. Even before then there were petty attempts to separate the religions from government, but they were doomed, of course, to—"

"Why, why were they doomed?"

"Pass a law that says a virus may not infect you. Will the virus respect your law? As long as religion exists, it will eat away at all that's good in the world. Even now it lives on, it tries, waits for an opportunity. There are still believers. With it banned, all that's different is the virus cannot exist in the open air, and that does quite a bit of good, actually."

It seemed a bit vicious to Violet. Religion was as dead as the dodo. It was almost funny to beat the dead animal so cruelly. "Not a fan of the old superstitions, are you?"

Balder understood her amusement. "I saw it up close. What to you is a line from Snorri was to me the death of my family. I saw Catholicism make its penultimate stand in the Americas. They burned my parents alive, for no reason beyond their lack of faith in a pile of lies that deserved no faith. I saw my friends and their families tortured into belief, pushed so far beyond their wits that they gave in and became as zombies to a name that was truly no more than a name and a system of cruelty." His serious candor gave way to a grin. "Yes, I am biased. Few have such a bias. Even here you will find some believers in some old myths. Even Alf suspects there is more to death than is apparent. He believes in metempsychosis. It seems a harmless belief, and in him it is indeed harmless. You might say rightly that some religious beliefs are more virulent than others. Religions like Nazism and Christianity have proven more aggressive than Thelema or Buddhism. But even those mild absurdities could lead to atrocities. Imagine if one in power believed an old nemesis was reincarnated in some random man, because of star charts or hepatomancy? Would they then attack a person, or perhaps a country that had done nothing at all?

"What I say, I say only so you know what to do when you come across it in its violent form. You will see men and women beg to be martyred. You will see people kill over no more than a line in an old book, and some of those lines would have us put to death for dressing as another gender or drinking the wrong wine. Do not expect logic from them. Do not ever try to reason with them. I find it best just to kill them."

"Got it," she answered. She thought to tell him his last comment sounded like the same kind of irrationality he was condemning, but there was something more important than religious squabbles. She had to hear now, without delay. "What's the Orange Gang?"

"I thought you'd never ask." He grinned. "You know most of it already, rather dull material from rather dull police. I know what they've told you about the birth of the color-coded sponsored crime organizations in 2222, and the resulting ultrafunded, ultracorrupt police crews of 2223 that captured most of them and stuffed them in the superjails built for them in 2224 by the companies that had suggested the color-coded crime organizations in the first place. It's all true, to be sure. Here is what they never told you.

"Wulfgar isn't just a criminal genius. He is Napoleon, Hitler, Genghis Khan, and Alexander of Macedon. Or he would be, if not for us. He is one of those men—perhaps one is born in each generation—who, if given the chance, will take the world entirely. To date he has been kept in check by our calculated destruction of his avenues of progress, and by his idiot brother. The cops dared not tell you, or perhaps they merely don't understand, that when you killed Hrothgar Kray, you broke one of his restraints. But you built a new one. Wulfgar is no longer susceptible to nepotism, but he is human, and a twin, and he is surely vulnerable to the anger and madness that his brother's death might inspire. Left to his own devices, he will work logically through them. He is strong enough, smart enough to do that. But you are now in the best of all positions to see that he does not.

"A genius is only a genius by the grace of fate. He has been made by the things that have happened to him and can be unmade by others. The most brilliant men alive, and he is one of them, are still men, and men are flawed, men are faulty! Our minds evolved to survive, not to govern or think. Wulfgar is an unstoppable train of cruelty, greed, and lust for power. He can't be stopped, but he can be derailed—"

"Why can't he? You could kill him!" Violet's anger at the cops was coming out at Balder. She knew it, but she didn't stop it. She had to know. "Why the hell haven't you killed him yet?"

Balder wasn't angry. He was glad to see her a sentence ahead of what he told her. "Chaos! We could have killed him when he was young but had no reason then. Now when we have reason, it is because he has power, so much power he is dangerous, so much power that if he died today, his gang would be plunged into chaos."

"Let it!"

"How big do you think the Orange Gang is, Violet? How many lives does it affect?"

"Couple hundred people, and fuck it, we can kill them too."

"Seventy million men, women, and children."

Violet was floored.

"Only a couple hundred know they are in the gang. That's the rock in the pond, but the ripples of what Wulfgar controls can wash over the banks! Seventy million people work for his interests, in companies related, dependent, or in opposition to him. If he died today, and we have calculated this precisely, the police in Danmark would become a genocidal force in weeks. Most of Italia would be seized by GAUNE and its population enslaved. Wulfgar is the only reason they haven't begun a hostile takeover. The goods are too damaged by his gang to justify seizure. Wulfgar has so deeply wedged himself into the world, that if we pulled out that splinter, it would bleed to death."

Violet took it all in.

"The world is complex, you see, and what is complex is fragile. This cold war, this tangled web beneath the skin of the globe, is a slim thread away from going hot, hot as a global thermonuclear war. We are one such thread, but Wulfgar is another. These threads are invisible, lest they be cut, so there's no shame in not having recognized them until you yourself became tangled against your will. Nonetheless, that gossamer web is real. To break it would wreck all of society, and as I'm sure you've been told, we don't fuck shit up.

"But what if"—his eyes grew wide—"Wulfgar betrayed his genius, betrayed his gang and his greed? What if he fell like one of the lesser Caesars? Then slowly, controllably, the world might recover. Now, what might make a man, a strong brilliant man, collapse like a common jealous lover driven to kill?"

Violet began to see wheels within wheels. "If some bitch killed his brother."

"And a spectacular bitch she would have to be! Men and women come to Valhalla from all kinds of problems. Vibeke came here from prison for the death of her father. Easy to kill, the only result of his death was that many children won't get molested. The problem that brought you into our sights is a particularly tricky one. We offered you revenge, but that doesn't mean you can go kill Wulfgar today. Not even after great training. No, your revenge must be a work of brilliance to dwarf his own!"

Violet felt as if he had just thrown a walrus on her.

He saw her concern. "You are smarter than you think, Violet. Not smart enough to take him down alone, but you have a ravine of us to help you. Together, we will drive him to madness, turn him to a pathetic jelly, and watch him lose his power, and I dare suggest you will enjoy that far more than a microwave to his head. And then, once he is nothing but a speck of dust, you will push the last rage from your lungs and blow him into oblivion."

Violet liked that last part. She really, really liked it.

AFTER LUNCH and a walrus relocation with her team, Violet met with Valfar for a short lesson on how to survive the arctic climate should she get stuck in it. His accent fell away with the link, and she found him rather agreeable. Still, he had a habit of going on tangents that went over her head, link or not. In what was to be a talk about frostbite, he ranted angrily against membrane, loop and string theories, and praised the discovery of the odo particle, the shapeless sublepton that kept quarks in order.

"Yah, neh, now the cat's out of the box!"

Through those sticky zones of his lesson, she waited for the next meeting to come. Alf would give her the first lessons on how to survive the underground of spycraft and violence she would work in.

He would teach her in depth: tailing, surveillance, capture, stealth, evasion, escape, cover stories, disguises, detection, defense, offense, interrogation, interrogation resistance, codes and exchange, code breaking and interception, special vehicles, technology and chemistry, weaponry, explosives, psychological manipulation and defense, linguistics, recruiting, and some matters of trust that went beyond catching someone falling backward with their eyes closed.

"How," he began, "do you know you can trust me to, among other things, teach you accurately?"

"No idea."

"Exactly. Aside from hearsay, the only reason you have to trust me right now is because you have no real reason not to. You came and met me as soon as you got here. I have displayed no intention to harm you, and you may surmise that because I have stated my intention to teach you and use you to our ends, I would not mislead you. Often, you will get nothing more than this from people you will need to trust absolutely, with almost no time to question or justify it. Naturally you have instincts, but they aren't always reliable yet. You need to master the composition of your instincts to the point that they are always right. What do you think forms your gut feelings?"

She considered, then replied, "Mannerisms, actions, nervous ticks, obvious falsehoods, tone of voice?"

"Yes, but not at first. Your first impression of anyone you meet in the real world will almost always be based on sight. If someone has gray skin and big silver eyes, you can gather they are probably Cetacean. It won't always be so obvious. You have to take into account what you expect to see. If you're in the ocean, you can expect to see a Cetacean, but if you see one basking in the sun in the desert, there's something treif. More subtly, if someone claims to be one of us, at first sight, how do you know?"

"Check if they're in a suit, or if they aren't, should they be, vice versa? Is the suit black or camouflage if they're working, do they have any marks or modifications we wouldn't have? Are they in good health…? Are they pointing a microwave at me?"

"That last one would be a good starting point. Now, these will not apply to individuals undercover, but we will address that another time. What gives someone away as a threat, aside from that last point?"

And so it went on. The early discussions were followed by demonstrations or tests, in this case identifying people at sight. She was surprised to find that this was not done online, with an infinite availability of possible test cases, but in the caverns, under different lights and situations, even crowds of Valhalla civilians who seemed to enjoy her tests as a form of ravine recreation.

She excelled in all forms of the game. She caught on to a man who was in all appearances Alföðr but was given away by an inverted antenna. Soon her teammates were invited to the games, though at first they weren't on her side. She found Vibs and Veikko in disguise and found the one disguised woman in a row of undisguised unfamiliar women. The only test she missed on the first day of this activity was when Veikko turned out to be the bad guy, Violet having dismissed him simply because she already knew him and did not see the signs that he was readying a knife behind his back. This failure stuck in her head far better than any of the lessons she got right, and she would never again let familiarity stop a proper scan.

Alf took her back to his library at the end of the day, which indeed had more genuine paper books than Violet had ever seen—she had never seen one, save that on Vibeke's bed. He offered her the freedom to enjoy whichever she chose, but she had to admit, "I can't read text. It was just an elective at Achnacarry."

"Ah, nothing uncommon these days, but you may find it worth getting used to. There's a good deal of it offline and advantages to be had in our line of work."

"Of course, just seemed a bit…."

"Outdated? Quite quaint indeed, but I find some old things are worth keeping around…."

She was worried she might have offended him until he spoke again.

"I do not mean myself, though I'm happy to be revived time and again. But perhaps there is something to be said for so antique a tool as a Bowie knife?"

She was happy to hear him approve of her choice and wondered what his tarantula might turn into. She was about to ask when another question cut in line.

"Snorri mentioned that you—that your body could change shape?"

"Yes, though he was kidding about the blender. Reassembly for the public realm aspires to make an amputee or temporarily dead person as close to how they were as possible. The silver lines you see across my own skin or other members' is an attempt to use the occurrence to improve ourselves."

He demonstrated by raising an arm with one of the telltale silver seams. His arm disconnected along the seam to reveal mechanics inside that would not only make it very strong but allow it to extend a full meter, rotate 360 degrees, and hide some small objects. He saw that she was astounded and reassembled the arm.

"This arm also houses a laser guidance and weaponry package, some personal keepsakes, and a projectile cannon."

He pulled back his thumb like part of an old shotgun and she heard the mechanism load a cartridge.

"The other arm is less impressive. It serves only to connect my hand, which is still real. The worse the state the medical bay finds us in, the more they enjoy loading us with their latest gadgetry. You would be both shocked and amused to find what they put in my left pinky toe."

But he did not tell her that day. The lesson ended at 1530 with the day's paranoid focus on recognition and awareness still squirming through her sulci.

As night fell, V team and a junior instructor, Øystein, left the complex. They flew south to Vadsø. Violet was surprised to be leaving. She'd assumed the next few days, if not weeks, of her life would be spent exclusively in the pit. It was both reassuring and alarming to be back in the busy outside world. The streets of Vadsø were quite alien to her. It was cold, and people wore thick clothes. After a day of learning to spot hidden meanings in clothing, this was intimidating. Was she to be tested out in the open? Of course she was. What was the use of learning it all in a safe place? She was learning to spot hidden weapons and the telltale signs of violent minds to avoid them in places like this, not when she was safe in the barracks.

She was not told what to expect. Neither member of her team gave away anything but the subtle unspoken suggestion that they too had been taken outside for this same test. She became more and more aware as time went on, anticipation growing for whatever might come. She waited, she observed. She saw the man carrying a mirror. Why did he have a mirror? What threat did a mirror hold? What would he be carrying it for? Who would have a mirror on the street? He walked away, down an alley. They approached the alley, and she was ready for him to do something; she couldn't guess what—but he didn't. He was gone. Was this a threat missed, a threat passed, or some guy with a mirror on the street?

The four entered a beer hall. They drank beer. Violet had not been given any training in poison detection so that couldn't be it. They wouldn't do that to her unannounced. But they would, obviously they would, nothing would be announced in the real world. It would just come. She observed the team drink from the same pitcher without caution. She did the same. Øystein began to talk about something, some small talk that went in one ear and out the other. He was talking, she knew instantly, to distract her. She managed to pick up the points of his spiel, just enough to answer questions on his words if she was asked, but stayed aware of the surroundings. More aware than ever, that had to be the trick, the test du jour. Could she pretend to be a normal girl in a beer hall while still picking up on the threat to come?

Time passed, but the threat waited. It was sadistic, this test, holding back for an hour, for two, as they wandered the streets and warmed themselves by the artificial fireplace. Her mind was so overworked by the time they left the hall that she could have recited the nature of every man, woman, and child there. She knew one man was probably a fisherman from his odor and modified hands. She knew that one woman was very angry, but probably not dangerous, as her anger was focused only on one of her husbands. Vibs and Veikko were giving no signs of danger, nor was Øystein, whose only fault seemed to be his habit of repeating the same punch lines for the wrong jokes.

They returned to the pogo, and she knew this was it. If they were about to leave, it would happen now. She was more cautious, more tense, her heart beating faster than the night her parents died. She was ready for anything; she was on top of all things, prepared to fight, kill, or face any foe. They got onboard and flew back north. Øystein left them at the lounge, and they went to the barracks. Nothing happened.

"What the fuck was that?" she demanded.

"We got beer."

"Yeah, what were you expecting?" Veikko grinned.

"Something! My brain was on overdrive. That wasn't a test?"

"Well," said Vibeke, "if your brain was on overdrive, you passed the test. Get used to it. You have to be in that state of mind without cease. That's the point."

"If there were a point, which, of course, there wasn't." Veikko savored the revelation. "We were just getting some drinks."

"You're sick. They did that to you too, didn't they? After all the trust crap shoveled into your heads, they throw you outside and see if it stuck? You did the same thing, right, brains on fire, scared to death?"

"Yeah."

"Yup."

"Bloody hell!"

They laughed, they relaxed, but Violet's mind didn't return to normal. It never slowed down again. From that day onward, her state of attention never waned or remitted. It just grew more and more acute, and that acute state grew less and less frantic to maintain. The next morning Alföðr asked the same question—what formed those first impressions? From that night alone she had a hundred more answers.

Alföðr then focused on focus itself. She had attention, but attention was a general state. When focused onto one object or goal, it became a weapon, a tool, a vampiric suction that desiccated anything of its guile and left it a clear window. This was surveillance—the art of denuding anything she wanted to know. She performed brilliantly. She could pick out the important conversation in a crowd. She could pick out the important words in a conversation. She could pick out the hidden meanings behind words and the implications of hidden meanings. She felt concerned that with so much material flooding her mind, her memory could suffer. It did the opposite. She could recall more and more, everything she needed at will. Soon she found the artificial memory partitioning that she had become accustomed to in school to be more of a nuisance than simply remembering what she had to remember. With that came a respite from all the thoughts that used to buzz around her like flies. She became sharper and sharper, stronger and stronger. It happened fast.

When they went to Vadsø the second time, she had the ability to enjoy her time with friends. She enjoyed the opulent decor of the Gilded Grildeaux, though the radiators they sat by were hot, so she removed the collarpiece of her suit and set it on the table. Violet even joined the conversation but didn't neglect to catch the man sneaking up behind her chair. He had no chance to aim his toy water pistol at her.

She saw him in the reflections, she smelled him in the air, she felt his presence like a slap in the face. It was so obvious. She also knew he was not a real threat. She could hear the water slosh in the weapon and smelled no hint of accelerant, and more importantly, she caught Veikko smirking with anticipation. She hoped she would not come to such a conclusion in error in the future.

She was not to have any rest tonight, though. The man she caught fled, and Øystein asked calmly, "Are you going to let him get away?"

Team V gave chase. Violet spoke to Vibs silently over the link as they ran through the slushy streets.

"I haven't been taught chase and capture yet."

"We have."

This was her first lesson in teamwork. This was the time to trust her two teammates blindly and follow their lead. Violet was still not in prime shape. She could run, but a stitch was threatening to form in her side. She knew her lack of stamina could hurt the team, so she linked them her status. They heard and told her what to do. When they arrived at an alley with two exits, Violet took the closer as Veikko took the farther escape route over some crates. Vibs gave chase. Veikko reported the subject headed for Violet. Violet reported again that she had not learned capture yet. She saw the man running for her corner. She hid. Vibs responded to her by voice.

"Just kick his ass, Vi!"

She heard him come close, and she sent her foot into the void beyond the wall. This hurt a lot when a man came plowing into it. It hurt him a lot more. She got a better look at the assailant. Ozymandias from Othala team. He seemed unfazed but clearly in pain.

"Owwww. Bloody kick was better suited toward a real bloody enemy, Violet. Tomorrow you learn some bloody restraint…."

Violet felt some guilt at having broken her instructor's ribs, but that guilt was pacified when she entered the lounge to the light applause of several slightly older trainees. Many a team had performed aptly on their first chase, but nobody had broken Ozzy's ribs in their first week. That was second week material. Beyond all the chatter and good humor was the pleasure that hit her when she saw Vibs' and Veikko's faces. They looked like her parents when she'd earned a high grade, or when she'd solved her first Kal-toh. Violet had never felt happier in her life than she did that night.

Then Veikko handed her a Thaco suit collar. She didn't recognize it at first, but then she saw it was her own. She had left it behind. She might have been a neophyte but was ashamed at the neophyte mistake.

"Don't sweat it, Vi. What you drop, your team picks up," he said. She understood what he said literally but didn't recognize the truth behind it. Violet had so little tolerance for any weakness in herself, she couldn't comprehend that she was bound to have flaws, even in Valhalla, even on missions. It didn't register in her mind that teams are teams for a reason. Thus began a splinter in the backbone, a dim fear that she was the weak link. She didn't know about that splinter, and she didn't know why she felt for a moment like she had at Achnacarry. She didn't know that whatever she dropped, literally or metaphorically, her team would be there to pick it up.

SHE LEARNED what she did wrong on that night (not much) and what she did right (much). At Ozzy's suggestion, she did indeed learn restraint in attack. Sparring was taught by her teammates. After dealing with a walrus that had somehow wedged itself into a heating vent, they headed to the gymnasium and found a free dojo. Veikko walked onto the mat and bade her to follow. The sparring arena was nearly identical to that at Achnacarry, a firm mat floor, wooden walls, and a variety of weapons on the walls, though the weapons here were more varied and less fake.

Vibeke sent out a quiet link around the base. "New girl sparring."

Violet suddenly felt two dozen knocks at the back of her eyes. She had let people peer through her eyes before. Her parents used to look in from time to time, but now she was receiving requests from all around the ravine, mostly strangers amid the teams, all waiting to see her spar. She let them in for fear they might try to hack their way in midmatch. She could see Veikko's face twitch from even more incoming viewers. Vibs got them too. Everyone wanted to see what the new girl was made of. Violet prepared herself and bowed like she had in the army. Veikko bowed too. It must have been a universal custom.

Unlike the silence that had lease in Achnacarry, Veikko linked in to the wall speakers and started a music program.

"What's all this, then?" Violet asked.

"This is sparring music from the twentieth century," he answered. Vibeke rolled her eyes; she didn't like it either.

"I don't like band era music," Violet said as the old music picked up.

"You will. It's fun, and the lyrics—"

"It's going to have people talking in it? Veikko—"

"No, no, it's good. The lyrics are appropriate."

Violet paused to listen to the unwelcome vocalizations. She heard a man say something about "smacking his bitch." Violet gave Veikko the nastiest look she could. Vibs shook her head, having dealt with it before. Veikko just laughed.

Violet began sparring with a roundhouse kick that sent Veikko to the mats.

"Oh, you're right," she said, "the lyrics *are* appropriate!"

She didn't waste any more time talking. She only mouthed the word "bitch." Veikko jumped up and fought back, and Violet thwacked him back to the ground just as easily. Vibeke appeared to enjoy the spectacle, and Violet might have admitted that the music was suddenly much more fun than silence. Veikko came back harder and harder. Half of his moves were feints; the other half were trick moves and flips that seemed better suited to a jester than a fighter. Still, the two had a damn good match. Violet thought so at least; she won every scuffle.

Veikko spoke, out of breath. "Okay, okay. We didn't all have commando training."

Violet retorted, "Should I get Dr. Niide for you? Your ego looks sprained."

A sinister grin spread across Veikko's face. "This room has an analgia generator. Want to see who goes to the doctor first?"

Violet gave a nod, and Veikko linked the generator on. Violet took up a solid offensive pose, and Veikko directed her to attack with a twitch of his fingers. She did. She fought no differently without pain than she did with it, but Veikko fought more savagely. He didn't fall away when she delivered a good hit—he just kept coming. That way it took her minutes, not seconds, to pound him to the floor.

"Training! All army training," he complained. "Let's see how you do with something you haven't trained on."

Veikko grabbed some gloves from the wall. Vibeke covered her face in shame.

"You know how these work?" he asked.

"No, but I'll still kick your arse," Violet said, laughing.

"Field knuckles." He put on a pair and ground his fists together. They sparked. "When they hit flesh, they make a small field. Amplifies the power."

"Neat."

He threw her a pair, and she put them on. He looked her over and grabbed another set of contraptions from the wall—foot fields. There was no interface; she just had to punch or kick. Veikko beckoned her on, and she threw an exploratory jab. Veikko had no need to experiment and hit her right in the chest. It didn't feel like a punch. It was like getting hit by a cannonball. The force bent her in half, stole her breath, sending her crashing into the wall with terrible speed. There was no pain with the generator on, but she knew it would have been excruciating. She took a second to catch her breath.

Veikko seemed concerned. "Shit, Vi, you all right?"

She nodded and stood up again. She breathed in, breathed out, and gave Veikko the same smug signal he'd given her to start. He shook his head in surprise and got ready to fight.

Her first punch connected and sent him flying, but he was ready and came back with a hit that fractured her arm. Without pain, she didn't even notice. She hit back and broke his cheekbone, then his shoulder. Vibeke linked to the med bay to get ready for the results of a field fight. The two continued smashing each other with smiles on their faces. It was a new level of sparring, one as rewarding as Violet dreamt it could be. When she hit, it was like conquering an army. When he hit her, it was a taste of blood and agony, agony without pain, and that was all the crazier. It was all fun and games until someone lost an eye. It was Veikko, whose cheek gave way completely and sent his right eye rolling across the mats.

"Stop, stop. Shit, where'd it go?"

"It woll—" She couldn't talk right. Violet was suddenly aware that they might have done more damage than would be prudent. "It wolled ower there," she said, pointing. Her finger didn't extend. *Uh-oh*, she thought.

Vibeke ran to a corner where the eye had ended up. Nurse Taake, who Violet recognized from the med bay, ran into the room and began prepping the eye for reinsertion. Another nurse she hadn't seen before followed. The link labeled her as Nurse Kampfar. She began scanning Violet.

"Good game, Vi," Veikko called to her.

"Yaw, it was good. I won," she mumbled as her tongue continued to swell.

"Don't rub it in. I was going eas—Ow!" Taake, perhaps annoyed at their candor, turned off the room's analgia generator. Veikko grasped at his cheek. "Oh chainsaw gutsfuck, that hurts!"

It didn't hit Violet at first, so she thought she must have surely done better. Then the pain flooded in. From her chest, her back, her tongue, all over, it began to creep in. She felt faint for a moment but didn't come close to passing out. The pain was insistent. It wouldn't let her lose consciousness. She shouted involuntarily, as if her broken mouth had to yell to stay alive. Mercifully, she had some degree of control over what she said.

"I cweamed yo ass, Veikko!"

"Names of Odin, give it up," he begged.

Violet let out a horribly painful laugh. "Could do it wit one awm!" She couldn't stop laughing, as if she were drunk on the pain. Everyone but the nurses got infected. Even Veikko laughed as the frustrated nurse worked on his optic nerve. As Kampfar paralyzed Violet's mouth, stopping her laughter, she felt every onlooker behind her eyes unlinking. They were all leaving, having seen the match they came to see. But nobody was linking to her to comment. At Achnacarry they had all criticized a match. Here they just vanished.

They couldn't have left for disinterest. That had been the most brutal fight Violet had ever fought. She suddenly felt a nausea that had nothing to do with the injuries. She had just screwed up big time. How could she not have known she was going too far? Looking at Veikko's wounds, it was clear everyone who saw it had left sickened. The new girl had just proven that not only was she too nasty for Achnacarry, she was too nasty for Valhalla. What would they do to her now?

Violet remembered the years of punishment for the slightest playground scuffles. It wasn't a question; she was about to be punished more terribly than she ever had before. If Valhalla was so far beyond Achnacarry in every other respect, how would it punish its own? What the hell was she thinking? How could she have been so damn stupid? She was finally somewhere that made sense, and on her second night, she had beaten a man into—she looked at Veikko. He was a mess. And everyone had seen it. Violet felt sick. She had just pulverized the first friend she ever had.

Luckily, the nurses were complaining to each other, and their words were reassuring, though they weren't intended to be.

"Just like everyone in T team, always their first week!"

"T was nothing, remember P? Pickles and Pustule?"

"Oh, that was the worst; we never did find all her teeth."

"I mean Pustule. I'm the one who had to wake him." He stared straight at Violet as if to blame her. "They got into the sonic scimitars, and he lost his arms, bled to death on the spot. I put 'em back on and started him up again, and the dumb bastard picked up his sword and went after Pickles again."

"What a night, and the next! The next night he died again. The damn fool just didn't stop. Sparring! You damn kids and your thirty-five VVPS!"

"Always on the first night, yeah, Vibs," complained the nurse. "Yeah, I'm lookin' at you."

Violet's mouth was almost working; she had to ask, "Why—whd yw do?"

Vibs cringed and looked to Veikko, who was smiling past the pain. "I might have disemboweled him. Just a little."

"Yeah," said Veikko, "but we weren't even sparring yet."

"Well, you heard his damn music."

Vibs shrugged. Violet's eyes watered slightly, and not from pain. It took the medics more than an hour to restore the two to working condition. They begrudgingly gave Violet and Veikko a couple of portable analgia generators to clip to their jumpsuits, and those covered the last bits of healing their bodies had to do on their own. The trio went to dinner and laughed about the horrific brutality customary of a first sparring bout in Valhalla. Violet was far from unique, having required the nurses, and she learned there would be far more to come.

THE WALRUS that had previously crammed itself into a vent seemed to have escaped its cage and gotten stuck in a civilian's door. Though the three walrus details on her first day were at the high end of frequency, there had been at least one every day since Violet arrived, and Veikko begrudgingly explained why.

"It's Tasha. She set off a sonic charge on the other end of Kvitøya as soon as she heard my team got a third. Sent all the blubber running for the ravine."

"Why would she do that?" Violet asked.

"Why indeed," said Vibs, staring at Veikko.

"I might have, uh, well…."

"The night Veikko learned how to sneak into secure buildings, he snuck into T team's barracks."

"I thought it was S team's."

"He found the first female in the room, thought she was Skadi, and proceeded to—"

"At least let me tell it. I was trying to get a laugh out of her. Did her hair in an afro."

"A two meter afro with keratin resin. It was so big and so solid she couldn't get out of the room till they cut it off. With a tank-mounted grinding beam."

Veikko went on with pride, "That's why she has short hair now," and less proudly, "and why we have a walrus a day."

"Two today," reminded Vibs.

"One today—it was the same walrus twice."

"So what other tricks did you try to play on poor Skadi?"

"Not many. I saved the best for you two."

Violet said softly to Vibs, "More and more I like those field knuckles."

As they slept, Veikko gave an account of the lengths he had gone to to make Skadi laugh. He had programmed her morning news logs to greet her with the archaic informal, "Whuzzup, Beotch?"; he had set S team's door image to show an ancient video file of an austere prairie dog, and recited his entire humor memory partition to her in lucid sleep. Then on his second day of her acquaintance, he had taken an enamel buffer from med bay and programmed his teeth to change color as he spoke, reduced her team to giggles with his impression of a drunk Cetaccan, programmed Alopex into the likeness of a two hundred kg bald man (without changing her voice), and vowed solemnly to tie his balls to a goat if he had to to make her laugh. He admitted that he had not yet resorted to that last-case scenario, but Violet offered to help him find a good strong goat at any cost. As morning drew closer, the conversation turned serious about the nature of what she would be training on the next day.

As soon as they woke, Veikko asked, "You said you could fight me with one arm, right? Is that what you tried to say?"

"Tried—my tongue was apparently disconnected."

"Well, you'll get to try. Today you start injury training."

"Injury training?"

"We can get hurt in this line of work. Badly," said Vibeke. "They teach you what everything feels like, how to tell a pierced kidney from a flesh wound, how to know how badly damaged you are, and how far you can keep going with every possible disability."

"There's a variety of pain simulations, and some are actually kind of fun," said Veikko. "They have Dr. Niide remove one of your arms or legs, and you have to fight. They'll take off fingers and show you how to operate a microwave without them. They'll also kill you for a few minutes so you know what it's like and won't be afraid of it."

How stupid, Violet thought. "I'd kind of prefer to fear dying."

"No, no, not like that, just the sensation," explained Vibs. "Dying feels pretty damn weird."

"But why should we know the feeling? If we die, we die—there's nothing to know."

"Because we don't always die by mistake," Vibs pointed out. "Playing dead's part of our arsenal of disguise."

"You have to know when and where you can die safely, for how long, how to orient yourself once you come back, much more."

"Is it safe?"

"Oh yeah, you won't be dead long," Veikko shrugged. "It's all done in med bay."

Violet would have continued her protest on the utter idiocy and uselessness of such a thing, but the fact both had done it before her raised a more intriguing question. "So what's it like?"

"I never got the white light, but I hear some people get it."

"I got it a little," said Veikko. "Then it turned red and this big horned red guy threw me in a pit of fire and shit."

"Death, Veikko, not the time you tried to cook."

"Oh no, nothing there. Just dreamless sleep. The hard part is the drug they use to kill you. It's not painful. It just lets you control it. It won't kill you unless you give in, and you won't want to give in."

"You're right," Violet snapped. "I don't want to give in. It's pointless. Absolutely fucking pointless."

Veikko thought for a moment. "Here's how Alf explained it to me." Veikko suddenly spoke with Alf's voice. It was beyond an impression; it was acting on a surprisingly high level. "Two reasons: one, if you're gonna kill people, it's only right you know what you're doing to 'em. Reason two isn't just moralistic drivel: No matter what fate the Norns spin, dying is the one thing you know absolutely that someday you'll do. Best to practice."

"I disagree about practice," Violet said. "I don't like it."

"It's death," said Vibs. "You're not supposed to."

Violet went to med bay intending to argue it to the last, but as she formulated the arguments, she became less convinced of them. Everyone in the teams had done it, even Vibeke, who Violet had to admit was right about everything else. It was harmless and safe, if dying could be described as safe. But what convinced her most was the fact that she was so adamant not to do it. She was afraid of it, a fear that was likely to cripple her if not dealt with, and here, now, they were going to take that fear away when she was safe with those she trusted most. By the time she walked into med bay with her teammates by her side, she was resolved to die if it was the last thing she did.

When she lay on the table, she was less determined. In her mind, she wasn't afraid, but her body told her otherwise, as she was shivering.

Dr. Niide mumbled, "Don't worry 'bout shivers.... Everyone does.... Important thing's your Tikari. It's safely chested?"

She nodded.

"Good. If you die without it, it dies too, or sometimes goes ronin. Ronin Tikari are dangerous, mmm, very dangerous. Won't be happy with us for, mmm... killing its owner." He picked up a hypospray. "Here's the toxin. Painless, completely painless. Like falling asleep. You'll be tired, but if you don't let yourself go, you won't go. You'll just be tired for... ever...."

Violet was about to start asking questions. She was suddenly very curious about how the drug worked, what it was made of, who invented it, how the hypospray worked, what grades Dr. Niide had at 133rd in his class. She could have asked questions until she died of old age instead. But Dr. Niide had already given her the toxin. She was suddenly very tired.

It wasn't so different from falling asleep, but it had a very final feeling to it. That finality was what she had to overcome. For all time, death had been final. Now it was not. It was much like the first time Violet tried to swim, when she'd had to make herself dunk her head under water. Everything inside her had told her not to do it, but after some hesitation, she'd remembered that it was what she was in the water to do. The instinct not to submerge was ferocious, nearly impossible to fight, but she'd mastered it and forced her head under the surface, and she came back up with water in her ears. She did it with ease every time she went swimming after that. She was in med bay to die. She would wake up again. She forced herself to let the drug take over, to let her heart stop, and she fell into nothingness.

She knew she was dead as soon as she was alive again. She had been dead. She knew that and was therefore not dead anymore. She was in med bay, and for some reason she was relieved that her ears weren't full of water. She opened her eyes to see Veikko and Vibeke beside her. She was home safe in Valhalla, Hall of the Slain. She laughed to herself. They'd named it exactly what it was. She was happy, a warm giddy sort of happy that she hadn't felt before. She was happy to be alive again, and though the feeling would never stand out as it did that moment, it never left her completely. For the rest of her life, she had a subconscious sense of value, and a conscious sense of just how nice it was to be alive.

"The first time is the hardest," Veikko said.

"You died again?" Violet asked.

"No," he admitted. "But how can it be any worse?"

Knowing that Veikko and Vibeke had done the same formed a connection deeper than anyone who hasn't died could understand. It was a bond that ran deeper than family, and in a less personal way, it extended to every other team. Even Balder, who had never died in combat, had done this. The notion that a team's first death in battle was to be celebrated also began to make sense: there was much to celebrate in coming back from the dead. An hour after her death, Violet began the rest of injury training with the recognition simulation, where a variety of wounds were fed into her brain so she would know what had happened if she felt them. Some wounds were so painful that she wished she were dead again.

Veikko was elsewhere throughout the simulations. Only Vibeke was by her side. Violet was kind of glad he wasn't there to crack jokes. She felt what it was like to get microwaved—hot. She felt what it was like to get shot—hard. She felt burns and freezes and blades and hits. She felt the loss of each organ, the puncture of an organ, the breaking of a bone, the resetting of a bone, and a horrible variety of every kind of harm it would do her good to recognize. She even got to feel what it was like to drown in boiling acid, which felt oddly similar to showering with army napalm.

One advantage of all that pain was that she did not undervalue the rest of injury training under analgia. The fact she didn't have to feel the pain behind a lost limb was heavenly now that she knew just how much it hurt to lose one. She almost felt sorry for Veikko's eye. Almost. Dr. Niide spent the rest of the day removing parts of her, deactivating parts of her, crippling parts of her. She didn't get to spar with Veikko at a disadvantage. He was still on another training job. Vibeke fought with great skill and didn't go easy on her for the loss of her legs or arms. Violet learned how to fight when cut in half. She learned how to think with a sluggish, contused brain. She learned every limit, and beyond the unsettling feelings, she was surprised at just how much she could still do.

When they turned on the pain again, she was amazed at what she could do despite it. No matter what they took off or broke or removed, she could still fight on. Deprived of limbs, she could bite someone to death. She realized she was damn near invincible, and that pain, though annoying as hell, couldn't stop her. After a short while, it couldn't even dissuade her.

Injury training also included desensitization to things like blood and fire. She learned to run through, stand in, and see through fire. The same three went for blood and gore, all simulated but still terrible to behold. She didn't question the need for it but hoped she wouldn't find herself in reality wading through so much viscera.

The remains of injury training were mostly classroom material. Most of it they link-loaded into her: The range she'd be able to limp, the force she could exert with a broken hand, the rate of blood loss and time to unconsciousness. They simulated link damage and how it could be overcome, as well as how it would affect her Tikari. This angered the Tikari greatly, and it was a bit hesitant to leave her chest for hours after.

They also cleared up one thing that Violet had never understood. Every child was given skull armor. She thought skull armor would stop anything, microwave or projectile or impact, but in fact, it was mostly there to make people feel good. As skulls develop, the armor had to shift to accommodate the sutures and became weaker. It would lessen impact for an adult, but it was really meant to protect kids' heads from falls. After that, like most safety features in the world, it didn't make one safer, it made one feel safer.

THE DAY after injury training was over, they gave Violet another task that was more appalling than death training.

"Kill training," explained Vibeke, "is not about the methods of killing. K team will teach you those. This is a single exercise we go through early because we need to know if you can do it. A good amount of our work puts us in positions where we have to kill people, and if you can't bring yourself to pull the trigger or raise the blade, you need to quit now before you end up in a place where it might get one of us killed."

"I've killed three people. Are you really saying I have to murder another just to prove I'm capable?"

"You killed three people in defense, instinctively. Sometimes, we're assassins. That's just how it plays out. You need to know what it's like to take a life in the field."

"I can't believe they'd have us murder people just to train."

"We do. It's that important. Whoever you kill will die so that—"

"No no no, don't justify it like that. I know the greater good crap, and I know it's wrong, and I know you know it too. Life isn't worth so little."

Veikko chimed in, "Noble but wrong. There used to be millions of people on earth. The biggest village had a couple thousand. If anyone died, a universe was lost. Maybe it still is, but in so many universes.... Being one in a million means there are twenty thousand of you. The only value you have is for people who know you, and even they can find another with a fast net search. But you work for us. Your life isn't worthless to us. Theirs is. Kill them."

"Wrong, wrong, wrong. I will not kill an innocent human being for training. Not ever."

"Who said anything about innocent?"

That changed her outlook. The people Vibs and Veikko killed for training unquestionably needed to die. Veikko killed, painlessly, a pirate who had tortured more than thirty families to death without reason, a sadist who would torture more kids if he went on. Vibeke killed, not painlessly, a serial rapist who targeted girls and boys with his surgically modified drill penis. She cut if off before she killed him, and Violet had to admit that even a cruel death might be warranted sometimes. She quickly understood they didn't kill for training alone. That was just a simultaneous objective. Valhalla didn't kill people unless they really needed to die. It was a mission that had to be done.

"Still," she admitted, "I wish you had me do it before showing me how it feels to die."

"Exactly why we do it in that order."

Recruits were spared the crisis of having to choose who to kill. When G team found a new recruit, they immediately began finding people for them to kill. Violet's psychological and historical profile dictated that she should be assigned to kill Alex Deramus. Alex was one of the Orange Gang's most horrible henchmen, a close friend of Hrothgar's who would have joined him for her father's murder had he not been drugged out of his gourd at the time. He tortured, he murdered, he did just about every nasty thing a man could do to a sizable heap of people, all in the name of Kray.

While Veikko and Vibeke worked on their own education with Alf, O team escorted Violet to London. When they came upon Alex, he was stalking a stray cat. Violet wished she could have come to him while he prepared to murder a family of three, one just like hers. But she did like cats. Kill training, as they still called it, had to be personal but it also had to be safe. They didn't send young Valkyries to kill people who had a chance to kill them back. Thus it was a perfect opportunity to use her Tikari, as was tradition.

All five humans stayed in a distant pogo as Violet put her focus completely into the insect. Her eyes rolled back, and her second link glowed bright, but only to the eyes of anyone with a Valhalla link—no outsiders could see the immersion glow. She flew to the pavement behind Alex's feet and felt what it was like to hunt. The day before, she'd thought if she had to kill a man, it would be a time of regret and fear. It was instead exhilarating. That worried her. The little moral sense left in humanity told her it was wrong. But it wasn't wrong. She was going to kill a man who was about to kill, well, a rather scruffy cat, but he was still Alex Deramus, and he still had to die.

So the little metal bug jumped and took its killing shape and stabbed him through the back of the head, and then he was dead. And Violet felt no regret whatsoever. She thought she must be a monster. She thought about Alex's parents, how they must feel. She remembered what they'd told her, that he'd killed his parents long ago by stabbing them in the backs of their heads. She tried to think of the pain he must have felt but knew he felt nothing. It was better than he deserved. She said his name to herself again and again. Alex. Alex Deramus. She couldn't feel a thing for him. She gave up trying to make herself.

The Tikari returned with blood on its wings. O team flew her home, where they watched the news logs: "A monster was killed today;" "More bodies found in his basement;" "Victims' families praise the vigilante who did the deed." Violet didn't feel pride either that night. No remorse, no pride, nothing. She just felt like she was doing her job.

Having learned to kill and be killed, Violet was now ready to learn the expansive variety of ways to do it. She met with K team the next morning. Kabar would teach her everything she had to know about her Tikari. He taught her how to use it in knife form, much as Sergeant Cameron had. Kabar's own Tikari link was broken the day he arrived. Knowing how personal an injury that was, Violet didn't ask any more about it, nor did she question why he still used the same deceased thing as his knife.

She learned in depth just what could be done with a Tikari, to do all Veikko had boasted was possible. In knife form she was taught how to throw a blade, and only when she had mastered the technique was she told that it had a self-balancing gyroscope for throws and could in fact be made far deadlier by deploying rocket thrusters in midthrow, and if necessary, shift its weight to turn corners and return to her hand. It was quite capable of following a target around the globe, killing a person, disabling heavy machinery, reprogramming linked and unlinked computer systems (even having its own web avatar, where it could pass as a human, albeit a quiet one), and she learned that in an emergency the poor animal could be left as a mine to detonate with a blast proportional to its size. She vowed never to use this feature.

She excelled at its use as a knife, but as much as she loved the gizmo, she was quite ineffective with it in bug form. She could stab a guy in the back of the head, but she couldn't make it do the amazing things a Tikari was supposed to be capable of. She couldn't make it do the aerial acrobatics, she couldn't make it do the precise carving, she couldn't make it do a thing she wanted.

"And that's because you keep trying to make it. Don't make it. Let it," said Kabar. "Trust the Tikari. When you pick up a glass, do you force your hand to make the exact movements? No. You just pick up the glass. Now, boomerang your Tikari through this slot and slice the apple in my hand."

After med team reattached Kabar's hand, he let Violet move on for the day. She met with Kalashnikov, who taught her about her microwave.

"The Valhalla standard microwave is far more complex than the weapon you used on Kray's men, or even your standard military issue. This microwave can fire a dispersion field, a scattering field, a diamagnetic tractoring wave, a conventional magnetic beam, as well as a heavily variable microwave beam. That beam can be adjusted in intensity to warm gently or melt gold. It can project a beam with a radius of eighty degrees or .0000001 degrees."

He showed her meticulously how to do everything he said. He also warned her about what might happen if she did.

"Any beam will set off a microwave detector. Even the tractoring wave. Now—that tractor. This weapon can lift a five-thousand kilogram weight, but your hand can't. If you try, you'll break your wrist. You cannot use a fulcrum with a microwave beam, so you must pay attention to what you're trying to do with it. Don't let its range of abilities make you forget your own limitations. Now, let us discuss its use as a grappling hook. First, you turn the flux pin...."

After he showed her how to pull herself up a cliff, Violet moved on to Katyusha, who began to show her the variety of special weapons in the Valhalla arsenal. She showed Violet a few rocket launchers, excision grenades, razor darts, variable motorized spears, chemicals, derezzers (devices that interrupt the electrical activity in a human brain, knocking one unconscious for a minute or a comatose eternity), explosives, and other weapons. It would take Violet months to get to the most amazing weapons that Vibeke was learning. Humans had invented too many ways to kill each other to be taught all of them in a couple of weeks, and Valhalla had all sorts of strange and amazing devices for that purpose in stock.

Katana told Violet about the weapons Valhalla did not have. They didn't stock nuclear weapons, but she taught Violet how to disarm them if she had to. They would never even suggest using a wave bomb but would stop one from going off at all costs. Violet learned how the bombs worked and how to take one apart with her bare hands. They showed her footage of what omega waves did to people, which almost reacquainted her with her breakfast. They did not teach her how to put the bomb back together, as they had with A, H, N, and F bombs. Some things are just too horrible to ever reassemble. In disarming all warheads, she learned which wire to cut, how to recognize that wire in any bomb independently of color code, and how to stop the ubiquitous red timer on every instrument of destruction that had one.

P team began to teach strategy. She learned to find an opponent in mazes that she herself did not know the layout of. She learned how not to be seen, how to be seen just enough to send them running toward her team, and how to recognize those trying to pull the same trick and to discover who wanted her to see them for all the same reasons. N team showed her vehicles. They taught her to fly a pogo as if it were a tank, and a tank as if it were a skiff, and finally she got to ride on a skiff without breaking any of her own bones. H team taught her Internet basics, defense and offense, and search features she never imagined possible. They also taught her what the Internet lacks.

"How do you discern what any building in the real world holds?" asked Hellhammer.

"I look at the link logo and ask; then I know."

"But you won't always have a link, and net logos can lie. How do you know?"

She didn't, so they taught her.

Fehu team taught her so many gadgets and gizmos that she had to put some of the information in her partitioned memory to learn later. She learned uses for familiar tools and weapons that she had not imagined, such as how Valhalla's hammers could magnetize and demagnetize metals and how goggles could start fires and matches reveal invisible ink. She learned how any link antenna could broadcast jamming fields. She never got around to reading written letters. Some things were just too daunting and too useless to justify the effort.

Her training grew more specialized. She learned to use her Tikari to spy ahead as she ran; she learned faster methods than uplink to communicate with her partners; and soon the three left the tunnels and villages to chase and sneak around in exotic locales demanding special techniques. She learned how to run on ice with and without her jumpsuit's cleatable soles. She learned how to scale skyscrapers and wade through magma. She learned that Vibeke was quite skilled at reading text, and that the book on her bed was titled *Personal Narrative of a Pilgrimage to Al-Madinah & Meccah* but never learned why Vibeke would read such a thing.

The training teams let her watch all missions in progress and required her to watch quite a few. Slowly Valhalla was revealed in all its unrevealable glory, as were some of its associates. Other bases across the world worked together as needed to be heroes without recognition. There were seven hidden cooperatives with their own hierarchical systems, though it seemed all had the same respect for Alföðr that Valhalla did. Valhalla was in many ways the core of the underground, and its history and politics took several days for Snorri to summarize. But Violet soaked it all up.

As she learned more and caught up to her mates, the team did more together. Spotting fakes in the caverns gave way to more field tests and even field fights. One night when they chased a target down a flight of stairs, they arrived in the basement to find him with five friends. They attacked and ended up broken in half with faces smashed by boots and skin ripped off by rough cement. The lesson that night,

Alföðr explained, was knowing when to retreat. Veikko and Violet reviewed their failure in the med bay's advanced healing generators, while Vibeke remained mostly silent.

"You had the fat guy until the thin guy shot you," said Veikko.

"That's not the point. The point is to know when you're beat, and we didn't."

"You'd think they could just tell us," he complained. "Not make us learn it the really hard way. I mean, that was my nose. I needed that nose, I used it daily."

"The new one looks fine," Violet reassured him.

"Yeah, but still…."

"They're sadists."

"Amen."

"I fuckin' had that fat fucker."

"You know, they never taught us point one about escape," Veikko noted. "I've been here longer than either of you. They did all this shit to me in the same order with different people, but they never told us how to escape."

"They do tend to teach us things after we fully comprehend the importance of them," Vibeke explained.

"There's something to be said for fair warning."

"And for surprise. This isn't like grade school. It really shouldn't be."

"Easy for you to say. You still have your goddamn nose."

"Shut it, Veikko. You didn't get shot in the back. How did I leave my back open?"

"You thought Vibs was covering it."

"I was covering it," she protested dully. "Then I woke up here."

Veikko shook his head. "Damn. We really sucked, huh?"

"Yes," Vibs confirmed. "Yes we did."

But they did not again. That was to be their worst failure in field tests and most teams had far, far worse. Mishka told them one day as they dissected roaming land mines how F team, a couple of Fs ago, had failed to clear a transport vehicle they'd stolen in a training mission and came under fire from non-Valhalla criminals—experienced yakuza who intended to kill them. The detectors knew it, and instructing members came in with force and saved all but one of the team.

"Fuchi, a tank with the sweet, silly personality of a child, had only been there six months, hadn't even seen her first arctic winter. That's the training nightmare they tell us all about."

It was uncommon for people to die irreparably in training, but it happened. Cautionary stories like F team's kept it from happening on the heaviest missions. Violet's mind wandered. She was less concerned with F-team history than she was with the way Mishka rubbed Vibeke's back.

After their failure in the basement, V team learned escape. They learned evasion and the most basic, crude methods of remaining hidden and moving silently. Only when they'd mastered the techniques employed by feudal Nippon and aboriginal America did they receive training in the technology that made those methods obsolete. They didn't learn camouflage-suit settings until they didn't need them anymore. They weren't given auditory dampeners until they could steal them from the storage tower unheard. They learned to wake at any shift in room tone and how to get a full night's sleep in under half an hour, if required.

Violet learned about cover stories, disguises, and survival skills on her own, her teammates having learned them before. She would catch up to them within the month. Survival training entered places she did not expect to need to survive. They even taught her all she needed to know to endure and even navigate without a link. In one test she was given her basic gear, flown blind for hours and then left alone in a hole. She knew to put up all-collar masks against anything from poison gas to a vacuum, which was good because she found upon standing that the hole was on the surface of the moon. She lived for seventeen hours in the Sea of Tranquility, which she found refreshingly tranquil. It was also quite simple as far as Valhalla tests went, given they dropped her there only minutes after explaining the importance of an immediate vacuum mask in unknown situations. They had left her well equipped compared to other tests due to the potentially dangerous climate. They didn't want her to die again unless she was as dumb as a moon rock. As soon as the shuttle arrived and let her in the airlock, she asked the pilot if anyone had ever failed.

"If anyone fails that," he said, "they get what they deserve. Not Valhalla material."

She was about to question the conviction of his boast when they lifted off. In the cold lunar light she saw two rocks that looked very much like bodies. She felt no need to press the question further.

The pilot was kind enough to swing a bit off course to see the corona behind the moon, which was pretty but smaller and more distant than she'd imagined. When she returned to Valhalla, she went over her stats. Analysis showed that with the manner of energy expenditure and rationing she'd employed, she would have survived twenty-four days. Abandoned underwater or trapped in ice, she could have lived nearly half a year, given the proper tools and pills. Abandoned on any surface on Earth with nothing but her suit, she could survive indefinitely. Violet was becoming very hard to kill.

She was also getting better at killing. She gradually came to an understanding with her Tikari, as well as an understanding of sparring limits with Veikko, moving on to the finest forms of karate, judo, tae kwon do, yoga, Spetsnaz system, MoQ'bara, and so on. This training evolved into martial arts developed around guns, microwaves, blades, beams, brutal tricks, and poisons and pitfalls to employ in the most desperate of times.

V team learned interrogation in all its forms. They learned how to torture along with an education in why they should never do so. Torture was useless for information because it was unreliable. It was just as pointless for striking fear because it produced anger instead. Obviously, they were not to torture anyone for their own pleasure unless the fucker just totally deserved it. They learned the uses and misuses of truth drugs and brain hacking. Violet finally learned the cerebral bore, which she was sad to learn was merely a portable brain-hack antenna and nothing as gooey as it sounded.

They learned the problems and solutions presented by diverse methods of keeping silent. People could kill themselves to avoid divulging information, but a postmortem brain hack could fix that. People could erase their memories. They learned to reassemble them.

And then came the unexpected problems, as they learned on assignment: Having caught their man on a chase in Vadsø, they proceeded to question him on the spot. Veikko put on his angriest face and barked, "Tell us your name!"

"Never," the man shouted.

"Tell us now or we hack in!"

"Never!"

Vibeke readied a cerebral bore.

Veikko continued, "Last chance! Tell us your name!"

The man faltered. "Schmelgert Helgerzholm!"

The trio looked to one another. Veikko barked back, "Tell us your real name!"

"Schmelgert Helgerzholm. It's Schmelgert Helgerzholm!"

Violet stared at the desperate man and asked, "Really?"

"Lesson over," laughed Øystein over the link. Their next lesson taught them to recognize the truth they uncovered, however disturbing and unbelievable it might turn out to be. Later that night the trio dined with Schmelgert Helgerzholm and his family, who enlightened them to the long and noble history of the Helgerzholm line and their custodial duties in the Valhalla ravine.

V team began to study the moral implications of operating outside all laws and oversight. Veikko often challenged Alföðr's wisdom on these matters and always got a specific and clear response. His questions were never avoided or answered halfheartedly.

They learned how to use people without telling them they were being used. They learned how to destroy minds with only a select few words ("I love you" being the most pernicious), and how to sell guano to bats. Their mastery of the human mind came more from mastering their own over the course of training than from any simple psychological technique. Their arsenal of psych capabilities came to encompass violence, fear, hate, love, sex, lies, and a dose of historical oddities like long-forgotten Crowlean theory and the long-long-forgotten art of patience. Violet asked outright just how they would learn to use sex.

"You're female," Vibs told her. "Instinct covers sex."

"I mean as a weapon," she said.

"You're female," Vibs repeated. "Instinct covers that too."

Veikko cringed.

There were reminders from time to time that the more experienced members were not training, but performing important and dangerous duties. There was an alarm one day as the team was dealing with a small walrus calf. V team had never heard a real alarm before. It didn't make any sound in the real world, but it resounded across their links. They managed to find their designated blue-level alarm cavern, and they waited for the all clear. It seemed someone had been followed back to the base after a mission in Russia. The small clan that followed them was unprepared for an entire base and was wiped out in seconds upon arriving, but still—their elders were not infallible. The base was not invincible, or as the walrus hunt resumed and reminded them, impermeable. Shit still happened and it still hurt when it did. That particular shit reminded Violet to ask Alf some questions she had neglected.

"They killed all of the intruders, didn't they?"

"Yes, they couldn't be allowed to escape once they knew what and where we were, obviously."

"Why weren't they held prisoner?"

"Because we have no prison. We take no prisoners."

"Why?"

"The simplest reason is that if someone wants to do us harm, we think it best not to keep them here where we sleep and keep all our weapons, however securely. The people worth imprisoning here are the ones most capable of breaking out."

That made sense to Violet. Something else didn't.

"Why don't we seal off the walrus hole? I'm not objecting to the walrus detail but isn't it a security risk?"

"A very slight one, perhaps. We're certain the rampart covers it when raised. But there are also advantages in having a secret hidden entryway."

"So you know where it is?"

Alf thought for a moment, then smiled. "Actually, in all my years, I never got around to pinpointing it. Consider it your first mission."

Chapter VI: Bayern

"SAY WE use some sonic charges to clear the ice," Veikko suggested, "and it just happens to collapse whatever we find. It's not like Alf would have us digging it back out. No walrus hole, no walrus detail. We'd be free!"

"Alf would certainly have us digging it back open," said Vibs, "and if he didn't, it's plain to any Cloutier fan that you'd die someday for lacking it as an escape route."

"Cloutier?" asked Violet.

"Author from the 2060s. His writings had so many twists of epic proportions and unlikely poetic justices that his death at the hands of his frustrated readers was judged worthy of his own works. But poetic justice isn't limited to Cloutier, especially when Alf tells you what to do. If you ignore him, you'll pay for it."

"Robot," Veikko accused.

"Besides, didn't you have some foolhardy plans for the next walrus?" pushed Vibeke.

"No, I found the right sedative, but I can't find a good way to get it into Skadi's bunk. And I can't find a funny wig for it either."

Veikko's sophomoric pranks were standing out in contrast to his other new project. He had started writing a new regular column in *Håvamål*. It almost always offered a polemic alternative to conventional wisdom, or at least to Alföðr's. Sometimes he went so far as to challenge the entire concept of Valhalla's subtle ways in favor of sweeping reforms of world problems.

Violet had only learned of the column when Vibeke had read her a quirky snippet from the text version. Violet wasn't particularly interested in the political complexities that *Håvamål* tackled, so she quietly ignored it online, but she did enjoy watching Vibs read the text. Vibeke looked enraptured by the paper, with the same deeply focused expression people had when immersed in the net or listening to Alf speak in person.

V team would take a place at his table or at Balder's whenever there were spots open. Balder would tell stories of seducing Phobosian Dissidents and fighting hordes of Christians with only a sun-bleached donkey mandible as a weapon. Alf would speak his concerns about the running dry streak: Valhalla hadn't been involved in a critical international incident or saved the planet in a full eight months. Balder hoped that this was a sign of retardation in the world's violent cycles, but Alföðr held a more pessimistic belief that it was an exceptional calm before an exceptional storm. When Alf spoke, his few words were always definitive and tended to end most debate. That's why he often maintained his silence, allowing a good spirited argument to go on around him with open ears and a subtle grin.

Violet steered the team back on course. "First we have to find the hole. How do we do that? By the time Aloe spots a walrus, it's already to the ground floor."

"Not necessarily," said Veikko. "She reports them as soon as a surveillance node spots them. But most of those nodes are deep down in the ravine or covering the open sky. That's how we know they can't be just falling in. Actually, most of the time she spots them from the eyes of a linked resident. As soon as one of us sees one, she knows."

"Like if one woke up with S team," Vibeke snarled. "What would that accomplish again?"

"It already made you angry, Vibs," Veikko said, satisfied, "and you're cute when you're angry."

She looked to Violet to back her up, but Violet wouldn't argue. Vibs was very cute when angry but the expression never lasted.

Vibeke returned to the subject at hand. "We need to tag one of them. Follow them in."

"Umberto," said Violet. The three-ton beast with a chipped tusk had been caught five times that month. He was among the slowest-moving of all the return customers. They always found him partway up the wall, suggesting that he never got far from the entry point before he was seen. It also meant a long, slow chase to the cages with him every time.

Veikko approved of the idea. "About time the lug did some good. I'll get a tracking pip from storage."

The trio took a lift to the topside terrain and proceeded to employ their most basic skills to find their walrus. The sun was surprisingly bright for midnight. It was a strange sight to Violet. The days grew longer and longer in summer until one night the sun failed to submerge behind the horizon. It stayed in the sky without cease, dipping low but never leaving. Good for tracking.

Their target was presumably a member of one of the pods that stayed close to Kvitøya, so they began with a survey. Aside from learning a great deal about walrus loitering patterns, they found Umberto at the western coast. They patiently waited for him to finish his display of machismo to a lesser bull, and then Vibeke sent her Tikari to land gently on his plentiful back fat and inject the pip therein. Back in the ravine, they told Alopex to monitor the pip and inform them should it come within twenty-five meters of Valhalla.

That done, they returned to their training. There was little left for Violet to learn before she caught up to her teammates. Only a few finer points of injury training remained. She headed to med bay, where she was taught to recognize a variety of stings and bites. She learned which stings would paralyze her, which would kill her, and which would hurt like hell for no reason at all. Next she felt a diverse array of bites, from the debilitating shark to the annoying but harmless birds, and that of the domesticated canine, which was far worse than its bark. She had once wondered why her arcology banned the animals. She didn't anymore.

Finally when she checked her memory partition of training assignments, she found it devoid of single-person projects. She had caught up to Veikko and Vibeke and would spend the rest of her training with them. She'd thought the moment would come with an added sense of accomplishment and belonging, but she felt there was something left to do. Something she had forgotten. There was something she had been meaning to learn since she arrived, something they could teach her… but its name was out of reach. It was distant, behind her, as far gone as her family.

She let the sense fade and sought out her team. Veikko and Vibeke were working on special weapons and tactics. Violet found them scaling a wall with ropes for a simulated incursion. They were already up the wall, so Violet switched to her Tikari's eyes and flew up alongside them. Veikko saw her first.

"Ewww, there's some kind of giant gnat following us."

Vibeke recognized the Tikari and joked, "Gross, smash it before it gives us some disease."

Violet playfully landed on their ropes and lifted a wing as if to cut them.

"Shoo fly, don't bother us."

"Yeah, bug off."

Violet linked to them from below. "I'm done with single training. You're stuck with me from now on."

"We're doing an incursion on P team right now for special weapons and tactics. Scout for us."

"You got it." She linked and spied ahead. P team was expecting Tikaris and kept their own zoomed in and solely focused on Vibeke and Veikko's chests, with an order to report a launch. Of course they were not watching Violet, nor her airborne friend, so she managed to sneak in and scrutinize the room.

They might have complained about V team cheating had they not done so well together. After Veikko and Vibeke stormed the room with perfect knowledge of what was waiting for them, the EPF analysis marked them at 99.999998 percent efficiency. Nobody really blamed them for knocking a pencil off the table, so they were marked flawless. The only sense of failure was Veikko's, owing to his inability to come up with any jokes about how Violet's fly had helped them on a SWAT exercise.

AS THE team waited for Umberto to sneak in again, they continued to train as a trio. Like the rest of Valhalla's teams, they could predict each other's every movement, every response, and they became a powerful force in the simulations, tests, and light duties. Together they managed, one quiet, bright night, to dominate the På Täppan heap for nearly half an hour. They were only deposed when S team showed up, and having four perfectly coordinated members to V's three, they sent the trio back to the floor with a few broken bones to remind them how far from complete they were.

After standard post-På-Täppan med bay repairs, they joined S team for a midnight snack.

"How goes the walrus hunt?" asked Snot.

"Dull," answered Veikko. "We got a pip in one of 'em, and now we get a five-day dry streak. It's like they all gave up."

"We can plant a sonic—"

"No thank you, Sigvald," Veikko interrupted.

"We're enjoying thc vacation from walrus wrangling," said Vibeke. "What are you four up to?"

"Another sort of walrus hunt," said Svetlana.

"In a way it is," Sigvald agreed. "Valfar found a hole in the armor around special arsenal seven."

"The one with the detector problems?" Vibs asked.

"The same. He patched the hole, but someone's trying to get in."

"Who?" asked Violet.

"Our best guess right now is a citizen. Might be some kids who want to play with our toys. SA7 holds most of H team's experiments, some of the really crazy stuff," Sigvald explained.

Veikko meanwhile engaged in an all-out footsie campaign on Skadi, who fought back expressionlessly, her mouth belying the good humor with which she pinned Veikko's legs to the floor.

Sigvald went on to describe the techniques with which they scanned around the arsenal and how they were fortifying the building in case it was a sign of more of a problem than local kids. "It's strange, because everyone on a team can get in. We just link in to the door, and it logs what we put in or take out. Obviously nobody has invaded us all-out, but we can't overlook something small scale. If someone out there has plans for what's in there, we have to see that their plans fail miserably."

"Plans failing miserably." Violet's memory was jogged. That was one thing she hadn't learned since she arrived—not training, but curiosity that the cops wouldn't satisfy and Valhalla's hacking systems could. She excused herself from the table and ran to the com tower. She summoned Alopex and hardwired herself into the tower broadcast network.

"Alopex, open Kyle City Scotland Police Network."

She saw the log-in silo for her old local police.

"Bypass all security."

For the Valhalla system it was as simple as that. Alopex set to work and broke through all the police security without a problem. The secret file icons stretched out before her. Alopex kept watch for anyone who might happen to link in on them unannounced, but even if a tron program was listening or a gelatinous blob came in looking for hackers, it would have a hard time recognizing them as anything but another program, a harder time than typical police security could handle.

Violet set to work finding her father's files and opened them to see forty tan folders and one red one.

"What's in the red folder?" she asked.

"Hrothgar Trap Files," it told her.

She wasted no time in opening it up and stealing its entire contents. She heard the file names as they transferred.

"Opening Logs—On Hrothgar Location; On Family Safety; On Plan Failure; On Nelson MacRae Fatality; On Nelson MacRae Cadaver Disappearance; On June MacRae Fatality; On Violet MacRae Survival; On Information Withheld From Violet MacRae; Closure Logs."

The penultimate file was a promise of the greatest magnitude, and in her anticipation she forgot the file about her father's missing body as soon as the link passed it. She was finally going to learn exactly what she'd wanted to know since the day her parents had died. She didn't forget what she'd learned about stealing files.

She fled the police net first—no need to wait around there. She had Alopex run all the antitrace programs and virus/trojan protocols that ensured Valhalla couldn't be traced by any sort of spy program the cops might have kept in their secret files. She did it all correctly and patiently. It took exceptional calm to back it all up in the Alopex mainframe, to label and note what it was and why she'd stolen it. Then, finally, she opened the file and saw exactly what the police didn't want her to know. She finally understood why they'd kept it from her.

Her father had known that Hrothgar would only come in person to kill a traitor he truly hated, and perhaps only if he saw some pleasure in it for himself. Nelson had researched the massacres that Hrothgar attended personally and found that the only sure commonality that warranted the man's attendance was not the degree of betrayal or the stature of the family killed, but that they had a teenage daughter. Of the few officers trusted to entrap Hrothgar, Nelson MacRae had the only one. He volunteered to infiltrate the Orange Gang, to act so sloppily as to get caught, and to trap the man with his own family. Hrothgar was meant to discover who he was and where he lived. He was meant to break in on them that night.

They suspected Orange Gang rats in the force, so Nelson couldn't risk setting up emergency detectors to be monitored by the common personnel, nor could he station guards who might have informed Hrothgar of the plan. He couldn't even warn his family. The Orange Gang's ears were so wide reaching, and Violet's father was so cautious. He could only calculate as accurately as possible when Hrothgar would arrive and tell his few loyal trappers to arrive at the same time. It would have worked perfectly if one of Kray's cronies, Alex Deramus, hadn't bowed out. Without stopping to pick up a fourth man, Hrothgar arrived seven minutes early.

Violet should have hated her father for it. She should have felt betrayed, angry that he'd used his own child to catch a villain. But anger never occurred to her. Her father had thought Hrothgar dangerous enough to warrant going all the way, and he didn't shrink from the best way to do it, not for her, not for his family. It meant risking his wife and daughter as bait to catch this man, and he didn't pass the responsibility to another cop. He didn't play it safe and miss his chance. He condemned his family to death or worse because it was the best way to rid the world of Hrothgar Kray. Violet was overwhelmingly proud she had finished it. As for Nelson MacRae, her dad was a heartless bastard, but he was a tough heartless bastard. Violet admired nothing as much as that kind of will. He was her dad, so she'd always loved him, but now she finally understood him. She could finally love him for the man he really was.

She logged out and found herself alone in the com room. Her first instinct was to remain alone, to absorb what she had learned and come to terms with it all. Her second instinct told her that she wasn't subject to any such need. She felt concern once again that she wasn't feeling what she should be. What she had discovered was already sorted into the parts of her brain where it belonged and the emotional barrage it might have provoked didn't come. *Heartless of me*, she thought, but she no longer wondered why she was so unfeeling: She got it from her dad.

So all that was left for her was to head back to the cafeteria, take her seat, and finish her green putty and tan hemispheres. She had been away only seven minutes.

"Was everything all right, Vi?" asked Vibeke.

"All was well," she said. It clearly didn't satisfy her audience. She thought she was lying when she said it but quickly realized that there was nothing wrong. She had only gained a fuller perception of past events. *Ancient history*, she thought. She could tell the crowd at the table but saw no real point to it. What she might say could not be unsaid, so it was best not to bring up her findings. Vibeke and Veikko probably knew already; they would have hacked the Kyle police back when it happened. They didn't tell her because they wanted her to learn it for herself, in her own time. They wouldn't bring it up unbidden purely out of courtesy. She wouldn't mention it for the same reason.

"What did I miss?" she asked.

"You missed," recounted Vibeke, "Veikko telling an obscene story that offended the ethnicity and gender of everyone at the table, me stabbing him with a putty spork, and Svetlana explaining the traits of the hole growing in SA7's wall."

"I also blew a bubble in my soup. Fifteen centimeters high," Veikko bragged.

"Where'd you go?" asked Snot.

"Com tower," she answered honestly. "Some loose ends."

Her tone must have told everyone she didn't want to talk about it, and none pushed. Svetlana went on about the mysterious hole and offered to send all the info to V team's common dreams. Though they were used to monitoring missions in progress for training, this was an even more appealing offer. The problem was a small one, but it was unsolved, and they were being offered the clues. That night as they slept, they dissected every fragment they were sent, coming to the same conclusions S team had already posted and bumping into the avatars of several other teams studying the same material.

A sort of contest was emerging between junior teams to see who could crack the riddle first. Violet gave it her fullest attention, she knew, so that she wouldn't have to think about what she had learned in the com tower. It was resolved, over, she reminded herself. There was a reward to be gleaned from this new mystery and none to be found in dwelling on the bare and uncomplicated past. Staring at chemical scans of the old broken detector and the SA7 hole, she thought she was beginning to see some sign of a pattern, some dim light of significance on the horizon, something that was almost a clue.

Alopex interrupted the mass viewing of the SA7 files at 0550.

"Tracking pip has entered alert zone," she said. Violet and her team wondered for a moment what she was talking about, but then they all remembered they had a mission of their own.

By the time all three were suited up and out of the barracks, Umberto was already well within the rampart zone. Alopex gave them a map by link that overlaid their vision, showing the tracking pip location as a bright-green dot. Once they walked into the open air of the ravine, they saw his dot right near the southeast edge of the wall. Umberto was still on the surface but was surely coming to his secret passage into the ravine. They hopped onto the power system branches and climbed fast up to the top levels. They defuzzed their feet and walked closer to the dot.

They saw the dot drop about twenty meters behind the rocks. He had just entered the compound. The only room carved into the rock around them was a storage room, number one, the highest up along the walls and also the least used. They noted and recorded that the landscape outside the room would indeed allow a large animal safe, albeit clumsy, passage to the lower levels of the ravine.

Veikko opened the door, and the trio entered. Umberto's dot glowed so large and brightly from the Alopex link that they told her to turn it off. The dot disappeared, and Vibeke linked to her teammates to ask for motion recognition. Alopex sent back a stream of information. "Motion at twelve meters."

That was past the back wall. There must have been a tunnel behind it. They approached, and the motion readings continued to grow closer. Ten meters, eight. Their heartbeats grew slightly faster. He was coming, but there was no visual or auditory contact. Seven meters, six. Still nothing. It would break through the walls anytime now. Five, four. Impossible, it was reading inside the room. Three meters. They didn't see it. But there was a sound. Veikko looked up. He saw heavy ceiling damage. Two meters.

Vibeke sent her Tikari up through a small hole in the ceiling panels. She linked Violet and Veikko in to its eyes. Darkness. One meter. The Tikari saw a great gray shape just before the ceiling gave way. The entire panel seesawed down to let the giant animal roll down into the room. He righted himself and gave a loud snort of recognition. Alopex glanced through their eyes and stated the obvious.

"Veikko, Violet, Vibeke, Sector 1F. Walrus detail."

Vibeke's Tikari swooped down from the ceiling as Umberto flopped happily off the panel and let it swing back into place. After V team wrangled the giant to his private coach and removed his tracking pip, Alopex sent him back to the surface, and the team returned to the storage room to finish their job.

Violet tractored the panel with her microwave to swing down and let them up. They set their suits to glow gently and illuminate the cavern over the ceiling. It was big enough for any walrus but too small for artillery or anything beyond personnel to walk through. It sloped up through glacial carved rock to a crevice in the surface, which, though, well hidden, would be quite easy to fall into if one lacked proper fingers. It was a perfect walrus trap to funnel its quarry directly into the hole in the ceiling. A quick Tikari flight confirmed the rampart would seal off the gap when raised.

They linked their findings to Alf, who expressly forbade them to erect any kind of barrier to prevent the walrus details of future recruits. Vibeke linked back to him a design she had whipped up that could lock the ceiling panel in place in an emergency, which Alf was happy to consider. But there were matters more pressing than their accomplished mission.

"Come down to special arsenal seven," he told them. "There's been a development."

THE DEVELOPMENT was a new hole in the arsenal wall—made by explosives. This was no prank by local citizens but an act of war. Skadi stood above the crowd, an easy task as she was roughly two meters tall, and briefed the gathering teams.

"The breach was made by at least three heavy thermite charges. Most of the detectors in the area have been broken, all by simple bludgeon. Detectors inside were deactivated by the heat from the thermite, but one was far enough away to stay alert. We set the detectors yesterday to give only silent alarms to S team, but the intruder was scared off nonetheless, possibly on recognition of a working detector. They fled before grabbing their intended target.

"They did manage to steal part of it, thus revealing their intention: Mjölnir, a magnetic weapon system designed for massive incursions into armored bases. Composed of two projector cannons and a magnetic generation core that charges conventional projector cannon ammunition, with enough force to collapse any susceptible materials on impact, turning metallic armor into a crushing force against the armored. Whoever got in stole the cannons and two spares but not the core. The cannons are dangerous in themselves. They are, after all, cannons, but they're nothing more without that critical generator."

Skadi looked over at V team. "We have a lot of work to do, V team. If you're done chasing pinnipeds, we could use your help." They were indeed done chasing pinnipeds and were most eager to help. S team was going to find out who did it. T team would find where the stolen weaponry had gone. V team would study exactly how they had gotten away with it. Elder teams would monitor. It was an important and disturbing occurrence but not one that merited their direct attention. Elder teams rarely worked on anything short of, as Veikko put it, "pure fucking Armageddon." They were quite happy to let the junior teams work on something real.

Vibeke demanded that they treat the smallest of the allotted tasks, "As if it were the Warren Commission." Violet and Veikko both linked up to learn what the Warren Commission was, while Vibeke did all the work. That evening they reported their findings to S team.

Veikko said, "Vibeke learned that Mjölnir was stored in the northwest corner of the special arsenal bay. Protective measures were as follows: the core generator was stored in a special rubber coating within a lead safe within a detector field. There were six detectors, five of which were deactivated or damaged immediately during the incursion. The last went off, starting the alarm, while the intruder disabled two of the five locks on the lead safe. At that point they escaped with only the cannons.

"The cannons were stored in simple locking mechanisms next to the generator, with individual semidetectors, all of which were disabled by microwave blasts. Each cannon weighed forty kilos, and the generator weighed nearly 300 kg, suggesting that heavy-lifting mechanisms and a transport vehicle must have been present.

"Flying vehicles are capable of working their way down to the caverns but not inside them, and certainly not to the special arsenals, so the transport would have logically waited at the east tunnel gate. Vibs confirmed that when she found the east tunnel gate torn off the walls. A carriage system was found damaged under the left door; readings confirmed that it was used to haul the cannons and was of a size capable of moving the generator had they taken it. The carriage was painted white, unlike Valhalla's equipment. When we commandeer such machinery, it's always stripped of paint and gold plated, so it must have been from outside.

"While Violet and I were still linking up the Warren Commission, Vibs concluded that at least three people were involved—one to run the vehicle, one to disable the outer alarms, and one to simultaneously begin breaking into the lead safe. They had equipment of their own, including at least one vehicle, one carriage, and extensive incursion tools. They had knowledge of the inner layout and some knowledge of the alarm and detection systems, presumably having broken them previously either in a failed attempt or in research of our reaction to a minor incursion. The intruders now have four projector cannons. The fact that they tried to steal the generator suggests they don't already have one."

S team was impressed. Veikko continued, "Violet and I concluded that Oswald acted alone."

Skadi laughed, and for the rest of the night Veikko strutted around the ravine with a sense of accomplishment far greater than if he had discovered the identity of the thieves, hunted them down across the globe, and killed them all using nothing but his pinky finger. Vibeke was quieter about her accomplishments, so as Veikko and Skadi walked the floors hand in hand, Vibeke and Violet went to find Alf in his library, where Vibs detailed her plans for a walrus door they could control.

"Brilliant work, Vibeke," he said. "I'll pass it on to H team to build."

"Then V team will install it?"

"Yes, but we will be leaving the mechanism in the open state." He smiled with a teacher's expression. "It's good to keep young teams busy with such things."

"So we're condemned to it for another eon?" Violet asked dejectedly.

"Not necessarily," he said. "Exclusive walrus detail is reserved for teams with three members. You'll reschedule tomorrow for applicant analysis. They found someone for your fourth bunk."

G team discovered him in Bayern. His name was Kristian. He was nineteen years old. He was very tall. He had blond hair and a muscle surplus. His family was alive, but he was distant to them. They were not on speaking terms. He had never killed anyone but had on many occasions defended weaker people at great personal risk. When he saw a child being beaten by her parent at a mall, he beat the parent to the ground and proceeded to lecture him on child abuse until authorities arrived. When a man with whom he argued was needlessly assaulted by one of his own companions, he broke his companion's arm. Many other similar instances showed him to be a far more philanthropic fellow than was common for Valhalla. His motives were less in the pleasure of violence than the pleasure of justice: an uncommon find in the ravine but not one to be discarded.

He had been tailed for nearly two months and received the clean bill of everything from G Team. V contemplated him for a week. They watched him at work, hauling boxes of tofu across sorting floors. They watched him at home, where he ate, slept, and masturbated over five times a night. They watched him online, where he read mythology, watched ancient cinema, and masturbated over five times a day. He was a happy sort, though he had few friends. G team had already dealt with the nitty-gritty of his abilities, so V team's observations were less about the necessities of Valhalla and more to decide if they liked him on a personal level. Violet liked him because he kept things simple. He didn't buy tons of decorations. He didn't need or eat expensive foods and so on, yet he seemed content with what little he had. Veikko admired his strength and good humor, laughing at his sardonic comments to oblivious coworkers. Vibs had no clue why she liked him, but darned if she didn't look forward to meeting the guy.

The trio logged in to black avatars and found Kristian in the lobby of a red-net bordello as he left—one does not approach a man with major life changes on his way in—and gave the greeting that Miss Manners suggested for approaching a man in a brothel with unspeakable underground work.

"What are you, spies?" he asked.

"Yes."

"Are you good spies or bad spies?"

"Good, we think."

He seemed humorously disappointed.

"Do I get to see the world, meet new women from exotic locales, and sleep with them in the line of duty?"

"All three are possible, if not likely."

"Are there girl spies?"

"Yes, about half of us."

"Great," he said, "I'm in."

And so he was brought in. R team headed out to Bayern as the trio watched by link. Like Violet's brief dagger fight, every recruit got their chance to die from the outside world in a manner appropriate to their needs, or if they had no specific needs, their wants. Kristian had shown his greatest appreciation for battle with those who posed a threat to the weak. He was protective and had even enjoyed a good deal of online sexual fantasies involving damsels in distress. Rebecca made first contact, and Kristian seemed to know what was coming before the others arrived.

"Please tell me you're on our side," he said.

"I am. So are they," she informed him as Ragnar and Ruger gave chase. R team had planned to pick him up quickly, letting him rescue the lady at the cost (onlookers would believe) of his own life. That should have been a pleasing way for Kristian to leave the outside world. What complicated matters was that he had not only a taste for heroism but for action. Kristian wanted his apparent demise to have a good degree of spectacle.

The wild and gleeful chase that ensued across the small Bayern village confirmed G team's description of his great skills and will to action. He took Rebecca leaping from the streets to the slanted shingled rooftops of ancient shops and into windows and vats of brewing beer, then into an antique motor vehicle that he managed to hot-wire and drive at deliciously unsafe speeds, until Rebecca reminded him that they had to get caught at some point. He safely parked the car by spinning it into a tight yet parkable space and took her to hide in an alley where he said they should kiss to appear as a couple of lovers and not the objects of the chase. Rebecca stated that nobody in the entire known history of nonfiction spycraft had ever successfully used such a ploy. He responded that they did, after all, need to be caught and kissed her passionately until the pursuers arrived. But style forbade he just let it end there, not when an artificial ski slope was only meters away. In the end Ripple had to pilot their pogo to the edge of a cliff that Ragnar managed to outski them off of. They flew from the edge of the outside world into the safety of a Valhalla transport and headed north with the pleasure of the most overdrawn chase a prospect had ever given. Kristian and Rebecca saw no reason to stop kissing on the way home.

He selected the name "Varg" within an hour of landing. Then he proceeded to make light-spirited passes at both Vibs and Violet and took his absolute rejection by both with a hearty laugh and an unspoken assumption that both were lesbians. That night the four spoke much as Vibs and Veikko had spoken to Violet, answering his questions and enjoying his naïveté about the world, which he had no clue required any underground to keep it safe and sane, having joined only for the thrill expected in the business. He stated he was happy to meet at least one English spy among them, to which Violet responded that she was Scottish, to which Varg responded that he thought all the best spies were English. Vibeke came to her defense and declared that the best English spies were best played by Scots. Violet had no clue what it meant, but it satisfied Varg, and Vibeke's defense almost made her blush.

Violet watched as Varg took his tour with Valfar, whom he not only understood but proved capable of conversing with on matters that Violet didn't even bother to link up. They argued about the mass of photons, Valfar suggesting that they had none and Varg laughing that they had to if they got caught by black holes, and that they were merely "very light." Valfar laughed at the remark and went on to explain how it would make the postulates of some relative theory obsolete. Varg replied that it would indeed, and that E did not equal MC squared, rather the square root of Y. When Valfar asked him the root of Y, he replied, "Y nought." Both laughed, and Violet cursed her lack of attention in school.

Varg was fitted for his suit the next day and selected a reflective gold finish like Balder's. He and Balder seemed to relate on a level reserved for a very select group of badass men. Even on matters of belief, he seemed in line with the elder, as Violet found out when she asked, "Why don't you talk to your parents?"

"I didn't live up to my name," he said.

"Varg?" asked Veikko.

"Kristian," he answered. "You know Balder's views on the old religions?"

"Yeah."

"Mine are similar."

"Why?" asked Violet.

"They all think sex is bad. I think sex is good. Very good. It's just… so damn good. If they're right and I go to hell, that's fine, because I've spent my time in heaven. And by heaven, I mean in—"

"Thank you, Varg, we get it," Vibeke interrupted.

"I don't," said Veikko, though he quite clearly did. Varg remained quiet, though. For all his apparent disregard for manners, he was careful not to offend. Similarly, for such a tough guy, he was unpredictably worried about the Tikari surgery and more so about the resulting new pal. As he would need to get the procedure done before he could sign back in to his old porn haunts, he walked on into the medical bay and did what had to be done. Though Varg walked back out with a spring in his step, they failed to spot a dagger or mechanical bug, but he wore a heavy new bandolier. The bandolier twitched. Varg let down his arm and the bandolier grew centipede's legs and crawled off his shoulder to his hand, where it formed itself into a massive claymore sword. He let the Tikari shift its shape just enough to show them that the sword could extend its length. He held the sword with pride, then let it crawl back to rest.

"You just don't do anything small, do you, Varg?" Veikko remarked.

Varg gave an innocent shrug, a silly gesture with one hand facing up and the other hand down. He said, "Balder has a caterpillar, you know. It's nothing new."

"I didn't know that," said Veikko. Violet and Vibeke didn't either. "What's his turn into?" he asked. Varg paused for a moment, then shrugged again.

Having his link back, Varg became acquainted with Alopex and quickly relogged in to some of his favorite sites. He did not have time to spend at most of them. Being in excellent shape, he took quickly to På Täppan and nearly made the summit on his first attempt. By now the four, even Veikko with some reluctance, could make a genuine team effort to take the hill. The severe injuries of their first uncoordinated attempt as a quartet gave them time in the medical bay to get to know each other even better. As they told Varg of their early training and assignment, he was saddened that he'd missed the walrus detail. He was fond of anything bigger and thicker than himself.

He approached death, injury, and kill training with great courage that didn't completely hide a sensitive streak. He was willing to die and get hacked up and feel pain beyond anything he had ever known but he was hesitant to kill for the first time. G team had to pass over their first pick, one the rest of V team would have happily murdered. He was a dreadful man who they confirmed was planning arson and kidnapping, a wastrel who lived like a parasite and gave back nothing to the world but bad odor and littered syringes. But Varg insisted on someone else. They found a random murderer, and Varg entered the field and killed him quickly with his sword. Even then, he disliked the act and viewed it as a sadly necessary duty. He never sparred to the point of horrific injury as so many had before him. In the sparring dojo with his team, he admitted he simply couldn't bring himself to hurt his friends.

"That will be your undoing," joked Veikko.

"I can live with being undone," he responded with a smile. "Hey, when do we learn to use sex as spycraft?"

Violet, having asked the same question, answered, "We don't teach what your DNA already knows."

"But maybe," he pleaded, "you could help me study a little?"

"We monitored you, remember? You've had enough practice."

Violet was amused that he had asked almost the same thing she had in so many words. She turned to Vibeke and inquired, "Does everyone ask that?"

"I did," she said.

"Me too," added Veikko.

"Same here," called Mishka from the next mat.

"As did I," added Alföör, who had been watching from the door. He bowed into the mat and signaled Varg to spar with him. The two fought in a way Violet had never seen. Varg was a capable fighter, but as he picked up speed and the will to fight seriously, Alf began to abandon normal fighting tactics along with the shape of his body. He would surprise Varg by extending his arms past their expected reach, revealing something of his cybernetic redesign. He would flip toward and from Varg with bionic speed and power. Even reorienting himself in ways that a human with his original skeleton couldn't. A crowd gathered to watch. Varg adapted to every trick and on his first serious match, tied the master of the ravine, three tags to three.

"Well done!" Alf applauded. "Next time I'll fight fair."

Varg trained at the same rate as Violet had and proved most proficient at Internet duties and psychology, using the latter to bed four different local women in a week and a half. After the first mind-altering study of attention and focus, he left for Vadsø in a state so nervous he twitched like a cat. Violet linked to the others to ask if she'd looked so worried on her first test. They responded that she had, and Varg's clever covert hack into their conversation made him even more concerned about what was to come. When nothing happened, he broke into laughter and tackled his pals with a good-natured roughhouse roll through the elevator lounge.

By the time the sun set again, Varg was well on the road to being a skilled warrior. He seemed so crucial to the team that they had no recollection of how they'd worked without him in the past. If there was a problem, he knew the answer, and if he didn't know the answer, he could generally find a way to hit or kick the problem hard enough that it fixed itself. He booted one machine back into order that turned out to be a projection system designed some forty years prior (and forgotten soon after) as an entertainment system. That made him very popular with the nonspy population, and soon he was using it to project his favorite ancient cinema on the smooth white western ice wall every few nights. Violet found these displays to be incomprehensible and archaic. Some were so old that they were two-dimensional and one even lacked color. Veikko loved every one of them, but Vibeke preferred to read, and Violet preferred to watch her read.

They took Varg through most of the same teamwork exercises they had done previously, including a descent into a basement where they were supposed to surrender. Perhaps as a result of Varg's enthusiasm, they forgot to surrender again. Instead of bearing a painful defeat, though, the quartet took on the superior opponents and won.

"I think we were supposed to lose that one," Vibs remarked.

"Oh yeah, surrender and stuff," added Violet.

"Fuck that, we kicked fuckin' ass!" shouted Veikko.

"Bloody balls, V team…" moaned Ozzy.

Øystein tried to sit up on his broken coccyx. "How are you supposed to learn when to retreat when you win everything?"

"Sorry," said Varg.

"Don't say you're sorry," called Veikko. "You saved my nose!"

Varg had no clue what he was talking about, but the cheer was infectious, and he bore a grin as he carried members of O team to med bay, one over each shoulder.

Owing to the difficulty presented by training so skilled a team, Balder filled in for Øystein on their next training chase. That gave Øystein a chance to recover but did nothing to diminish their overdeveloped abilities to hurt their instructors. Varg caught Balder by brute force long before he was supposed to and took him down with such energy that he broke Balder's neck. Balder didn't die but admitted it might have been the closest he ever came. After he was patched up by a very surprised medical staff, Balder and Varg were as blood brothers.

Varg had learned in his first weeks that he and Balder were cut from the same stock. In their conversations and lessons, they shared opinions and tastes, priorities and reasons for doing what they did and didn't do. One of the reasons surprised Violet when she heard it.

Since Varg's arrival she'd noticed that he didn't fit the common amoral Valhalla style. He went out of his way to protect the weak. He didn't take pleasure in beating the shit out of everyone and was sensitive enough not to kill his first recommended target. That worried her until she overheard him speaking to Balder.

"Why," Varg asked, "wasn't I kicked out when I refused to kill G Team's first find?"

"Because I insisted they keep you," Balder replied flatly. "Because I know why you refused."

"You do?"

"I watch G team's findings as closely as your team. You didn't hesitate because you were afraid to kill. You refused because he didn't fit your idea of justice. That's not common here, but it's good to have around."

"And they told me about the Geki…." Varg added.

"You don't need to worry about them. It's not in your nature to do anything that would provoke them. Of course, Alf wouldn't tell you that. And he didn't tell you that the man you refused to kill never committed the crimes he was planning."

Varg lit up. "So he changed? He turned straight?"

"No, I killed him myself."

Varg laughed at the dark humor of it. Violet never related the conversation to Veikko or Vibeke and didn't dwell on it herself. But she did pay closer attention to Balder. His stories were like a peek at who Varg might become. She imagined Varg's eagerness in hearing the same tales must have hinted at Balder's character in his youth. Those who saw them together even remarked they had the same smile despite the vastly different shape of their heads. Varg was quickly becoming Balder's protégé, but the new V team member admitted, as they turned in for the night, that he never really knew the man until he had almost killed him.

"Must be a guy thing," said Vibeke.

"No," said Violet, "I think I know what you mean." She reflected a long while before she spoke again. "I never really knew my dad until after he died."

She dived into a dream state and the other three followed. She let them see deeper into her mind than she had let anyone before, laid bare her parents' deaths and her peek into her father's police files, and told her team just how she felt about him. After she told them about her father, she kept speaking as a new concept crawled out from the folds in her cerebrum.

"The strange part is, he's not the only man I respect for that kind of willpower. My dad sold me out, risked me, put me on a hook to catch a guy who had to be caught at all costs, and Hrothgar turned out to be a pathetic thug. Not even the brains behind the Orange Gang. But his brother is still out there, still in charge. Wulfgar lost his brother, and he didn't sell himself short by coming to kill me. He didn't stick by his family and go for revenge. He's better than that. He's just like my dad, just as smart, just as strong, just as ruthless. I've never met the man, but

I feel like I know him. I respect him. That cold cunning streak I got from my dad, that I love so much about him—Wulfgar has it too."

There wasn't much for anybody to say. None of the four even knew what it meant, if anything. But they talked on through the night. They spent all of their dreams together, time devoid of arguments or ill will or any of the cares of daylight, where training slowly gave way to work. As a full team, V was finally ready for small low-risk missions outside the base. Their first venture would be remembered in Valhalla as the bloodiest maiden voyage a team had ever faced.

Chapter VII: Udachnaya

"S TEAM says you did some fine work," Balder began. He had called V team in their dreams to have them come to his office right after they woke up. They were expecting a new training routine—one that, given the recent trend, would surely break someone's something or sever a body part that ought not be severed. They were quite relieved when he explained their new task. It was a real mission and, compared to training, a walk in the park.

"One of our sister camps has a Mjölnir system similar to our own," he continued. "They want consultants on our break-in to redesign their own security. We need S team here on our own case, but you're quite familiar with the methods used as well, so you'll head to Siberia tonight and stay there until recalled. Your contact in Trubka Udachnaya is named Dmitri, from their De team. He's twenty-eight and recognizable by his black hair with a gray streak. He'll meet you in the blue flower patch. When you land, exchange coded greetings, then shift your links to the Udachnaya network. Vibeke, as you handled most of the analysis"—Veikko and Violet tried not to look utterly useless—"you'll be head consultation. Varg, you keep my kids alive. And team—" He smiled. "—Don't Fuck Shit Up."

Mishka spotted them leaving his office and jogged up to meet them.

"Heading out to my old stomping grounds?" she asked, putting on an extra thick accent in case they had forgotten where she was from.

"Ja, any advice?" said Varg, oblivious to the fact that she was speaking to Vibeke.

"Yes, borscht means beet juice, and don't try to speak Russian. And you, pet"—she took a step toward Vibs—"try not to get intimidated around all those big muscular Udachnaya boys."

Vibeke didn't have a response. Varg spared her the need for one. "What's wrong with big muscular boys?" he asked.

Mishka didn't enlighten him. "Take care of yourself," she said with a last glance at Vibeke before she walked away. Varg watched her go.

"You know, I don't think she's attracted to me at all," he said.

"Lucky you," said Vibs with a smirk, and they headed to the pogo pad to depart. Gastric butterflies began to join them as they walked. Despite the finest training and the most detailed outlines, and despite the assumption that this would be a totally benign assignment, it was still their first mission out on their own. With the butterflies came another sort of animal in Violet's belly, a predator that hoped beyond logic that something might go wrong and give her a chance to show off. She knew nothing would happen to allow her to try out all her new skills on a first mission, but there was an appeal to heading out to a strange land, invulnerable with her team, into the unknown.

As they walked onto the pogo pad, their uniforms turned the dead tan color of Udachnaya soil, with flower-blue shoulders, the first genuine mission camouflage they got to wear. Violet remembered one trip to London when she was young. She'd walked around the city with her parents, seen the sights, and heard the sounds as she had a few times before.

The megalopolis had been peaceful in an odd sort of way. It was busier and far more crowded than Kyle, but it felt the opposite. Back home pogos bounced at high speed from one deflective road panel to the next, and people wandered and trotted along in droves. London was so full that pogo lights blurred into still lines, and humans packed into solid states becoming mere texture.

It was a comfortable place where even the outdoors had felt like a lobby with a ceiling too high to see. It was a safe, easy realm.

Her parents, after linking briefly to one another, told her that they were going to see an opera. When Violet protested that she didn't want to join them, her father said something that took her by surprise.

"You're not invited," he said. "I'm transferring fifty euros to you. Have a look around, be safe, and link me if you need me." Then they left her to her own devices, and the world was no longer safe.

The comfortable London of seconds before was suddenly both frightening and exhilarating. She did no more than walk across the street and eat dinner, but it was the most exciting day of her life thus far. She hadn't experienced the same feeling since then, not in a fight for her life nor in training for the wildest things. But she felt it as her suit changed color. She felt it as they boarded a pogo and called for clearance for departure. She could sense the same feeling in her team. Varg, of course, had more important considerations.

"They neglected to tell us in briefing how many girls there are in Udachnaya."

"I'm sure," said Veikko, "you'll find a waiting menagerie of buff Siberian women, Varg."

"I'm sure you won't," Vibs interjected. "Udachnaya is all male."

"Barbarism!" Varg cried. "Why would they do that to themselves?"

"Tradition, I suppose?"

"Sickening. Where'd you hear it?"

"I read their history on Alopex. They're a good deal more utilitarian than Valhalla. They have no lounges, no gymnasium, and you won't be setting up another Wednesday movie night, that's for sure."

"I suppose not everyone gets to stay in the golden hall."

"Anything else we should have looked up for ourselves, Vibs?" Veikko asked.

"I'll let you know if anything comes to mind."

Violet thought for a moment. "Why do we gold plate everything anyway?"

"Doesn't tarnish or rust," Vibs replied. She really seemed to know everything.

Vibeke closed her eyes and rested against the side of the seat. The hangar controller sent them on their way. The vehicle was on autopilot, there being no risk in a trip to a random flower patch in Siberia, and no way for a human pilot to discern which field they were to land in. To avoid any would-be trackers, they took a scenic route that snaked far south of the direct line, so the trip was long and quiet. Violet stared out the window at the world below. Vibs was online, reading. Varg had fallen asleep within minutes of lift-off, and Veikko amused himself by stacking survival gear on Varg's head.

Violet, too, eventually drifted off. She stayed asleep for most of the trip. Bored sick as they bounced gently past Smolensk, Veikko pulled an air horn from his Varg stack. Sometime later he held it to Violet's ear. While the pogo flew over the Ural mountain range, a terrible noise emerged from Veikko's horn that echoed across the peaks. An instant later, Violet was wide awake, and Veikko was bleeding badly from his nose and cheek. He dug through the survival kit for med gear. Violet looked out the window as the mountains came to an end.

She had always imagined Siberia as a wasteland of ice and snow, like Svalbarð but flat. In summer it was nothing of the sort. There were endless fields of flowers. At the speed they were flying, the fields must have been dozens of kilometers across, without interruption, without any sign of civilization or heterogeneous life. Just flowers. Orange, red, purple.

They set down on a sea of blue petals. The flowers stretched to every horizon with only one miscolored dot, a man in a black jumpsuit. Dmitri stood exactly on target. Veikko woke Varg, who had somehow slept through the air horn, and led the team off the pogo with great formality, eager to look good on his first job. Veikko walked up to Dmitri, head raised, shoulders back, and forgot the coded greeting.

"Something about a purple sun and red snow?" he asked.

"When the blue sun melts the red snow," started Vibeke, annoyed.

Dmitri spoke loudly and quickly. "Right, yes, purple water runs uphill. Are you satisfied, yes? You have the right man standing in the middle of the blue flower patch eighty kilometers from the nearest nothing? I see you are, yes. Let's get on with it and spare the next five poems. You Norsk and your poetics, none of that here. I am me, you are you, we get to work now, yes? Yes."

He knew the greeting better than Veikko, at least. They parted with Alopex and withdrew their links from the Valhalla system. Dmitri took them to a small, nondescript hole in the ground. There was no elevator. He simply jumped into the darkness. They all followed and fell some distance to a tube with an inertial conveyor. They didn't feel the jolt of an instantaneous two hundred kph acceleration. They just watched the dark surroundings fly past. They stopped as abruptly at the edge of a gargantuan spiraling walkway, which fell far deeper into the ground than Valhalla's ravine.

It was clearly an old mining pipe. The soil looked so old and decrepit, it would never support life again. Overhead they could see the camouflage canopy, fake blue flowers like a dark sky in a field so expansive that a surface search team would take years to find the fake patch. Their suits matched the colors perfectly, in contrast to the Udachnaya locals, who like Dmitri wore flat black and looked at the newcomers' boastful garb with disdain.

Like Valhalla, a walkway was carved into the walls, but unlike their native ravine's, this massive road was the only path there. They didn't use the walkway to spiral down to the bottom; rather, Dmitri led them to slide down the steep dirt slope between loops, kicking up a thick tan cloud. The few structures inside had giant proportions, all black and bereft of any style, just utilitarian square slanted walls, jutting up from the sides of the pit like giant black fangs from the earthen maw.

Dmitri pointed out each tower, only one of everything. The only hangar was big enough to hold their entire fleet. Their one barracks held all their men. It stood attached to the only mess hall. They continued past it down the loose sandy slopes. It was a jelly-legging route straight to the bottom of the spiral, where the pit dropped off to a steeper hole. Deep inside, at the base of the hole, one arsenal held almost every functional weapon in the outpost.

Dmitri continued, "We only have about ninety people here, and only thirty-two of them are in trained teams. This isn't a genuine base, yes, more of an arms storage facility, and if they went for our best, strongest base first, we fear our Mjölnir system is a prime target to fill in their missing pieces, given they lack a generator and we have so many."

"So many generators?" asked Veikko.

"Yes, we have twelve generators and forty-four cannons."

"Odin's beard," he said.

Violet linked quickly and silently to Vibeke. "Odin's beard?"

"That thing on Niide's face. Men used to—"

Dmitri went on. "We took the precaution of moving the generators to the deepest, most secure part of the arsenal we could fit them in, which is to say third level. They used to be in fourth. Our engineers have set up more detectors, and we have live guards stationed, along with a partition of Prokofiev. Ah yes, Prokofiev. New kids. I need to link you up."

He gave a burst of information from his link, catching their antenna signatures and relaying them to his net. They felt the intrusive flood of a new network coming into their heads. Like Valhalla's, it lacked ads and immersive qualities in favor of an AI.

Prokofiev introduced himself: an anthropomorphic wolf in traditional Russian garb. He was not fully rendered like Alopex but seemed a more fitting computer system for Udachnaya. His voice was egotistical for a computer. He spoke almost musically. "Welcome to Siberia. My analysis shows our generators are protected with far more than your estimate of three intruders could penetrate, my security designs are theoretically flawless, and I look forward to seeing what a quartet of Westerners can add to it, if anything."

When they crossed catwalks to the arsenal, they found Prokofiev's attitude to be quite justified. Beyond the general security stood a barrage of detectors that could spot a dust mite even if that dust mite were invisible, holding perfectly still, and equipped with signal jamming hardware. Beyond the detectors were two tall men with Gatling shotguns. Beyond the men were two-decimeter-thick vault doors, and past those there were ultrahigh-voltage barricade fields. Within the fields were the generator safes, each one protected by its own FKMA robot—intimidating metal beasts with dual plasma cannons. Each robot had been relieved of its treads and was bolted directly into the generator housings. If someone by some miracle did manage to steal a generator, they would take an angry robot with it.

As Varg admired the sheer masses of heavy-metal bulk, Violet and Veikko kept their mouths closed in astonishment that they had been sent to this grand stronghold to improve what Violet thought were the most impressive protective measures she'd ever seen. Vibs had other ideas.

"First the robots need to go. The FKMA models can be hacked even with binary lattice shields. Prokofiev?"

"Yes?"

"Do they have BiL shielding?"

"No."

"Call in some engineers. Let's get 'em out of here," said Vibeke with great authority. "The detector field is double redundant in at least nine places. Let's get someone on those and move them to the next outer ring, where they'll do some good. Keep redundant scanning only on susceptible areas behind the door and in the corners. What kind of armor does the inner arsenal core have? Prokofiev?"

"None."

"At least four welders and some gear for us."

As the rest of V hid the fact that they shared no part of Vibeke's inspiration, Prokofiev called in men to do her bidding and work began. Vibs revealed weak point after weak point and seemed to know exactly what each point needed. Most of the impressive, broad measures Udachnaya had taken proved either too little or too much in the wrong places. As efforts began, Veikko and Violet found their roles and set to work. Varg didn't even try to steal Vibeke's conceptual thunder. He just picked up a hydraulic wrench and started in on the robots. Everyone was impressed at the end of the day by Vibeke's catches of every flaw and her truly inspired retrofitting designs. Dmitri looked at her as if she were a tiny firecracker that had just blown up a bridge. He caught Violet by the arm and asked, "She's always like this, yes?"

"No," Violet answered. "She must be tired from the trip."

When they retired for the evening, Vibs admitted that she was as surprised as they were: Her brains had never been so useful in the past.

"And how did you know about the robots?" Varg asked. "BiL shields don't cover them?"

"Not those models," she explained. "They're open on the bottom. They could be broken into with a linear broadcast from underneath, and the arsenal had a floor below. We'll need to check out that floor tomorrow after breakfast. If they have breakfast here."

"They will," said Varg. "The comforts are few, but they're sure to be big."

"Like the bunks?" Violet remarked as they walked into their new room.

"Yeah," added Veikko. "Why do we all have king-sized beds?"

"With no bed sheets…," Vibs said as she looked over the massive mattresses.

Violet found a gap under hers. "They have sheets, in the big giant rusty drawers."

Indeed, the big rusty drawers built inside the beds held great thick sheets, which were unwieldy due to their size and heft. That seemed the motto of Udachnaya—big and not always for the better. The team spoke of how they must appear to the others, soft pampered little kids playing warriors, telling the locals how to do their jobs and so on. Modesty was disallowed, of course; they were there to improve the security, so they had to point out the shortcomings. But there was some degree of surprise as to how much had come up short. Halfway through talking, they realized they were all asleep. The Udachnaya lucid dreamscape was identical to the plain black bedroom, so they hadn't noticed the change. They agreed to change the surroundings, on Veikko's suggestion, to a Pacific island beach. Vibs dialed up beach chairs, Violet lowered the gravity, and Varg called back to Alopex for "Program Varg 36D" that conjured a surplus of naked large-breasted native women for the background.

"So this is life on duty," he said with a wide grin.

"It could be worse," remarked Veikko.

"It will be when we start work on the roofs. We need to test the load bearing—"

"When we're awake, Vibs. For now I'd prefer either making fun of cultural differences or staring at Varg's background work."

"Boys. You could be fighting women for your lives, and you'd still be staring at their chests."

"You used to spar Mishka," said Veikko. "Tell me you didn't notice with, well, the sheer size of them…."

"Sure, they're great targets, and she feels it when they get punched. Then she gets angry and breaks your skull."

"Come to think of it, has she ever lost a single round?"

"Never, she's impossible."

"Katana is impossible," said Violet. "She took on all four Fs simultaneously and won without a scratch. Even with Balder, she holds her own."

That got Varg's attention, briefly, "They say Alf and Balder used to have epic day-long sparring bouts," he said.

"There would be a sight."

"Sure would…."

And so they went on until the sun finished its circuit.

PROKOFIEV WOKE them as rudely as an air-horn blast and directed them to the eatery. Breakfast was as big as they'd expected, full of genuine meats and eggs and greasy salty potato products. The unusual foods made their bellies happy and talkative and keen to expel noxious fumes from one orifice or another. Then it was time to plan out more security measures that they (Vibs) had invented overnight and set to work. Work went on through what would have been lunch, if anyone there had needed it.

Moving heavy artillery out of the rooms to be altered took time. The microwave arrays alone took two hours. Organizing the security force to watch over the work took another hour, but it was necessary. If anyone tried to break in while the arsenal was in disrepair, they'd have to face the whole ravine of men to get there. The team never felt safer than they did surrounded by rows of men with Gatling shotguns.

Rebuilding the lower floors and new roofs was so involved that even the biggest of the Udachnaya men were getting tired. They planned another two days of heavy labor, then testing, then more labor. After that, they would stay for a couple more days of debugging and simulations, and then finally they could return home to the luxury of Valhalla and be done with this monster of tasks.

By the end of the first full day of work, a good portion of the deconstruction was complete. Walls that had to be replaced completely were gone and the vulnerable parts of the roof were ready to come off and be replaced. The sun hadn't set overhead, but it was past the walls of the pit. The blue canopy made it dark enough to require artificial lights for roof work. Udachnaya used ancient sodium-vapor lights, which turned everything perverse colors. Their eyes played tricks on them, so nobody noticed the gentle rain of blue petals.

Only when a strange wind tickled the back of Violet's neck did she shut off her microwave's welding beam and look around. Vibeke and Varg were already looking for the source. Veikko found it and signaled for them to look straight up. When V team looked skyward, they saw the canopy tearing open, pulling back like curtains to reveal the dual blades of a panzercopter, shaped like a giant hornet, painted completely in white.

Alarms began to sound. This was not a friendly craft. The flawless white paint gave it a sinister aura; the sodium lights made it glow angry yellow and cast its recessed armor into harsh shadows. But it was clearly covered in paint. White paint, same as the thieves' carriage. Prokofiev abandoned his lupine graphic and began highlighting routes into the special arsenal. Native teams followed other alarms to their battle stations. Dmitri and his team descended with V into the arsenal, jumping down through the holes they had spent the day making in its roof. Violet followed her teammates through what few walls and doors were still intact. They headed for the second level down, where they'd stored the Mjölnir system during retrofitting. As they sealed the last hatchway from the open air, they caught their last glimpse of the copter extending drop lines. Six of them. The inner arsenal doors sealed.

The sounds of antiaircraft fire echoed from outside. They all ducked away from the walls. Dmitri shouted to Vibeke, "Did your analysis predict they had armored air support?"

"No, everything we saw pointed to three intruders with minimal hardware."

"There were six lines on that thing yes, and it takes two to pilot! Prokofiev, update."

Prokofiev appeared, but before he could speak, the link went dead, the lights went out, and communications went silent. The only sound was from the fight outside. Seconds later Dmitri turned on a glow patch on his shoulder. V team took his cue and set their uniforms for illumination. There were eight people in the arsenal. Dmitri's team didn't appear to have any plan. They could only hope for the guards outside to defeat the intruders. Everyone just watched the ceiling and listened to the fight going on around them.

It was just like a day in training when P team had taught V team how to discern various types of fire from the sound. Violet could make out the Udachnaya projectile cannons, the Gatling shotguns of the guards, the panzercopter armor deflecting them, faint microwave hums from artillery-sized batteries, the flight noise of drone missiles, the impact of missiles, and drop charges. She saw that her teammates were listening to the same sounds and coming to the same conclusions about the level of battle going on around them. They were caught in an all-out firefight, the kind people died in without so much as a chance to fight back. They all knew it was a possibility, but only Veikko said it.

"Well, this team was short-lived," he stated over the team link, coded so that the Udachnaya team couldn't hear.

"We're not dead yet," replied Violet.

"Tell me that in ten minutes."

"I will," she said, "They wouldn't have sent us out if they didn't think we had a chance."

"They didn't think we'd run into panzercopter troops."

"Because we told them it was three thieves," said Vibeke. Even over the link her voice wavered. She had come up with the estimate, now proven wrong. There were at least eight on the copter, in a far superior position. The enemy had come in a craft made for war, made for the old, tough wars. N team had told them in training how Valhalla wished it had a panzercopter, how the things could take out an army base, how they could massacre a city, how one had killed everyone on E team when E team had been armed to the teeth. How only the most besieged companies like the YUP still used the things because they were overkill for anyone else. There was no doubt that the craft had an edge on Udachnaya and from the sounds outside, it was busily annihilating all the guards stationed to protect them as they worked.

"Maybe it's survival of the fittest," Vibs reflected. "Our team got it wrong, so we'll die for it."

"That may be," said Violet, "but I plan to live for at least ten minutes just to prove Veikko wrong."

Violet wanted to say something comforting to Vibeke, anything to relieve her of the responsibility of that three-man estimate. She could have admitted she'd been no help, that nobody in Valhalla thought otherwise, but it was all too petty. She wanted to move on, to abandon the subject. To say something noble, stoic. "And I don't know about you, but I died to the outside world with a sword in hand. I'm going the same way if I'm dying for good. When Alf gives our eulogies, I'm gonna make sure he does it proud."

"Damn straight," said Veikko with a nod.

"Works for me," linked Vibs.

"Forget your eulogies and forget ten minutes," said Varg aloud. "I'm gonna live forever."

He stood up and drew his microwave. A petty weapon compared to what was outside, but in Varg's hands, it looked like it could save all of Siberia.

Dmitri walked up behind him, hauling a crate. He spoke aloud. "The only thing we know for sure is that they want what's in here. They're going to come in. You know how to use these, yes?" He pried the lid off the crate to reveal ten of their Gatling shotguns. Another crate revealed as many drums of shells.

Varg called back, "Oh hell yes."

They passed out guns to everyone, Dmitri and one of his men held two each. He spoke again. "And you four, Valhalla, don't use your bone bugs unless you want to lose 'em."

Questionable advice, but they weren't about to argue. Training took over their minds. Panic didn't set in; it didn't even threaten them.

They took the best strategic positions in the room and dimmed out their suits. The room went black. Gunfire outside had ceased. All was silent. Had the troops outside ended the threat? Could it all be over already? They would wait for the link to come back on before making such an assumption. They would hold their positions until relieved and assured the situation was over.

Violet set 99 percent of her mind on tactics. The last percent was still dwelling on their underestimate of the intruder forces—they'd put it at three, and now they knew it was at least eight. At least eight people with a panzercopter, a craft even Valhalla didn't wield. A formidable nightmare. Violet heard an angry buzz, a tractoring force from outside. The entire top floor of the arsenal tore off to reveal the panzercopter, four more panzercopters, and a descending force of thirty armed, gas-masked personnel, all in heavy white armor.

"Oh fuck!" shouted Varg.

"*Chyort voz'mi*!" yelled Dmitri. Everyone in the shredded room seemed to shout an old native curse. Violet was inspired by no obscene exclamations. Before she was hit by the shock of seeing such a powerful opposing force, she saw the gas masks, and training demanded she be prepared for a gas attack. She pulled up the aerotoxin-coat shield from her collar and sealed it against her nose and mouth. The rest of her team did the same quickly after. The Udachnaya teams lacked gas-masking uniforms.

Dmitri's men opened fire immediately, spraying the intruding force as they dropped in. The spray of Gatling shot hit the intruders' body armor like hailstones, bouncing off harmlessly. Only when a spray hit the rubber joints in their armor did it disable a limb. Varg opened fire sparingly, targeting their neck fittings as best he could. The rest of the team followed his lead and managed to take out two of the enemies as they descended, knocking a couple of others' weapons from their hands. Intruders were beginning to make the ground, and as soon as they landed, they could deploy heavier armor. Shields sprouted from their forearms and the torso joints were no longer vulnerable. Violet focused all her fire on legs, knee joints, and ankle joints. She disabled one man, but it was little progress. The landed enemies did not return fire. They kept their heaviest shields to the team and headed straight for the generators.

Dmitri called for them to fall back. They started to back up, checking carefully behind them as they had learned. When they looked back, they saw Udachnaya teams hauling something out from the ditch around the arsenal. Artillery. Though the panzercopters had destroyed Udachnaya's antiaircraft batteries, the microwave arrays from the arsenal were ready to go, having been moved for retrofitting work. V team took cover by the arsenal foundations, and the sky lit up with ultrahigh-intensity waves. Two of the copters lost electrical power and fell to the ground. Three remained in the air. Two of those airborne began an assault on the new arrays. One moved in closer to the arsenal.

The landed troops had already affixed cables to one of their target generators. More troops on the copters pulled the cables up along the drop lines and affixed them to clamps. Varg stepped up and sighted the clamps with his microwave. He was on target, but beams weren't enough to sever the cables or clamps. The panzercopter lifted the generator and some of their ground troops with it. Once in the air, the troops lowered their shields and started firing at the microwave arrays. Varg and the Russians were forced to take cover again.

The two other panzercopters successfully obliterated one of the microwave arrays. Working together, they headed for the remaining unit, which let loose all it had on the northern copter. It drifted back, its field rotors partly scrambled from the attack and having trouble holding their airfoil shape. The other copter began firing, sending the Udachnaya team running for cover away from their overheated array.

One copter was about to leave with a generator. The other generators sat in the open. Vibeke shouted through her mask,

"Armor! Metal armor! Start one up!"

V team ran for the remaining generators. Dmitri and his men started unloading a crate beside them. Violet started one of the systems, while Vibs and Veikko hooked up the cannons. Varg lifted the cannons with his bare hands and pointed them in the right direction. Dmitri arrived with the contents of his crate: the manual targeting hardware. His team began wiring it in. Other Udachnaya teams saw them at work and headed back to the remaining microwave array. They retargeted at the enemy escape route, but the array was still so hot the chambers were on fire. They would only be able to keep a burst going for a few seconds.

It was enough. The Mjölnir system was up, and Dmitri's men targeted the panzercopter carrying the stolen generator. Violet looked around at the intruders. Something was strange. They weren't firing at her. The copters were firing to suppress and disperse, but not massacring the teams in the remains of the arsenal. On the ground, the men had weapons but didn't use them; they kept their shields up and despite losses, they weren't shooting. Violet thought it strange enough to comment on. "The intruders! They're not firing at us!" she called out.

"They will after this!" shouted Dmitri as he triggered the generator. Varg was knocked off his feet when it fired, but the bolts hit the copter right on its belly. In milliseconds the ten-meter craft became a fist-sized crumpled mass with its crew crushed inside. V team felt their metal uniforms flex for an instant when the magnetic field hit. The generator and troops fell to the ground. The troops didn't put their shields up. This time they drew their Gatling shotguns. The big Udachnaya microwave array targeted them. Then one of the remaining copters appeared to break in half. Its cockpit and motor segment held still as the back half lifted like a skunk lifting its tail, exposing two nozzles. They fired a glowing cloud at the microwave array. It was blinked out of existence along with six Udachnaya men. The copter lowered its troop hold back into place and flew for the arsenal.

Every armored enemy on the ground was now firing at them. The two deactivated copters had also restarted their electronics and began to lift off. Dmitri and Varg retargeted the fallen generator and fired, smashing it. Dmitri called to his men,

"Break out explosives! Destroy the other ten generators." He targeted another copter with the system, and Varg fired. One of the bolts hit but the other missed. The magnetic field failed to form and the craft was only knocked off course. Three copters were hovering overhead. The fourth was gaining altitude and covering their escape route, but there was nothing left to fire at in the canopy hole. If they wanted out, they could get out.

Troops were back on the ground, and the ones that weren't crushed in the fall were pissed off. They continued to fire with their microwaves. Several Russians were hit. Varg dropped the cannons and found cover. The rest of Violet's team hit the deck with another member of De team. The two other Russians stood and shot back. They targeted necks and killed three more of the intruders before they were killed themselves, hit by so many microwaves that chunks of them were vaporized. Four of the remaining enemies seized the generator in use and began affixing new cables.

Dmitri pulled out a remote and hit some buttons. The bomb he had affixed to the generator blew, sending the troops around it flying in four directions each. Other Udachnayans began detonating their own bombs. Six of the generators were destroyed, five of the enemy troopers. Debris hit one of the copters and sent it off course, crash landing in the dirt. It was undamaged, though, and began revving up for takeoff.

Four troops were approaching the arsenal foundation. The copters had the surrounding area covered. V team had no avenue of escape. They only had their Gatlings and even odds. They nodded to each other, an unspoken agreement that there was nothing to do but fight face-to-armored-face. Before they could spring up, the approaching troops were hit from their flanks. Three more teams of Udachnaya soldiers flooded in amid heavy fire from three of the copters. The link came back on and Prokofiev blinked in.

"V team, follow Ef and Ya team to the engineering silos. Kha, Tse, Che to continue engagement."

They followed the AI's plan. More troops were dropping in from another copter. Udachnaya teams were taking over the ground battle. As they followed Prokofiev's path, they saw intruders hold a line around their new target generator, one of three left. One copter was covering the enemy troops, one was awaiting the cargo, and two were laying waste to the pit. They didn't fire to suppress and protect anymore; they fired to kill everyone they could.

Heavy fire from the copters made the run a desperate one. Microwave blasts turned streaks of sand into glass. Giant shells sent puffs of dirt into the air and cut an Udachnaya man in half. The blood and guts to which they had desensitized themselves in training were accumulating all around. It looked like the simulation, but it wasn't graphics; it was the men they'd eaten breakfast with. A horrible sight, they kept running through a gruesome alley, ducking shrapnel and taking cover when the microwaves hit something explosive. Violet looked back as she ducked behind a fallen wall. She saw the generator almost ready to rise. Russians adeptly blew the heck out of it, but another generator was already set up to go—one of two left. Nearby, the FKMA robots they had set aside were getting carted into one copter as it awaited its primary target. Spoils of war.

The evacuating teams entered a tunnel and began climbing up to the engineering complex. As they made their way up, one of the copters unleashed an assault on the building. Walls fell in on the tail end of their group. The tunnel was broken and bent, so those behind them were slowed by a sudden rise in the terrain. Violet and Varg ran back to pull men up the jagged cliff, but only one man had not been crushed under rubble. Violet reached out to take his arm, but both of his arms were gone. They stared uselessly at each other for a second. There was no way to help him. The tunnel would break in less than a second. She and Varg moved onward into the building. They sealed the door as the tunnel collapsed. They would find no rest indoors.

They came under fire again from troops in the building, firing with Gatlings they must have picked up from Dmitri's fallen men. Machinery around the room sent shot ricocheting in too many directions to predict. It was mayhem. Violet took cover behind a giant lathe. Everyone else took cover in an alcove opposite her. They did so because the troops were moving toward Violet's hiding place.

One of the intruders kept a suppressing fire on them. They knew they had singled out the weak member of the pack. They were moving in to kill her. *Stupid*, she thought. Every damn soldier had gone one way, and she'd gone the other. Her own Gatling was long out of ammo. Her microwave would do nothing, not even to their joints. She had nothing else to fight with. She saw one man approaching, hunting her. She looked around for anything that could help. She found nothing.

Tikari! Tikari, dumbass, she cursed herself. She ejected it from her chest and took hold of it in knife form. Its AI buzzed into her brain; it wanted to fly out and kill the man coming for her. She suppressed its thoughts. She couldn't use it like that here, not like this. She still hadn't fully mastered it in training, and now wasn't the time to risk it. *A thousand reasons not to*, she thought. Dmitri had even warned her against it. She couldn't do it. She had to wait for the man to come, and then she would go for the neck. He wouldn't expect it. It would work.

Or it would have if two Russians hadn't jumped out to save her. They came over the lathe with nothing but spent Gatlings they used as clubs. They pounded the armored invader to the floor. The other intruder fired at them, killing one instantly, shredding the other's back terribly. Violet couldn't let it go on. She darted past the lathe, keeping under the enemy's field of view, and stabbed the shooter in the ankle. He fell, and she stabbed him in the neck. He kept fighting. She stabbed him again, again, and again until he stopped and blood leaked from his armor. She looked back to the others. The surviving Russian had taken the attacker's gun and crammed it behind his armored visor, opening fire inside his helmet. Violet's rescuer looked at her, smiled, then dropped dead.

Two men had just died because she'd gone the wrong way, because she couldn't trust her Tikari to do its job. She sensed that the Tikari was pissed at her for it. She shut it up by stowing it in her chest, still bloody from the fight. It was a sickening, dirty feeling to have his blood under her skin. The feeling wasn't half as bad as having two dead Russians on her conscience. She turned her brain off to it. She would feel it later; she'd learn to trust her Tikari later; she'd clean it off later. Vibs stood over her. They were still on the run.

Once in the silo, she saw several Udachnaya men uncovering what they had come for: a mortar and armor-piercing shells. The unit was under repair, but they knew how to use it in this state. A panzercopter was still hovering outside, letting loose a barrage of conventional gunfire at the complex. The walls held against it. Prokofiev told Ya and V teams to await orders while Ef team set up the mortar and opened an embrasure, then began launching shells, not on the nearby panzercopter but on the cargo craft. They hit it with two shells and broke the cables, but the copter remained. It moved out of the way and another took its place. Men began rewiring the generator yet again.

V team kept to the back of the bay, out of the way. Violet was standing still and couldn't bear to have a moment to think about what had happened. She had to do something. "What was that spray," she asked, "that got the microwave array. What was that?"

"Antimatter," said Vibs. "Not a generalized antimatter blast—that would blow up half the planet. The weapon works by scanning a target and arranging antiprotonic particles—"

Varg interrupted. "But not true antiprotons."

"Right," Vibs said, "but they use the exact solution that will annihilate the target, no more. It's an uncommon weapon because it takes a long time to scan, and any working computer with a sensor can see it coming and set up a defensive field long before the scan is complete. Even our suit fields could block it."

She was talking in full explanatory mode, fast. She was doing it, Violet knew, because she couldn't stand still either, because she needed to avoid thinking about her own mistake. Nobody on her team could bear to let in Violet's idiocy or the men it had killed. Even Veikko was trying to talk about the damn antimatter gizmo.

"It's called a Kraken system. Has a twenty-minute recharging time. They won't use it unless they have to. Don't worry."

He was saying "don't worry" to himself. All four were worried the more they considered it. They were trying to take their minds off the disaster, and all they could talk about was how it could get worse. Then it got worse. The copters were getting tired of their quarry getting blown up. There was only one generator left, and all four copters and about ten armored men were gathered around it, not letting anyone in. They were out of range of the half-assembled mortars, so Prokofiev was sending men about the silo to assemble something that could reach them.

Dmitri walked into the room from another bay, carrying equipment. All four V teammates ran to help him, to do anything they could. Dmitri sent them for parts, and Prokofiev told them where to dig. Violet ran to the north end of the bay for recoil springs. She delivered them to Varg, who was helping to assemble something that resembled a slingshot with a field projector for power. It could lob mortar shells all the way to the generator.

Varg took charge of aim. A massive Russian man loaded a shell, and Varg let loose. The field projector kicked in as the springs hit their apex and sent the shell flying past the copters. They reloaded. One of the enemy must have seen it, because one copter broke off and headed for them. Varg fired. Another miss. And again, a hit that did little damage to the coming panzercopter. It drew close enough to hit with the more accurate mortar. Varg didn't even ask for the mortar. He just picked up a shell, ran to the window, and lobbed it by hand. It hit the windshield and exploded harmlessly. He threw another; it missed. He threw a third, and it hit one of the rotor caps. Without a cap, the field rotor suddenly extended infinitely from its spinning emitter. It connected with one of the Udachnaya buildings and stuck like glue. The copter suddenly spun out of control. The thing had to eject its front emitter assembly and fell to the ground. Che team stormed it and slaughtered the crew.

Veikko gave Varg a complex high-five ritual as Violet looked out the archer's hole. The chaos continued in and around the arsenal. Dmitri's men were fighting hand to hand to keep the intruders from hooking the last generator. Tse team was blowing up any enemies they could spot. Varg and Dmitri spoke by open link. Dmitri had a plan to aim the slingshot. Violet didn't understand him, but Vibeke did. They set to work and in under a minute had hooked the carriage holding the sling into a Prokofiev hardwire port.

With targeting information from Prokofiev, Varg loaded five mortar shells into the sling and launched another volley. Several of the shells hit the new cargo-copter-to-be and cut it in half. Three copters down. One was busy firing what it could at the men holding the arsenal; the last deployed new cables. The slingshot team called for its coordinates.

Prokofiev calculated, but before it could respond, the other copter left the fight and headed for engineering. Prokofiev alerted them to an antimatter spray solution forming in the craft, adding that the silo's shield generators were down. This meant "Run!" They did. Everyone ditched their positions and fled the silo before the spray hit. The Valhalla few turned on their strongest deflective fields. Their suits sucked the energy out of their bodies and put it into thin spheres around them. The amount it stole rendered Violet cold and tired almost instantly. She barely saw half the building cease to be. The rest caved in around her. Prokofiev disappeared again.

Violet was alone, stuck in a mess of debris. She called out for Vibeke, Varg, Veikko, and Dmitri, but the sound of her voice echoed at her like a mocking refrain. Her link couldn't get through. The antimatter weapon had contaminated it all with a form of radiation that jammed the signal. At least, she hoped that was why she couldn't contact them. She kept her defense shield on in case of another attack or further crushing debris. It drained energy from her so fast she could feel the cold.

She pushed around on the wreckage, but it was all rock solid, more than solid—it was pressing with great force against the vacuole that her field made in the avalanche of twisted metal and sand. She had to keep the field on. *Fine*, she thought. If she fell asleep, she wouldn't have to think.

But she couldn't fall asleep. She sat in the space for an hour, tired, sick, and freezing but unable to pass out. Her brain got the better of her. She had failed in every way she could have failed. She had seen men die for her mistakes. Her entire team could be dead. She couldn't link to them, couldn't hear them, couldn't even dig her way out. She might be trapped there forever, to die for her pathetic misdeeds.

TWO HOURS later, the twisted metal ceiling twisted more and revealed the night sky. Veikko's look of relief to find her was comforting. Varg and Vibeke stood nearby. There were no panzercopters, only the ruin of Udachnaya and a pile of dead intruders in payment for one magnetic generator, successfully stolen. Udachnaya had lost nineteen men and nearly all its defensive capability in the attack. Prokofiev was operating at a quarter capacity, and the enemies had accomplished their objective. V team found Dmitri in the remains of the medical bay, where medics were busy dealing with dozens of men in dire need.

"That was not three men with minimal transportation! Are you four okay?"

"Yes," said Veikko. "Have you contacted Valhalla?"

"Prokofiev has sent word, but our link to Alopex is gone, so it's a cable transmission. Don't worry, I'm sure they'll call you back before you have to clean this mess up."

Nothing was further from their minds (except for Varg, who would later admit his pleasure at not having to reassemble their base). Now that the chaos was over, they had only more time to think, and thinking about it hurt them all. There were a hundred times they could have died and a dozen they didn't know how they survived. The medical team gave them a very quick triage and some radiation shots, then got back to work with the dying.

"Actually," continued Dmitri, "it is likely they'll vaporize the place and find another. Our little gangs have a very pragmatic attitude toward losses, but we shall see. Once our wolf returns home—"

Prokofiev appeared, at horrible resolution.

"Valhalla requests immediate return of V team by pogo. Teams D and E will arrive within the hour with arms, a contingent of engineers, and a medical detail. Vladivostok and Abu Simbel are on standby for assistance. All bases on second degree security lockdown."

Dmitri said. "That means you need to get back now. If your pogo doesn't arrive in their projected window, they'll shoot you down. Liev will escort you to the tube. Liev?"

"Dead," called a medic.

Dmitri smiled a hateful, sarcastic smile. "Well, then. You know the way, yes?"

They did know the way. The conveyor system in the tunnel was down, so they had to walk. When Vibeke reminded them of the time window they had to make, they ran. What had taken them seconds to travel before took almost five minutes at full running speed. They came out at the pogo and piled in out of breath. Veikko hit the controls, and they took off into the night. Nobody spoke on the trip home. Veikko played no tricks. Varg didn't sleep. Violet didn't look out the windows.

She felt shame but didn't feel crippled with emotion. This time she wasn't worried that the coldness was insanity but relieved that she was numb to the matter. This was part of life now, not a family disaster but her job. She would be shot at more. She would see more die, people she knew. She would kill more. How many had she just done in? She had no idea. There would be no cops to tell her what she had accomplished this time. It happened as she imagined war must have felt back in ancient times. You kill anyone you can on the other side.

After dwelling on it for an hour, she found the whole thing philosophically compelling. Beyond the shame of their prediction of three men—she cringed as she thought of it—beyond the shame of her pathetic failure behind the lathe, beyond the soreness and pain she felt, there was a part of her that felt… satisfied? Had she enjoyed what just happened? She couldn't admit that, but the fact remained, something had happened, something big, and she had been a part of it, for better or worse. She lived. Her team lived. Survival was quite an accomplishment, really. She did not let herself imagine how she would feel had any one of her team not survived.

When they started their approach to Valhalla, Alopex appeared in the cabin and told them to delink and return to their home network. They all disconnected from the thin dying Udachnaya link and let the clear, sharp Valhalla link flood into their heads. It was like a shower for Violet's brain. All the slimy grit of battle left her mind, cleaned away by the fluffy white fox. The pogo fell into the hangar, and their suits turned back to their native colors. Only once their old colors were restored did Violet notice they were covered in blood and debris.

Chapter VIII: Geki

ALOPEX LED the team to a small chamber next to the pogo pad, an industrial-sized sonic shower. She directed them to take earplugs from a slot in the wall, then sealed the door. A deep rumble began to sound from the showerheads. The dirt and blood and scraps of debris that clung to their uniforms and faces fell into the air, so thick they could see it dancing and floating to the walls. Violet was suddenly eager to clean her Tikari, but holding it up to the shower would only clean its blade, not the blood she had stuffed with it into her ribs. That would have to wait.

As soon as they left the shower, Alopex told them to head for Alf and lit up a path along the floor. They followed in silence. There were few people along the way. They didn't see anyone from the teams. Violet wasn't sure what was to come. There would surely be a heavy debriefing and investigation, but how would people act around them after what had happened? Part of her said nobody would raise an eyebrow, that this was business as usual to them. Part of her said that such modesty was the worst form of conceit, and that she and her team would be treated as wounded children, coddled and hugged and pitied. The idea of Alföðr acting in such a way was grotesque. Mercifully, he was quite the opposite. They came to him on the ravine floor.

"So, how was Siberia? Weather all right?"

Violet didn't know if it was a joke. She looked to Veikko, who seemed afraid to laugh if it was.

Alf went on. "You're all wondering if there was more you could have done, if it was your fault. Get over it. You did fine. When a team of your experience is faced with a threat on this level, the best you could be expected to do was stay out of everyone's way. But of course, Udachnaya's protocol was to use whoever was closest to the guns regardless of their survival probability. Thirty-six died in that assault, more than half of them our allies. The enemy gained their objective and did it by catching us totally off guard."

"We told you...." Vibs was almost stuttering. "We told you it was probably three people...."

"Here, it almost certainly was. There was no panzercopter fleet here, no drop teams. They most likely sent a select few here because they had someone on the inside and knew how to get in and out. They wanted to steal without waking the giant. This gave them the added benefit that if they failed in their mission, we would underestimate their capabilities. Only when they failed did they use brute force, and at an advantage."

"There's a double agent here?" asked Varg, clearly more excited at the prospect than afraid.

"Almost definitely, in the population or, I fear, among the teams."

"What do we do now?" asked Vibeke.

"You four go to the medical bay and get a once-over. D team and E team are heading out to Siberia with Balder. S and M are attempting to track the invaders with our most expensive gadgets and gizmos, including one machine that costs over, well, no matter. C team is internal affairs. They'll want to ask you all about what you saw, a full and most likely repetitive debriefing. Then you will be interviewed by... another interested party."

He said the last words in the tone Violet's parents had used when they told her bad news. It was disconcerting coming from him, as if he felt sorry for them having to meet that "interested party." He could laugh about the weather in Udachnaya, but he was dead solemn about what was to come. Violet suddenly felt like the disaster wasn't at an end.

Alf headed for his library. V team headed for the med bay. As they walked north toward the bay and gym, they began to see crowds. Residents and teams were standing, staring as they passed. Violet couldn't make out what they said and linked to each other. Condemnations? Pity? Whatever they were saying, Violet didn't like those whispers. There was no way they were anything good.

They came to the med bay, walking under a cantilever of the gymnasium to the entrance. Most people from the gym were out to see them, staring as they entered. There was only one person in the bay. The link called her T. Nachtgall, nurse third class, junior grade.

"Dr. Niide and the senior med staff are en route to Udachnaya. They said you weren't too beaten up. Uh, are you?"

All four shook their heads.

"Okay, um, I don't have X-ray eyes. So...."

She meant they had to disrobe. Violet was never more aware of the medical bay's transparent front wall. Who the hell, she wondered, designed a medical ward, realm of the colonoscopy and catheter, with a giant transparent wall? The crowd from the gym hadn't the classic decency to disperse as V team stripped off their suits for exams. Violet felt like she was in summertime Scotland again.

The four sat on their respective exam tables, all unclothed and all growing certain they did not need to be. Varg alone sat without the least degree of modesty, and the others sat trying not to stare at what he had reason to be immodest about. The nurse approached Veikko first. He held up his arm for dermal regeneration on a bad scrape and asked for a muscle patch on his shoulders. Vibeke needed nothing. The nurse came to Violet, who had one request.

"I got blood in my Tikari port."

"You're injured there?"

"No, I stabbed a guy, put it back in."

"Ewwwww!" shouted the nurse.

"Yes."

"That's really horrible!"

"Yes. Can you clean it out for me?"

"No!" she shouted as if she had taken offense. "Why the hell did you do that?"

"I was in a hurry. Why can't you do anything?"

"Like what? What am I supposed to do that you can't?"

"I don't know," she said, growing irate. "Disinfect it? Wash the port out? Test me for.... cholera or something?"

"No, just go... go shower or something. And don't do that again."

"Thank you so fucking much," Violet barked as she hopped off the table and grabbed her suit. She didn't bother to put it on; she just marched as fast as she could out of the med bay. The nurse moved on to Varg, who alerted her to a sensitivity in his inguinal ligaments. Violet marched out of sight of the crowd and into the gym, empty with everyone outside staring at the med bay. The gym washroom was also empty, and beside the sonic showers was a water sink with a water hose. She ejected her Tikari into the basin and gave it a thorough cleaning, let it shake off, then put the hose into her chest. The water froze her ribs and lungs, but she didn't mind at all. *The more it hurt*, she thought, *the cleaner it got*. The metal parts of her port stayed cold after she was done, a discomfort that lingered after the Tikari jumped back in.

She dressed and walked into the På Täppan room. The hill was only a meter high without the three-meter people heap on it. She sat on the empty hill and cursed the inept nurse, the transparent wall, the crowd. The whole damn day. The whole damn mission. It was a joke to Alf, disgusting to the nurse. How could she even talk to her team about it after her failure in the machine room? Everything about it was rotten, like a dead rat in the walls, stinking up everything and impossible to find and excise. Violet didn't know how tired she was until she noticed she was asleep, in the lucid dreamscape. If she were dreaming, she knew one thing she could talk to without shame.

"Alopex?" she called.

"Yes, Violet?"

"What the hell happened?"

"Please make your inquiry more specific."

"What happened in Siberia?"

"Analysis is underway. Early findings suggest a devoted strike force attacked Trubka Udachnaya in order to obtain weaponry they were unable to steal in a previous incursion here. The force consisted of at least thirty-four and no more than forty-four individuals, five panzercopters, and extensive light armament. Udachnaya responded with heavy artillery fire, incapable of full defensive capacity, and improvised attacks including semifunctional batteries and use of the targeted Mjölnir system. The strike force showed 92.9 percent efficiency, with Udachnaya forces responding with 88 percent theoretical efficiency and 32 percent active efficiency. Infiltrators succeeded in the theft of one Mjölnir generator, seven Gatling shotguns, and two FKMA robots. Abnormalities in the strike included extreme heavy armor and excessive offensive commitment."

An obedient little fox. Not a single word outside the analysis, cold and robotic, almost like Vibs. Almost like herself, Violet thought. "What was abnormal about it?"

"Armored aircraft are limited in the amount of shielding they can carry and still fly. The enemy panzercopters had 800 percent of optimal shielding, as well as Kraken assault systems. Flight capabilities were significantly impaired. Personnel carried heavy armor atypical of land assaults, as well as contingency gear that was not deployed, including—"

"Gas masks?" she realized.

"Affirmative."

"Why would they have gas masks if they weren't using gas? Have our Russian agents ever used toxic gas?"

"Negative. Toxic gas has not been used in any Udachnaya or Valhalla assault, or any known dispute for over thirty years. No suggestion of its use has been implied or threatened in twenty years. Gas masks of the style deployed at Udachnaya are used currently only for deep gas-giant mining operations, methane-carbonizing reverberator assembly, sexual fetish and disguise, algae farming in toxic env—"

"Likelihood of disguise purpose in attack?"

"Under 10 percent."

"Why?"

"Deduction based on purpose in disguise. There is little likelihood the attackers would be recognized by our forces or Siberian allies."

"Update to include factor: one or more members of Valhalla or Udachnaya are double agents."

"Calculating."

As Alopex worked, a new avatar appeared at her side, a giant brown tarantula, watching her with several eyes. He spoke to Alopex in a recognizable voice. It was Alföðr.

"Alopex cancel calculations, delete record of last query, code by identity."

"Registered and deleted," said the fox.

"Clever, Violet. That's how I got it. I set Aloe to alert me if anyone asked the same question. You see, if we have a double agent, we don't want Alopex to alert them that we know, do we?"

"Got it, sorry."

"Don't apologize for brilliance, even if it only takes you halfway. For now we must answer to our dreaded elders, you to yours and I to mine. Head to C team's office with your team."

He blinked out of the room before she could ask whom he would report to. She awoke, and then headed through the crowd outside the gym. Veikko was regaling the multitude with an explanation of how he had downed two of the panzercopters with only his Tikari, which nodded assent on his shoulder. Vibs was standing with Mishka, who appeared to be asking her for the real story. They both saw Violet and excused themselves from the crowd to join her.

"Where were you?" asked Vibeke.

"I met with Alf." She left out the rest.

Veikko asked, "What did he say?"

"Report to C team's office."

"Right," responded Vibs, looking around. "Where's Varg?"

Varg was visible with the nurse in med bay, probably thanking her for the exam and offering to repay her in kind.

"You want to get him?" asked Violet.

"No," said Vibeke and Veikko together. They linked to him to report to C team. The message went into a storage file in the back of his mind, and the three went without him.

C TEAM'S office felt like a room in Achnacarry. Their uniforms were all green, the walls were all covered in maps, and the four Cs stood as formally as regiment officers. Claire, Cato, and Cassandra all stood behind Churro, who had been called the coldest, most bitter man in Tijuana before he arrived, and the coldest, most bitter man in Valhalla after.

"Where is Varg?" he asked.

"Med bay," said Vibeke.

"We can wait," said Cato in his Australian accent, clearly annoyed.

"It will be a while," said Veikko. "He's got some major swelling going on."

"We'll see him later," said Claire. "Let's get on with it."

Churro stepped aside and let his team go to work. They each took one of the three. Cassandra spoke to Veikko, Claire to Vibeke. Violet allowed Cato to link in to her head to see her memories. He would interrupt her thoughts when her memory grew blurry or he found something unusual. He always spoke as if he blamed her for the faults in memory.

"What is this? Why did you run behind the lathe when the rest ran to the right?"

"It was a mistake," Violet admitted.

"Yes, it was a mistake. Why did you make it, mate?"

"I don't know. It was a mistake."

"Right. And this?"

He pushed her memory further and watched her stab the intruder.

"I stabbed him."

"Right. Why didn't you send your Tik for him?"

"I was nervous. Dmitri told me not to."

"Well, you didn't follow Dmitri past the lathe. Why listen to him, then?"

"Because I fucked up. I know I fucked up, I told you I fucked up. It was a total disaster from beginning to end. I didn't know what was going on. It was the craziest fucking hell I ever saw. Okay?"

"Yeah, mate? That *you* ever saw. I've been to Tunisia. You know what's there? The Unspeakable Darkness, mate. Claire and I saw the UD gang slaughter half our pals from Abu Simbel. You know what the gang looks like, the UD? They're monsters, beasts like demons, all painted black and sewn together by the skin. They roll at you like spheres of limbs, like a shoggoth, they are. Horrible. And we watched them kill forty men. Forty men like that, no mercy. None at all."

"Fine." Violet tried to sound submissive. "You win."

"Not a contest, mate." He shook his head slowly.

It went on, with Cato's smug comments on her memories, on her mistakes, rubbing salt into every wound. Oddly, the experience made her feel better about what had happened. The more he tried to break her down, the more she realized she didn't deserve it. When her indignation topped out and she was ready to challenge him to a field fight in the gym, Cassandra and Claire called them back to reality. Vibeke was clearly more rattled than Violet had been, but Claire appeared to be most forgiving and understanding. Veikko had stayed stoic, giving Cassandra every detail with utter detachment. To Violet's surprise, Cato spoke as if she had made him proud.

"Violet did a damn good job, stayed alive, took out a couple nasties. A good girl."

"Agreed, the three—four of you," said Claire.

Churro nodded. "Well, that told us just about nothing."

"I told you it wouldn't," said Cassandra.

"Thank you, V team." Churro stood and addressed them with enough formality to suggest that the meeting was over. Violet was surprised when he asked, "Now, do you have any questions?"

"Yes," said Vibeke. "Have D and E learned anything?"

"Nothing. The fleeing troops were far gone when they arrived, and the remains have yielded nothing. The equipment was so modified we can't trace its sale, and the bodies were all rigged with decay accelerators. They were dust before we could take genetic readings or anything else of use. S team is hunting, M team is scouring the air for any path, but all we know is that they headed southwest with the generator. We don't know how far, though. Basically, we know nothing."

"And Udachnaya?"

"Not a total loss, but a great loss. We don't know what will be done with it yet."

Violet was more concerned with local events. "Alf said he had to meet his superiors. Who did he mean?"

The Cs looked to one another. They gained the expressions of parents readying their children for vaccinations. Cassandra spoke with cold composure.

"*Svartedauden*—the black death. The Geki."

"Not just for Alf, I'm afraid," taunted Cato. "You'll head to Alf's library. He should be done by now. They'll be waiting for you."

Veikko said, "Geki? We're going to meet them?"

"Yes," said Cassandra. "It will be worse than Udachnaya."

Somehow Violet didn't believe that prediction. Claire spoke up. "Don't worry about it. They have no reason to harm you, and the feeling you'll get is just a side effect of being in the room with them. Just answer honestly, and it will be over soon enough."

"All set, then, on your way," added Cato. "And nuke Tunisia."

Violet hadn't been at all worried until Claire gave her reassurance. The three Vs headed to the library. They said nothing on the way. When they arrived, Veikko, walking first, paused at the door. Rather than knocking, he froze in place and looked back at Vibs and Violet. His face was pale. When they took a few more steps, they knew why. It was not like any sensation of cold or tense air, but something attacking the highest levels of their consciousness. They were all terrified, suddenly and for no reason they could describe. They all knew rumors of the Geki but could not account for the sudden bludgeoning from an emotion all three had long since mastered.

Violet had never been so afraid before. She didn't know that fear could strike like an animal, claws pushing between her ribs. Her heart was beating fast, too fast; her breathing sped up too. The fear she knew from childhood, from death training, from Udachnaya, was all stunted by comparison, like some sort of dwarf version of what she was experiencing at the library door. She felt shame at the feeling and terrible discomfort. She wanted to run, to get away from the door, but she couldn't even move. Paralyzed, they never managed to knock. Alf opened the door. He looked solemn. He hid it well, but they could tell he shared their apprehension. It was true; even he was afraid of them.

He quickly whispered why. "We think it's some sort of link trick. They broadcast fear everywhere they go. It will pass when they leave," he said and waved them in.

In the center of the room stood two tall black cloaks. The cloaks had no open faces, and whatever was under them didn't move. Violet made her way to the library's sofa, a soft comfortable seat that felt like stone to her that day. She tried to think analytically—who would want to cripple people with fear like this? What could the Geki want? She tried to think of anything to distract from the fear, but she couldn't do it. Her mind was powerless.

The three sat together, and Alföðr stood behind them. Then the Geki spoke. They spoke not only in deep, loud voices but in link transmission as well. Both the cloaked things spoke at once, and it registered in every corner of Violet's mind, as if she were not only hearing it from a speaker at each ear but remembering it, even speaking it silently to herself.

"Where is the fourth?"

The question struck Violet as if it were the most important question she had ever been asked. She had to answer it. She had to tell them honestly, immediately or something terrible would happen. But she couldn't. She knew she couldn't because he wasn't asking her. The question was directed to Alf. She had only caught the edge of the wave.

"He is still in the medical bay," said Alf, speaking as if admitting to a crime at the end of days of torture. Then Alf surprised her. He didn't just answer; he went on. He asked, "Is there reason to believe he can tell you what these three cannot?"

There was silence. Absolute dead silence, not even the high-pitched note of blood in her eardrums. The Geki didn't move. They didn't seem to discuss it. Then they spoke again, and this time the question was to Violet, directly and inescapable.

"Did you recognize any of your attackers?"

"No," Violet stated as clearly as she could. She had to say it clearly. Once she said it, the pressure of the question faded. It was like a bone getting set in injury training. Amid the pain was a sublime pleasure of relief, as if the answer had repaired something deep within her.

"No," Vibs shouted beside her. Veikko said nothing. He was frozen in place. Violet could feel the pressure growing on him. Why didn't he speak? She knew how it felt to answer quickly; how could he wait? She could sense it growing, getting worse. The blood left Veikko's face, turning him white, almost blue. The fear was still on Violet like a vise grip. And the Geki were moving. They weren't walking, just moving. They got closer to Veikko. The sight was vile, like watching a man slowly torn to shreds, worse because she knew it was his mind getting ripped open. Violet wanted to close her eyes, but she couldn't.

"Did you recognize any of your attackers?" The voice was now booming. Though not louder in decibels, it was like getting stabbed in the ears. The voice hit with bruising force and kept pushing its way inside their chests, as if not answering would make the blade real and kill them. Veikko broke into a cold sweat. He looked like he was going to pass out. He shouted "No!" at the top of his lungs, like an apology, like he was begging. Alföðr stepped forward.

"Not so deep, Geki!"

They moved back. They didn't walk, but they didn't float. Their motion was so subtle Violet began to doubt they were even really there. She wondered if they would still be there if she turned off her link. Then she knew immediately that she could not turn it off. They had forced her mind open and would not allow her to close it. The very thought of trying to turn off the link hurt.

"Do you know who they were?"

"No."

"No."

"No," she shouted. They had all answered; it would be okay.

"Guess."

The word was horror incarnate. It was far worse than anything at Udachnaya. It was all the things she had never felt afraid of there, now hitting her in full like paying a terrible debt. She didn't think she could guess. She couldn't think at all. She didn't even know what it meant, but she said, "It was one of us!" She didn't hear what Veikko or Vibeke said. Her vision was blurred, dark, her skin was freezing as the Geki spoke again.

"Thank you for your cooperation. We are watching you."

Then the cloaks were pulled away like a magician's handkerchief to reveal nothing below, shooting upward and disappearing. And it was over.

THEY WERE shaking, but the pressure was gone. The fear was a memory that faded mercifully fast. Alföör sat beside them and exhaled. It was another sickening feeling to see him at that moment was disturbing—he looked weak, tired. It lasted only an instant before he was back to himself, a powerful figure in control.

"It is most regrettable that you had to meet them. Most regrettable. Not only because they are terrible to behold, but because if they are here, bad things are afoot. Worse than the events of Udachnaya alone. The Geki do not care to involve themselves with the petty squabbles and stealings of underground clans. Veikko, tell me, did you try to resist them?"

"No, no, I couldn't. I didn't want to. I just... froze...."

"I did the same when I first met them," he reassured them. "I couldn't speak though every fiber of me wanted, needed to. Horrible."

Veikko transmuted his agony into anger. "So that's what enforces the treaty? Who the hell are they? What are they?"

"Rumors abound," said Alf. "They are Geki. All else is speculation. Take time off, relax. You'll find the gym back to its usual state of good-humored bedlam. The cafeteria should have Jumja sticks tonight. Take all the time you need, enjoy yourself. Tell Varg how lucky he is to have missed it."

"And Udachnaya?" Vibs asked. "What about the attack? What do we do?"

Alf seemed amused. "We consider what we do. Any ideas?"

"No, I just—"

"Me neither. So you think, I think, and we wait. Don't assume there is always something to be done immediately. That urge for activity is a remnant of panic, nothing more."

Little else of use was to be said. They didn't feel like playing gym games or even eating. They headed for the barracks and lay in their beds. Violet fell asleep instantly. They called up Alopex and asked her to get Varg. He logged in from sleep somewhere in the medical barracks. Their post-Geki demeanors oozed out from their avatars, and Varg quickly lost his postcoital grin. They explained.

He responded, "Sounds horrible. Even Alf got it?"

"Yeah."

"Fucking brutal," Varg said, unable to give a better consolation. Another avatar knocked at the room list. Balder. He was online in Siberia, having just then fully restored Prokofiev and set up new defenses. They invited him into the dreamscape, where he was happy to see them alive.

"Once I heard you were under attack, I drew up a real impressive, deep speech for any of you that survived—how it wasn't what you wanted to hear in dark times, but you weren't meant to be heroes yet, how you survived and that was more than any of us could have hoped. But I don't have a damn thing for you since you joined the battle and took out two panzercopters. At least, that's what Dmitri tells me. Ah, and Varg's throw! You really just stood up and threw shells at its rotor, Varg?"

"Yes, I'm fucking awesome." Varg nodded.

"And damn lucky, Varg, if you missed the debriefing." He turned to the others. "I heard you met with Geki? You all okay?"

"Yes, unpleasant fellows," said Vibeke.

"What did they ask?"

"If we recognized them. That's all they cared about, and if we knew who they were."

"And they made us guess," interjected Violet. That was the worst of it, when they'd forced speculation out of them like squeezing the last drop from a crushed fruit. "I told them—Is the Siberian link secure?"

"Mine is," said Balder.

"I said I thought it was one of us. I'm not even sure I knew what I was saying. Alf suspects someone on our end, but—"

"No, I told them the same thing," said Veikko.

"Same here," agreed Vibs. "It's like they sucked it from the back of my mind. I don't even know if it's accurate. They didn't ask what I meant, if I was sure. They just took what they could and left."

"That sounds right," said Balder solemnly. "They're quite unconcerned with our methods. They have their own way about it all. They may not even care who it was. They may only want to know if you knew. I couldn't venture to say."

"Have you run into them before?" Varg asked.

"Mercifully, not often. Though I've seen them in action, ages ago when I failed a mission and they took over. I guess they thought it was important. I saw them annihilate three buildings with fire. They controlled fire like we control Tikari. And the fear…. Enough about the black plague. Try to forget them and be proud of yourselves! With your experience, we wouldn't have put you against a kid with a slingshot. This was an unwinnable battle for Udachnaya, a near full alert for everyone else. As of yesterday you were a junior novice team recommended only for light peacetime work."

"And now?" Varg asked hopefully.

"Now, you're a junior novice team with heavy combat experience, which is uncommon, to say the least. The last time we listed a team that way was posthumously, for Ingwaz team, a rune we retired so as not to think about the poor bastards. Never even found their faces."

"So now we go back to engineering jobs and training?"

"You do. I trust you won't mind? Have you had enough battle for the time being?"

"Definitely."

"Absolutely."

"Yes."

Varg shrugged. "I'm up for another one."

THE NEXT day their only duty was a single walrus removal. Since Varg had joined them, the walrus detail had rotated through the runes, finally coming back to V team to reunite them with Umberto. They found him in one of the cafeteria storage bays, where he had wandered into the compartment of purple patties and eaten so many he couldn't get back out. While Violet and Veikko broke part of the wall to move him, Varg managed to divert the beast's attention by rubbing his whiskery cheeks, provoking a deep sort of belly laugh that scared the heck out of passersby.

After that they began the light risk-free work they were supposed to have done as a junior novice team. To the delight of all four, the first involved explosives. An old battleship hull had floated too near to Kvitøya for comfort. After T team had confirmed that it was not housing five panzercopters, V took over and flew in with two thermobaric bombs. Vibs and Violet set them, Veikko flew the pogo to a safe distance, and Varg detonated them. Once they had finished, they felt almost disappointed that nothing had gone wrong with the mission.

Things had returned to normal in the North. V team learned new tricks, some of which they recognized: Varg from old movies, Vibs from old books, Violet from old games, and Veikko from missions he'd observed before the rest of his team had arrived. Violet doubled her efforts to control her Tikari in complex operations. Kabar told her again and again that she was trying too hard. He said it was all about trust, but she trusted the thing. She just couldn't get it to extend its handle flaps to change direction.

"Don't try to extend the flaps. Just try to fly to the left."

She sent the Tikari flying. She wanted to fly left, so she extended a flap—and the Tikari fell from the air.

"You're trying to walk by programming your feet again. Don't program, just do.

She threw again, and again, but the poor thing fell every time. It was starting to get annoyed with her. She wondered if Tikari ever rebelled against their humans. She asked Kabar.

"They're three-rule safe for their owners, not for anyone else. It will never hurt or disobey you, but you can have troubles. R team did once, Ruger, I think. George wouldn't—"

"Who's George?"

"They named their beetles John, Paul, George… and…. I forget."

"Ringo?"

"Ah, they told you?"

"No, but I get the idea. What happened?"

"George, like Ruger, developed a real lazy streak. Dr. Niide reprogrammed the Tikari to be more proactive, but they couldn't reprogram Ruger. Little bug kept poking him in the lung when he lagged behind. But you don't need to worry. You need to practice. Throw and think left."

She threw then thought left, and the Tikari went perfectly straight.

A week later she had made little progress. As they flew a pogo south to excavate a tunnel for H team, Violet tried to steer the conversation toward her troubles.

"Did you know that R team named all their Tikari?" she asked.

"Yes, after saints, I think," said Vibeke. "Mine's named Bob."

"Sal," said Veikko.

"Pokey," added Varg. Pokey lifted his mechanical head at the mention of his name. Varg turned to Violet. "What's yours?"

"It doesn't have one. You never mentioned yours did, any of you."

"We didn't?"

"Yours doesn't?"

"Who hasn't?"

"I haven't," Violet admitted.

"Well, what do you call it?"

"Nothing," she said. "It's like a body part. We don't name our parts."

"Actually...." began Varg.

"Don't," warned Vibeke. "So come up with a name, Vi."

Veikko agreed. "I suggest Schmelgert Helgerzholm."

Though the shape reminded her of Sergeant Cameron, and R team's logic suggested "David," her Tikari was soon named "Nelson." Not long after, Nelson was capable of turning left on command.

As Violet progressed again with Kabar's training, V team completed task after task, mission after mission. Varg got to use explosives again when they adeptly blew up a bridge to help M team catch an assassin. They flew cargo pogos for L team's theft of weapons from a company who was best not allowed to have them. Under Alf's direction they completed a dozen odd jobs and once, for H team, they got to test a new apparatus that made land skiffs capable of flying upside down. After proving the devices' functionality, they spent the better part of the day skiff racing. Violet tied with Varg but came in second due to an overly complex tie-breaking procedure.

As they completed missions, analysis was coming in about their possible specialties and suggested duties. The team as a whole showed particular skills in rapid analytic response, physical abilities, and due to one mission that skewed the averages, wartime armed assault, defense, and battle tactics. Everyone knew where the skew came from, but nobody denied its accuracy. As soon as Balder returned from Udachnaya, he took over the majority of their training and supervision. K team continued to teach them more and more advanced weapons, and they continued training in infiltration and general espionage, but V team was heading for a life in offensive operations.

One day V team found they were no longer the most junior team. W started up when a sixteen-year-old named Ibrahim had the worst coming-of-age party ever. G team, who had only begun to monitor him as a possible recruit, saw him sold by his parents to a Somali labor company, where within hours he was beaten within an inch of his life just for having a small fungal growth on the bottom of his foot.

Ibrahim's first bit of job training was how to operate a heavy forklift, and nobody on G team was surprised when all his attackers were found impaled on that very machine. R team got him the hell out of there fast. He came in wounded and frightened. They had no chance for the proper explanations and offers and doubted he would adapt at all to being the first member of the newest team.

He likely would have become a rescued, relocated, and forgotten resident of Kvitøya had Veikko not barged in. Having been a first himself, he knew some of what the kid was going through. Raised in a family of sea lovers and thrown out in an emotional gorefest, Veikko also knew something about what Ibrahim had already gone through. He didn't know the rest but he went out on a limb, and they became close friends. Veikko in the coming days would practically raise the kid, and that made Uncle Varg and Aunts Vibeke and Violet close to him as well.

Before he had been there a week, Ibrahim resolved to join the Valkyries. As the first W, and unaware of his aunt's history, he picked the toughest W name he could think of: Wulfgar. After Violet coughed green pudding across the table, he asked if there was a problem with the name.

"No, just haven't heard it in a while," she said quickly. "Bad memories."

"I can pick something else," he said.

"No, no, it's fine," she said, trying to clean the green pudding off of the table, chairs, and Vibs.

"Not Wulfgar. It was a bad omen," he said.

"Agreed," said Vibs.

"Wart," suggested Veikko, after the foot problem that had gotten him into their company. Violet thought to say the term was a bit dubious, but Skadi and Snot were at the table, and Snot thought it was a great name. So Wart he was, and W team began to train. Veikko stood by him in death and injury training and took to calling the boy "Grasshopper." Nobody was sure if the name came from or inspired Wart's grasshopper Tikari. Nobody questioned where he got the idea for a fire-yellow suit like Veikko's or what gave birth to his growing sense of humor.

Violet also took something from that dinner conversation: The name Wulfgar had affected her far more than she wanted to admit, and she was quite relieved he didn't keep it. She hated herself for reacting the way she did, for caring about it at all. She didn't want a name to surprise her, to feel like a pin stuck into her side. She had been in Valhalla almost six months. Her team agreed—it was time to call in a promise from when she'd joined.

"I want to go after the Orange Gang," she told Alföðr. "We're not the junior team. We have battle experience and offensive ops training. We can take the whole gang down."

"Ambitious after your first taste of blood, aren't you? Have you discussed this with your team?"

"They're itching for it."

"And how itchy are you?"

"You know why I want to. I can do it dispassionately, without acting from hate. We can plan it out, make certain it doesn't break the planet. We know how to do this. We're ready."

"I will not insult you by saying you are not. And I think observation of the OG might be in order, indeed by your team. I'll discuss it with Balder. In the meantime I think you can begin to prove your abilities on some similar but less ambitious marks. There is certainly no shortage of them."

Balder agreed it was a waste to use V on minor demolitions—although Varg would sorely miss it—and routine activities. He began to note low-level gangs and criminal organizations they could practice on. He didn't look for safe projects. He looked for gangs that had to be taken out. He looked for challenges and lined up some serious work for V team to do. He noticed that almost every team logged in to look over his notes. All Valhalla was eager to see the survivors of Siberia show off their talents.

Chapter IX: Jylland

AS V team slept, Balder joined their dream to give them the options he had found for their first mission. "First, we have a breakout of mental patients in Montevideo. The local police have rounded up all but four of them, who have begun sending threats to Uruguayan citizens. Most of the threats are nonsensical and involve plans to kidnap the elderly and ransom them for cat and dog pelts. A straightforward search and capture."

"Where's Uruguay again?" asked Varg.

"South America. It's just outside the hot zone," said Vibs.

"How far outside the hot zone?" asked Veikko. "I'm not in the mood for equatorial air."

"It's past the really bad stuff, maybe three hundred and twenty-five kelvins this time of year."

"No, thanks. What else? Something cooler."

Balder called up his notes. "How about Sverige? A band of body modification surgeons went rogue and started breaking into people's homes, giving them beautification treatments while they sleep. We think they're still working professionally, forming a sort of secret society. A confide-and-go-seek job."

"I refuse on principle." Varg laughed.

"I thought you might." Balder flipped through some icons in his notes. "There's a serial killer in Cologne—"

"Is that really what Valhalla deals with? Murderers and psycho surgeons?"

"That's really what junior teams deal with, Veikko," Balder explained. "You don't get to save the world in your first year. That's in your third year. In your first year, you get to deal with serial killers in Cologne." He checked over his notes. "And that one just got caught. See what happens when you argue? Okay, what else.... Here's one from your home company, Violet. G team is watching another Scot, possibly for W team, and they found some Americans openly recruiting mercenaries. They're not totally inept, so they've avoided police recognition. We don't know what they intend to do, but their chatter says it'll be illegal and medium scale. Research and reaction gig."

"I'm all for it," volunteered Violet.

"Same," said Varg. "Where in Scotland?"

"Inverness Industrial Zone."

"I'm game."

"Agreed. Let's check it out," said Veikko. "And Americans too! I've always wanted to meet real cowboys."

V team took a pogo southeast toward Inverness. Varg and Veikko discussed cowboy movies in the hopes they would offer insight into the American mind. Vibeke gained a better idea of what to expect by looking over the short dossier Balder loaded into their heads. Violet piloted. She was born in Inverness, where her parents had lived for about a year before they headed for the arcology in Kyle. Violet had visited the city with her dad to see the old castles and the stuffed remains of Nessie but remembered little of either. Now she was headed for the industrial zone, the largest expanse of factories and refineries in the highlands. She set the pogo down atop a chemical factory with a broken link label. It manufactured either exfoliants or defoliants. It didn't matter which. She chose it for the flat roof with no detector cameras.

In the alley below, link icons visible only to Valhalla links labeled the targets. The icons from G team pointed to three men walking together. The first task was to find out exactly what they intended to do. As they were recruiting openly, V team elected to approach them and offer their services. Violet, Varg, and Veikko slid down a light pole alongside the factory, out of sight of the targets. Vibeke stayed in the pogo and sent her Tikari along to watch. She would provide intel from the nets and keep a bug's-eye view of the situation. Varg would keep watch from a street perspective and stay ready to move in closer for rescue or a fight. Violet and Veikko followed the men to a factoryside bar. They walked in as Varg stood outside the door. He linked in to Violet's brain and watched from her eyes. Veikko linked back to Vibeke, "One tall male with hat, one short male without hat, one bald male to his left. Anyone outside?"

Vibs gave the area a quick search for any other G-team-labeled people.

"None," she said. "Go for approach."

Veikko and Violet walked casually to the marks and Violet, having the only local accent, spoke first.

"Hear you're hiring."

"Sound waves are slow," said the bald American. "We have all the mercs we need."

Violet didn't miss a beat. "There must be something you still need, or you wouldn't be out here."

The bald man linked to his friends. His link was encrypted, not as thickly as their own but enough to hide his words from Veikko's subtle attempts to listen in. The man turned back to them.

"You got any problem with bending laws?" he asked.

"We don't mind bending, twisting, or snapping them in half."

"You know the territory around here?"

"I'm a native. What do you need?"

"A place to land a couple subs and someone to bring their cargo in under the radar."

"That we've got."

"How much?"

"We get 5 percent of the value of your cargo."

The man grew suspicious and linked to his pals again. The short man said, "You must really need our business. Why so eager?"

Violet's lack of knowledge of standard criminal rates had alerted them. She couldn't think of what to say. Veikko's link protruded into her mind, just as encrypted as their opponent's. "Ideology," he suggested.

Violet spoke quickly. "Well, we hear you share our sympathies."

Thc tall man looked irate. "What do you care? How many Scots lost any cash last week?"

Vibs immediately began searches for major financial shifts in the last week. The Irish-American Coast Consortium had just lost all its submarine shipping rights to Cetacean shippers. She linked Veikko her results so fast there was no break in the conversation's cadence when he spoke up in an Irish accent. Veikko's accent was so spot-on Violet had to conceal her surprise. Not only did he sound Irish, but he acted it, as if every year of his life had been spent soaking in the subtleties of culture and phrase. Even his facial expression was different, as though every muscle had reset itself into a County Cork countenance.

"I'm not Scottish," he shouted. "I'm Irish, and it was my family, if you have to ask. My family had everything invested in the Coast Consort, not to mention four years of our lives and a lot of hopes pinned on that feckin' thing. So when some damn Scot—no offense, dearie—steals our lanes to sell them to the clatty fish, I'll have a damn thing to say about it."

The growing suspicion in the Americans disappeared. Violet let Veikko do the talking and watched as he exploited every hint they gave. Like a master negotiator, he knew just what to say to make them comfortable, to feel safe. He did it so subtly Violet couldn't follow it all. She could only marvel at the ease with which he took them in. In only four minutes the Americans took Violet and Veikko into the alley and spilled the entirety of their plans.

Veikko even managed to get the bald man to give up the carrier signal of the coming subs that were to unload derezzers bound for the offices of their enemies. Vibeke loaded it into the pogo's computer. When Veikko asked if they intended to disrupt their enemy's hard drives, the bald man volunteered that they wanted to disrupt their brains as well.

"All too easy," Varg linked from around the block. Now it was time to sneak in, identify the heads of the plot to learn how deep it went, and seek out the hidden members. Violet began to think of the days to come, genuine spy work, but it would be tedious. Veikko thought the same and didn't intend to wait so long.

"I want to know just who I'm dealing with. When do I get to meet the rest of ya?"

"On arrival," said the bald man. "Jason is on one of our subs. You'll see him on landing."

"Ya got everyone on those subs?"

"Everyone but Kevin in Dublin."

"Everyone, ya say?" Veikko smiled. The American nodded. It was crude, sloppy, and simple, but Veikko had just done all the research they would need to make the enemy operation unfeasible. The police could handle the rest, the grunt work of arrests and investigation. Many a mission V team had observed in training had ended as such. It was the style of most Valkyrie teams to end the threat and leave cleanup to the local authorities. V team would be no exception. They didn't bother to shift the conversation gently or gradually move the men into traps. Varg simply came forward, pulled out his microwave, and stunned all three Americans, then cursed that he'd forgotten to say "Draw."

The team hauled them into the back of the pogo. With the American recruiters in the cargo hold, they sped out to sea. Having the carrier signature, they found the incoming subs with ease. Violet was about to start discussing what to do about the subs when Varg seized the weaponry controls and started shooting. Neither Veikko nor Vibeke said anything against it, so Violet assumed he knew what he was doing.

He did. A short blast from the pogo microwave cannon disabled the subs; another couple welded their hatches and cargo bays shut. Both subs surfaced immediately, and Varg shoved the sleeping Americans ungently onto their decks. Vibeke sent an anonymous link to the UKI coast guard with all the information they would need to capture and detain the belligerents. The mission was over. It was brief, fast, and to Violet's mind, dull as doilies.

When they came back to Valhalla, they headed straight for Balder's office. He and Alf were waiting for them. Violet tried to think of a polite way to ask for a harder assignment, something that might fast-track them to the Orange Gang job. Balder spoke before she could. "I suppose we don't have to tell you analysis gave you a 100 percent on that one."

"We could have done it in our sleep," said Veikko. "I thought you wanted to challenge us?"

Violet couldn't have put it better. It had all gone so well that she felt almost left out. It was as if the Americans had wanted to get caught. She wondered briefly if that might have been their covert intent but admitted there was little chance of it. Sometimes sloppy, simple enemies meant no more than sloppy, simple work. She hadn't even gotten a chance to do much of anything. She'd just watched her team function like clockwork around her. Had she been slow? Could she have done more? In the short time before Alf spoke, Violet pushed such negative possibilities aside in favor of recognizing a job well done. She would do more when she had more to do.

"A challenge?" Alf smiled. He whistled for Alopex, who darted into the room and opened up a video graphic for all to see. It was a news log. The news program said, "—Local police forces are at a loss. There are at least twenty rebels armed with microwave rifles. We have confirmed that they have a low-yield wave bomb. We don't know where they got it, but the omega wave signature has been confirmed by satellite. They have just given us their demands. They say if IBC prisoners are not released immediately, they will detonate the charge. They've already killed—"

Alf broke the transmission off. "IBC was a bit of a joke until today. A rogue company arrested en masse for beryllium theft, illegal mining, trespassing, and the like. It seems the few that weren't caught have turned terrorist after their fall, the last pathetic grasp of petty thieves made complicated by their possession of a wave bomb. Our own intel suggests they bought it on the Nikkei underground. E team is looking into that side of it. Anyhow, you said you wanted a challenge?"

"Maybe not that big," began Veikko. "We just finished the last one. We haven't had time to—"

"Rest?" Balder laughed. "Silly boy, you asked for a challenge. If the PRA rose from the ashes and blew up Mars, you'd have the job! Get off your ass and save Canada! I'll load the background into your heads before you get there."

A wave bomb! Violet was surprised that they were about to get a real assignment, an important, dangerous one. And right after their first joke of a job. It was what she wanted. Even Veikko, behind his complaints, wanted it. They would head out at once, right after Violet made sure of one thing: "If we succeed on this," she said to the elders, "we get the OG next."

She meant it to be a question, but it wasn't a question that left her mouth. It was a deal. She had just spoken as if she were their equal, and the military chunk of her mind told her she was about to do ten thousand push-ups for it. The splinter of pride that had wedged its way in after the success of the last assignment had just expanded beyond its welcome. Balder and Alf looked at one another.

"If you succeed, you get the OG next," said Alf. Violet's deal was legitimate and accepted. The splinter of pride was now infected and swelling rapidly. The team headed for the pogo pad.

"If you fail, they set off a wave bomb," Balder shouted after them, "and you get sold to a sideshow!"

Violet was reasonably sure that if they failed, Dr. Niide would spend the time to make them humanoid again. Still, she was sobered by the idea. They were going up against something major. As they flew over the North Pole, Balder's transmission dumped news logs, company history, criminal profiles, and tactical building maps into their heads. He also gave them solid analysis of the situation and his recommendations on strategy. At the same time, they felt something else linking in to their heads. There were dozens of new visual requests flooding in. Half the people in Valhalla were going to be watching from V team's own eyes.

The team linked to one another on high local crypto so as not to be overheard by their observers. They agreed to follow Balder's plans to the letter if they could. They didn't want to show off. They didn't want to take risks. They wanted to do as they were told and survive. The risk this time wasn't a sub's journey away. It was an immediate and truly deplorable threat waiting to turn a neighborhood in British Colombia into the unthinkable. On reviewing the information, Violet had no doubt they could succeed. It was, in theory, not too difficult given their exceptional training. But they had to get it right. They would get it right. When the gravity of the situation seeped into her mind, Violet smiled. This was exactly what she'd always hoped for. She looked over Balder's intel with the utmost focus.

They arrived to see a solid perimeter. The cops had done their job and evacuated as many as they could and then made sure that nobody was getting in or out. That included V team. Police across the globe knew as little about Valhalla as Violet's father had. If they were recognized as the Hall of the Slain, they would be considered a greater threat than the terrorists with the wave bomb. V team had to do its job despite the cops, not with them. And as Alf had warned her, "We never harm the police. Not unless it's a crooked cop, or a matter of survival, or we feel like it."

They landed on a skyscraper just outside the police line. They were unseen. All eyes were on the thirty-sixth floor of the IBC headquarters. The roof of their landing skyscraper was about even with the roof of the IBC building, high above the streets but beneath the midcity walkways and decks. V team left the pogo and looked in on the enemy. They saw twenty men in strategically poor positions around that single floor of the building. Windows were intact and made of beamproof glass. It wasn't Tikari-proof, but if the terrorists saw knife bugs killing their men, they'd likely set off the bomb. V team would need to disable all the men simultaneously. They had to go in.

Balder's analysis showed a reasonably safe route in that the enemies shouldn't be able to see, roof to roof. They wasted no more time on observation. Varg went first. Using part of an overhead pedestrian overpass as a grappling target, he used his microwave as a tractor and pulled himself up over the IBC building, swung to its roof, and dropped down. The police would definitely see him, but that was no concern. They wouldn't want someone going in, but they sure as hell wouldn't do anything to make the terrorists aware of them, including fire on V team. Violet and the others swung over and landed alongside Varg. As she landed, Violet ventured a subtle hack into the police links. They were frantically trying to figure out which police agency was making a move. Given their bureaucracy, it would be thirty minutes before they figured out it wasn't authorized, let alone not one of their own.

Vibeke sent her Tikari over the side of the roof to watch the enemies from outside. All twenty were still in place, and nobody was acting as if to suggest they had been seen. Veikko began to cut through the roof with his microwave. He made a sizable hole, and Violet tractored the loose chunk of roof to set it down quietly inside the building. They used it like a step to get down. Violet and Veikko headed for the nearby stairwell. Varg and Vibs took the elevator shaft. For the first time since heading to Udachnaya, Violet felt that uneasy anticipation. This time there would be violence. There was no question about it. They weren't heading to blindside submarines or knock out idiot cowboys. They would have to disable twenty men together or get wave bombed. The fear of mutagenic omega waves was half that of returning home (hauled by an elder team, inside out) to the disappointment of the ravine. Horrific spontaneous mutation was bad enough; failure was far, far scarier.

They all took positions behind the doors into the thirty-sixth floor. Vibeke linked the team in to her Tikari's eyes. The layout of the floor was as Balder's plans showed—no walls, just a honeycomb of cubicles with short dividers. Vibs sent the Tikari around the windowed exterior. Aside from the spinal columns of the building that housed the stairs and elevator shaft, there were no barriers. When they came in, no enemy would miss the sight of them and no enemy would be hidden from their microwaves. Whatever happened, it would happen fast. Violet knew that was in their favor.

From the Tikari's eyes, they could see where the men were positioned. A few stood by the bomb; most stood near the windows. The elevator and stairs were at the northwest and northeast corners. There would be little risk of crossfire. As per Balder's suggestion, wide stunning beams should knock out the lot of them. Violet and Varg would fire the opening shots, then Veikko and Vibs would be ready for anyone who stayed awake. Violet and Veikko were closest to the bomb, so she would focus on the men most ready to activate it. Veikko would disarm it. The Tikari showed every man standing and in safe stunning range. Every domino was lined up perfectly to fall. It was all going as easily as Inverness.

Vibeke gave the signal. She and Veikko zapped the doors off their respective positions, and Violet and Varg hit the terrorists with the widest stunning beams they could. They knocked out sixteen men, including all those near the wave bomb. Veikko ran for the bomb to secure it. Violet confined her beam and shot at one of the remaining four men. Varg used his Tikari as a sword to disable two men with ready microwave rifles. Vibeke sautéed the last belligerent's heart in his chest, and the room was silent. Veikko pulled the guts out of the wave bomb and used his microwave to boil and render harmless the omega-active fluids. Violet and Varg checked every part of the floor for more men, confirming they had stunned or killed them all. Vibs recalled her Tikari.

The incursion had gone flawlessly—so flawlessly that Violet felt like something had gone wrong. This was supposed to be the tough mission. It wasn't. Their decision to go by the book had just led to another perfect, uninteresting nothing of a mission. If everything they did was to be so simple, Violet wondered if she would continue to enjoy her new life after all. She pushed the thoughts from her mind and got back to cleanup. Cleanup—she felt like a damn janitor. They pulled steel ribbon from the dispensers built into their Thaco armor and tied up the disarmed enemies. Police links were trying to make out what had happened inside.

The cops could scan that the omega bomb was neutralized, so they would be coming in quickly. Time for V team to leave. They tractored their way up the elevator shaft and emerged onto the roof. Two police teams were coming up the walls, but too slowly to catch V team. They swung back to their pogo and took off before a police vehicle could make the air. It was over, no mistakes, no undue risks, clean, simple, and successful. So why was Violet so unfulfilled? She wondered if she was so cruel, as those childhood tests had said, that she had to see (more) blood to feel content. She felt something was terribly wrong with how morose she was, more so with the three happy faces around her.

As they passed the North Pole, Balder linked to them, "News reports the police have taken over, four terrorists escaped. Twenty in custody, omega safe. Well done, V!"

"Well done?" Veikko bragged. "We said challenge, damn it! Never been so bored in my life!"

Vibeke chimed in, "What, what? I just woke up. Did we do something?"

Even Violet wasn't above pride in another job well done, but she couldn't think of anything clever to say. She didn't feel like saying it if she did. She let Varg indulge his immodest streak in her place. "Now what was that you said, Balder? About selling us to the circus sideshow? Was that so we could show off our freakish giant balls? Our mighty and pendulous, gargantuan…." He continued at length.

Violet ignored him. She had other things on her mind. She wondered why the police couldn't have done what they just had. Surely they had their own specialty teams, their own methods of disarming something so dangerous as a wave bomb. She knew as she thought about it that the mild curiosity was a sort of intellectual modesty. She couldn't let herself indulge so hedonistically in another line of thought: the one she wanted to, the one she had begged for and finally earned. It was time for revenge.

On the flight home, they all began to feel the weight of a long, active day. However disappointed Violet felt, however eager for what would come next, they had all just gone through a solid day's work, and their bodies were exhausted. Arriving late in the night, V team got to rest at last. They were paid one of Valhalla's highest compliments from the populace: They were ignored. It was far better than the attention they associated with Udachnaya, even better than it might have been if people had come up to them with words of praise. It was as if they were saying, "Yes, you have done a good job, but it was your job and nothing out of the ordinary. This is what we expect of you." To Violet, that was oddly bittersweet.

All four fell asleep easily. As soon as they were out, they called Alopex and told her to get Alf and Balder. After a few more minutes of Varg's testicular boasts, Alopex arrived to take them into Alf's dreamscape, an ornate ancient mosque called Hagia Sofia. Violet tried to speak subtly. "We're ready to do something important."

Alf's tarantula avatar scratched its head. "I am sure, Violet, that the unscrambled brains in Scotland and the unscrambled bodies in Canada are important to the would-be victims."

"Sure," she said, less subtly, "but the cops could have handled that crap."

The old splinter that made her deal and not question was stronger now. It had worked before, and she had just justified it in action. Her team had just done all they were asked. She would press for the Orange Gang this time, right after they told her why a Valhalla team, junior though it might be, was doing the work of lowly cops. "You kept the police off it so we could have a go, didn't you?" she said, almost an accusation. Then something felt wrong. Not her boast, not her demand, but the word "lowly" in her mind. Suddenly her father's line of work was beneath her. She felt a tinge of regret for thinking it.

Before she could reroute her train of thought, Balder spoke up. "We might have neglected sending a few bits of intel to delay their response, but we certainly didn't go out of our way. I was hoping to see your death-defying escape from the police after they mistook you for terrorists. Escaping from police is good practice in nonlethal force."

"I think," Varg hinted, "one of us might be eager for a specific assignment."

Vibs chimed in, "The other three of us might want it too."

And Veikko: "I could really go for some fresh-squeezed orange juice right now."

Her team shared her feelings, and to a girl who lacked friends growing up, that meant everything. Any thought of regret for her unspoken overdose of pride died then and there, and she grinned in her sleep. The big brown tarantula folded four of its arms. "Balder, any objections?"

"None at all. We haven't had a team observing them since D left for Siberia. You're clear to observe."

"To observe," repeated Alf.

"And if we discover they're planning an imminent thermonuclear holocaust?" pushed Veikko.

"We are your elders, Veikko, not your commanders. You don't need our permission to throw some shoes in the deuterium."

There it was. They were not her commanders from Achnacarry. They weren't even teaching programs from school. They were elders. Experienced men who respected her. She could bargain with them. She was supposed to. She felt slow for not having known it before. She asked with confidence, "What constraints does 'observation' involve?" Observation was less than she wanted by far. Gathering intel might be the first step in taking down any gang, but she knew it wouldn't satiate the bloodlust she was cultivating.

"Don't Fuck Shit Up, V. Beyond that—" Balder looked to Alf's avatar. "—we're not the sort of elders who 'constrain' our own teams. I believe that 'observation' to this tarantula once involved blowing up a warship and several yachts."

"Ah yes," he said, "the *Nimitz*. The great grand-elder Borr wanted me to 'observe.' He neglected to say if I should observe it under normal operations or observe what it did whilst exploding. The latter proved more interesting than the former. That said, V, you know the treaty." He leaned in toward them. "And you know very well who will enforce it if you go too far."

V team withdrew from the elders' dream and rested in their own. They didn't begin planning that night. To earn the job was enough for one day. That night they talked about Veikko and Skadi, about Varg and his conquests, about how well they could all do at the once insurmountable På Täppan hill, and about trivialities that were suddenly funny in proximity to the great significance of what was soon to come.

IT WAS the first mission of the team's own design and initiative, so it was the first they got to name. Project names, like teams, went by alphabet. This being the team's first mission, it started with an A, and being their first attempt to name a mission, they came up with the edgy and outlandish name of Alpha. They would be mocked for their lack of creativity for the duration of the project.

D team had been keeping an eye on the Orange Gang until recently, when they had been dispatched to Udachnaya. The all-female team had not only monitored the gang for action that would need Valhalla's attention, but they had plotted out the gang's history and organization to such detail that V wondered what was left for them to do. The teams linked from Alopex to Prokofiev. D team dumped heavy loads of their findings into V team's brains in new partitions to be studied at their leisure. Then they came to chat more casually.

"How's Siberia?" asked Veikko.

"Dull work, but it's going fine," responded Deva. "The flower canopy is back up and morale with it. Udachnaya's in shambles, to be sure, but we're putting it back together. Slowly."

"Very slowly," added Dani.

"So you really want our old job?" asked Death. She never took her time in cutting to the chase. Online she was an imposing dark figure who looked like a Geki with an ankh necklace. In person she was an imposing dark figure with a jet-black Thaco suit and a moth Tikari that, unlike her team's simple fly knives, turned into a giant scythe. Her namesake might have envied her look, if not her child's voice.

"We really want your old job," said Violet. "Wulfgar killed my parents."

"We know," said DeMurtas, "but do you really want to watch him day and night? You know you can't just kill him. It would wreck half of Italia."

"It would, but you won't get the chance," interrupted Dani. "You'd get torched if you tried. In case nobody told you, the Geki aren't just keen observers like us. They're omniscient, inhuman, and aware of everything on this planet. They're gods."

"So are we," said Death, "to normal men."

"Point is," Dani continued, "nobody will flambé you for deactivating a wave bomb. You're stepping into responsibility here. Tread lightly at first."

"We will."

"Absolutely."

"At first," whispered Violet.

"Good," Death cooed in her helium tone. "I'd hate to scrape you off fate's grill. The Orange Gang is tricky to keep tabs on. They know what they're doing. As soon as you get a Tikari into one of their meetings, they meet somewhere else. As soon as you get a rat, they bring out the rattraps. They'll kill off half their men before letting you get an intel foothold."

"Any tips?" Violet asked.

"Well, it's a family affair," Deva began. "Wulfgar and his brother were tight, and his men trust their families, rightly so. They won't take newcomers outside one of their members' families without high, high recommendations. And they won't take people outside Danmark without a whole lot more."

"Our best streaks came from the old tricks," said Dani, "Flies on the walls and bugs in the soup. We managed to get Dorian in for almost a month, but they kept him in the dark, so there was nothing to learn. He did a great job and dug deeper and deeper, and before he could even meet Wulfgar, Hrothgar found him snooping. A sad day, but DeMurtas is a capable replacement."

"Dorian lasted," Death said, "as long as he stuck to dead drops and rare contact with the team. Once, maybe twice a week. They caught his link at the last meeting, and we don't know how. Haven't tried an insider since. I wouldn't link out if you get someone in, not until you know how they got Dorian."

"We were planning to replace one of their high-level men," Deva revealed. "Have Niide modify one of us into a duplicate and infiltrate from there. We were in no hurry, as all the high-level OGs are male, and none of us wanted to wear the phallus to penetrate their ranks. Luckily Udachnaya grabbed our attention before we might have tried. One of your boys can try, if he's got the…."

Varg was about to speak, but Vibeke thought it best to cut him off. "Guts."

It was something to consider. V team knew they wouldn't be content observing from bugs planted on lowlings. There was no shortage of options. But Violet wanted to know more about one specific aspect of the gang. "What do you know about Wulfgar?"

Death smiled. "So brazen, Violet. You don't hide it at all. Did you know that I joined when Hrothgar Kray killed my parents? Back when he was heading up the Purple Gang. Yes, he was a nasty little man back then too. This is back when all the color-coded gangs were still sponsored by the state, test cases to see just how much illegality a company could get away with funding. My mother was a whistle-blower in Gang Green. I'd wanted to kill Hrothgar for twenty years. How old are you, Violet?"

"Eighteen in three days."

Death loomed closer. "I'm not jealous, Violet. But I understand you very well, and I owe you some thanks. Yes, I am thankful that you did it. I say all this because you may have to do the same. You might not get to kill Wulfgar. You might have to wait a decade to see someone else do it. When the time comes, darling"—her light candy voice was as deep now as a Geki's—"don't get in their way."

Violet let the idea soak in.

"As for Wulfgar," Death went on, "he's guarded by a small band of people he trusts. He doesn't trust people easily. You'd have to save his life or bring him the head of his worst enemy."

And therein lay V team's advantage. The head of his worst enemy was resting on Violet's shoulders.

As Varg stayed behind to flirt with Death, the rest of V team began to delve into the mindloads of information provided by D team. Violet didn't look forward to the study, having failed every history class she took. She was surprised to find out how much she enjoyed it. It was all so much like her dad's bedtime stories, but more than that, it was her dad's job. He must have gone over every historical fact she was now studying. He must have hunted for some bits of information she now possessed. So she learned about the color gangs, the rise of the Krays in separate colors, the betrayals and consolidations and takeovers, and imagined her father learning the same. She let information trickle in from D team's memory partition: the turning of political tides and gang wars, the slow shift from Danmark to Edinburgh and Italia, the preservation of Hrothgar's work ethic of crucifying victims and traitors.

All the while she imagined her father making notes, and Death just over his shoulder, waiting for her chance at vengeance that never came. She pitied Death but respected her, the will she must have had to wait so long, and the will to persevere after some little brat took her prize. Violet knew she had stepped hard on Death's toes and was thankful she hadn't held it against her. Violet tried to make that will her own. If she had to, Violet would wait twenty years. If it was someone else's fate to take Wulfgar down, so be it. Thinking back on Balder's speech, Violet knew it would very likely be someone else who pulled the trigger. Valhalla couldn't do it without disrupting the order of things. But she could weaken the gang, rot away its supports, cripple it, and then see that once all was lost, Wulfgar would get shot by some petty thief as he lay defeated in the gutter.

As soon as Violet had solved Death's riddle of wills, planning began. They wanted to begin where D team had left off, with infiltration at a high level. Veikko was the master of disguise, so he would be the one to go in. He could do it by handing Violet to Wulfgar. Simple enough, but Wulfgar would surely kill Violet. She secretly liked that bit. It meant she would be celebrated as the first mission death for V team. They plotted out his most likely means of killing his nemesis and outlined a plan to see that she died safely and could be retrieved and resuscitated without too much risk. Veikko would then ingratiate himself with Wulfgar and prove himself a loyal and useful servant. But how to make contact with him again?

Planning went on for the better part of October. So did daydreaming. As much as she worked out the specifics of communications and conferred with Death over a game of chess, Violet imagined the fall of the great gang. She let herself drift into ambitious fantasies from time to time, never letting hubris kick in or mistaking dreams for plans, but indulging in the sense that she was about to embark on the greatest of deeds, and of memorials. Great potential outweighed great peril in her mind.

Violet no longer felt guilt for thinking of her dad as a lowly cop. She was about to do what he never could. Where police could try only feeble arrests and then only at the cost of so many lives, V team was working up the plans to strip the gang bare from the inside out. She didn't feel guilty for having pride in what she was doing, and she didn't feel the boredom of her previous assignments. Every step of the plan was like candy for her ego.

They could get a top-level spy into one of the nastiest criminal gangs, and though many around Valhalla muttered that they might bite off more than they could chew, the plans were flawless, and everyone knew that V team could do everything they outlined. Vibeke anticipated so many potential problems that Alopex would report them hourly to the masses to be considered. Varg solved so many that few had a chance to add their thoughts. The team worked hard and relaxed harder in the gym, where the På Täppan pile was now subject to their tyranny. The chaos of the pile was like a living, broken testament to their quick teamwork and strength. Then as they slept, they attacked the chaos that could foil the observation that would take down the Orange Gang.

"What if he tries to kill you the second he sees you?" Veikko asked.

"Varg needs to be there," Violet decided. "He'll have to follow us. That will be hard. You know we'll be taken somewhere they think is untraceable."

Vibeke affirmed what was becoming a mantra. "We have to think on our feet."

"What if we send them some meat and see where they drag it?" Varg suggested.

"Unreliable but worth a try."

"When?" asked Veikko. "The timetable is crowded. We can't do it close enough to our first move to do any good, and the schedule is full there."

Vibeke finally said what they were all beginning to realize. "We need another team working for us."

Veikko wanted to give Wart something to do, but he was only just beginning to train. Mishka and Marduk volunteered as the rest of M team (Mortiis and Motoko) was busy on a two-person fact-finding assignment in New Guam. Violet finally had a chance to get to know Mishka better and was surprised at how well they got along. In a rare offline chat when Mishka was cleaning her butterfly/shuriken Tikari, Violet noticed a strange insignia on its wings, a line intersected by two straight lines and a slanted one.

"What is that?" she asked.

Mishka said simply, "A Russian cross."

"Why a cross?"

"Because I'm Christian," she said. Violet wasn't entirely sure what that meant. She knew it was a religious sect, one that Balder despised. As for the specifics, Mishka might as well have called herself a Huguenot. Vibeke occasionally mentioned reading a book about Christianity and its schisms, Catholics, Protestants, Mormons, Khlysty, but Violet failed to listen when she elaborated. She knew so little that she asked Mishka flat-out, "What does that mean exactly?"

Mishka stopped working on the butterfly. "It means I believe in a god, a forgiving one." The idea was peculiar but extraordinarily comforting. Violet admitted why. "I suppose we all do plenty that needs to be forgiven."

"We do. Here, take this." She handed Violet a small leather-bound book. "You can read all there is to know in here."

Of course she lost Violet with the word "read."

Marduk was an odd sort as Valhalla boys go. He spoke little and spoke softly when he did. He mostly just did what Mishka asked. He was a fast and skilled fellow to be sure, and he seemed to zelig the traits of whoever's company he held. Around Violet he was eager to do the job, around Varg he picked up a slight macho streak, with Vibs he was all brain, and with Veikko he was playful, even given to humor in his own quiet way. Around Mishka he was the purest of emulators; even when they parted, he would maintain her love of Mussorgsky.

With all the teams in Valhalla giving input, obstacles in the plan crumbled and every conceivable possibility was soon accounted for. Alopex began devoting a major partition of herself to monitoring the gang's influence on the globe. If V stepped on any toes that might radically shift company actions, she would be able to catch it. Every team member would look out for Violet to see that her sacrifice would be neither pointless nor permanent.

Before sending her to Scotland to pose as her former self, Dr. Niide implanted her with all sorts of undetectable tracking and monitoring gadgets. When Varg pointed out that "her fly was open," the medical staff sealed her skin over the Tikari port so as to make it invisible. Her second link would attract no attention, as double links were common enough. With it intact she'd still be able to use her Tikari in an emergency, albeit with a painful launch. Violet was also implanted with several dozen hyperanalgia packs, so that at will she could block out the pain of months of torture. Every unnatural component was checked and double-checked to stay invisible to any scan Wulfgar might try, including vivisection. If need be, her Tikari could make any of three subtle escapes, welding its port closed as it did so to leave a normal-looking chest cavity. Only two of them involved severing her spinal cord.

Orange Gang studies gradually turned from history to current events. It became clear to V team that Wulfgar was done scouring Scotland for the last MacRae and was looking globally for any possible lead as to where she might have gone. Only recently, his men had killed a couple in Prague who claimed to have found her so as to collect a reward. Obviously they hadn't really found her and no reward was paid. The couple was dumb enough to insist that she had been killed in her apartment after Achnacarry and then demand payment. Though the police believed it, Wulfgar was quite aware that his own men had not caught the girl.

Vibs tracked down the deceased couple's online movements and discovered that they had come across an odd sort of personal ad, a rather obvious one, if criminals knew what to look for: "Missed Connections 655321 Scotland—Kyle—posted by Orange W, 'seeking a girl who made the news, you all know why. Will pay for help in finding her. Reply to Orange W Monitor at Ognet.'" The door was open.

VIBEKE STARTED by breaking into Kyle's police network. She loaded Veikko's stats and picture into a new officer profile named William Rickman. Will was getting a transfer to Kyle's witness protection division with top-clearance access. If the cops checked his background, they would find his complete service record and all the bells and whistles. Before departing, Veikko mastered his police persona, talking with experience in the field, knowing specifics of his life in and out of cophood, and somehow holding his face in such a way that he looked thirty years old.

He walked into the forty-first Kyle precinct as Will and enjoyed the ritual doughnut feast. Vibeke kept a well-hidden uplink going as he made friends, completed simple work for his chief, and spent some time snooping through old files, should the right people be watching already. He looked at Violet's case and allowed the police computer to record him doing so. He found the high-security log about her going to Achnacarry, saw that she'd been kicked out, and then he saw the bit Vibs had just added to it stating that she was still in Achnacarry city, skulking around outside the gates of her would-be camp, having faked her death with only a few top-clearance cops months before.

So Will Rickman recalled an old missed connection ad and replied to it. "Found little purple riding hood, still at grandma's house. Will give the address to big bad wolf in person. Meet at straw house in Plockton 1150 Monday?"

He got a response in under an hour. "Confirmed, little Pig. No address needed. Have the girl there and alive or I huff, and I puff, and I blow your brains out."

Wulfgar wanted him to capture her. So he did. Vibs watched the activities of the responding avatar and found that he had discovered the police records and false identity and was no doubt convinced of its authenticity. Will Rickman then traveled to Achnacarry, to the house of Sgt. Jack Cameron, who, the day before, had spotted his old recruit wandering the streets and invited her to dine with him. Violet had in that time told him what falsehoods he needed to know, so when Will came in and asked her to come along, any observer would see the crooked cop escorting Violet from a house in Achnacarry where she might well have been hiding all those months.

He took her to Plockton's rustic Straw House pub. She suspected nothing, or so it appeared. Then, as the crooked cop and his quarry drank, an orange pogo landed outside. Violet saw it and screamed. Veikko whispered his opinion that she was overacting. She shouted "Traitor!" at the top of her lungs and gave him a good kick to the mouth. Three orange-suited men came in to restrain her. Veikko complained about his split lip convincingly and called Violet a few ugly names, not just for the benefit of the gang members. Violet continued to fight and managed to give the traitorous officer another solid kick in the mouth, also for more than the gang to see. The orange men hauled her out of the pub and began trying to stuff her into their pogo. Will the cop followed after, shouting how he'd like to kill her for breaking his lip twice and using some very impolite words, for realism's sake, of course. Violet, for more realism, called him some even worse names and thrust her foot out for one last hard kick to his mouth before they gave her a hypospray.

Through one of Niide's implants, Vibs analyzed the hypospray substance as soon as it entered Violet's bloodstream. She could not risk an open link to Veikko, so she told the microde in his shoe to give him two tiny shocks, meaning "safe sedative." The man then offered the hypo to Officer Will.

"You travel asleep," said the happy gangster. "Trust me, you'll get paid, and more."

So Will let them knock him out. He woke up in a plain office in a plain Dansk skyscraper. There were four men in the room: a doctor dutifully shrinking Will's lower lip, which had swollen to four times its original size, so that he could speak; one man standing to the right of a big orange desk; one standing to the left of the big orange desk; and one man behind the big orange desk. Veikko recognized him immediately but was surprised by his smart, respectable presence. Veikko's false identity—he told himself it was just the false identity—hoped that someday he could appear just like the man before him.

"I owe you a great debt of gratitude," said Wulfgar.

"And of cash, I hope you recall."

Wulfgar smiled broadly. "That too, and I will not break my word. You will be given riches to last a lifetime. You will be rewarded, to be sure, but my men have looked over your employing swine. They saw what you did. They are hunting you."

"I expected it."

"So you did, and came anyway. You may leave with your earnings in any form you like, or you may work for me now."

Will Rickman was in. Only one concern was left. He asked, "What did you do with the girl?"

Wulfgar breathed a sigh of triumphant relief. "All I wanted, my friend. I tortured her to death while you slept."

Veikko could not contact Vibs via link yet; he couldn't take that risk. He didn't hear the tale of Violet's demise.

SHE AWOKE tied to a thick pipe with heavy-duty plastic cord. Her link was active but jammed. When her eyes refocused, she could see one man standing before her. At first she thought he was one of Wulfgar's men, someone sent to represent him. But the man looked just like Wulfgar. She reasoned that it was Wulfgar, but the idea didn't take hold. The man didn't fit her notions of who he would be. She knew he was thinner and cleaner than his brother, but his demeanor was completely reversed. Hrothgar had been a thug from eyes to heart. This man might have fit in at a wine tasting or a play. He had an expression like Alf's, smart but not smug, wise and mature, but above all reserved. Restrained. He crouched down to her level. When she looked closer at his eyes, she doubted his identity again. His eyes were those of a kind man, the eyes of a child's doll or nanny program. His voice matched when he spoke. He sounded nothing like his twin. He even hid his accent.

"Do you know who I am?"

"Kray," she muttered. She didn't want to say more until she knew she was back in character. She convinced herself she was doomed, not in control. It wasn't a hard role to play.

"Yes, and do you remember what you did to me?"

If she had been scared, she'd have hidden it. She wouldn't have sounded scared. "I fried your brother's head off."

"Yes, yes, Violet, you did. You killed my brother."

"He killed my family. We're even."

"Were justice not blind, she might have seen it that way." He put a hand to his lips, a gesture of bemused consideration. "But justice has no power here. I have all the power here. And I see a sad, frightened little girl who tries to talk tough, who knows she has no way out, who knows what I am going to do to her. You may act now with some pride, some degree of hope that somehow someone will save you. But you will not leave this room alive. And you will not die fast. No, Violet, you will feel pain like no girl has felt before."

She allowed herself a subtle laugh. "And you'll talk and talk about it so long you'll die of old age before you get around to it," she said. It wasn't too far from how she might act if she were really cornered, and it would egg him on. Best to get tortured to death quickly so she could get back to work.

He stood again, his face more serious. A hint of his brother's cruelty seeped into his eyes and a tinge of Dansk into his voice. "Sad little runt, I'm going to peel you. Peel you like… like a—" His mouth formed a vicious grin, half snarl. "—like some kind of fruit."

He produced a knife. She activated an analgesic capsule. It dissolved into her blood and deadened her pain receptors. She suddenly wondered why she had done it. She had gone through so much in injury training, she could surely survive this, or at least try. Violet almost felt guilty for a moment, as if she had faked something that should have been more genuine, as if she owed Wulfgar that much.

That brief oddity of mind disappeared as soon as she felt the knife entering her fingertip, under the nail. She tried to act like it hurt. She remembered from training that losing a fingernail hadn't hurt nearly as much as she expected, so she might have underacted a bit. "Oh. Ow. How terrible, it hurts, kill me now," she muttered, realizing instantly that she might have given away that she was feeling nothing. He looked at her, amused by her lack of misery.

"Well, I suppose your time playing soldier must have toughened you up?"

She played into it. "You're a stuffed animal compared to the Camerons."

He laughed. "Then I'll skip the foreplay." He flipped a switch on his knife, and the blade grew red hot. Violet didn't make the same mistake twice. When he pushed it into her next finger, she gave a yelp. Not too much but something to convince him she felt it. It worked. He continued with her fingernails, then toenails.

She let out a few crocodile tears and acted half-defeated. "You're sick," she said. "You're a sick fuck."

"Yes," he admitted proudly, "yes I am." He began cutting off her fingers. She acted better. He bought it. Without the pain, the sight of what he was doing still got to her, as did the silence. Balder had said she could get under his skin, that she could rot away the foundations of his mind. By the time she was five fingers down, she decided it was a good time to begin. She gave a couple of shrieks and spoke with a shaky, pained voice.

"I didn't torture your brother, you know. I just flushed his head like the shit he was."

"That was a toothpick, Violet. A toothpick against a tank. I am a tank." He took her other hand.

"You are. He was a moron. What kind of mobster gets killed by a teenager?" She made sure to give a waver to her voice.

He cut off her thumb. "The careless kind." Her index finger. "The kind given too much power without earning it." Her middle finger. "My brother wasn't a great man; I won't try to claim it." Her ring finger. "But knowing one's family to be beneath him doesn't make their death any easier." Her pinky. "And it doesn't make this pile of digits any less rewarding."

Through it all she let him do his work, whimpering and wincing as she thought she might have done half a year ago. Back before injury training, before Achnacarry. If Hrothgar had done her in back on that day. Wulfgar tried to pull her right foot toward him. She kicked with it, not enough to hit him but enough to free it for a moment. She used her toe to push at the pile of her fingers. She poked one of her middle fingers upward in an obscene gesture and gave a pained laugh. Wulfgar laughed too.

"Keep it up! I like spirit in my prey. I'm enjoying this so much more than I thought I would."

He leaned close to her face. She thought he was about to kiss her. She recoiled. He could hack off any part he liked, but that would be going too far. *It would be wrong, incestuous*, she thought, then became concerned that she thought it. *How twisted is my mind if a kiss is worse than loss of limbs?* But she was right; it was wrong, deeply wrong. She was relieved when he went for her neck and bit.

It wasn't as wrong as a kiss, but it wasn't exactly proper. He bit very hard, breaking the skin and doing severe damage to her left sternocleidomastoid muscle. His teeth were unnaturally sharp, cutting almost as cleanly as razors. *Like an animal*, she thought, *like a predator evolved to rip meat from bone*. She was bleeding badly when he withdrew. His face had lost its gentle appearance once dripping with blood. He wore an obscene expression of pleasure and relief, as if he had just enjoyed the bite more than he'd expected to. Violet was offended by the look. It was the sort of look one expected from a lover, not a biter. She forgot she was supposed to be in pain. She was enraged.

"You sick old fuck," she said. "I knew your brother was a pervert, but you take the fucking cake!"

For a second he looked hurt. She had hit the right nerve. Wulfgar didn't want to be his brother, and then and there, he was. He was the worst of his brother. He felt ashamed, she could see it. So terribly ashamed that he would have done anything to wipe that revelation from his mind. In his desperation he fled into vice. He fled into the love he had for Hrothgar and called it respect. He fled into the pleasure of the flesh before him. "Cake," he muttered, caressing her neck wound.

"Eat me," she barked. He did. He gnawed on her neck, nibbled at her shoulder, and started biting her hard enough to take off skin. Violet was utterly disappointed. The man chewing on her had lost all decorum, all sensibility, and gone animalistic. Despite the detachment of the analgia and presence of mind she had cultivated, Violet felt a sharp prick of terror. To fear being eaten alive was so deeply ingrained in her mammalian brain that it tried to break in on her. She beat it back down and kept her mind on her devourer.

He showed the sort of bestial disgrace that a man can only show to a victim he knows he'll soon kill. The shame would be too deep otherwise. He looked pathetic, desperate, starved. Violet didn't know how much lower a man could get than sucking on her arm wounds, a far cry from his first impression. *All the better*, she thought. *When he sees me alive, he'll bear the shame of it. It will be like a mirror held up to him at his ugliest*. He bit through the tendons in her wrist. She screamed out in false pain to hide a laugh within.

Then she grew woozy. Blood loss. It was time to pass out and continue another day. She expected him to doctor her up, keep her alive for some time, and enjoy more torture. He surprised her, though. Just before she passed out, she could see something click behind his eyes.

He collected himself, stood up covered in blood, and swallowed the bit of arm meat he had just torn off. Her arm was wrecked utterly, chewed through. Her hand fell off from the damage. And Wulfgar, covered in blood, looked ashamed of it.

Violet had won this little encounter. Both knew it. The destroyed body held a victorious mind. In her last moments of consciousness came clarity, a spotless window into the man: He was afraid of what the broken girl had turned him into, and he didn't want another day of it, not another second.

Violet passed out. Wulfgar wouldn't let her do it again. Torturing her was beneath him. The pleasure of it degraded him. No more. He picked up his knife and stabbed her in the heart, then walked away.

That made Varg very happy. He didn't like his role, but he still carried it out with skill and composure. After Dr. Niide had grown a brainless Violet body. Varg took the lifeless double to Plockton, where he watched the Orange Gang kidnap her. He followed them stealthily to Jylland, where they unloaded her at a gang warehouse. He snuck in, watched them tie her up, and monitored their link to Wulfgar to come and get her. He analyzed the link and found Wulfgar must have been about ninety kilometers away, so Varg had time, and his part proved uncomplicated.

He ran into the warehouse and took note of the surroundings. It was a messy place, one with few security measures. He brought the fake Violet in and arranged some crates and junk into a good hiding place from which he could see his real teammate. Wulfgar arrived and woke her. Varg took out his medical tools and prepared himself for the ugly task to be done. As Wulfgar vivisected the real Violet, Varg matched every act on the facsimile, thankfully not with his teeth. He stood ready to intervene should Wulfgar try to damage her brain, but luckily he just stabbed her in the heart, and that was satisfactory. When Kray left the room to inform the garbage detail, Varg made his move. Within seconds he had freed Violet, and taking care not to drip blood in the wrong places, he set the wolf's leavings on a cushioning field and pushed her into his hiding place, replacing her with the fake.

Men in orange suits came for the corpse and left with it just as quickly. Varg took his deceased comrade to the pogo and flew her to a temporary Jylland med bay. There she was repaired and restarted with great ease. Dr. Niide was on site with new skin, limbs, and a new heart. He did not need to use any of them, Wulfgar's techniques were old-fashioned and did little real damage, aside from mutilating and killing her. The doctor even complimented Varg for keeping her severed fingers and toes in order. Violet woke up with Varg standing over her intensive-care bed. He had tears on his cheeks. She wiped them away.

Violet spent little time checking over her repaired form. She wanted to get on with the mission. Niide had done a fine job; only her left pinky was a bit stiff, and the doctor repaired that with a pinprick. He reopened her Tikari port and removed the monitoring chips. Her Tikari was happy to get out after seeing Wulfgar's blade pass right beside it to kill its owner. Dr. Niide insisted that a Tikari could not be traumatized. Violet knew better.

The medical pogo headed north. Varg left Jylland for København to rescue Veikko should his part in the venture be compromised. As per the plan, Varg headed first to a statue of a little mermaid on the shore. He took a fluff bomb designed for a big blast and minimal damage and set it to blow the statue a few centimeters off its rock. He headed for cover and set off the blast.

The instant Veikko was at home in his new Orange Gang apartment, he opened up a news link. His new gang roommates watched, though none questioned why. The man would surely want to see if his actions had been newsworthy. But he only looked as far as an article stating that a local mermaid had survived a small explosion. To Veikko that item meant the survival of someone else entirely, and he was most relieved.

Vibeke met Violet with a tight hug as soon as she got back. That hug was worth every second of torture. But something was amiss back at home. There was no celebration. Violet knew that the first combat death on a team was usually celebrated like a sort of birthday, but nobody seemed to give her a second glance. As N team walked by, she asked about the lack of festivities.

"Oh, you didn't really die. You planned it," shouted Neurosis.

"Yeah, we all saw the plan," seconded Nails. "You should have died in Udachnaya when you had the chance."

"Oooh, look at me," mocked Necrosis. "I'm mutilated!" He ejected his Tikari and made it cut off his hand. "I'm tortured!" he jeered as he kept the bug slicing up his arm like a cucumber. "I'm dead, celebrate me!" He dramatically raised his remaining arm. The Tikari stabbed him in the heart. Violet was shocked at the lengths he had just gone to for the joke.

"Damn, Violet," said Neurosis, annoyed at her, "now look what you made him do. He does this every damn time."

"Every time," agreed Nails. "Loves attention. Come on, let's gather him up."

N team dragged his parts off toward med bay, and Violet sighed a frustrated sigh. She had been proud of her sacrificial act and now felt utterly deflated. She was tempted to steal a slice of Necrosis's arm so it would come back short, but Vibeke held her back.

"Well, I thought it was impressive," she said. Then she kissed Violet on the cheek. The torture, death, and disappointment were suddenly a distant memory, and Violet was the happiest girl in the north. They headed to the cafeteria for a postmortem snack.

Over the next week, Violet and Vibeke spent their time in the safety of Valhalla, getting reports relayed from Varg, who was never far from Veikko. The team had never discovered exactly how Dorian's link had been caught, so they elected to play it safe with Veikko's communication. With several hundred forms of link cryptography out of the running, they resorted to dead drops across København, or when Veikko could manage it, a note sent by "post," an ancient occult system of text transfer unknown to all but the most cunning spies. When the reports came by paper, Vibeke would read them to Violet, which Violet saw as an unexpected benefit of her illiteracy. The first report came a week and a half after Violet's death, by which time, Veikko boasted, he was already Wulfgar's right-hand man.

"All goes well. Herr Kray welcomed me with promises of wealth and power. He offered me work with the gang to compensate for the loss of my police job, though they still call me "Little Pig." I proved myself trustworthy by murdering several of my former police buddies, a task for which I used the cold-flame setting on my trusty Valhalla microwave, ensuring their survival and a good show of fireworks.

"As per the plan, Varg ambushed us shortly after and tried to kill Wulfgar with a fluff bomb. I gallantly jumped on the bomb and disarmed it. Varg gave them quite a chase—the man loves his grenades. That, along with my extraordinary charm and good looks, has allowed me to cuddle up with the big bad wolf. Even from the start, he stated and restated his gratitude and regaled me with the story of how Violet died—the highlight, of course, being when she finally stopped speaking, a moment I sorely missed seeing.

"From this raw material, I forged a grand friendship with Wulfgar. He lets me call him Wolfy, Big W, or my favorite, Growly Magoo. Lies aside, I really have grown close to the fellow, or so he thinks. At all times I use this favoritism to sow distrust, envy, and low morale among his men. One of his advisors has become so annoyed by my candor (I'm sure you can sympathize, Vi) that he spoke back to Herr Kray quite rudely and has been sent to 'manage distant interests' for the gang on Venus. I have not yet learned about said distant interests, because I've been too busy collecting intel on the deepest secrets of the gang. I have done so, because I am awesome.

"So now, let me tell you ladies, safe as you are in the north, all that I have uncovered at great risk to myself."

The first note and all after were chock-full of gang plans and acts of cruelty and illegality. In weeks he had more info on the gang's intents than D team had gained in years. Factoring the new information into Alopex revealed that the gang was both smaller and crueler than previous estimates. Veikko continued embellishing his reports with more quips about how much Wulfgar claimed to enjoy torturing Violet to death.

She and Vibeke looked over the reports and condensed them for Alf and Balder, made their notes well into the night, and analyzed the intel in the bunks, reclining together on Veikko's empty bed or in the gym. Nothing helped to break up the monotony of analysis like a good sparring match. The two watched the sun set for the last time that year on October 26, sitting out on Austfonna, one of the last ice caps. Vibeke said it was a good place to avoid the bustle of the ravine floor and told Violet how, when she first moved to Tromsø with her father, the polar days and nights had driven her insane, though not nearly as much as he had.

Violet asked, "That's the one you killed?"

"Yes," she said. "Quite a terrible guy. I only have two really clear memories of him before I stabbed him to death. In the first, he couldn't be bothered or approached. He was working hard on something online, not immersed but intent and busy. I remembered thinking that this is what grown-ups are—they do work, they do important things and have no time to play with kids. I hacked into his vision with a trick I'd learned from a girl named Angela in school and saw he was playing Tetris. It was funny."

The sun passed the horizon. Vibeke continued. "The other memory was when I invited Angela over for the first time. She came over and we played for a while, but after a few minutes he asked to see her in his room. I thought she might have done something wrong because of his voice, but I didn't know what. But she went to his room, and I thought I heard them talking for a while, but then they stopped. In a couple minutes I went into the room, and I saw them.... I closed the door partway so they wouldn't see me, but I kept watching. I couldn't stop. She didn't cry, but he did, and I could swear he said my name." Vibs thought for a long time. Violet had nothing to say, nothing to compare.

"I'm really very happy to be here now," Vibs said as the sky grew dark. She was leaning against Violet's side. Their suits were wooly against the cold and had complex internal temperature mechanisms that should have made them feel the same homogenous warmth all over, but Violet could swear Vibs felt very warm against her, and the arctic night's cold was feeble by comparison.

Over time, Veikko's reports became more and more depressing. He was sending back horrors of gang life and collecting priceless information, but he was only observing. He observed as they killed people, he observed as they cheated and stole and raised hell for companies in Italia and Danmark and UKI. But they were cleared only for observation. They downright hated observation, uselessly watching crime after crime. One day Vibeke remarked how much easier it would be to observe a smaller gang. To disable the gang and shrink its numbers would be a good observational tool. The team agreed.

Strict observation gave way to subtle action. It wasn't so different from walrus detail. They closed off all avenues of escape and made sure the gang moved toward the cage. When Wulfgar planned to assassinate the CEO of Dansk Fiber Optic, Veikko made a dead drop to Varg, who sent the info to Vibs, who contacted Mishka, who with great style and efficiency foiled the plans without letting on in any way that someone knew about the attempt. Alopex monitored and found no significant global change. When Wulfgar ordered his men to take over an industrial district in København, they found the area defended too well to make an attempt. When they tried to sell kidnapped victims to chop shops, Mishka and Marduk saw that the doctors who ran the shops were caught before they could buy.

Whenever Wulfgar made a move, he was thwarted by means so mundane that he never had reason to believe it was anything but a streak of bad luck. As his luck grew worse, his trust in Will grew stronger, the man who had such great ideas, who managed to keep the gang alive through one disaster after another, and more than that, spoke to him in his most depressed states. Who would act as a psychiatrist when he needed a shrink and a bodyguard when he needed a bodyguard. But most of all, Will was a friend when he needed a friend.

All Valhalla praised their efficiency and results. Alopex monitored no dangerous shifts or takeovers. Everything the gang did led to another lesser criminal enterprise taking their place or a company blocking chaos's way. Alf himself saw their action as an homage to his boating days. It was a fine operation in every way. And it went on and on without losing its potency.

It went on and on so long it stagnated, and the team in charge of it got bored again. Violet could have asked Alf or Balder how to cope with the boredom of a job well done, but she didn't want to cope with it. Neither did Vibs, Varg, Veikko, Mishka, or Marduk. They had crippled the Orange Gang, reduced its numbers over several weeks to less than forty men.

Veikko was so smooth in convincing Wulfgar to fire or kill his men that he was never even associated with their loss. He organized revolts and fights between factions within the gang that resulted in the deaths of many and the desertion of many more. He maneuvered Wulfgar into committing lesser and lesser crimes to compensate for his losses in manpower, and he exploited the loss of morale by making sure the news logs got wind of the most pathetic arrests.

Veikko finally sent a note to Valhalla expressing Wulfgar's misery when four of his gang were arrested for "conspiracy to loiter." Though the crime was in fact arson, Wulfgar was nonetheless miserable to lose 10 percent of his remaining gang.

The gang was a pathetic trace of what it used to be. It was high time to end it. Violet and Vibeke considered what might provoke a Geki response. Alopex confirmed that the gang was now small enough that its total destruction would have little effect. Italia was totally free of the gang and prospering in the grips of an elder Mafia that had welcomed it back. Still, they would not kill Wulfgar. Though the gang was only thirty-six men strong, though Alopex had read every net source and tracked every individual, it might still have unforeseen connections.

As the mission was one of "observation," (they giggled at the word) they decided to "observe" what would happen if Wulfgar and his last men disappeared. After all, they could observe him better in jail. Valhalla didn't have a jail, but Vibs suggested it might need an excuse to build one. Then they could watch what might become of his lesser known, looser allies, those on Venus or the Americas, and annihilate them too. Then perhaps he could be killed.

Technically they needed no permission for the capture. They didn't need to keep Alf and Balder appraised of every move they made, and it was far easier to ask forgiveness than permission. Violet knew she was approaching a line. She knew they were going a bit farther than they were supposed to, but they had done that already and the ravine had loved them for it. And how many would-be victims in Danmark loved them for it without knowing? Violet had done exactly what Balder said she could. Her team had taken Wulfgar down to the level of a petty criminal. Veikko reported that Wulfgar had actually cried when Lars, his old number-two man, tried to kill him with a drug overdose. "He probably cried," Veikko reported, "because I replaced Lars's drug with concentrated estrogen." Vibeke made a note to disembowel him again when he got back.

The new, brief planning phase paid little attention to the distant remains of the Orange Gang, the rumors of members in America or Russia, on Mars, Venus, or Luna. Veikko still couldn't confirm there really were any, and if there were, they would be driven underground by Wulfgar's disappearance. V team decided it was unlikely any would try to find him again, though all agreed it would be pragmatic to destroy as many of the remaining thirty-six as possible in the events leading up to his capture. Even Death herself was proud of V team, and pride was infectious. *And anyway*, Violet told herself, *it's only capture. If something bad happens, we can set him loose again. With a personality hack in his brain.*

So the day came. Trusted adviser Will recommended a night at the opera to calm Wulfgar and as many of his men as he wished to take along. He knew Wulfgar's tendencies so well he had to feign surprise when Wulfgar had the idea to take all thirty-six, and had no doubt the man would pick *Hemlighet om Runor*. In fact, he had already signaled Vibeke to tip the police that Wulfgar would be attending.

Thirty-three men showed up for the performance. Perhaps the others had already abandoned ship. Twenty-six police officers were in attendance. For the small venue, that meant only five civilians were present that night, and they bolted as soon as the fireworks began. It was a peculiar sight to Veikko, who watched from the empty mezzanine: Everyone in formal wear, police highlighted by link sirens, and the Orange Gang highlighted by their clumsy attempts to escape. Half the gang was cuffed and welded to the floor in seconds; a couple were zapped, a few beaten by police who were overeager to score their first major blow against the gang. A total of twelve escaped, as did Veikko, but no group of thirteen counts the traitor ex post facto. Needless to say, Wulfgar was among the survivors, and Wulfgar was at the end of his rope.

Valhalla had anticipated around fifteen escapees, and by the time they reached the safe house, Veikko was well on his way to implementing the plan to dispose of them. Having met Wulfgar right outside the theater doors, he spoke of revenge from the start.

"We still have weapons," he rallied. "We still have men!"

Wulfgar was quick to add, "And we have the tank from the Roskilde job. We have a tank, and we know where the pigs live!"

The planning lasted only half an hour, there being little to plan. The remainder of the Orange Gang would take every resource they had left in the country, a few microwaves, a few rocket launchers, a seventy-year-old treaded tank, which the gang used mostly for sewerside transportation—and they would lay siege to the police headquarters. The two members who had been arrested before in that district knew the layout and knew it was crammed in between enough newer buildings to make it blind and inescapable on three sides. If they took the cops by surprise, they could annihilate them before they could haul out their own arsenal. This fault was exactly why V team made sure that particular police force incurred Wulfgar's wrath.

Will was in charge of preparations for the assault, of course, and before they left, he diligently checked every weapon and vehicle, making certain all the microwaves were uncharged, all the bullets were duds, and all the rockets lacked fuel. And then they marched. A tank rolled through Amagertorv for the first time since 1945 and up to the least strategically positioned police station in København.

The police were scared shitless. For the last few months, it had been open season on orange hats and this previously unheard of little station had received the tip to take the gang down for good. So they had and times were bright, until they saw the tank. And the men. And their weapons. Chief Namier felt like he had been punched in the stomach. Soon he would be remembered posthumously as the fool who had taken on the nastiest gang and suffered the nastiest death for it. Wulfgar shouted the order to attack.

And nothing happened. Triggers were pulled left and right, buttons were pushed up and down, and not a round flew, not a beam sizzled, and for some reason the barrel fell right off the tank's turret. Some of it was Veikko's expert sabotage; part of it was the suppressing beam that Varg was firing from a pogo overhead; part of it was the ineptitude of Jan Tsang, who had the one loaded clip of the bunch but had loaded it wrong. It took Namier a few seconds to understand that the siege was impotent. As soon as he did, he called in every man with every microwave in the station. With a crazed expression of relief and bloodlust, he ordered them to fire.

The tank exploded. The men exploded. The street under the men exploded from the heat of twenty police microwaves set to wide field and full power. Namier laughed in an insane howl as burnt flesh rained down on his uniform. The Orange Gang was suddenly a gang of two.

Wulfgar had turned his back as soon as he'd heard the click of an empty weapon. Veikko was at a distance, watching where Wulfgar fled. He linked quickly to Varg's pogo to inform him that the target was heading to a nearby alley.

The pogo fell from its position and past traffic to cut Wulfgar off. It landed only meters away from him. Veikko followed to cut off his only escape. Wulfgar saw the traitor for the first time as he truly was—and bore no expression. As soon as it registered, Wulfgar decided in cruelty that he would deny this traitor a look of rage. He would make no move nor put up any fight. He hated the man too much for that, and more than that, admired his skill. He turned his back to Veikko and his drawn microwave and faced the pogo. Its door opened to reveal something even more shocking. Someone he had killed not too long ago.

Violet stepped out of the pogo with Vibeke beside her. She looked into his eyes. He recognized her but didn't look surprised, or as ashamed as she had hoped. He was more reserved than ever. Not broken or defeated at all, though she might have been disappointed if he'd broken down. She walked up to him and demanded his knife. He calmly took it out of his coat pocket and set it on the very fingers it had once cut off.

"Did you know, Violet, that I once kidnapped the finest surgeon in the city to have him implant explosives in the marrow of both my personal bodyguards to detonate in just such an instance as this? I have the detonator right here." He raised his hand to show off one of his rings. "One is dead in that pile behind me. The other, I'm heartbroken, never showed up for the opera."

He pressed the ring. Somewhere, kilometers away, Mehmed Parker burst like a melon.

"And I am left alone, at your mercy. Well played, girl. Well played."

He knelt, and he thought. His admission of defeat wouldn't fool them for much longer, if it had at all. He had only seconds to pull out his Thunder 5 revolver and only time to fire one shell. There was the girl who killed his brother. The boy traitor who had destroyed his gang. And some girl he never saw before. Wulfgar was not dead, and therefore these masterful children didn't want him dead. They must need him alive. Perhaps they knew about Venus and needed to question him? Then he needed to know too. He would have to get under their skin and learn what they knew. Yes, there was only one choice. He would cause pain to the two he knew, and if he survived, he would exploit it cruelly.

His arm moved with lightning speed, and as soon as Violet had fired the stunning pulse, the shot was passing through Vibeke's neck. The splatter was enormous, the heat of her blood intense on Violet's cheek. For a brief moment, Violet had no idea what was going on. Vibeke fell to the ground, her head only half connected to her body. Blood covered her chest, the street, everything.

They hurried to throw Wulfgar's unconscious body into the pogo alongside Vibeke, with whom they took far more care. Vibs was awake and looked perversely happy enough for her injury. They had just ended the gang and taken Wulfgar into custody. Varg gave Wulfgar a hard twenty-five hour sedative and broke off his antenna. He then took the pilot seat and headed back for Valhalla as fast as the pogo could fly. Veikko tended to Vibs with the greatest care and skill.

Violet held Vibeke's head in her lap, trying to estimate how it would have lain with a full neck. Violet tried to apologize, to tell Vibs she was sorry for how it went down, to tell her she was going to be okay, but no words came. Violet couldn't speak, she was so worried. She didn't know why she was worried. It was only half her neck, comparable to injuries some sustained in training. But Violet felt as if she had betrayed Vibeke with the stupid plan, her idiotic pride, and all the crap she had felt so smart about as it had gone down. She had let her ego bloat that past month. She thought herself worthy to bargain with the elders, to tempt the Geki, to take down the whole gang single-handed. She didn't think that way anymore.

She thought instead that ending the gang would mean nothing if she didn't have Vibeke to share it with. However it turned out, however better the world was, however triumphant she might be against her grand nemesis Wulfgar, it was meaningless with Vibeke hurt. Memories of lounging around with her, looking over intel, came unbidden to her. Memories of how Vibeke's arm pressed against hers in Veikko's bunk, how they caught each other out of breath sparring in the gym. How they laughed in anticipation of the pleasure of annihilating Wulfgar's last men. That pleasure had been utterly deflated, killed, and Violet knew it was because she felt more for the friend lying injured in her lap than she felt hatred for Wulfgar.

She admitted that until the recent plans and projects, Wulfgar hadn't even meant that much to her. She only felt so much because she had friends at last to share her feelings with, friends worth letting into her mind. And now she had a weakness for them that she never had before. She had become vulnerable, and for someone who had never been vulnerable for a second in her life, it was terrifying, more than the Geki or anything she had ever faced. Violet had felt a kiss on the cheek that made her feel warm in the frozen north, alive after she had died. She was devastated to admit she'd risked the girl who gave it to her on so small a nuisance as Wulfgar Kray. She only knew the value of that life when it was bleeding away rapidly before her.

Vibeke died on the flight home.

Chapter X: Austfonna

THERE WAS much rejoicing in Valhalla. After Vibeke was patched up and jump-started, a process taking Niide under ten minutes, she was the celebrity du jour in the ravine. Greeted by citizens and teams alike, she was paraded from the med bay as the first battle-death of V team. Mishka gave her a strong hug and a light slap to the repaired part of her neck.

"I knew it would be you, I just knew it!" she laughed. Eric presented Vibeke with a new collarpiece for her armor. S team had taken the old bloody collar to hang from the med bay windows, declaring the consummation of V team's training.

Varg asked what it had been like. Veikko asked if it still hurt. Both jogged by her side, more proud than envious. Alf and Balder applauded. Valfar called out a compliment that even Alopex couldn't translate. T team approached, Tahir pulling a small metal object from his Thaco collar as he walked. He approached Vibs and held up the trinket—a little magnetic coffin. The crowd went quiet for him to speak. "For Vibeke! May she rest in peace!"

The crowd cheered as he stuck the little coffin to her new collar. "We've passed this on since D team. I earned it when I got pushed—"

"Fell!" yelled Toshiro. "You fell in!"

"When I was thrown by gravity herself into an industrial bottling machine. I present it now to you, Vibeke of Valknut team, for gallantly getting your neck shot to shit in the line of duty. May it be the first of many such grisly deaths, and however often you might break your neck, may you never lose your head." He leaned in close but still spoke loudly. "Keep this coffin safe for Wart. He should earn it in a day."

Wart giggled when she looked at him. Necrosis pushed past him to shake Vibeke's hand. Death, who'd started the tradition, whispered something into Vibeke's ear that made her laugh. It was all laughter, whistles, and cheers. Violet could hear it as she walked to a janitorial shed and grabbed a carriage system. She was relieved to be away from it. Someone had to drag Wulfgar from the pogo, though she wasn't sure to where. She was just desperate to do something so she wouldn't have to watch the party.

Nobody knew just why Violet was in so dark a mood, least of all her. She had seen Vibeke get patched up, seen color return to her face with new blood. Vibeke was as good as new, but the sickly feeling of her death stuck to Violet like slime. It was clear from Vibeke's waking remarks that she didn't blame Violet. She didn't even think of the possibility. She was just as happy as the rest to have ended project Alpha, captured Wulfgar, destroyed the gang, and earned the neat little magnet on her suit. But Violet did blame herself. She would all but set the sleeping bastard free if it could take back what had happened. She loaded Wulfgar onto the carriage and hauled him from the pogo.

Staring at him asleep, she wasn't interested in killing him. She didn't feel any hatred toward him. Certainly not over Vibeke. That hatred she reserved for herself. She wanted to work, to move him somewhere safe. But Valhalla had no jail, no brig, nothing of the sort. Every room there locked from the inside. Had they avoided any injuries, they probably would have elected to hand him over to the Kyle police. He could stand trial for all she cared. But now he was in Valhalla. Violet took him to the only lockable cages in the ravine that could hold him—the walrus cages.

Celebrations went on. She could smell the cafeteria cooking up something special as she passed. What the hell would they do with him? *Not send him all the way south to the cops*, she thought. Someone could break him out from there. Who might, she didn't know. She didn't care about loose ends just then. She just thought it better he stay there, where they could watch him. She unloaded him into the cage on the far right of the cluster and locked it by link. She informed Alopex to keep that cage off the crane, so it wouldn't be unloaded topside by mistake, then gave Alopex the information to treat him as she would an animal injured on capture: to keep him fed, watered, and locked in so securely he couldn't possibly leave. Then Violet was done with work and left alone with her thoughts.

She kicked the cage as hard as she could. She kicked it twice more in frustration before she slipped and fell on the rocks. She sat there for some time, angry as hell. She was upset enough about Vibeke but even more angry at herself for feeling it. If she felt so strongly about the death of a teammate, she was screwed in this line of work. Valhalla was meant for people who celebrated trifles like this. She called herself weak. She called herself stupid. She looked into the cage and saw Wulfgar sleeping, snoring, and couldn't think of what the hell he'd done that was so important he had to get caught. It couldn't have been just her family. It couldn't have been general crimes or mayhem. *Earth is hell*, she thought. *How is he any worse than the status quo?*

Yet she had forced the situation to catch him. It was hubris, bloodlust, petty revenge that killed her teammate. But she knew nobody would blame her. Nobody would berate her; to everyone involved, even Vibs, all was near perfect. Balder linked her a compliment on their success in taking down the gang once and for all.

"I've seen many a gang go down by our hands," he said, "but this will be the one to review! Training will reference this for ages to come as a prime example—"

Alföðr joined the link. "I don't know about that, Balder. Trainees might get their hopes up higher than they can handle. This was quite an ambitious first effort for a team."

"I'm sorry," she said, knowing the words to be a heavy understatement.

"For what, Violet? You broke no rules. The Geki haven't shown up. Why aren't you in the cafeteria with us? They made special brown wafers that taste like nuts, chocolate, and milk all at the same time!"

Balder linked again. "Ambition ain't bad when it all works out, Violet. Speaking of which, where did you stick Wulfgar?"

"In a walrus cage. I know we don't keep prisoners, but—"

"Excellent idea. We'll discuss his future tomorrow. Come, join us. Your team misses you." And the link ended.

Not enough to call me themselves, she grumbled to herself. Of course she wasn't trying to link to them either. What could they say? Veikko wouldn't understand a shred of it. Varg would only lament that

Valhalla celebrations lacked any kind of orgy. The one person who might understand was Vibs, and Violet wasn't going to share the bad mood with her. She had done enough to her for the day. Violet cursed loudly and lay back on the rocks, staring up at the icy walls, and wallowing in self-disgust. She had learned the last bit of that old cycle: if you do something wrong, someone will yell at you; if you do something very wrong, they talk softly or not at all; and if you fuck up beyond all measure, you punish yourself. She'd never guessed that the last would be the worst.

Violet fell asleep there on the rocks. Her link was dimmed at the time, so she didn't go into lucid sleep with the rest of the ravine. Nobody came to get her. Her team cared for her deeply but agreed as they slept that she had to work through something on her own.

"Must be a chick thing," said Veikko.

"I'd understand it, then," answered Vibs. "It can't be jealousy. I mean, she was sad she didn't get to die first, but she wouldn't be this upset over it."

"I don't know, that little coffin is pretty cool," said Varg.

"Actually, the magnet stiffens the collar a little bit."

"Keep it. The dead should get rigor mortis," Veikko mused.

"What's Mortiis got to do with it?" asked Varg.

"No, not Mortiis from M team, part of decay."

"Oh, that's why you smell so bad," said Veikko.

"Shush. I'm worried about Vi."

Veikko was concerned too. "Alopex, where is Violet now?"

"Violet is in sector 86-E, in proximity to—"

Vibs canceled the response. "She must still be staring at him."

"Or asleep off link."

"Or she's pining for a walrus that's out of her league."

Varg spoke up. "You know, if I had just caught the guy who killed my parents, if someone had killed my parents, I'd be there too. And the man tried to eat her. They clearly have issues."

"He never told me he tried to eat her." Veikko mulled it over. "It doesn't seem his style. He's dignified, that guy. Respectable. Crime is just his business. He's a CEO like the rest of them."

"Then company men are all monsters," said Vibs. "Here's what I'm wondering: What do we do next?"

They spent the night debating it. There were other gangs. Veikko thought it would be a good sophomore effort to end oceanic piracy. Varg had some humanitarian ideas that Veikko and Vibeke found in poor taste. Vibs didn't really care that much just what to do next. She was preoccupied with Violet's state. Varg was right, there were issues raised by having one's worst enemy so close at hand. But Violet was strong, she thought. She could handle him.

"HELLO, VIOLET MacRae."

It was daytime, the dim twilight day of November in the north. Violet woke when she heard her name. She sat up on the rocks. Her back ached from having slept on the hard, uneven ground. She knew who was talking and glanced around to make sure there was nobody else around. She turned and looked into the cage. Wulfgar was back to the kind, dignified man he liked to appear as. He was covered in the grease of the walrus cage, stained with some blood, but his face showed no hint that he was imprisoned. Violet saw through the exterior and recognized the animal within, the degenerate soul stained by their last meeting. She felt quite in control of him.

"Just Violet now," she said simply.

"What a shame. We should never lose our family names. It's akin to losing our families."

"I can thank you for that."

"And I you, Violet."

Polite conversation felt like a waste of time. She had more important things on her mind but she started with the least of them, a minor oddity that had bugged her when she'd confronted him last. "Why weren't you surprised to see me alive again?"

"Oh, I was. But this is the Hall of the Slain, isn't it? Yes, that's who bought you from the orphanage. Who gave you the chance and the tricks to break into my gang? You forget that to the vulgar world, you had died once already. I wasn't fooled only because they claimed it was my own gang that captured you. I had no idea just who was faking your death.

"Then I killed you with my own hands. Had I known you kept the boogeymen behind you, I'd have killed you more permanently. Live and learn. Or learn nothing. You speak to me now, and you'll fall victim to my own mistake. You're letting me, me of all people, live. Have I not earned death at your hands? Why do you keep me alive in this cage that smells of fish breath?"

He was right, but he was also making up his bold words as he went along. He was still in the cage and she was safe from him. She had no reason not to speak honestly, "In case we need you to tie up your gang's loose ends. We might not need you at all, but your death can't be undone."

"You of all people should talk, having died twice now. I won't beg you for death. I don't want to die. But your idiocy amuses me." He thought for a second. "Yes, I am very amused."

Violet had nothing to say.

"You seem so morose for a victor. Does my capture not satiate you the loss of your parents?"

"I suppose it does," she lied.

"Then what's eating away at you, girl?" He crouched as close to her as the cage allowed. "Come and tell your mortal enemy your deepest psychological vulnerabilities."

She wasn't about to. He went on. "Then let me tell you the source of my amusement and pleasure. It isn't merely your tactical error of letting me live. It's so much better than that. You see, I wanted revenge. I wanted to torture you to death, and I got to. And it was good. I was very happy."

He was lying, and she knew it. Even then she could see the hidden shame that he had enjoyed it too much, as his brother would have. But then, no man can truly despise himself for feeling pleasure. He was ashamed, but shame for a man so perverted as this might be just another vice.

"My revenge," he said, smiling, "wasn't as empty as yours. Never mind your own reasons. I was tumescent with joy as I relieved you of your fingers. And your hand. The only slightest fault was, like you said, death cannot be undone. Life is one of those possessions you can only steal once. I thought I could only kill you once. I'm so happy to see you all sewn up, so I can tear you open again."

She could fight back with one thing he didn't know. "I had analgia. I didn't feel any pain at all. I faked every scream."

"All the better. I can do it right the second time." He studied her for a moment, tried to see through her facade, to see what she was thinking. *Try it*, she thought. *You're powerless. You have no idea who I really am or how I work.*

She was wrong.

"You're depressed right now because your friend got shot. Yes, your simplicity betrays you. You lost a friend."

"She's fine."

"Then I'll kill her as you watch. And the rest of your new family. Such an extended family you have here. They'll all suffer so much, so much at my hands.... You think you feel bad now when your sister-in-arms survived? Think how you'll feel as she dies painfully because of you. Think how your superiors will weep at my feet, how they'll dwell in agony at your mistakes, and how their eyes will stare daggers into you in disappointment and shame for trusting you, before I pluck those eyes out." He stood and looked down at his pants. "Dear me, I've gone hard again. Come closer, girl. Finish me off."

He was disgusting, to be sure, but that didn't bother Violet. Nothing he said really got to her, because she had already told herself far worse. There was a peculiar satisfaction in hearing his threats and taunts. The more he tried to hurt her, the less she hurt. But she had seen quite enough of him for the day. She turned and walked away. He didn't call after her. She walked to the steps leading away from the walrus cages and was surprised to see Cato.

"Violet, congratulations, mate!"

"Thanks."

"I came to see the prisoner. You know, he's the first prisoner we ever had here. Big man outside too. I thought I'd see how he was holding up in a cage. Some animals just die in captivity."

"I'm sure you can lend him a hand," she said and jogged toward the barracks. She found herself in a better mood than the day before. Despite Wulfgar's poor skills as counselor, Violet's visit to him served a purpose: She finally felt like a minor team injury was worth it to take the sick bastard down.

WINTER BROUGHT snow, more than Violet ever thought could fall. She spent some time alone outside the ravine, watching the flakes collect, thinking about Wulfgar in his cage or about Vibeke. She knew why she had felt so terrible that day, so afraid of Vibeke's loss, and decided that the way she felt for Vibs was a liability in their line of work. They could be friends, they could be close friends, but she knew part of her wanted more. That part could be very dangerous in a battle or—

She heard crunching. After months in Kvitøya, she knew the sound meant footsteps in the snow. She heard a voice from behind her.

"You're lucky you have that furry suit."

Violet turned around to see a man of about twenty-five. He was bundled up in a thick jacket like one of Valfar's. He sat on the rock beside her.

"I'm Nergal," he said. "Civilian. And you're the girl who caught Wulfgar Kray."

She nodded.

"He killed my mother—well, his men did. So thank you."

"You're welcome."

"I never knew my dad. Alf's been like a dad to me. Ever since I joined up."

"You're on a team?"

"I was on N team. It didn't work out."

"You're retired, then?"

He laughed. "So to speak. You have a very stressful job. Too stressful for me, and not worth the Thaco armor. I was going to take N team on a mission to destroy the Orange Gang. Didn't make it past Death's doorstep. She told me what I'd have to do, and I just couldn't do half of it. I couldn't do most of the shit we set out to do. Have you met Sappho or Samoth, formerly of S team?"

Violet shook her head. Nergal went on, "Same deal there. But damned if we'll leave the ravine. Once seen the promised land, right? But I had to find you after this. Just to say thank you, thank you for doing what I couldn't, what the world couldn't do. We all owe you so much."

She suddenly felt angry, despite his kind words, or perhaps because of them. "That's a bit much, isn't it?"

"Nah," he said, standing. "It's just a little note of gratitude from his victims. I wanted to deliver it on their behalf."

He walked away. Violet turned back to the cold expanse. She resented the man, however kind he was, however natural his words might have been. She tried to think of why and decided it was because he claimed to represent "the victims." She wasn't a victim. She wasn't even fighting for victims. Deeper down, though, she knew she was more bothered that he seemed perfectly happy as a civilian. Someone who had trained and fought as a Valkyrie could simply stop one day and live a happy life. That meant she could too.

What if she could leave the team and still be perfectly content with herself? She had her revenge; now why shouldn't she retire? She could stay and see her team, when they weren't working. She could see Vibs and watch her grow distant over time. *No*, she thought, *it would be agony. I'm not a victim nor a civilian. I'm not Nergal or Samoth, and I don't run away.*

Violet knew what she had to do. She tracked down the part of her that wanted Vibeke as more than a friend and killed it as if it were another enemy on the battlefield. *It is an enemy,* she thought, *quite literally. It's the most dangerous enemy I face because it makes me weak.* Violet had the mental discipline to make it a precise and effective assassination. That part was dead and buried under the snow. Something Wulfgar said about death's permanence rang dully in the back of her mind.

But Violet was happier for the moment and headed back into the ravine to see the people she had so recently shunned. She found most of them enjoying one of Varg's ice-wall film projections. Not one person mentioned her stay in the doldrums. Their eyes were all on the spaceships on the wall. The night's show was the second part of an ancient series that intended to predict the future, a vision of half a century to come made over two centuries ago. Violet doubted that such pretty spaceships would be floating through such distant nebulae so soon, but she still grinned when one blew up the other and found herself moved at Spock's funeral. She blamed the bagpipes.

Once again she felt at home with her team, in dreams or in the gym. The På Täppan pile was conquered, but with the mission accomplished, the enduring occupation was light fun. The team had mastered so many forms of personal combat that sparring was like a duet, improvising off one another and enjoying the odd sensual cocktail of pain and pleasurable contact. Violet and Vibeke spent a lot of time sparring. Varg and Veikko seemed content in the bleachers. Veikko spent much of his time off with Wart. Thankfully Veikko never had too much free time, or he'd have surely returned to his pranks. When Violet caught him modifying a target-range microwave to spray silly string, the team thought it time to start more assignments.

They didn't plan another massive gang takedown, partly because the biggest gang was already taken down. They joked about taking on the yakuza or Unspeakable Darkness, but the fact was they were a bit sobered by project Alpha. They didn't want to take on the worst of the world that year. They wanted to refine their skills.

Mostly they assisted other teams, owing both D and M for their help. Mishka, Marduk, Mortiis, and Motoko found use for them in preventing an assassination in France, where they got to track and catch more talentless American assassins and see Paris, the Eiffel Tower, the two-kilometer-high Sarkozy glass atrium, and the site where the Cathedral of Notre Dame once stood. Marduk explained that it was destroyed and not rebuilt in the single most malodorous sewage explosion of all time, one of the events that led to mandatory dispersion-field toilets in megalopoli. Vibeke mentioned that the dispersion field's safety components had been bought up and price hiked in an early scheme of the Purple Gang, leading to substandard, fragile safety features on some European models. She didn't need to remind Violet that the Purple Gang was then run by Hrothgar Kray.

After D team returned from Udachnaya, they began an advanced surveillance operation in Argentina. V team offered to assist, but there was little to be done. Before she left, though, Death took some time to talk to Wulfgar. Violet was surprised when, the next day, she listed plans for a brig on the Alopex bulletin. A rather humane brig, in Violet's opinion, considering who would be its sole prisoner. Aside from jokes about Death's merciful side, the ravine set to dreamtime debate and design. Alf posted only one note in the discussion, stating, "We have never held prisoners here for extended periods of time. It seems to me unwise to begin." He did not state any opinion on what to do with Wulfgar, nor did he argue further when the ravine decided to build the brig.

One day Galder and Gehenna approached Violet at lunch. Galder spoke plainly. "What do remember about Heather Lyle?"

"Private Lyle? From Achnacarry?"

"Yes," said Gehenna. "We've been watching her for W team for a while now."

"Well, I kicked some of her teeth out. She might not like me."

"She actually never blamed you for that," said Gehenna. "Though she thought you were insane, she also thought you were, as she told a Sergeant Cameron, 'One badass babe.' Once she got new teeth, she completed training at Achnacarry and proved herself in the combat-free military world. While stationed in the Israeli craters, she expressed concern for you and sadness at your faked death by the Orange Gang."

"But the station," said Galder, "wasn't easy for Heather. Her individualist tendencies put her on the shit lists of enough officers to land her in trouble again and again. When she became disillusioned with the pointlessness of her career, she tried to leave, but her contract was so Machiavellian as to leave her stuck in the service of Scotland and its subsidiaries. When they gave her twenty-four-hour medical cleanup duty, the last bonds she had to her sad employ snapped, and she deserted. Desertion means if she's ever caught, she'll spend the rest of her life in slavery so unspeakable that I won't speak of it, but this is a Grade-A Achnacarry commando, and Valhalla's not about to let her go to waste."

"Subject to your approval," added Gehenna. "Wart has given his."

Violet didn't have to think long. Veikko looked forward to getting a "daughter," and Violet looked forward to seeing former Private Lyle again. V team saw R team in their dreams the night before pickup and asked if they could come along.

"You can bring her in," said Ragnar. "We wanted to go to Türkiye for Anma Günü tomorrow."

So the Rs took their holiday trip, and V team headed for Edinburgh. G called them in flight to tell them to make haste, as the police were on their way to pick Lyle up. That was a benefit if they could time it right. The cops would see her die and close the files on her. She wouldn't get the luxury of an epic chase like Varg's or a knife fight like Violet's, but they expected she wouldn't mind.

Heather was sleeping atop a mountain crammed with memorials and statues, at the top of an ancient rock staircase named Jacob's Ladder. Jacob's Ladder was covered in drunk vomit and trash, so the cops were making a slow ascent. V team landed their pogo behind a tall conical monument and Tikaried the air to get multiple views of the situation. Heather awoke and spotted the incoming police but didn't run. Violet was surprised to see the state she was in, homeless and desperate, and if she wasn't going to run, she looked quite ready to fight. Veikko's Tikari saw the police were well armed. Vibeke gave their precinct a quick hack to see their directive. It was a brutal one: "Subject is highly trained and highly dangerous. If given any resistance at all, shoot to kill."

Violet wasted no time and made contact. Knowing exactly what an Achnacarry-trained soldier could do when taken by surprise, she called to her as she approached.

"Heather Lyle!" she shouted.

Heather turned around, expecting to see more police closing in. When she saw Violet she was surprised, to say the least. She called, "Violet? Is that really you?"

"Yes."

"No it's not. You're dead."

"Faked. I found something better than Achnacarry. You can join us or leave with the cops."

Heather pushed aside her disbelief. "Gee, let me think. Okay, you. What do I have to do?"

The police were nearly to the top of the stairs.

"We have to convince the cops you're dead. You need to run from them and take cover under those pillars. They're going to get knocked over in one minute. We're gonna pull you out half a second before you get crushed. They won't see it."

"You will?" Heather didn't seem to believe it. "Violet, if you really are Violet—"

"Trust later. It's death or the cops." Violet disappeared into the shrubbery. Heather knew she would have died anyway rather than go with the police, so the offer was golden. She saw them come up the stairs. They ordered her to freeze. She did not. She took cover by the pillared monument and sure enough a blast, courtesy of Varg, knocked the monument off its rocks and onto Heather. The instant Varg had triggered the blast, Veikko tractored her out with the pogo microwaves. He did it so fast it nearly broke her neck, but she landed far from the police's view, and Veikko had a med kit ready for the expected whiplash. He quickly sprayed some fragments of burnt flesh cloned from Achnacarry's records to supply a "body." Violet and Varg rendezvoused with their Tikaris and boarded. Vibeke kept her hack active long enough to hear the words "suicide bomb" reported, then cleared them for takeoff.

From the back of the mountain, the pogo flew low into the traffic of Edinburgh. Heather looked at the team around her, her heart racing and mind reeling.

"So I'm dead and you're the angels?" she asked.

"Demons, sorry. You're going to hell."

"Shut it, Veikko. My name is Vibeke, this large blond fellow is Varg, and Violet you know. We're spies."

Veikko continued, "And we're gonna remove your sternum and turn it into an insectoid—"

Violet gave him a backhand to the face.

"Oh!" said Heather. "You really are Violet!"

The flight gave them time to explain what they would have online, given the chance. As Heather was on the lam, she'd kept her link off, making both W recruits "raw catches" who didn't know what was coming. Vibeke had been such a rescue, so this was Veikko's third experience at welcoming such a person. His humor was terrible as usual, perhaps even worse, but it did seem to break the ice and set Heather at ease with all that was to come. As Heather came to laugh about her fears, Violet admitted there might have been method behind Veikko's madness. She failed to regret the backhand.

Veikko explained the rune system to Heather as they flew, and by the time they landed, she had dropped the first letter of her old name in favor of the new. Wart and Weather met that night as Veikko watched from his link. Weather got the same Tikari as Wart, a grasshopper that formed a mek'leth knife. As Wart's suit took the yellow shade of Veikko's duotone suit, Weather's took on his reds. Veikko volunteered again, as he had with Wart, to handle their training, but that was still O team and P team's job. Easy as it was to forget, V was the most junior team and not yet cleared to train new recruits.

AS VIOLET slept, Alopex knocked at her brain. "V Team, I have news."

"Report." Vibeke and the others joined.

"Four military targets in Africa have been attacked by a Mjölnir system. Readings suggest the generator from Siberia was used. Targets had little or no significance to company disputes or strategic locations. Political tensions have risen but not erupted. Teams D, E, L, and N have been reassigned for investigation and renewed tracking options. Junior teams (V team) to remain inactive until further notice."

The kids stayed indoors for the rainy days to come. This meant a redoubling of training, sparring, exercising, and above all, conjecture, and rumor. There were minor Mjölnir attacks in the logs every few days, but no pattern emerged in the targets. Alföðr admitted he had no clue as to the purpose of whoever stole the system, beyond the destruction of bases in Africa. They considered every possibility from a violence-for-pleasure-seeking gang to a superior force just beginning to flex its muscle. But the fact remained—someone among them was involved. Someone right there in Valhalla. C team was hunting them around the clock, and V team was invited back to C's offices to tell them the same things they'd told them before. Cato paced back and forth across the room.

"Why, Violet, did Varg not come to our offices immediately after the events at Udachnaya?"

"Ask him."

"I'm asking you, mate."

"Because he was busy flirting with a nurse."

"And that's why he missed the Geki too, right?"

"Right."

"Do you really think the Geki would let a man miss his debriefing because he wanted to bed a nurse?"

"Do you think they'd ignore a man they thought was betraying us? Varg killed a dozen of them. You're grasping at straws," Violet retorted.

Cato stared at her. "Yes, we are. Here's another straw: Why didn't the intruders open fire at you until you fought back?"

"Clearly we were too pretty to kill."

Cato laughed. "Internal Affairs means everyone here hates me. I don't need you to like me, but I do need your help. Like you said, grasping at straws. Try to think, Violet. Was there any reason they might not have come in shooting?"

Violet gave it some genuine thought. "Because they didn't want a fight? Because one of them was from our camp and didn't want to kill the junior team. Because they wanted to save ammo. Because they thought they had superior forces. Maybe they just don't like killing people like—"

"Like we do?" he sat backward on a chair. "Not related: Why didn't you kill Wulfgar?"

"Geki."

"If there were no such thing, you would have?"

"No. His gang might have connections we haven't seen yet, lines we didn't cut. He was a big man once. His disappearance might bring up problems we couldn't solve with him dead."

"Alf's words. Balder's. Wise, but not your own. Let me tell you a little bit about m'self. If not for the Geki, I'd destroy Tunisia. Utterly. I'd nuke it, wave bomb it, burn it, drown it. I'd salt the bloody earth."

"Why?"

"Not your business. Point is, I would. And I won't be going there again lest I can. So when I see you just talking to that man, I have to wonder. Why?"

"Not your business."

"That, Violet, is an ass thing to say."

"I couldn't agree more."

C team wasn't the only team pursuing an investigation. Back in the barracks, Violet wondered aloud with her team about every question Cato had asked. Why didn't they come in shooting? Why gas masks? Was there really someone from Valhalla there with them? And if there were, who the hell was it?

"It was Cato," said Veikko.

"Oh, that would be nice. Then I could shoot him."

"He's not that—well, okay," Vibs admitted, "he is that bad, but it couldn't be him. He was meeting with Balder when it went down."

"Alopex," Varg called up the fox, "list all Valhalla citizens and team members unaccounted for during the Udachnaya incident."

A huge list of icons appeared. Varg waved it away and continued. "Let's say it was a team member. Citizens don't generally blow things up; that's why they're citizens. Alopex, list unaccounted members."

Another list, still huge. Vibeke said, "Remove any members with active Alopex links at the time."

The list shrank substantially. A dozen icons floated around, all of members who were not linked in to the Valhalla computers.

"Label list as possible conspirator list six and close."

The list disappeared. Veikko scratched his neck and nose, then said, "Our recruiters couldn't have missed a previous loyalty, right?"

"It's beyond unlikely," said Vibs.

"So they must have been recruited by the enemy while working for us."

"Unless it was an association that we knew about but didn't consider dangerous. Loyalty to a legitimate group that turned violent?"

"We don't induct people if they have so much as a weekly chess club," Veikko stated.

"I was in prison chess club…," said Vibs.

"What about surviving families?"

"Alopex, display members with surviving family."

There were thirty-seven icons.

"Limit to local base." Sixteen icons.

"Venn with list six of possible conspirators." Three: Veikko, Varg, and Mishka.

"Well, I didn't do it," claimed Varg.

"Me neither," added Veikko.

"Why are you two even on the list?"

"All four of us are listed because we were there, unlinked to Aloe," said Varg, "and my family is alive, if you can call it living."

"And Veikko? I thought your parents were dead," asked Vibeke.

"No parents. I have an older brother," he answered. "He's in a Cetacean colony. I can't stand the syphilitic son of a bitch, so there's no real connection. And I can absolutely rule him out of any violent plot. He would consider violence to be 'improper.' He's one stuck-up fish. A total *peräevä*. Who's Mishka got?"

"She never mentioned anyone to me," Vibeke declared with certainty. "I know her pretty well too. Odd."

"Want to deploy some of your covert interrogation skills, Vibs?"

A giant brown tarantula appeared in their chat. "You're very clever for such a young rune. I do hope you'll someday learn that what you discover might have been considered by your elders before you."

“So you already checked into her family?” pressed Vibeke, eager to hear his results.

The tarantula scratched his head. “As it is, no, it never occurred to us. I suppose youth has its advantages. I don’t even remember having a family.”

“So you’ll put C team on it?” asked Violet.

“Unsubtle,” he said. “Vibeke, I think you have a capacity to talk to Mishka subtly without calling undue attention?”

“She’s a close friend.”

“Was that a boast of capability or a lament of having to research ‘a close friend’?”

Vibs wasn’t about to leave that one in doubt. “Alopex, locate Mishka.”

“Mishka is in the gymnasium, sparring pad four.”

“I suppose you can all watch.” Vibs disappeared from the chat and walked to the gym. Alföðr and the rest of the team monitored from her eyes as she walked. She entered the gym and found Mishka fiercely defending attacks from Marduk and Mortiis. Vibs watched. Mishka saw her and proceeded to show off her most flamboyant moves, sending one man to the mat and the other into defensive mode. She flipped onto Mortiis and caused him to forfeit before she broke any bones. Mishka linked to the men. They nodded and left. Mishka glared with a grin at Vibeke as if to say she was next. Vibeke bowed into the ring.

“We haven’t done this for a while, have we, Vibs?”

“Was starting to miss you.”

“You must be a masochist.”

She launched a halfhearted kick at Vibs.

“I know you’re a sadist…”

Vibs fired a volley of punches at full strength but failed to connect.

“Come on, little girl. Aim for the soft spots. You display weakness.”

She tried again, more fiercely, with no success.

"Harder! You went soft sparring that Scottish *korova.*"

She kicked Vibs in the face. They could almost feel the pain over the net. Vibs dropped to the floor, not in pain but in tactic, and kicked Mishka's feet out from under her.

"Da! That's better."

Mishka launched another, more dangerous attack, taking Vibs to the floor, pinning her.

"And then you let me back on top. Soft, soft meat. You've been tenderized without me. Get up."

Mishka didn't let her up. Vibs struggled.

"Tender meat. Kjøtt. K-J-O with a silly Norsky line through it—T-T. Admit it."

"*Nyet*.... H-E-T, nyet."

Vibs tried with all her might to get up, but Mishka kept her down with what looked like little effort. She stopped trying to get up.

"Weakling," Mishka whispered in her ear. "You never should have left me."

"Who said I left?"

"I do." She sat up to straddle Vibs. "You may have a full team, but you needn't spend all your time asleep with them or leave the smart half of the gym for the jocks in the pile."

"I came back, didn't I?"

"You came back crawling."

Mishka leaned in face-to-face. The four watching through Vibeke's eyes instinctively flinched. A question suddenly occurred to Violet that she hadn't asked Alföðr previously. She linked to him out of Vibeke's hearing, "Is there any actual Valhalla policy on dating between ranks?"

The tarantula patted her on the back. "I'm flattered, Violet, but you're much too young for me." He turned back to watch. Mishka was a centimeter from Vibeke's ear.

"What do you want from me now, kjøtt?"

"Just to talk."

"I can't talk when I'm busy sweating. Let's shower off and get dinner."

So they did and so they did. It took an eon of banal small talk before Vibs could maneuver the conversation past current events to past events, to past missions and inductions, to life outside, to the subtle question it was all about.

"You got any family left, Mishka?"

"No, all dead."

Vibs was back within minutes of a proper farewell. Alf and her team were waiting in the real world now, back at the barracks.

"Are we sure she's lying?" Vibs asked.

"Positive," answered Alföðr, tapping his fake eye with a spear tip. "I can spot them from kilometers. She has family, and she knows it."

"Who?" asked Varg.

"Aloe lists her as having family in some logs but not others," said Vibeke. "Doesn't have anything else. Did G team skimp on the job?"

"Never," Alf said with confidence. "If Aloe's records aren't complete, someone deleted them."

Violet thought for a moment. "Then how can we—"

"In my records," said Alf. The team followed him to his library, where a tarantula Tikari emerged from his chest and climbed to a high shelf. It pulled out one of the many paper volumes and set it down before them. Its innards were a nightmare to Violet—the exact reason text was such an impossibility. She had all the information she needed to read text loaded into her in school, but there was a difference between loading and learning. As she looked over the list of letters in her memory, none of them resembled the scratchy curly forms in the book. They merged together and formed messes that Violet couldn't imagine were words. Yet still, Vibeke pointed to one of them and said, "Mishka."

Alf read on. "One brother named Sasha, family name Suvorov. At least, that's what it was when Alexandra Suvorova joined us. We lost all record of Sasha shortly after she joined. I believe he got professionally hacked out of net existence."

"What are the chances she and her brother were there, in Siberia?" asked Violet.

Alf quickly added, "Alopex, closed-line security recognition, apply."

Alopex spoke on highly localized encryption. "Records show Mishka on assignment under water and out of link at the time. Margin of error 30 percent, probability 60 percent."

"So it's likely?" asked Veikko.

"It's a distinct possibility" said Alf, looking most concerned.

"Vibs," Varg asked, "would you put it past her?"

"No, no not at all. Who else would have let us live?"

Alföðr nodded gravely. His Tikari nodded with him.

V TEAM now worked for C team. Violet wasn't happy about that. They worked for C team because Vibeke was in the best position to squeeze Mishka for information. Violet wasn't happy about that either. She might have killed off her own interests, but that didn't mean she could stand seeing Vibeke upset or in Mishka's arms.

Obviously they were not to give any hint to Mishka of what they knew, if they knew anything. Violet's first impression of Mishka had been vaguely hostile. She didn't know exactly why, but in the last months, Violet had given up that irrational mood in favor of Mishka as a good friend and a woman she could trust. Now every sinew of friendship that had developed between them was strained, ready to break.

She knew Vibeke harbored feelings far deeper, had known her longer, and faced a more personal betrayal. How personal, Violet still couldn't stand to ask. But V had an assignment now: observe Mishka, and if the opportunity allowed, find proof of her innocence or guilt. This time when Alföðr said observe, Violet would be content to just observe.

The whole team found great difficulty in watching someone so close by. They would have gladly traveled across the globe to spy on someone they never met in favor of monitoring someone they knew well without their knowledge. It was next to impossible, because they were recognizable and not naturally around Mishka all that often. They volunteered to help M team on every mission, simply because they had no work during the lockdown. So they piloted their pogos and scrubbed their tanks and debugged their avatars but saw nothing of any use. As other intel teams sent back data by the kiloquad, V team alone logged nothing and nothing and nothing again. That meant C team started breathing down their necks, pushing for them to send Vibeke after her ex-girlfriend.

The night Vibeke had first arrived in Valhalla, she'd been in poor shape, having been rescued from a very real prison riot in which they'd faked her death. Ragnar and Ripple had deposited her right into the med bay, where the bones in her feet, legs, and chest were fixed. She woke up in a bed so like that of her childhood that he was convinced she had been brain hacked. With her, Veikko gained the humor and tone that best invited new recruits. He also developed a fatherly composure, himself only months out of the family from hell. But when Vibeke began to train, it was Mishka who taught her the ropes. Mishka taught her Tikari tricks and sparring strategies. Mishka shared her knack for reading on paper. They ate together at every meal and spoke of le Carré and Fleming and Cloutier. In dreams they wandered computer dreamscapes of Nizhni Novgorod and Norge terrain together, pointing out where they'd grown up.

Vibeke told her how she was born Vibeke Dyrsdatter in Stavanger in 2212 to a single mother, whom she'd watched struggle financially and emotionally. She'd been thrown from school to school and net to net, and she'd seen her mother broken by man after man before settling for the worst of them. Vibeke had watched him destroy her mother, sending her into a mental asylum and stealing custody of her daughter. He took Vibeke to Tromsø, where he treated her the same way he'd treated her mom, and for lack of knowing a better way to live, she let him, until the day he went so far she had to stab the man to death, lest she see another friend fall victim to his lusts. She lost the last friends she had anyway when they sent her to jail, and in jail she was thrown to criminals who made her father look meek, and she lived in that hell until the last riot, when Valhalla came for her.

Mishka shared her own childhood stories, siblingless stories about Sundays in the most beautiful of Russian churches, cathedrals made of wood without nails to hold them together, only the flawless workmanship of monks hundreds of years before, where she saw ikons made of enamels and ivories long since extinct. Soon Mishka confided how, in that beautiful world, she'd suffered survivalist parents who'd kept her outside in a cage, who'd never let her get a link or go online or learn anything but weapons and exercise and how to hunt for her dinner. If she hunted badly, she didn't eat. But she taught herself to read.

Vibeke couldn't help but love her. And now every tale Mishka told and every aspect of her that had made Vibeke fall in love was an act of betrayal. Violet had never seen in the outside world how cruel love could be when it turned. Nor had she cared for anyone so much as Vibeke before, or felt such empathy for one so hurt.

Vibeke now had to seduce Mishka back to keep an eye on her. She buried her emotions so deep Violet feared they might never surface again. Vibs went to Mishka, softened up after their sparring match, and they talked. When they talked in dreams, the team watched through a special division of Alopex that Alf divvied off for them, which Mishka wouldn't be able to sense. By day they monitored with Violet's Tikari, the smallest of the bunch. They kept out of Vibeke's eyes lest Mishka sense them within. Though Varg was hurt by his inability to punch or kick Vibeke's pain away and Veikko wished he could have spared Violet the duty, she had to watch through her insect's eyes and relay it all to the others. She had to be the one to scrape the privacy from what Vibeke most wished could have been private.

Vibs did well. If they still gave out awards for acting, Vibeke would have won hands down. Violet watched them fall in love again gradually, convincingly each day. Then she listened to Vibs toss and turn with rage every night. Vibeke managed to talk about Udachnaya so casually, so subtly that Mishka never picked up on what she was doing. Vibs communicated carefully designed fragments of a puzzle that would assemble subconsciously in Mishka's head to suggest that she could forgive whoever was behind the attack. She could perhaps even help the attackers in Africa if she knew what they were up to. Nothing happened at first, but by the time the puzzle pieces were all stuffed into her head, and Mishka and Vibs were nearly sexually active, some progress began.

Violet's Tikari followed the two for a walk in the moonlit meadows of Austfonna, hidden in the iridescent blue fur grown by Vibeke's suit. Mishka finally spoke the magic words.

"Did you know I had a brother?"

Vibs played her part adeptly. "You didn't have a brother. I know you. You were the only one."

"Not quite. He's a lot older than me. I always thought of him as a sort of uncle. I didn't meet him until I was almost fifteen, and only then when I could get away from my parents. They wouldn't admit he was theirs. If they saw him, he was Sasha, just a boy they didn't know. They even had his records destroyed by a professional hacker so that nobody would know their shame that they gave birth to this brilliant, silly man. But he followed me from birth when he could, introduced himself when I was hunting a sable. He caught the animal with his bare hands and broke its neck for me."

"Do you still talk to him?" she pressed. "Do you know where he is?"

"He fell into debt and got sold by Gazprom to an African military. They were going to use him in some Congo fight, some tribal war turned despot company match. He proved himself the hard way. He took villages for them and stole equipment from superior forces. He reinvented guerilla war in the jungles."

"Amazing."

"He is. And he's taking over the continent. Slowly, he's taking the entire continent. He—"

Vibs couldn't keep hiding her knowledge. Luckily Mishka couldn't keep her secret anymore.

"I'm so sorry, Vibs. I didn't want you in Udachnaya when he broke in, but he had to. He needed the weapon to take UNEGA outposts along the river. But if you could see what he's doing—Sasha is taming that vile land. He's turning it into a peaceful, controllable civilization. It has to be done, and he is the only man who can do it. So I gave him what he needed. You have to understand, Vibeke, this is more important than—"

Vibeke put one finger on Mishka's lips and showed such forgiveness in her eyes as to melt any last barrier between them. She kissed Mishka full on the lips, whispered in her ear, and held her close amid a sea of ice. Back in the ravine, Veikko shuddered with pride. Vibeke had outdone his finest disguise. Violet shuddered with something very different. Something she'd killed was coming back from the dead. Varg stood up and shouted a triumphant, "Yes!"

In the coming days, Vibs professed her allegiance to Mishka convincingly. She learned the rest of the strategy, most importantly how Sasha needed another generator badly. The Congo bases were armored with meter-thick steel, and it was the only way to conquer them.

They knew the plot. It was time to deal with the plotters.

Chapter XI: Suqutra

"DID YOU ever read her little book?"

Vibs looked at Violet for a moment, trying to think of what book she might mean. "Oh, the bible? Yes, in jail before I met her, they passed around a lot of banned books."

"What's in it?"

"Creation myths, tribal history, lots of rules."

"Rules that she lives by? Any we can use to our advantage?"

It was a good idea, but Vibs looked amused. "I don't think she obeys them too strictly. I can think of a few she breaks quite often." Vibs reflected on that bit with a knowing expression that rubbed Violet just the wrong way.

Where the Orange Gang's destruction had been a pleasure to plot, there could be no happy ending to this project. No matter how it turned out, it would be a sad day for Valhalla, and the longer it went on, the more frequently Vibeke had to bear Mishka, and Violet had to watch her do it skillfully. Skillfully meant Vibs looked happy, in love, in ecstasy, and each of those resurrected with a vengeance the feelings that Violet had buried. They'd never put her through jealousy training, so she didn't know how to counteract its effects.

C team didn't care. Not that she ever brought it up with Cato. The Cs were all about reports and progress. Even as Violet and Vibeke slept, Claire was in the dreamscape listening to their chat about Mishka's book. She didn't add anything useful, didn't suggest what to do or help in any way—V team was working for internal affairs, not with them.

"Did the book," Claire interrupted, "suggest anything about her sense of justice or priority that would shed light on her brother's actions in Africa?"

Conversations in the night were turning into work. Violet floated back and watched Vibeke's avatar think. How, Violet wondered, could Vibeke's avatar, a little green worm with glasses, have the same expression Vibs had when she was reading in the real world? How could it be so oddly alluring when it was just a mathematical facsimile of her presence online? Violet reminded herself that she was supposed to be thinking about Mishka, as Vibs was.

Vibeke explained, "The book's full of contradictory philosophies, some warlike, some pacifist, some wildly insane, and some plainly logical. It says nothing of the sort of people who follow it. There's no hint of how she works in there."

Claire was disappointed, another feeling that came across through an expressionless avatar. Claire's was a black chess pawn. Cato's was a white knight. He came toward Violet from behind the pawn, moving a step to his side and two in her direction. "Violet? Any thoughts?"

"None you want to hear." She unplugged and let herself dream offline. They were getting nowhere anyway. That used to be okay, she remembered, even after Udachnaya. V team wasn't expected to contribute all that much to the plans of other teams. They were the new kids, there to learn. Now nobody in the ravine thought of V as a junior team anymore, so when Vibs was assigned to determine if Mishka was a double agent, it was expected that she would, in so doing, install herself as a double agent. She was a mole before she knew what she was underground to do.

So C team pushed, and when V team didn't move fast enough in any inspired direction, C team began to plan for them. The haphazard organization of project Alpha was eschewed in favor of a hard logical list of necessary steps and their ideal executions. They had to figure out exactly what Sasha was doing. Vibeke was the one who had to do it. She took on the task admirably. Churro had no problem devising a way to simultaneously prove Vibeke's worth to Sasha and his army and install yet another agent unseen into their midst. Violet volunteered. So did Balder, and his qualifications for advanced stealth surveillance outweighed hers by several hundred missions.

After Udachnaya, anyone with a Mjölnir generator had dismantled it and destroyed the special parts. The only working copy left was the prototype, constructed by H team at Valhalla. After the first break-in, this generator had been moved, only Balder knew where. With a sudden need for a decoy generator, H whipped up a new one in secret, but instead of a functional copy, this was a Trojan generator. In place of its proper magnetic components, it had only one working system—life support. It held all the right materials to trick a scan. The support system's electronic signatures were made to pulsate in the same manner as that of a real Mjölnir generator and to disguise human life signs. Thus Balder would be delivered into the core of the enemy stronghold.

The plan was to force a situation where Mishka would need to openly defect and leave Valhalla, and where Vibeke could prove her false loyalties and follow. They would be allowed to steal the fake generator, so they had to design a situation irresistible to Sasha, but not so obvious that he might suspect it. The fake generator would be moved to Antarctica along a route designed with a subtle weak point, the Suqutra archipelago in Yemen.

As they carried the generator, they would pass through the territory of Yemeni Utilities and Programming—the YUP, a draconian company notorious for rewriting its contracts in the middle of jobs. They would believably give Valhalla their allegiance one day, then rescind it the next as they flew through, having done exactly that two years prior and ruining one of Mishka's first assignments. Her hatred of the YUP and its enforcement army, the Yuppies, was sure to solidify their decision to take advantage. It wasn't hard to predict her response to their attempt at a hostile takeover of their cargo. V and M teams would have been the likely choices to carry the real generator, so it was no stretch to assign them for their known traitors and double agents to be.

Valhalla's pals from Karpathos base would play the role of the Yuppies. Two Karpathian teams, Theta and Omega, would come with hovercraft painted in Yuppie colors just as Sasha's men, presumably in their panzercopters, engaged the Valkyries to take the generator. Churro allowed two possibilities—they would try to take it by force, or Mishka would reveal her loyalties to facilitate a bloodless steal. Vibeke began trying to convince Mishka, as soon as they got the transport job, to shuffle off their Valhalla loyalties publicly and leave with the generator. Mishka was receptive, but Vibs couldn't be sure she would do so when the time came, not if her brother's men allowed for a nonlethal, covert grab-and-go.

To ensure that Mishka couldn't remain innocent, pretending to fight her brother's men, the Karpathians would attack her helicopters before the cargo pogo. They were armed with semifluff charges to make giant semiharmless fireworks. That would force Mishka to either defend the attackers or take the generator in the pogo to its destination, while abandoning the rest of their teams. Cassandra diverged from her team on that point, stating that the handover couldn't possibly go so predictably. She had nothing to add on how to ensure the ideal series of events.

Mishka, while planning the theft with Vibs, had revealed Marduk as an ally. This changed little, as M team was not briefed on the true nature of the mission. M team was as tight as V team, and there was no opportunity to brief Mortiis and Motoko. Their genuine desire to protect the generator had to be negated by V team, and covertly so.

The night before the mission was to take place, V met the teams from Karpathos briefly online. Vibeke was in a separate dreamscape with Mishka, so she had the briefing stored in a memory partition to look over while awake. They went over rescue procedures that would be necessary for Balder should anything go wrong. Churro and Cassandra, present as a rook and a bishop, planned each step and accounted for the enemy's most probable and all conceivable actions and reactions. After the Karpathians delinked, C repeated outlines with V team thoroughly. All felt it was a good, strong plan, but Cassandra told them not to rely on any of it to go down remotely as expected. She said just as they woke up, "No plan ever survives first contact."

THE PLUTURUS family had always been rich. As far back as Cetacean records went, they had always been pillars of the undersea civilization. Ionas Pluturus was the most famous, as the founder of the Ionian colony near Patmos. He was not only a pioneer but a leader of the school. He protected his colony against the violence of humans, and with the riches he made as a privateer pillaging the enemy's ships, he funded and revolutionized gill surgery and nictitating membranology.

He instilled in his offspring the belief that one day, all life would return to the sea. That belief passed all the way down to his great-grandson, Pelamus Pluturus.

Pelamus had inherited a submarine fleet painted in black and yellow, his family colors. Every ship was richly decorated on the interior with fine wooden carvings depicting the family's past accomplishments, present abodes and holdings, and future plans and aspirations. It was one of the most opulent and beautiful fleets in the Mediterranean. When his parents died, that fleet buried them at sea, and Pelamus took charge of the familial empire. He didn't quite follow in his father's footsteps as a genetic scientist. He and his sister Nuala found more appeal in stories about their great-grandfather—the ones about piracy.

Leaving the Ionian colony in the care of their younger siblings, Pelamus and Nuala set to sea with plans to annihilate the human vessels that harassed their rural zones, to pillage the Red Sea spice routes, to make a name as the Cetaceans who wouldn't stay underwater. They wanted to be the names remembered for turning the tide on humanity. Sadly, on their first venture under the Jolly Roger, the small band of bullies bumped into a YUP security patrol.

The Yuppies sunk two of Pelamus's seven ships, crippled his flagship, and in so doing killed Nuala. He stood helpless on the bridge as he heard the breaches crack the deck below and crush everyone in the torpedo chamber. Pelamus won the battle and destroyed the security patrol, but at so great a cost that his mission in life fell to the wayside of his desire for revenge. He forgot the designs carved into the walls of his captain's quarters and set course for Yemen to make an example of the first YUP ships he found. Then of the second, and third, and on and on until the whole company would be remembered only as the first savage casualty of the great uprising that ended life on the surface.

IN THE last days of November, the sun still tried to light the northern skies during the day, but it didn't do very well. It was dark gray at noon when H team dredged the fake generator, passenger inside, from a hiding place deep within the ice of a glacial wall. V and M hauled it to a bay where the cargo pogo waited. Violet was briefly distracted on the way by a brig being assembled. It looked weak and escapable. She made a note to inspect its plans when they got back.

The cargo pogo lifted off and headed sluggishly south into daylight. The journey was sickeningly quiet, anticipation killing small talk before it left their mouths. They crossed Norge and Europe, crossed the Mediterranean Sea and Arabian Peninsula. As soon as they passed into the Yemeni airspace, Mishka dropped a pellet into the sea. The pellet opened on contact with seawater and made its broadcast across the waves, literally in the waves—a waterborne signal that would not travel in interceptable air. Four panzercopters emerged from the sea, now painted with brown Yuppie colors. As Churro hoped, the enemy was pretending to be company interceptors and had dropped their extreme armor accordingly. Now they were only "lightly" armored unstoppable death machines. Four of them, when only three had survived Udachnaya. Sasha was building one hell of an army. The cargo pogo links activated and shouted forth the copter's demands.

"You have entered YUP airspace. Identify yourself and prepare for cargo review."

Varg gave the standard response that would remind the YUP of its Valhalla contract, knowing full well the YUP had never been told any such thing. "This is cargo pogo URS5MA, delivering an electrical generator to Chronos Inc., YUP Subsidiary 1442."

The copter went quiet as they pretended to look up the information. A real YUP patrol, as there were such things in the area, would then know they were impostors, having never been told of such a delivery. Only Sasha's men would respond to the statement as if it were legitimate.

"Info confirmed," they replied. "Prepare for inspection."

Everyone on both teams agreed to allow the inspection, each for their own secret reasons. Mishka and Marduk knew they would take the generator, Mortiis and Motoko thought that the YUP would merely check for contraband then release them, and V team knew they would take the bait.

The cargo pogo set down in the water and copters hovered close. Two landed on the water and extended plank fields to send a torrent of men aboard. This time they had no masks. Violet looked over every face, wondering which of them had killed men in Udachnaya, which she might have fired on. They looked over the generator and linked to each other with heavy encoding.

Finally, one man spoke up.

"Yeah, it looks like YUP has arranged another delivery service for Chronos Inc. We'll take this from here."

"This is security level eight," said Motoko. "We cannot let it off the pogo until it's signed for by Chronos."

"I'm security level nine," said one of the men.

Violet was suddenly aware that she didn't know if higher or lower numbers in YUP security protocol were superior. Then she remembered it didn't matter in the least. They had to take the thing somehow. Mortiis did not know that, and he became belligerent and said loudly, "You can have our generator when you pry it from our cold dead hull."

Each eager to get the job done without a problem, Mishka, Marduk and every member of V team all simultaneously suggested he back down. The two unwitting Ms were a bit surprised, along with the fake Yuppies. Violet stepped up, drawing attention away from the group call for pacifism and placing it on Vibeke, pushing her to reveal her Sashoid allegiance.

"Why, Vibs?" she demanded. "Why do you want them to take it?"

Vibs played her part and blushed. "No, no, that's not it. We just don't want—"

"I knew it, I knew it since Udachnaya! You're trying to take it yourself!" shouted Varg.

Melodrama treated their intentions well, but Violet knew it wouldn't hold without an escalation in tension. Veikko knew it too and dropped his broadcast pellet covertly out the door. It sent a signal to the Karpathos teams.

Within seconds, two hovercrafts with the same false flags and link labels as Sasha's copters came to the scene and demanded to know what was going on. To all eyes who needed to see, the YUP had just caught on to the game being played in their waters. This was the point where they hoped Sasha's men would take the generator and their double agents and run, so Vibeke forced the issue and betrayed her team, making Mishka and Marduk do the same. She held her microwave at Violet and continued the argument. "We're taking it because you won't use the damn thing! We're taking it because we can do some damn good. And we're taking it clean or covered in guts, so pick fast."

Violet had to keep herself from smirking at the hokum and ensure the defections as the Karpathians began to barge in.

"Who's 'we'?" Violet sprung her Tikari and held it to Vibeke's eye. Luckily nobody saw Veikko cringe as she did so. He and Varg quickly played along and took up fighting stances.

Mishka answered with her own Tikari, sending it to perch on Violet's shoulder, wings at the ready. Marduk followed her lead, and all three traitors were in the open. The hovercrafts got as close as they could fit into the crowd and broadcast a loud message. "This is the YUP! Everyone stop doing"—the Karpathians caught a glimpse of the standoff within the pogo—"whatever the heck you people are doing! Stand down!"

The Karpathians knew the plan, and they knew the standoff in the pogo would remain a standoff without them making a move so, as they shared the Yuppie garb of the panzercopters, a couple of Omegas boarded and sided with the like-labeled fakes. "Lower your weapons! And you, lower your… butterfly!" one demanded. V team and Marduk did so, but Mishka did not. That was in theory no problem, so the Omega went on asking the nearest copter soldier, "What are you here for? Home base didn't have you logged."

"Generator. We're supposed to take it from here."

The Greek happily sided with him and forced the situation. "That's it, then. Generator goes with the copters. You people come with us."

They had such fancy-looking weapons that not even Mortiis or Motoko disagreed. They began the move. Mishka explained that she and two of her companions were the generator technicians. V team glared at her to keep the illusion going, and the Omegas already knew why, so they agreed to let them fly with the generator.

All was on course for the traitors and copter troops to take Balder on their way and leave the Valhalla teams stuck with the bill. All the people and props were on their right vessels. Then the real YUP showed up, and wrecked everything as Yuppies were wont to do.

Despite heavy precautions to hide the internal matters from the real owners of the space, the Yemeni boats wandered onto the scene to find four copters and two hovercraft flying their flags clustered around a foreign craft in their waters. C team would hardly have been an elder team if they hadn't planned for this, so they had the hovercraft transponders matched to the company's signature. Sasha was not so great a planner, and the company read his fleet as a copter threat to two of their own hovercraft. Valhalla now had to protect the copters and double agents on their escape without giving away their true nature. That could happen by making the cargo pogo a greater threat to the newly arrived boats than the copters.

Vibeke and Mishka had made it to one of Sasha's panzercopters; Marduk and the generator were escorted to another by the Omegas. With all hostile eyes either leaving or not yet arrived, Veikko deactivated the pogo's flight safety features, and Varg took the cue to turn on the flight fields. Without the safety systems on, the fields extended with brutal force into the hovercrafts, knocking them into the air upside down. As expected, the company ships moved in to protect "their" men, and the copters with Mishka, Marduk, Vibs, and Balder escaped with haste. Violet couldn't risk a link to Vibs as they fled, so she only thought it. *Happy hunting, Vibs.*

Their escape was what C team had planned. But the other two copters stayed. C team had not planned for that. There was no tactical advantage in leaving them there and no way they could have foreseen it. Vibeke knew why immediately. She had read Mishka's little book. It was why they hadn't shot first at Udachnaya, and why they would even stay in Suqutra as protectors: Sasha and his men thought they were the good guys.

Noble as they were, the men in the copters remaining to protect their enemies didn't know which half of those enemies weren't enemies.

The instant the hovercrafts fell back down, they posed more of a threat than the company boats, so the copters opened fire on them with conventional microwaves. Men aboard the hovercrafts didn't know which copters their allies were on, so they dared not fire at any of them. The Yuppie boats assumed they were incapable of returning fire, so they did the honors and engaged the copters.

This all could have ended well had the cargo pogo just left and let the hovercrafts and Yuppies work it out, but they forgot Yemeni seas are subject not only to Yemeni law but Murphy's as well: The cargo pogo's field caps did not turn back on. When they tried to lift off, the vessel stayed still, and the wind and sea around it moved instead. The waves forced one of the floating copters directly into Omega's hovercraft. The Yuppie boat before them had no idea what to make of the malfunctioning field waterspout and ceased fire long enough to let the other copter blow them out of the water.

Violet watched helplessly as the last remains of the plan fell apart. The damaged hovercraft opened fire on the boat with a damaged microwave array and vaporized all the water beneath it, sending the remaining copter into a vapor cloud that didn't affect their hardware but rendered the pilot blind, forcing him to gain altitude lest he hit the other hovercraft, which also went blind and plowed directly but harmlessly into the cargo pogo.

For the next fifteen minutes, copters, boats, hovercraft and the pogo fired on one another, bumped into each other, disabled each other, and tried to hastily repair themselves. Chaos reigned supreme over them all. Finally, the genuine Yemeni boats gave up trying to figure out who was on their side and decided it would be easier to sort out with everyone dead. They fled and called in air support, which came immediately from the company's air fleet: six panzercopters, all identical to Sasha's.

The panzercopter that had plowed into Omega's hovercraft made the air just in time to get lost in the crowd. Veikko and Violet tried to tell the hovercraft just to get the hell out of there, but the com traffic was as bad as the air traffic, and even the links were useless—someone was jamming. Who the hell would jam a situation like this? The hovercrafts followed the boats and let loose with every battery they had, which annihilated the company's sea force and infuriated their air force, who now stood ready to destroy anything that was not a panzercopter.

And then things began to get confusing.

PELAMUS AND his vengeful fleet arrived in Yemeni waters expecting to find typical company vessels carrying typical company cargo. Instead, his scout subs reported a small but wild battle near Suqutra. Most of the vessels involved appeared to be painted with YUP colors. Captain Pluturus didn't know what to make of the mayhem and was content to observe. He formed a line a kilometer away from the fight and watched. He tried to make out which side was which, but it quickly became apparent that those involved had little idea themselves. He tried to think of how such a battle could be swayed to his advantage.

There was a cargo pogo that seemed incapable of going airborne. It might carry something worth stealing, but it was the one thing there not labeled as a YUP ship. There were boats, all clearly YUP and most sinking or sunk. There were hovercrafts, also YUP, but they were shooting at the panzercopters, also YUP. The panzercopters were also firing on each other. Pluturus's post captains and commanders could offer little explanation. Cetaceans being a generally patient folk, he was content to wait and see how the situation sorted itself out. After ten minutes it became clear that, given the equal armament and armor of each vessel, that wouldn't happen soon enough.

Against his nature as it was, Pelamus decided to play peacekeeper. He ordered a jamming signal to break up the link communications. As he and his fleet lacked links and networks, this cut off any communication he couldn't monitor himself. The next step was to send a clear message that a new and superior force was present and wished to sort out the matter with words instead of weapons. As weapons were all the humans were presently aware of, he used his own to say hello.

All four of his boats launched surf torpedoes. A total of sixteen of the little monsters floated to the surface and began bobbing around the hovercraft, pogo, and floating chunks of YUP boats. They all sat on their fins, pointed at the sky. In under a second, any of the torpedoes could swim or blast off into any ship present, in the sky or on the water. As he hoped, the belligerents ceased their feud in order to figure out who had just won the fight.

VARG AND Mortiis were doing a fine job of repairing the field projectors. Violet had kept the copters at bay by firing when they came close, and even managed to cover the Theta hovercraft for a time. Everyone else aboard the cargo pogo hung on to the walls and tried not to get seasick. The instant Varg reconnected the last field plug and proclaimed the pogo ready to fly, Motoko spotted the torpedoes.

"Fields are back, we can go!" Varg called, then "We're good, we're online, we can go," and finally, "Why are we not going?" He closed the engineering panels and sat upright to see a spiny little cylinder flopping about on the water beside them.

Violet asked outright, "What are those?"

Motoko checked the defense monitors. "Torpedoes, at least a dozen of them in the water!"

"What's going on?" asked Varg.

"We seem to have been captured by a naval force," Veikko mused.

"And those aren't YUP," said Motoko.

"Then whose are they?" prompted Violet.

"No clue," she said. "Nobody dropped them."

Varg was at the flight controls, ready to take off. "All stop, then?"

Violet stuck by her artillery controls. She was a good shot. She could shoot one of the torpedoes if it was in the way. She might even take out two but wasn't about to begin unless it was their only option. She waited for a consensus.

"I say we stay put," said Mortiis.

"No," said Veikko, intending to punch through the stress with a mock American accent. "Damn the torpedoes, full speed ahead!"

"What kind of dumbass order is that?" demanded Violet, unaware of his jest.

"Don't you fucking read?" he retorted.

"No, I fucking don't. All stop!"

"Yes, all stop," he said, annoyed. Stress was running high, not only for those on the pogo. Omega's hovercraft didn't intend to stay passive. As V team watched, they fired with both batteries on the closest torpedoes. Theta followed their lead taking out three more, opening a wide gap in the torpedo net. Omega headed toward the gap; Theta remained as if to hold a door open for V team. Varg knew the signal and gently raised the pogo into the air.

Pelamus's front guard was sitting directly beneath Theta's hull. As they had disobeyed his implied order, he launched two more torpedoes straight up into their engine. On the surface, everyone saw the result. The hovercraft exploded from the inside in a great plume of fire, scattering its crew and mechanical innards across the water. Varg let the pogo flop right back down into the water. Omega set down as well. They might have escaped but weren't going to leave their allies behind.

The waters were still. Violet walked to the side of the pogo and looked out at the situation. She saw something moving in the water. Yellow shapes deep below, all of them moving in a serpentine line. As they grew shallower, she could see that they were segments in a great long line, a yellow-and-black mass. Then she could see the fins, jagged dorsal fins atop each segment. And she felt it. The pogo bobbed on displaced water—a very large amount of displaced water.

The YUP saw the shapes too and unwisely opened fire. Tired of topsider disobedience, Pelamus decided to make an example of them, one more clear than torpedoes had been. He emptied the collective bilges, and the sub leapt into open air to address the crowd. The great yellow-and-black serpent cleared the water, and with its weapons array lowered as a snake's jaw, he caught the offending panzercopter, cleaving it in half, then splashed down in a circle around the others. YUP-colored copters that hadn't fired weren't attacked, but the rest were quickly annihilated.

Pelamus was content with the demonstration but wanted to make it clear that his upper hand didn't end with one sub on the surface. He gave the order to break formation. Each black-and-yellow segment of the serpent disconnected from its neighbor and sailed into an encompassing formation, surrounding every topside craft with three individual craft. Icing the cake, his other subs came up slowly from the depths to surround the lot. Stillness prevailed again.

"Cetaceans," whispered Veikko calmly. "Pirates. They won't attack a cargo pogo till they know it's devoid of cargo."

The leviathans had shown such force and fury, it was clear nothing in the area could stop them. The few remaining copters slowly set down on the water as if to surrender. Omega turned off their floatation systems and came to a rest. As soon as everyone was on the surface, the torpedoes went belly up and withdrew their spines. They could still be rearmed instantly, but their message of reciprocation was clear. Violet didn't quite understand. "They have us. Why give a millimeter?"

Veikko answered, "Cetaceans are slaves to naval etiquette. Even the thieves are honor bound. They'll rescue the survivors and parlay. We'll be fine."

He was correct. Three other subs came to the surface. One began breaking into segments of smaller boats. Methodically, each miniboat made its way through wreckage to survivors in the water, picked them up, and allowed them aboard. As the boats got closer, Violet could see who piloted them. They wore suits like humans wore when they went underwater: yellow and black, lightly armored, with rubber fittings and joints. She couldn't see the faces behind the masks, which were painted with baroque detail, with jaws and fangs and tentacles and artistic flourishes that no land force would bother with.

Their actions were more efficient than their wardrobe. Once the living were aboard, half the boats reformed their sub. Another sub took the remaining hovercraft in tow; another strung up the two last copters as they floated. The last sub headed for the cargo pogo. Veikko motioned for everyone aboard to remain still as two suited Cetaceans began tying the pogo to their sub with some kind of line. It was the first actual braided hemp line Violet had ever seen outside of history class. It looked old and weak, but it did its job.

The Cetaceans stood guard as the subs began docking and extending gangplanks to one another. They drew closer and closer until all four were connected into a great barge, human survivors in the middle or on their tied vessels. One of the subs continued to change shape. The tower in the middle of the boat split down the middle and disgorged an internal chamber from its center. This chamber tracked across the top of the sub. Violet could see that it was carved out of wood. It was very ornate, more like part of an old castle than the bridge of any seafaring vessel she had ever seen. Its fine wooden doors opened to reveal one suited figure, his outfit painted with far more detail and carrying far more armor than the others. He stood and surveyed the humans around him, then walked up to the side of the cargo pogo with two guards. One of his cohorts spoke, his voice distorted by his armor. "Pelamus Pluturus, lord of the Mediterranean, lord of the depths of the Red Sea, lord of thieves, father of plunder, enemy of all human rich, and vengeance bound to slaughter the YUP!" He pounded his right boot, shaped to hold a wide flat foot, on the deck.

Then Pelamus stepped forward and said something that few land folk would have expected. "Permission to come aboard?"

Veikko fearlessly responded, "Permission granted, sir."

Pelamus came aboard. He looked around the cavernous interior of the cargo section and at the controls in the small cockpit and passenger section. He spoke with great formality.

"This is not a YUP vessel?"

"No, sir."

"Are you allied with the YUP?"

"No, sir."

"And your cargo?"

"Stolen," Veikko lied, "by the YUP."

"That was the cause of battle?"

"Yes, sir."

Pelamus stood still. He might have been smiling in his elaborate helmet. He might have been deciding to kill them all. After a few seconds of tense silence, he spoke again. "We should like to borrow your vessel to hold a gam and sort out the survivors."

"Granted, sir."

Veikko seemed to have made the fish's good side. He whispered to his team as Pelamus disembarked that he had not put them on friendly terms. He had only given him enough respect not to get killed instantly. The Cetaceans pushed every drenched survivor into the cargo pogo hold. Three suited captains came from their subs, one with two crew carrying a fine wooden table. The pogo proved a good meeting room. Its hold was large enough to accommodate everyone, and it kept out the noise of the ocean and twisting burning wreckage. Once all were seated and Pelamus's ornate chair arrived, he sat and spoke again.

"Who here call themselves Yuppies?"

A few people timidly raised their hands. Violet thought she recognized a couple of Sasha's men among them. Pelamus made a hand signal. His men stepped forward and executed every one of them with harpoon guns.

"Anyone else?"

Nobody raised their hand this time.

"Good. Now, who are the rest of you?"

Veikko stepped forward.

"My mates and I are from the cold edge of the north. We came as merchants, but Yuppies in the birds took all we had. Those birds have flown. The Ellines in the hovercraft defended us from the YUP."

Pelamus looked to the Karpathians. Everyone from each hovercraft was present, all alive, though some a bit crispy. Pelamus surveyed them and considered the situation. He said, "Then your cargo is lost. We shall have this vessel for ourselves. You may go free. We offer safe passage and medical treatment for your ally Ellines if you accept."

"We accept and offer all gratitude, sir," Veikko said with a slight bow of his head.

Pelamus nodded, a motion that suggested he had a very long neck under his armor. Then he kept his word. His men took over the pogo—after Varg made sure to wipe its memory core of anything Valhalla related—then directed the surviving Karpathians and Valhalla teams to the subs. The boats broke their tight barge formation as suited crew directed the humans below. Violet, Varg, and Veikko were taken with

Mortiis, Motoko, and a few Karpathians through dank, cramped corridors, through a maze of baroque decor that cramped the space even more. None of it appeared practical, all form before function, but on closer inspection Violet spotted functionality hidden throughout. They ended in quarters near the ship's stern, where their escort asked, "Destination?"

One of the hovercraft men responded, "All of us to Karpathos."

Veikko added, "If it should please your captain."

The escort stood up straight with a click in his finned heels and left. They spoke freely.

"I'm glad you know all that polite crap," Varg said with a laugh.

"I lived with that shit every day for my entire youth." Veikko grunted. "I fucking hate Cetaceans."

Violet whispered, "Don't say that too loud."

"Don't worry, their hearing's terrible in air," he explained.

"Well, we completed our mission."

"At the cost of two of our hoverfleet," said Omega's leader.

"And much of our skin," said a Theta. "How are the fish with human medicine?"

"Your men will be fine," Veikko replied.

"And my lunch!" said another Greek. "My lunch was on that hovercraft." He buried his face in his hands. "The first real food I bought in a year. How much is lost in war…."

The Omega leader patted him on the back. "We got off easy. Who the hell are these—these people?"

"Pirates," said Veikko. "No clue why they broke up a Yuppie fight."

"Pirates?" Varg laughed incredulously.

"No, no, sea pirates. An old tradition. They don't traffic information or bootleg entertainment. They steal cargo from intercompany waters."

"He said he was after the YUP," remarked Motoko. "Do they usually go for companies?"

"Never in their own seas. This guy's strange."

"You mean stranger than the rest of the fish," said Mortiis.

"Yes."

Violet felt very tired. She kept replaying the events of the day in her mind. It had gone haywire, but everyone seemed to be ending up in the right place. They had lost a cargo pogo, but Valhalla had five more. What, she wondered, did fish need with a cargo pogo anyway? From what little she knew of them, these were not what she expected. She had questions to ask Veikko but she stored them away in a partition. They didn't matter just then. All that mattered was that they'd survived the fight, that Balder and Vibeke were on their way. Vibs was gone with Mishka. The triumphant achievement of their mission goal seemed more depressing than failure.

After hours of slow sea travel, they arrived at Karpathos. They disembarked with great pomp and politeness at the island port and followed the Omega and Theta teams. The injured men who had traveled by another sub were all healed. Whatever Cetacean doctor lurked below the depths of the other subs was apparently quite skilled. With links functioning again, they sent an all clear to Alf. They received only a receipt and a request to return north. They followed the teams through a Karpathian forest, where a secluded elevator took them underground. Karpathos base had no extravagant views. It was all hallways and rooms and hangar bays, the last of which they went straight toward. From there they would take a pogo back home to await news of Balder and Vibeke with bated breath.

They all got some sleep on the way home, tired as they were from the battle and the tedious sea voyage. They were all so stressed and drained from the day that they failed to notice something about Pelamus's boat that would have given them cause for concern. Amid all the lavish decor and all the carvings, there were some panels that depicted Pelamus Pluturus standing triumphant over a burning, broken Valhalla.

Chapter XII: Congo

VIBEKE'S MIND was racing. As the aerial mosh pit faded away to the horizon and the sounds of that battle turned to dull thuds and thumps, she was left alone with Mishka. Marduk and the generator concealing Balder flew just under half a kilometer to their side. Aboard each copter were only two pilots, and a gunner, and the passengers from Valhalla. Their links were all turned off.

Vibeke felt powerless. Partly because her team was stuck in a fight that she couldn't join, but more so because of the extraordinarily powerful woman by her side. Vibs always felt weak next to her, pinned under her, even watched by her. Even when they might have been in love in the beginning, everything Mishka did was like a reminder of her superior strength and tougher mentality. Even the plain fact she was taller was intimidating. Mishka's very way of speaking suggested superiority—not egotism, just simple matter-of-fact power. Power she used without even trying: Every time Mishka touched her, it was like a stolen grope. Every time she caught Mishka looking at her, it was a deep, penetrating gaze.

"Eye rape," she'd called it once, talking to Violet as they planned the infiltration of Sasha's militia. Vibeke didn't fail to notice that when she told Violet how it felt, Violet quickly averted her own eyes away from Vibeke's body. Violet was, to Vibeke's mind, the exact opposite sort of person. She was strong, willful, everything good about Mishka but not as a threat, rather as a counterpart. She didn't mind when Violet watched her. And Mishka thought Violet was stupid, slower, a lesser version of herself. Maybe she was right, Vibs admitted. Violet wasn't as smart or strong, and that's why Vibs cared so much more for her. *A goddess is intimidating, but Violet is human*, she thought, *tangible and warm and human... and so terribly far away.*

Vibs reclined in Mishka's arms that whole trip, buff arms protecting her from the wind, hot breath on her neck. She'd never felt more alone. It was a not a woman but a mission that sat behind her, holding on to her. Vibs shut down whatever part of her brain could be called herself and focused on work. Work meant deception. So she rolled over to face Mishka and kissed her neck, let her head rest against Mishka's chest, and tried not to let herself admit that she felt safe there and loved.

Marduk, alone in his copter's hold, just stared at the big heavy generator he had stolen. He felt sad saying farewell to his old home in the north. He wished someone wise like Balder was nearby to help him through the shift.

VIOLET FELL into her bunk, as tired as she had ever been, and completely incapable of sleep. The room smelled like boys, felt half-empty, felt too big. All that lay on Vibeke's bed were two books. Violet tried to read the titles but gave up after a few attempts to match the letters with the images in her memory. She couldn't do it with the books on their sides. *Mishka can read*, she thought. *I can't.*

Violet hopped out of bed and showered, let the sound waves gently pulsate the dirt and grime from her, let the air cleanse away the smell of the Cetaccan subs. Then she left the barracks. She wandered the ravine and had never seen it emptier. Everyone was asleep. She even passed by Wulfgar in his cage, sleeping curled up like a kitten, snoring an uncharacteristically purr-like snore. The brig, half-assembled nearby, was still puny-looking. Violet tried to be useful by noting some design changes to be made but gave up before long. She didn't want to be useful that night.

She wanted Vibs and didn't care to hide it from herself. She couldn't admit what she wanted Vibs for, or just how overpowering that need was, but she knew that whatever was alive inside her was worse than she had feared when she had spoken to Nergal. It might have been the only thing Violet had ever encountered that she couldn't hope to control. So for that night when she was alone, when she had no mission or duty, no prospect of sleep or consolation from her team, she let herself hope and indulged every thought of what she could never do with Vibeke when she got back.

THE COPTERS landed at night, but it was still hot as hell, so hot that Vibeke's suit turned its rubber sections into netting and began puron cycling. She had hoped the enemy base would be something like Valhalla, but it was in every way the exact opposite. The base was small because it was mobile, resembling the body of an aircraft carrier sailing smoothly atop the jungle canopy, an ocean of treetops in the moonlight, swaying in a hot breeze. Vibs found it a most unnatural surrounding.

The panzercopters sunk into the carrier on massive flat lifts. Mishka and Vibeke hopped off and traversed the deck toward the island, a mess of artillery and white metal. The whole carrier was white, ghostlike under the moon. Every man on deck wore white, even one man with a thick black face mask. As Sasha spotted them and ran closer, Vibs could see it wasn't a mask but a thick, hideous beard.

He greeted Mishka with three kisses on her cheeks. He turned to Vibeke and offered the same, a bit more awkwardly. She let him hug her and rub his gangly wool pad of a face against her cheek, smiling all the while as if she had been waiting her whole life to get pummeled with the man's scruffy mug.

"Welcome to Africa!" he shouted, then spoke to Mishka in Russian. Vibs couldn't understand it without her link, and she tried to hide that she didn't care to. She did that well enough that he apologized and begged them to come inside and see the bridge, speaking as if he were inviting them into a gazebo for tea. He shouted to the men on the deck, ordering them to start hooking up and testing the new generator. Vibeke wished she could have seen Balder's escape, but she was obligated to follow Sasha and make small talk and convince him of her genuine love for her worst enemy.

Balder's generator was taken immediately to an enclosure on the beakhead, which held the other Mjölnir system. The new generator was to be searched and tested to make sure it was not a decoy carrying something so ill-conceived as a hostile agent. When Balder heard the men beginning to pry off the top lid, he spared them the trouble and popped it off, quickly stunning everyone around him with his microwave. He was relieved to find himself out of sight of any more than the men he had knocked out. He had brought ten cerebral bores and only needed three. He set one on each head and let his teammates back in Valhalla take over.

As Balder cut into the bow and began his covert stroll through enemy territory, his team began hacking into the brains of the unconscious. They recorded and copied everything the men kept stored in partitioned memory, then set to work charting their wetware. Within minutes, B team had convinced them that the generator was intact and functional, that they had never gone unconscious, and that for the next few days they would defend the honor of this inviolate generator. However poorly it worked, they would not let a soul but themselves open it for repair.

Meanwhile, Sasha sat down with Vibeke and Marduk in his ready room and spoke to his new recruits. "When I first arrived in Tanganyika, I went over the logs, African news, Congo history, everything. The big headline of the day was 'Nine bodies found beheaded.' Not somewhere in the jungle but right on the shore, right in the yard of my new owners. The next day, the headline was 'Nine heads found.' The next day it was 'Bodies do not match heads.'

"They sold me here for a petty tribal conflict, where one tribe got a man elected, and he planned genocide for his old rivals. And that sad state of affairs is the norm here. The world at peace? It's a lie, an absolute lie. This is not peace, not at all. Ages ago, long before our parents were conceived, this place was even worse. And in that diseased era—and I do mean diseased, for this land was infected with so many illnesses we couldn't read about them all in a lifetime—there were people called missionaries who came here to try to sort out the land, to teach the inhabitants.

"It was their burden, their God-given plight to tame this place. Of course, that ended with the banning of the church. Those who ended the church, they knew not what they did, and I forgive them, we must forgive them, but we must try to repair the damage done. That's why I'm still here, after that latest tribal conflict ended. And it ended because I alone brought Western strategy to its fights, to continue in their spirit—to fight no longer for their tribal honor but for their very souls. When I have taken the land, spanked the children, and brought them to silence, I will reestablish the church over this land as it was at its height.

"Like Spain," he declared with infinite pride in the name. "Long before it was owned by Portugal and long, long before it was owned by Asda or UNEGA, it was owned by a company called Vatican. And they knew how to run a business. They had a division, or perhaps a subsidiary, called the Inquisition. And it brought order, moral guidance to the land! Its CEO, Thomas De Torquemada, was a true genius of the era. Centuries before Trump"—he genuflected—"Thomas established systems that made use of any means to seek out people who didn't believe or didn't comply….

"That's who I am, Vibeke, Marduk. I am Torquemada returned in this most corrupt and wild era, in this corrupt and vile continent…." Sasha reclined in his chair and casually polished the peace badges on his chest, appallingly proud of himself. He went on and on.

Vibeke looked around the room as he spoke. It was full of old artifacts. Not weapons, like those in Balder's office, but organic remains. There was a pelt of something yellow with a mane, a basket made from what might have been the foot of some extinct monster, even sculptures made of what Vibs assumed to be walrus tusks, though she couldn't imagine a happy walrus in that weather. She did anything to try to distract herself from the implications of Sasha's words, because she was deathly afraid she might agree with any of it.

Mishka nodded along, impressed with her brother's way with words. It was easy enough in the end for Vibeke play to Sasha's ego, compared to that night when she would have to play to his sister's lust. It was all necessary, Vibs reminded herself. She had to stop this madman, and to do it she had to do what spies do. They put up with the heat by remembering their cool, cold home. They put up with the degenerate philosophy by thinking of how to annihilate it. She would put up with Mishka by—she would find a way, somehow.

Mishka took Vibeke to her quarters, luxurious for the carrier but hot and humid, sickeningly hot and humid even at night. The worst weather for sex. She had to do it to the sound of bugs scratching on the mosquito netting. She had to do it with the rat she hated more than anyone else on earth. But she did it, and did it well enough as to be believed. She was okay for a while, at least until she lay in Mishka's arms, pressed against her naked in the hammock. Then the insects stopped chirping, and the wind blew gently in, and she was left with nothing to keep her blood boiling, no annoyance to hide behind, only a cool breeze and an embrace she couldn't help but enjoy. Then she wasn't okay anymore. There was pain training, there was death training, there was kill training. But there was no training for love or hate, and no drug in her armor pockets to stop her eyes from watering. She was lucky Mishka mistook her tears for sweat.

The rest was easy by comparison. She observed Sasha's men working on the generator, declaring angrily when pressed that they almost had it working. She observed what she could of their course through the forest, but without a link, it was all just trees and bizarre howls from within. Mishka abandoned her Thaco armor on the first night in favor of a relaxed white jumpsuit. Though it wasn't as comfortable, Vibs stuck with her armor. It might have been questionable, but there was no way she would abandon it. So strong was her hope that she would be leaving any second that she wouldn't leave herself hunting through closets when she could be escaping.

Days passed. Vibeke gleaned little useful knowledge or intel. There was simply nothing to learn unless she could snoop around below decks, and that was Balder's job. That left her with nothing but free time with Mishka, whose libido seemed to grow by the day. Finally, in the hope of releasing some of the tension, she challenged Mishka to a sparring match. Mishka was delighted at the idea. Vibeke vowed to kill her any way she could in that match.

Of course, she couldn't. Mishka wouldn't let the match become anything more than a sweaty, playful romp. That would have been bad enough, but when Vibeke got a punch in, it felt so good she enjoyed it, and the instant she realized she was enjoying any part of it, her mind was wrecked. She felt dizzy, angry, pained, too many feelings to register as anything but misery. She ran for Mishka's quarters, the only home she had there. Mishka didn't guess why she ran away. She might have figured it out, but an alarm sounded first.

The false generator had been found out. Vibs welcomed the snap back into survival mode. It was time to go, and she couldn't wait to leave without saying good-bye. She turned her link on and sent Balder the alarm. Within seconds, the ceiling of Mishka's room let loose a shower of sparks, and he dropped in. His Tikari followed in caterpillar form and receded into his chest. Vibs stood up, strong as she could look, and spoke without a quiver in her voice.

"Collect anything good?"

"Tons, tons, and tons," he responded by link. "Ready to go?"

Vibeke felt as if she'd been harrowed from hell. "Fuck yes."

"Follow me. Take this," Balder said as he led her from the room. She expected to be handed something, but it came by link. It was a massive, complex map file. She loaded it into her vision as they ran down the white passage. Suddenly, an outline of the passage overlaid the genuine article. Balder linked again, "We'll need it later. These bulkheads have scramblers. We're heading for the lowest deck. They have a half dozen tanks hanging from this thing like offspring. Valhalla could use some tanks. I'll link you hot-wiring instructions in a—"

Balder was interrupted by the scramblers he had just mentioned. Though the map stayed the same, several of the square blocks that had formed the bulkheads fell out of place and darted across the hall to reshape the passageway. Instead of the right turn they were to take, it now went straight forward, and in it stood Mishka with four men in white armor.

Balder stopped fast in his tracks. Vibeke almost slipped on the smooth tile deck. She looked at Mishka and saw her face was livid, murderous. She stood so still time seemed to have lost its grasp on her. Vibeke couldn't move either. The terrible moment forced her to look into Mishka's eyes. Mishka knew everything, had figured it all out the instant she saw a hole where the generator's innards should have been. As she heard the alarm, Mishka tried to tell herself that Vibeke wasn't part of the deception, but now Vibeke stood there with Balder, transfixed.

Balder pulled Vibeke out of the terrible trance and pushed her to run back the way they had come. He broadcast a jamming signal that deafened Vibeke's link and, more importantly, the bulkhead scrambler controls. It could not affect Tikari links, so Mishka launched hers, not as a butterfly but as a spinning cluster of blades, toward Vibs' neck. It cut her hair as it passed and lodged in the bulkhead. Vibs and Balder ran past it and around a corner as it turned into a bug and pried itself free.

Mishka and her men were giving chase, audible like a stampede coming at them from behind. Vibeke ran, but she felt pulled backward like a magnet, not by fatigue but by rage. She didn't want to escape. She wanted to kill, to destroy that face that had stared at her, that was still burnt into her mind's eye. The throwing star Tikari came again and hit her in the shoulder, lodging in her armor. Again it turned into a bug and tried to free itself. Vibs acted instinctively by springing her own and sending it to get the thing off her back. It jumped forward from her chest, then gave a short rocket burst to strike Mishka's Tikari hard, knocking it back several meters. Vibs couldn't stop to let hers back in, so it flew alongside her, keeping watch for the other.

By the time she and Balder came to the lowest deck, they heard no footsteps behind them. Vibs thought they might have outrun Mishka's troop, but Balder knew otherwise. He motioned for her to stand back at the hatch to the outside. Vibeke checked the map and understood there was another route to the tank bay. Mishka could be right outside. Balder pulled some explosives from his armor and placed them on the corners of the hatch. Vibeke hoped Mishka was just outside when they blew.

They took cover, and Balder triggered the charges. The hatch shot away at a hundred kph. Hot African air flooded in as it flew across the tank-bay catwalk and fell to the jungle below. No sign of Mishka. Balder ran out to the bay and ended his link jam. He started sending Vibeke tank manuals as she walked outside.

They were under the carrier on a railless catwalk running fore to aft. Vibs could now see the carrier's eight legs picking their way between the trees. Small one-person tanks hung from the belly of the craft, each secured upside down. The tanks were clearly high-end. Each had four legs with ports for four more, heavy armor, and armament, all painted white. Balder began hacking into the first tank to his right. Vibeke's Tikari landed on her shoulder, keeping watch on the hatchway.

The hatch at the other end of the catwalk was intact. Vibeke took out her microwave and steadied her aim. She set the weapon to kill. Balder's Tikari crawled from his chest and jumped onto the ceiling as he worked. It leveled a scanning beam at the closed hatch and waited with Vibeke. Balder worked.

Suddenly his Tikari broadcast a warning to her. "Explosive bolts." Mishka didn't have to blast through the hatch. She was doing it as an offensive tactic. An instant after the warning, the second hatch blew across the catwalk. Vibs ducked at the message, and the hatch flew over her head by centimeters. She could see the armored men coming. Balder's Tikari fell from the ceiling and launched itself as a boomerang off to the side of the carrier. Vibeke began firing at the men, but her beams only glanced off their armor. Balder's Tikari had more luck. It continued its circle around to their necks, through their necks, and back to Balder's hand. The men and their heads fell from the catwalk.

Balder had activated the first tank. He wiped the blood off and chested his Tikari, then motioned for Vibeke to hop into the tank. She didn't. Mishka was standing in the hatchway. The devil's stare didn't work this time. Vibs was ready to fight. She linked to Balder, "Get in the tank. Get out of here."

He responded by voice. "That's my line, kid."

"Do it," Vibs demanded. "The bitch is mine."

Mishka heard her and did not like being called a bitch. Balder tried to step in front of Vibs, but she pushed him back toward the tank. Mishka ran, Vibs ran; Balder knew the score and got out of the way. Mishka and Vibeke both attacked in anger, so both were on their worst form. It was not at all like sparring. It was two sloppy attempts as murder. Both sent their Tikaris, and a razor-blade butterfly and a dagger-winged ladybug fought in the air by their masters, set on AI as their owners were so engulfed by hate that they could not control them.

Because the Tikaris were on AI, Mishka was able to do the cruelest thing a warrior from Valhalla could do to another. Vibs thought she was aiming for her head, so she blocked in the wrong place, and Mishka punched her target—Vibeke's second link. It snapped off and instantly the ladybug shriveled into a dagger. Vibeke screamed.

Balder heard the scream, but he was busy defending against a new torrent of Sasha's men, coming from the nearer hatch onto the catwalk. But he knew what had happened. There was no scream like it. He had heard it before, and his heart broke for her as she fought. And Vibeke fought on. Mishka's functioning Tikari attacked her and cut her skin to ribbons. Mishka attacked her and managed to break her right elbow backward, but Vibeke kept fighting.

She fought her way across the catwalk to her Tikari, only a dagger now, but a dagger was still a weapon. She slashed at Mishka, but the superior insect defended its master, leaving her hands free to attack. In agony in every way, Vibs fought on, growing tired fast as the fight grew futile.

Balder killed the last in a squad of oncoming men and ran for their fight. He didn't try to win it. He just took Vibs by the collar and dragged her to a tank. His caterpillar leapt from his chest to hold off the butterfly. Mishka kept fighting, but Vibeke could only kick at her. Vibs dropped her dagger on the way. Balder tried to push her into the active tank, but she broke free of his grip. She had to retrieve her dagger. She fell to the catwalk and raced toward it. She found it covered by Mishka's foot.

Mishka was out of breath from anger, not fatigue. Balder was standing ready to fight her. Mishka knew that if he and Vibs attacked together, she wouldn't survive. Balder knew that if he stayed to fight, Vibs would probably get killed. Vibeke, at that moment, only wanted the corpse of her Tikari. Their states formed a brief truce in which Mishka ventured to talk. "Why, Vibeke? We have so much to do here!"

"For Valhalla," she said through her teeth.

"For the fools up north? Vibeke, you and I loved—"

"You and I were nothing! You and I were a cover story! Valhalla was in our blood, Mishka. You betrayed us all!"

Mishka looked as though she felt sorry for her. It was a near motherly expression that filled Vibs with hate, because it was the expression she used to have as she taught her the craft. Mishka took her foot off the Tikari to crouch down. "You never had a real family. Sasha is my real family, as you could have been. Valhalla is nothing."

Vibs grabbed the blade and tucked it close to her chest, in pain that it wouldn't go in. In that pain was the clarity to speak, to give a warning to the monster before her face. "Valhalla won't forgive this."

"God will forgive me," Mishka said, resolved and sure of herself.

It broke Vibeke's cool again. "God? You have bigger things than God after you now!" she screamed. *"When I'm done with you, you'll envy Judas in hell!"*

Balder sensed that the brief truce was at an end. He couldn't let the fight go on. He pulled Vibs up and threw her full force into the tank. Mishka just stood there as Sasha arrived with another squad of white-armored men. Balder told the tank to raise its armor and drop to the jungle floor. As the tank's shield closed, Mishka sent one last dart at Vibeke. Not the Tikari that fluttered on her shoulder, but one word. "Weakling…." she whispered. Vibeke heard it, and the tank broke away.

The Valkyries could have stayed to fight on, to try to kill the heads of the traitor force. Mishka could have chased them. Sasha could have sent his whole fleet after them. But nobody made a move. War had been declared between the forces, that much was certain, but they left each other in pain so deep that the most basic pleasure of a fight had abandoned them. They were all drained of any will to fight on. For the moment.

Balder drove the tank across the jungle and across the Sahara Desert with Vibeke crammed into the small shield dome. She cried in rage, then cried in pain, then resolved her mind in hatred. Cradling her dead blade, trying to force it back into her chest, she slowly began to accept that it would never take its place within her again. Instead she vowed she would bury it in Mishka, the traitor, her most loathsome and ultimate nemesis. And her heart was at rest, its wounds sealed with anger and its fate sealed with purpose.

The tank galloped across the land all the way to the Sahara in only a few hours, as fast on varied terrain as most pogos were in clear sky. Balder slowed down and let it trot into the back of the cargo pogo Alopex had sent for them. Then he opened the shield onboard and set

Vibeke down in the passenger bay, asleep. He took out a first aid kit and treated what he could, her broken bones and cuts, but not even Niide would be able to fix the rest.

VIOLET WATCHED the pogo land. She and the team had run to the pogo pad as soon as they got Balder's link, a full explanation of what had happened. Violet didn't know what to do. The team was at a loss to help their comrade. They watched her walk off the pogo, holding her dead knife. They couldn't find any words to say. Vibeke walked right past them. They followed her to the med bay, suddenly grateful for the clear wall. Violet realized the wall might have been left clear not in mockery of those inside, but in compassion for those without.

They watched Niide check her over, saw the nurses fix her Tikari link, but nobody tried to take the blade from her. She just held it by her chest. Violet walked away. She didn't want to see Vibs like that. There was nothing for her to do there, not yet. She had waited days to see Vibs again, but now Violet felt utterly useless to her. She knew how to fight so many battles, to kill so many in so many ways, to accomplish feats of warfare most soldiers couldn't imagine, but for the person who needed her, she was nothing just then, completely worthless.

She wanted to find Balder. He must have had some use for her. She could process information, intel, something, she didn't care what. Alopex listed him across the ravine in Alf's library. She jogged over and noticed Veikko right behind her. Same reasons, she assumed. He stopped near the pogo pad and watched the tank walking down to the floor. He stayed with it to help. Violet continued on to the library. Alopex didn't list it as locked, so she pushed open the door.

She was hit by bloodcurdling fear and terror. The Geki stood between Balder and Alf. One of them twisted, moving slightly as if it were looking at her, though there was no face. Suddenly they flew upward into nothingness and the fear was gone. It was brief, short, done. That's what Violet told herself, but she still fell to her knees from the shock of it. She put her hand over her pounding heart and sat down in the doorway.

“That’s why you knock,” said Alf. Balder walked to her and lent a hand. He helped her stand up and directed her, not back to the door but to the couch. She sat next to Alf, who rubbed his eyes and brow.

“They didn’t ask questions,” Balder explained. “They knew everything Vibs and I had learned. As Sasha’s actions are more in our realm of action than their own, they will not act. They only came by to tell us that they will not interfere with any attempt we make to take them down.”

Alf grunted. “Pointless old farts, aren’t they?” He sighed, thought for a moment, and added, “They have their job and we have ours.”

“And what is ours?” Violet asked. “Have you decided what to do?”

“We decide tonight,” he said, looking at her with all the lenses in his MMR eye. “You are not with Vibeke right now… because you think you have nothing to offer her?”

She nodded in shame.

Alf went on, “We neglected to train you for that, didn’t we? Go to her and be there, that’s all. It will do her little good, but little is more than none.”

She stood up as if it were an order from a drill sergeant. She had something to do, orders straight from the top, and with that she could go back. She marched out to the med bay. There, through the clear wall, she saw Vibeke sitting with Varg and Veikko. Veikko had gone back instinctively. Violet would have to walk in and explain that she needed Alf to tell her what to do. It was too shameful to consider. She could imagine the scene and didn’t want it to play out. Vibs had Varg and Veikko. She had nurses trying to take her dagger’s bones for another Tikari. She didn’t need Violet stumbling to speak.

Violet knew it was fear. Not fear of pain or fear, like the Geki, but some petty weasel kind of fear that was keeping her away. She rationalized it, convinced herself it was instinct, convinced herself Vibs would be better off without her just then. It was all feeble crap, and she knew it, but she had enough willpower to make it real, and she didn’t enter the med bay. She walked away before they saw her. She hated herself for doing it all the while, so more or less subconsciously she wanted to punish herself for it. She knew just the man for that and walked right to the brig.

Wulfgar had been interred there only hours ago, as soon as Violet admitted the brig was impervious to escape and Alf gave the go-ahead to move him. Cato had told her in passing that Wulfgar seemed happy in his new cell, though she hadn't cared to hear from Cato at the time, or about Wulfgar. She'd only wanted to see Vibeke again. *How times change*, she thought.

The brig had a link label now that it was up: Gleipnir. Violet didn't bother to query Alopex for how it got the name. She was content just to hate it. Valhalla loved its bizarre old mythic names. *Call it the damn brig,* she thought. *That's what it is*. She walked past a couple of empty hexagonal cells and sat down on the floor across from Wulfgar's. She glanced at the bars, the detectors, the systems all designed to keep him in, the systems designed to keep him alive and prevent him from linking out (if he had a link). And in the middle of it all was a well-groomed man with friendly eyes, smiling.

"I love looking at you, you know," he said softly. "You tease me with yourself at my hungriest, and hunger is my favorite seasoning for girl meat."

"You like your new office?" she taunted.

"It's better than the cage but still smells like fish breath. Do I have you to thank for it?"

"You have me to thank for the buttresses, the lack of windows, and a few other security matters that the architects underplanned."

"It's not so different from København. I had to worry about the same things there, from the opposite side. But as long as I live, you're kidding yourself that you're outside the bars. You're in the cage too, girl."

"Could have fooled me."

"I did, I am, I will again. I love when you visit. I shouldn't be too distressed if I wake up one day to find myself a hundred years old and still enjoying your visits. So why now, purple cow? Why let me milk you?"

Violet had to think about it. She really didn't know why she was there, especially now of all times. She was sitting there aloof, talking to the one guy she most surely shouldn't be talking to. A man whom she was still painfully aware had digested some of her. She lied, "You put things in perspective."

"A purple cow full of a bull's shit. You still don't know," he laughed.

She was as clear to him as the med bay walls. Why the hell was she so desperate not to see Vibs? Was it because she couldn't bear to see her weak? To see her hurt? Because she was afraid Vibs might lash out at her? All the time Vibeke had been gone, Violet had held an odd sort of hope that when she got back, Vibs would jump out of a pogo and hug her. Mishka would be out of the equation. Violet might have even told Vibs… things. Her thoughts were fractured, discordant. She had no chance of understanding why she came to talk to Wulfgar when Vibeke needed her. So she asked her makeshift shrink, "No, honestly, I don't. You want to tell me?"

Wulfgar stood up. "It's because you never had time to adjust to life without Mom and Pop." He pointed his finger as he spoke, as if giving a lecture to a student. "Your army sergeants gave you a taste of parental compassion and order, but the leaders here do not. The place is relaxed and soft and gooey, like the old queers that run it. So I"—he placed his hands on his chest with great pride—"I, as the lone heterosexual on base, attract you like moth to flame, and I know even if you don't why the moth seeks the flame! Because it longs to get burned!"

She had only one thing to say to that. "Damn, you're weird."

"And you're cute, Violet."

Maybe she saw him from time to time to remind herself why she hated the guy. She certainly did at that moment. But then, why did she suddenly feel so much better when she spoke to him? She had the last time and now, she had a sudden will to go find Vibeke. She had the strength to apologize for not being there before. She could even say honestly where she had gone. She was happy Vibeke was back and ready to lend her a shoulder to cry on.

Violet walked out of the brig and headed for the med bay. As soon as she was out the opaque heavy door, she walked, clumsily, right smack into the first person passing by and toppled over on top of her. Only as she pushed herself up did she recognizc Vibeke lying under her.

"Happy to see me again, Vi?"

Violet pronounced a rapid series of apologies and exclamations of condolence as she tried to stand and help Vibeke up. She considered herself lucky she hadn't been stabbed by the dead Tikari. But to Violet's surprise, Vibs wasn't holding it.

"Where's your Tikari?" Violet demanded. Then she cringed. *Oh shit*, she thought. *Great way to say hello.*

Vibeke was so surprised at it that she laughed. Violet thought it was a sob, hugged her immediately, and spewed forth another string of apologies. Then, realizing how pathetic her words were, she stepped back, and leaned against the brig. She looked at Vibeke, tried to look her in the eyes. She looked broken, tired, angry, hurt, strong. In the strangest way, she looked sexier than Violet had ever seen her. The instant she thought that, Violet almost smacked herself to wake up. She finally got a couple of coherent words out. "Can I start over?"

Vibs nodded. Violet took half a minute to think of what to say, finally blurting out a useless, "Hello."

"Hi."

"Uh, how are you holding up?"

"I'm not a damn victim, Violet."

"I know, Vibs." She sighed.

They looked at each other for a while. Vibeke felt quite as useless for speech as Violet did. For the last few minutes, Varg and Veikko had coddled her to the point where she had jumped off the medical table and walked out. She didn't want to deal with the crap people gave to weaklings. She didn't want to deal with nurses explaining how they could make a new Tikari. She got so sick of them asking for it that she gave in to a sudden surge of anger and stabbed Nurse Taake in the leg with it, and left the poor thing in his care. *They're in med bay*, she thought. *They can deal with a stab wound.* Vibeke just wanted to get out of the friendliness and find Violet.

Violet wouldn't coddle her. Violet wouldn't try to convince her to move on or get a new Tikari. Violet wouldn't understand or even know what to say to her, but she would at least be Violet, and that would be something. So after their horrible reacquaintance, Violet and Vibeke sat down together against the fortified, buttressed brig wall and got a chance to breathe and finally talk.

"What were you doing in the brig?" Vibs asked.

"Talking to Wulfgar. It's easier to say the wrong words in front of your enemies than your friends."

"Fuck words."

Violet was somewhat surprised to hear her say it. She spent so much time reading them. She didn't know Vibs was merely fed up with consolations and took it almost as a justification of Violet's own lack of a use for them. Though she did wonder what had been sitting on Vibeke's bed while she was away. "What are those books on your bed?"

"Two of Mishka's favorites." Not what Violet wanted to hear. "I was looking for the right lies to tell her. Didn't get to use any of 'em. Aloe said you were with Alf before you came here. He say anything?"

"No, we'll all go over what to do tonight. Dreams, I assume. Today he was meeting with the Geki. I walked right into the scary zone."

"Oh, that sucks."

"Not as bad as your day."

"Maybe not." Vibs paused and rubbed the empty hole in her chest. "It wasn't the worst week of my life. It will all work out when we go to destroy them. I'm sure we will. And if the elders don't send us to do the job, I'll stow away…. I'm really going to enjoy killing her. I don't even care if we get her brother, or the tanks, or the hammer, or the whole of Africa. I'll make her pay for it all herself."

Violet tried to affirm what she said, to play along. Now wasn't the time to argue, just to subtly remind her that she had people with her, that she wasn't alone. "Valhalla will handle the rest. We'll make sure we get assassinations, even if they call it a sidetrack."

"Side? Valhalla is the sidetrack. Africa's the sidetrack. I love you like a sister, Vi, but I'd give up the team to get her. I'd have to."

Violet asked despite herself, "Like a sister?"

Vibs grew annoyed. "What would you prefer? You wanna fuck me too now?"

Violet was tempted to say "Maybe a little" but held back. She might have admitted that she wanted Mishka dead so she could have Vibs to herself, or even so things would go back to normal, if killing the problem could make them the way they used to be. *It could*, Violet thought. *If killing the problem didn't solve things, then what was the point of Valhalla?* Violet resolved to comfort Vibs subtly, to remind her she was still sane. "Don't let her turn you into a total mental case, Vibs."

Vibeke was full of finely directed anger. "Then don't let her get away. When we get to Africa, don't let her get away or die by any hand but mine. Then it will all go away."

"And if she escapes?"

"Then we chase her."

Violet remembered an old story about that sort of obsession, something from Varg's movies. It was about a guy who wrecked everything and everyone around him to get revenge. There was one classic line she never forgot. She repeated it to Vibs as best she could. "Chase her around perdition's flames?"

Vibeke was a little surprised and a little amused. "I thought you couldn't read those books on my bed."

Violet was suddenly very interested in those books. "They made a book from *Wrath of Khan*?"

Vibeke laughed. Violet didn't know why. She was sure she had just said something stupid. It wouldn't be the first time. But that didn't matter. Vibeke had laughed, and that was worth whatever mistake caused it. They sat in silence for a moment as Nurse Kampfar walked up to them, holding a Carlin blade with a ladybug-colored hilt. He handed it to Vibeke, who accepted it without a word. Violet looked at it in Vibeke's hands, a cold dead Tikari, still sharp to the molecule, though the med team had taken its bones. Her own bug stirred in her chest. It surely wanted to peek out, but Violet wasn't going to let Vibs see it. The sight of it could only hurt her.

Vibeke threw her dagger as hard as she could into the wall of ice near the walrus cages. It lodged almost six centimeters into the ice, impressive as she threw it sitting down. She got up and retrieved it, then threw it again. She hadn't thrown it in anger. This was practice. Her throw was powerful, accurate. Violet could almost see Mishka in the ice, so strong was Vibeke's intent.

She watched Vibs in silence, wondering if she had become a liability, if her desperation for revenge would cause problems. Violet wouldn't have said anything if it did. She decided that whatever missions came and went, whatever critical situations they got themselves into, it wouldn't be worth it to drag Vibeke down to earth. She couldn't try to change her like that, to tie her down. She could only fail and grow farther from her if she tried. And she wanted to stay close, even if she was close like a sister.

Vibeke, as she chipped the wall away with successive throws, wondered why Violet had asked "Like a sister?" She wasn't sure what could be closer, but then she'd never had a sister. Or family. Mishka was right about that. She didn't understand how Mishka saw her loyalties. She didn't really care. And she had read *Moby Dick* before she left on the mission. She knew even then what she was getting into. That's why the other book was *The Count of Monte Cristo*. Vibs had never bothered to finish its last quarter.

Mishka wasn't an animal, no force of nature. She was a perfectly killable, vengeable human being. Vibeke threw the knife again. It hit the wall so hard it shattered the ice, sending chunks sliding across the ravine floor. She wanted to go to sleep, not to rest but to meet with her team, with Alf and Balder, and begin planning. Violet wanted the same. Vibeke helped her up, and they walked to the barracks.

IN THE center of Minack Amphitheater stood Alf's tarantula avatar. To his left were the chess set of C team, to his right stood Balder, and behind him, in three obsidian avatars, his team. The theater seats were filled by teams H, S, T, and V. Violet had returned to using the old purple squid avatar she had as a child. Vibeke was present as a myopic green worm, Veikko as a ball of flame, and Varg as himself. Many observers from other teams floated around as transparent eyes just to watch.

They began the meeting with Balder's synopsis of the intel he had collected. Not only did his speech cover all Vibeke had learned, allowing her to stay silent, but he gave so detailed and exhaustive an account of Sasha's history, forces, and plans that Vibs couldn't imagine how he'd learned it all in only a few days. Even after all they knew, he dumped a sizable heap into their memories, along with maps and equipment diagrams.

Alf then began discussion of what was to be done. "At the least, I think we have an obligation to retrieve our weaponry and see that it does no more harm. Balder feels we should destroy Sasha's force and dismantle the military theocracy he's setting up across the continent. What say the rest of you?"

Hellhammer's avatar, a hellish hammer, enlarged to take the floor and spoke. "H team will capture the Mjölnir system."

"T team will steal a few of those juicy tanks," called Tahir.

"S team," announced Skadi's rock giant, "will destroy the carrier, unless Valhalla wants the thing."

"Nowhere to put it," said Alf. "Might as well blow it up."

Varg smiled. Nobody on V dared to speak before Vibeke. She floated up off her seat, enlarged her avatar, and said, "V team will assassinate the siblings in charge."

Nobody objected. She had her wish, and nobody outside her team even thought it a special one. That was just how Valhalla worked.

Balder spoke next. "My team and I will handle air support and transportation. Is R team present?"

A pistol blinked into the dreamscape. "Monitoring."

"I'd like you in proximity to the battle zone, two pogos."

"You got it."

The tarantula spoke next. "As you've taken all the fun duties, C team and I will be traveling to Africa to disassemble Sasha's regime. Has anyone anything else to say before we split up for tactical projections?"

A frog with a crown blinked in and spoke with Wart's voice. "New guy here. Um, are you really letting the most junior teams fight the fights while you work on diplomacy?"

The tarantula responded, "Certainly. This isn't advanced spycraft or anything so unevenly matched as Udachnaya, merely a battle. Diplomacy is the field that requires expertise. Wars have always been fought by children."

Wart didn't question it. Alf called for any last remarks. There were none. He said, "Very well. To your teams now. Let's refine this wild hunt."

Within seconds, every good name for a project was taken and posted. V team was left unaware that they were even supposed to name this one, so the few appropriate terms they could think of—Oskorei, Perchten, Herlathing, and Asgardsreien—were all taken. Having gained little creative will, V team called their part of the project Beta. They coordinated with all the other teams heavily, but focused most on cornering Sasha and Mishka onboard the carrier. The rest was routine murder.

Coordination took longer. V team ran their reasonably simple plans—go in, kill people, leave—by the others and got sound advice all around. S team suggested they do more for camouflage than let their suits turn white, so they arranged for Dr. Niide to tone their skin and hair white as well. Only the space around their eyes would be black, so as to reflect as little light into their eyes as possible. Though Veikko and Varg thought it made them look like corpses, Violet couldn't help but stare at Vibeke with her natural hair color reinstated. Varg caught her staring and necrophilia jokes ensued.

H team showed them how to pack extra explosives into their Thaco armor. The clips on their arms were good for small concussion bombs. The three triangular pegs on their backs could hold heavier thermite loads. Each had their microwaves, and they stuffed the other standard bits and pieces in the little squares across their chests. The inside of the toughest armor could hold even more, med kits and the like. All in all, they crammed into their armor twice as much as Eric designed them to hold.

T team suggested they devote extra practice to incursion jumping, as both Tasha and Toshiro had broken limbs on their last drop and had to sit out while the rest of their team fought. H team asked only that V stay out of their way. R team asked them to get tracking injection pellets, a matter of some dispute: It would make it easy for R to find them should they need to be withdrawn, but it would also make them easy to track should the enemy not jam their links. Every team elected not to have the pellets.

Then there was the matter of M team. Motoko and Mortiis were not invited, and they stewed about it terribly. Partly because they were still suspected by C team (and nobody else in the least), partly because they were not a complete team, and partly because there was nothing left to do after the initial duty allotments. They elected to handle tracking and monitoring. Balder's team usually did so, but they would be flying transports and battle pogos. C team didn't object, so they at least got to watch. Motoko reminded V team that Marduk was also a traitor to be dealt with, but Balder's intel suggested he had not been on the carrier when they departed. That left V team with one less goal and left everyone wondering just where Marduk was.

M team, in their monitoring duties, constantly followed the tracking nodes Balder had planted on the carrier. He had placed twelve around its bowels. Four had been found and destroyed, but the rest were working perfectly, and it was likely Sasha suspected that they were. So as planning neared completion on December 20, it was a bit of a surprise when they showed the carrier heading north toward Valhalla. The carrier was slow as snot dripping, and it wasn't much of a match for the ravine, should it make it so far. But the message was clear: If you don't hurry up and come for us, we will come for you. It was time to attack.

A brief debate ensued about what music to listen to on the way south. The votes were three for "Carmina Burana," twelve for "Ride of the Valkyries," eight for "Peer Gynt," two for "Pagan Prosperity," and one for "The Ballad of Roger Young," but as they had listened to Wagner's opus the last thirty-two times, Grieg won and the native

Norsk were happy. The teams headed for their pogos. H took a cargo pogo; V, T, and S took to the transport pogos, each piloted by one of Balder's team; and Balder hopped into the heaviest, most brutally armed battle pogo they had. It was almost a fair match for a panzercopter. Varg spotted him as they boarded.

"Balder!" he called, catching his attention. Just as Balder had told them before Udachnaya, Varg reciprocated, "Don't Fuck Shit Up!" Balder smiled, and the teams flew south.

VIOLET SAT in the transport section of the craft with her team. She felt a peculiar mixture of anticipation and camaraderie; she had never flown into battle with so many teams behind her. She had a sense that the day really belonged only to Vibeke, so Violet was but one of her supports. She found that position most comfortable. As for the battle to come, she felt on top of it. That feeling didn't fade at the sight of the carrier.

Sasha hadn't even made it out of the jungle when they arrived. As the troops flew in, the carrier turned and ran like a spooked wildebeest. Nobody mistook it for an escape attempt. It was a maneuver designed to give them time to launch their two remaining panzercopters, armored as at Udachnaya, along with an array of defense drones and heavy antiaircraft fire. The battle commenced. Balder began heavy fire and engaged one of the copters. Borknagar, piloting V team's transport, started firing with their pogo's light artillery to clear a path through the defense drones. H team's cargo pogo was the fattest target, so they were engaged by the other copter. Bathory quickly flew the T team transport under the jungle canopy to engage the tanks, seen dropping from the carrier into the trees.

As V team flew closer, they could see that the Mjölnir system was powered up on the carrier's beakhead. There were men around it, all in white armor, hunting for a target. Borknagar flew them in so close to the island that they dared not fire, but their deck was crawling with armored men. Borknagar linked to Balder one word, "Strafe."

Just then, the panzercopter that Balder had taken on burst into flames and dropped from the sky. He sped over toward the carrier and began strafing the deck. The battle pogo's dual GAU-80s started hurtling lead onto the men below, whose armor was nothing to the 40 mm rounds. Borknagar flew in close behind and took out a few more with the transport's punt gun. The carrier's artillery continued its assault. Borknagar skillfully ducked and dodged their microwave beams and rounds just long enough to dive at the deck. Violet expected to get butterflies so close to the jump, but they were strangely absent. She was hungry to get onboard and start the fight.

As soon as they came within five meters of the deck, Varg jumped, Vibeke half a second later, then Veikko, and finally Violet. She hit the air just as Varg hit the deck. He rolled past some bodies and pounced upward with sword in hand. Pokey unwrapped from around his torso and bisected an enemy who stood with his microwave aimed, sending half of him over the side of the deck. Vibeke and Veikko headed straight for the hatches to keep a path secure, throwing men out of the way with microwave tractor pulses. One unfortunate was thrown before the carrier's own artillery; pieces of him showered Violet as she landed and rolled. She stood to find the deck slick with blood. She too came up fighting, her white armor and hair speckled. She took stock of what had to be done. There were still men on deck. Veikko was readying thermite for the hatches. She and Vibeke took the offensive as Varg hopped into a forklift and firmly convinced its driver to get out.

Early link updates started coming in from the teams. Down below, T team was focusing on one tank at a time, their pogo unleashing an assault on the shields for one T at a time to drop in, displace the drivers, and target the next tank to be taken. In the sky, Balder was defending H team's cargo pogo from the last copter as S team aimed for the carrier artillery and drones. The sky was a chaotic mess. Veikko sent a short link that V was about to blast the hatches.

As soon as the charges were wired, Varg linked them to run from the hatch. Veikko was about to object when he saw why—Varg was driving the forklift full speed into the structure. They fled just as the lift plowed through, breaking off the hatch, the corner of the island, and a few panels of the bulkhead. Varg leapt onto the deck and the lift, with half the structure, flew over the gunwale to the forest below. Violet sent a link to ground teams. "Falling objects." That would be enough. Vibeke was already running full force into the exposed passageway, almost colliding with two armored men and a set of much thicker emergency hatches. Vibeke fought one of the men hand to hand. Violet zapped the other's joints. Once they were out of the way, Veikko found a use for his thermite charge and began melting through.

As soon as the edges of the hatches were molten, Violet set one of her own concussive charges, and the four cleared the immediate area. The charge went off, sending the hatch spinning into the passage behind it, dripping with molten metal. The hatch took out two armored men. Vibs and Veikko ran in to fight another three. Violet kept watch outside for anyone else coming in.

The deck was growing clear of men, and whoever was left was busy fighting off H team, which was coming in for a landing by the Mjölnir. The Mjölnir was beginning to fire, but nobody felt their uniform flex. None of the shots were connecting—good news as V team headed into the belly of the beast. Veikko sent a link update. "We're in." Not to be outdone, T team stated that they had caught their first tank.

As soon as the guards were dead, the passageway began to scramble. Blocks from the bulkheads began flying across to reshape the passages, turning them left, right, straight, up, down, and into dead ends. Violet was disoriented at first, intimidated at the mess they'd have to fight through. She and the others loaded Balder's maps. The true routes glowed as lines amid the frantic reassembly of the physical passageways. The disorientation ended just in time for Sasha's men to arrive and give resistance. V team dodged the flying bricks and zapped the occasional soldier within as they made their way toward the aft command deck.

Now they were in incursion mode. They covered each other and secured the shifting passages methodically. Unarmored guards attacked them to no avail. Lightly armored guards attacked them to no avail. As they penetrated deeper into the carrier, armored guards with grenades attacked them, also to no avail. Varg and Violet took the front and broke through everything thrown at them with fatal and efficient tactics, staining themselves with more and more blood to the point their camouflage was useful only for intimidation. Exactly why S team had suggested it.

Violet was growing concerned at the ease with which they were getting through. Albeit slow, their progress was without flaw or injury. They might have been meant to get in part way if there were a trap. She didn't have to link it to the others; they all knew. Balder's notes sprung into their vision from time to time to let them know where he had seen what as he snuck about. His little explanations were accurate about every detector trap, every guard station along the way, every internal defensive system and how it could be disabled. He really took the surprise out of life.

H sent out a link update. "Mjölnir retrieved, loading in progress." Other teams chimed in: B team reported both copters and fifteen drones down. S team was working on the carrier artillery. T team claimed two enemy tanks seized and one destroyed. Everyone on the outside was half done with their duties. V team reported that they were nearing the command center. Then a massive blast racked the ship. It shuddered and came to a stop, inertia sending all four Vs up against a bulkhead. A solid bulkhead—the blast had destroyed the scrambling system. It was a straight jog to the bridge.

Before them were four unarmored guards and two heavily armored hatches. To their surprise, the guards knelt and surrendered, placing their microwave rifles on the floor and backing away. V team let them go. Varg and Violet kept watch as Vibeke unloaded all her thermite onto the hatches, padded with some conc-foam so the blast wouldn't deafen them. Veikko kept watch to kill anything that came out at them. This was it, the last barrier before the siblings. Anticipation was at its highest in Violet's mind. No matter what the outcome of the next minutes, it would be significant; perhaps extremely good, perhaps extremely bad, but there was no chance of anything in between. Violet stood at full battle readiness, ready to be surprised by fighters or anything else. Vibeke set off the blast.

Before the smoke could clear, they fired off broad stunning beams and stormed the room. Varg ran in holding his Tikari high, and Vibs had her dagger ready. Veikko and Violet breached the command center, pointing microwaves into every corner. Nobody was inside. T team reported another tank captured. V reported nothing. The room was empty. They immediately suspected that this was the trap—that they were in a zone ready to explode or flood with gas. But nothing happened. They scanned the room with their eyes, then Tikari, then consulted Balder's notes. Balder linked to them directly, not to tell them what went wrong but to tell them he had just shot the last drones. Just about everyone was done but them.

Veikko linked to H to see if they had spotted Sasha or the command staff on deck. They had not. S team had seen no sign of Sasha or Mishka, just a great deal of carrier that S team was busily blowing up. V team left the room, weapons ready for more soldiers, but there were very few left alive. Violet began to wonder if Sasha and Mishka might have been among the armored soldiers they had passed or killed, a deception tactic. Vibeke was either thinking the same or listening to Violet's thoughts, because she sent a message out to T and S. "Check the faces of anyone masked." Vibeke didn't appear upset as she sent it. She was too focused on the job to feel any way about it; that was good: She was fighting from her mind and not her heart.

As they walked out of the bridge, Violet spotted an unarmed man in white, one Balder had seen while undercover and link-labeled for them as a member of the command crew. She grabbed him and held him against the bulkhead. The others looked at him and understood her intent once Balder's label loaded. Varg said in his deepest voice, "Where are they? Where are Sasha and Mishka?"

"Never!" the man shouted proudly. Veikko sprang his mantis Tikari directly onto the man's neck, where it crawled like a giant insect up toward his ear. The man was clearly unnerved by the thing and spoke again in a panic. "They're in cargo bay three, lowest deck, around the fuel tank with a Mark 17 Gatling array and several armored guards!"

The team looked to one another with slight surprise at how scared men could be of insects. Veikko's Tikari injected the man with a light sedative and hopped back into Veikko. The man passed out, and they followed Balder's map to the nearest lift. After checking it for traps and allowing some unarmed technicians to leave, they headed down into the belly of the beast. Stuck in the lift for a moment, Violet asked if she had heard correctly. "Did he say fuel tank?"

"Yes," replied Vibs. "Not everyone has a quarkamajig like Valhalla. It was in Balder's report."

"Yeah, didn't you look over what he loaded into your head?" chided Veikko.

"Did you, Veikko?" asked Varg.

"I almost thought about considering it," he admitted. S team linked that they had just destroyed the last cannons onboard. V team was now severely behind.

The lift display showed that they were approaching the base cargo bay, one massive doughnut-shaped room around the fuel tank. They refocused their microwaves to avoid penetrating the tank.

The instant the lift gates opened, Gatling fire came in. They were ready for it and had already ducked below the line of fire. Varg sent his centipede out and saw the lay of the land. Several guards in heavy armor, one Gatling array positioned just in front of the fuel tank, where they couldn't risk grenades. The centipede ran straight for them, below the sight of their masked eyes. Behind the array was Sasha, Mishka by his side—they had chosen the bay for their last stand. Vibeke linked the other teams. "Siblings sighted, base cargo deck."

"Backup?" asked Skadi.

"Bragging," responded Vibs. She was about to claim her prize. She nodded to Veikko, who took an ultralocalized heat grenade from his armor. He set it for a range of one meter and set it to go off no more than two meters from the Gatling array. He handed it to his Tikari and sent it in. The Tikari flew it out over the Gatling array. The armored men saw it and fired at it with all they had. Veikko displayed extraordinary evasive skills and dropped the grenade on target, fusing the Gatling barrels together and escaping without a single hit to his bug.

Armored men moved in on the lift. Varg lit a smoke cookie for cover, and V team moved out of it. They systematically attacked the leg joints of any armored men they encountered with microwaves, then Tikaried the neck joints and melted the enemy microwaves with their own. They moved quietly, employing not only the sound dampers on their boots and knees, but the techniques they'd learned months before, making themselves nearly invisible and moving past the guards with ease.

Violet found herself by Vibeke's side up against the disabled Gatling array, the enemy's last defense. Vibeke grasped her knife and

Violet her microwave. Violet stood first to cover Vibs as she moved in. But as she stood, she saw that Sasha and Mishka were gone, replaced by another six armored guards. They set to work fighting the group.

Varg and Veikko, approaching from the right, saw the siblings taking cover on the other side of the fuel tank, behind two massive crates. Varg linked it to Vibs as she fought. Veikko pursued them. As he rounded the corner, he saw what they were running for: another ten guards. These guards had the same armor but different arms. They had projectile miniguns and they opened fire, showering Veikko with hundreds of rounds. He ducked behind the crates and called for help.

Oddly enough, it was H team who responded to his call. Having taken the genuine, functional Mjölnir system onto their pogo, they left the thing turned on and resolved to help V team. In less than ten seconds, the entire side of the bay crunched under the Mjölnir's magnetic force. Most of the guards' armor did the same. What rounds were in the air jumped backward into the mass of metal with the weapons that fired them. V team's uniforms flexed painfully in such close proximity, Veikko's most of all. Then they were rocked by the shift in weight of the carrier as the hull gave way and the tight metal heap fell out over the side.

Vibeke and Violet ran over to the sunlit opening. The fuel tank was leaking slightly. Most of the crates had gone overboard. Standing between two huge crates that stuck to their places were Sasha and Mishka. They didn't run. Varg had a pretty good idea why, so he linked a hyperencrypted message to Veikko. The two sent their Tikaris along the floor toward the crates. Violet stood beside Vibeke with her microwave drawn to cover her. Then Vibeke did exactly what everyone knew she would.

Her team didn't expect her to run toward them out of rage. They expected it because it had been planned. They'd planned for her to run at the two because Sasha and Mishka would see it as the emotionally unstable member of the team moving out of position for revenge. Thus, they sprang their last trap early, and the team was ready for it. The giant crates broke open to reveal Udachnaya's stolen FKMA robots, so Varg and Veikko hacked into them through their Tiks on the floor and leveled the robotic guns at Sasha and Mishka. They didn't open fire and steal the kills. After all, it was Vibeke's birthday (in seven months).

Vibs charged with her team behind her. Sasha had a microwave, but Violet countered it with her own, firing a suppression beam as he shot at Vibs. Mishka launched her Tikari but Veikko's knocked it out of the way. Vibeke cornered her prey before the breach and attacked in flawless form, driving them toward the edge. Varg backed her up by engaging Sasha with his sword, keeping him at a disadvantage to allow Vibeke to fight his sister.

Mishka fought with the fury of hell. Vibeke, being quite scorned, fought with fury like nothing hell hath. Though Mishka was more adept at sparring, Vibeke had an attack she wasn't even thinking of. To Mishka, Vibs didn't have a Tikari, so she was caught off guard when she saw the dead knife coming at her. Vibeke thrust it toward her with a force that shredded the muscles within her arms and that strained every tendon and ligament and burned from every ounce of hate that had grown in Vibeke. The blade, beyond razor sharp, sliced into Mishka's eye as if it weren't there. The orbit of her skull gave way like shattered ice. The blade wasn't slowed at all as it left the side of her face and plunged into the back of her brother's neck, upward into his skull, cleaving his medulla oblongata in half. It lodged in Sasha with such force that he was thrown deceased off his feet, out the fissure in the carrier's hull into the trees below.

Mishka's scream was deafening. Vibeke stepped forward to silence the organ of its origin. Mishka was on the floor, crawling toward the rupture. Varg handed Vibs his own Tikari, which she raised high in the air. Suddenly, Mishka was engulfed in shadow. Vibeke was distracted from her by the absolute loss of sunlight from the hole. There was something gigantic outside, moving toward the carrier.

Violet tried to link out to Balder, but she was blocked. Something was causing a massive jamming force. Violet realized that was why they hadn't heard from anyone since H team had destroyed the hull, why they hadn't heard a warning about what was coming. The four Vs were all distracted by it. Vibeke herself didn't even see Mishka duck out through the hole and slide down one of the carrier's legs. It took them a moment to realize exactly what the thing was. First they made out the moving legs. Not the legs of their carrier, but of another just like it. Another giant white jungle carrier.

"Did Balder's intel miss something?" shouted Veikko. "How many of these things do they have?"

"No," said Varg. "It might not be Sasha's."

"Is it friendly?" asked Violet. She got a definitive answer when the second carrier opened every porthole on its side, revealed massive cannons, and opened fire on them. V team hit the fuel-covered deck as projectiles began annihilating the inner bulkheads. Panic tried to break into their minds, but all of them denied it access. Varg and Vibeke were already firing suppression beams over the fuel to keep it from igniting. Veikko was using his microwave to deflect shrapnel. Violet was looking around for anything that could give heavier cover when the cannons reached their position.

Her mind was racing, open to anything that popped into it to save them. She had no ideas. Veikko had no good ideas either, but being Veikko, that didn't stop him from joking that he did.

"Violet," he shouted, "you're closest—take out that carrier!"

Violet had been so intent on the new dilemma, and so ready for advice on the matter, that she took it as an order and ran for the hole in the hull. Veikko didn't even see her run until she was jumping from the breach. He suddenly figured out what was happening, and in surprise muttered, "She knew I was kidding, right?"

Violet did not know, nor did she hear him say it. She had already raised her microwave and leapt for the other carrier. Her team watched her go, thinking they would never see her again, questioning how she could be so foolish, so idiotic as to try—they couldn't even imagine what. Veikko cursed himself; he'd never imagined she would take him literally.

They were still between cannons, so Violet took no direct fire as she fell. She still felt a sense of dread as the thing drew closer. The sheer size of it was daunting, terrifying. She aimed her microwave at a point above the cannon portals and fired a full-strength tractoring wave. The force almost ripped her arms out, but she held tight, pulled her legs up and body tight toward the carrier, and swooped up toward the cannon bays. The gain was no comfort. She was alone against a giant.

She didn't have time to think when she rolled onto the deck. She was surrounded by six very surprised men in white uniforms. She reset her microwave for a wide stun beam a fraction of a second before the men pulled their sidearms, and fired. All but one fell. He was close enough to kick unconscious, so she did. She checked the area for anyone else. One man ran into the bay: Marduk.

She didn't spare him any thought beyond a confirmation that this was Sasha's carrier. Sasha's *second* carrier. He ran toward her at full force, just as Hrothgar Kray had ages before. Thus she knew how to deal with him: She took a step back, grabbed him as he ran toward her, and hurled him as hard as she could out the cannon bay, toward the other carrier. Maybe they saw him, maybe not. Maybe he lived, maybe not. She didn't care. She had to take out the carrier, any way she could. The expectation of survival diminished, and the expectation of success replaced it. The only way to go was inward.

She found herself running into another set of passageways, but thankfully not scrambled ones. Nobody was expecting her—an advantage. Balder's map reset on recognition that the new carrier had the same design. She tried to think while she was running, to take inventory of what she had to work with. The only explosive she had left was a single mild thermite charge, made to produce a lot of heat but little else. A man in one passageway spotted her. She shot him before he could realize what he saw. What could a thermite charge do?

It could ignite fuel. The carriers had fuel. They needed enough to fill panzercopters, tanks, and keep running themselves. She had seen the tank on the other carrier. It could leak. Liquid fuel. She was one deck over it. Even better. She changed course and ran toward a spot directly over the fuel tank. For an instant, she thought it unwise that Veikko had sent her in alone. The thought didn't have time to develop further. She was almost over the reservoir.

She slid down a ramp and made her way cautiously through the passage. Another solitary man saw her on the way. Another microwave beam took care of him. There was greater resistance at the leg-motion engine room, the room immediately over the fuel: guards with batons. They saw her as soon as she saw them. She toasted one, but the other man hit her with his baton. Searing pain exploded from the spot where it hit. The batons were doleos, nerve pain inductors. Pain was fine; it just made her feel like she was in training again. She zapped him.

The hatches opened by hand. There were two more men inside. Both surprised, both microwavable. The microwave going off in the engine room set off every alarm the carrier had. She felt the thing stop walking, saw the engine reverse direction. None of that concerned her. She set the thermite charge to burn down into the fuel tank. She set it for two minutes and used her microwave to weld it to the metal floor. Her microwave was beginning to overheat. She holstered it and broke off the detonator's interface. The bomb could no longer be disarmed by any known means. Time to leave.

As she ran from the room, she suddenly wished she had set it for ten minutes, owing to the ten men blocking her way back to the outside. And she was at ground zero. For the first time, she was truly afraid of a physical threat. Two minutes. Why had she set it for two damn minutes? Her microwave was still too hot to fire. She took a deep breath and surveyed the guards. They were all armed, but only with doleos. They were useless against her. Their only weapons were fear and pain, feeble weapons against Violet. As for numbers, it was ten to one. That wasn't intimidating; it was the same odds as her little fight in Achnacarry. She tried to think if there was anything strategically different. There was: this time she had a knife.

She ejected her Tikari into her hand, took the best stance she could, and ran at the crowd. The fools attacked one man at a time. She dug into the force like it was made of cobwebs. She cut off the first five arms that threatened her. The other fifteen began to strike her with the batons. It hurt like hell, and she couldn't have cared less. She plowed on through the mass, letting them strike her uselessly as she disarmed them left and right and dislegged those she could. She flipped over and under them in a balletic barrage, stabbing and killing whoever didn't get out of her way. She wasn't afraid anymore. They were. They saw only a whirlwind of death and dismemberment hurtling toward them, a wave of mutilation in affirmation of all they'd heard about the Hall of the Slain.

As she came near to the end of the ten-man force, she saw the rest of the passageway flood with another twenty. The sight hit her with a fragment of panic, a jab of concern that she couldn't possibly make it out in time. She wasn't going to live, but she wasn't going to stop. It's not like she had anything better to do in her last seconds. Still, she was already surfing over the first crowd with the difficulty of the sheer volume of the men, and this new batch would clog the passage further. Worse, they weren't armed with doleos; they had kukri knives. They didn't attack one at a time either. They all attacked her at once. She was utterly fucked.

If it were training, she might have hesitated to do the one thing she knew could give her a chance. She had never been able to give her Tikari so complex an order and just trust it to do its job. But this wasn't training. She was going to die and had exactly one way through. She raised the blade into the air, linked it to go berserk, and let go. The Tikari sprang from her hand so fast she couldn't see where it went. But she saw the first four men fall to pieces. The Tikari was orbiting her at a speed beyond sight, spinning and hacking its way through every man it could.

The mass was thinning, but not yet thin. Violet still had work to do. She had no knife in her hand, so she picked up the first kukri knife she saw on the ground as she cartwheeled past two shredded men and began to cut into the new heavy crowd. Soon a second kukri knife lay abandoned and doubled her armament. The Tikari anticipated her moves, spinning around her vertically, darting out to kill anyone who got too close to her. Again she flipped through motions as if in a dance, breaking, cutting, and beating her way through the thick pile. The bug killed eleven of them, she killed nine, and soon she ran out of men. She left the kukris in the last two and caught her own knife.

She clipped the bloody Tikari to her arm. The passage was clear. And it had taken only fifty seconds. She looked back for an instant on the passageway now piled with sixty severed limbs and a half-meter deep with blood. She too was painted red, unscathed and adorned in the innards of her enemies. She didn't dwell on it. She ran for the side of the carrier and found her entry point. The second carrier was stumbling backward toward Sasha's first. A jump would land her there if the carrier would stop for just a moment.

The thermite charge went off. In the moment that passed as the thermite gutted the engine room, the carrier crunched to a stop. Violet used the shift in inertia to jump nearly halfway to the hole she'd come from. She tractored herself to the oncoming gunwale of the original craft and swung fast to the breach in the hull, landing, rolling, and standing almost exactly where she had leapt from only minutes ago.

She stood before her team as the other carrier burst into flames and clusters of combustion behind her, twisting and breaking apart into a dead mass of burning metal wreckage. The main tank blew and a behemoth explosion erupted from its belly, shattering the deck completely. More explosions ripped across its skin as arms caches blew. She glanced back at the thing, crippled and crumpled in the trees. She turned back and saw Marduk, unconscious on the deck. She took quick stock of the situation. She was uninjured, and she was onboard a safe deck in the company of allies. Everyone was staring at her for some reason. They were looking at her as if she had just done something terrible, but she had done exactly what Veikko said. The last combustible fragment of the second carrier burst apart behind her. And her team still stared at her with open mouths. Just stared at her.

"What?" she asked. Nobody answered.

Chapter XIII: Valhalla

WHEN VIOLET figured out just why everyone was staring at her, she felt both rather stupid for having done it, and also so good for succeeding that her hands went numb. She was suddenly ecstatic to be the fool of the team because without that momentary lapse of judgment she wouldn't be where she was, before the astonished eyes of every team on the deck of the surviving carrier. Every Valkyrie present met her with cheers and applause, which she accepted with even less modesty than Varg might have.

Violet had been the center of attention before, but never for anything good. As T team gave a victory broadcast and the encryption on her link turned off, she got some fifty requests from back north to peek at her memory. She let them all in, where they could see all she had done and hear none of what she thought. Back on the deck of the captured carrier, Balder was ridiculed in good humor for having failed to pick up intel that Sasha did in fact have two carriers, hence his intent to steal a second Mjölnir generator.

"Second biggest mistake I made," he boasted. "The first was back in—does anyone care?"

"No," shouted seven Valkyries and twelve prisoners. Violet was vaguely curious but failed to ask when Vibeke caught her attention. She was coming up from one of the deck lifts. She looked happy but also preoccupied. Violet left her idolaters' company and ran over.

"Where have you been?"

"Seeing if Mishka was anywhere to be found. I think she must have escaped during the barrage."

Violet was suddenly very concerned. The day was a victory without question, but for Vibs, she knew that could all be for nothing. Vibeke caught Violet's expression and laughed. "Just means we have a chase to look forward to. Today's yours, Vi. Don't let some old hag get you down."

Vibeke meant it. Perhaps because she had just killed Mishka's brother, perhaps because Valhalla had four new tanks to play with, perhaps because Violet had totally just hacked through thirty guys to annihilate a giant jungle carrier—in like two friggin' minutes—Vibeke simply couldn't feel any regret for one fish slipping through the net, even if it was the catch of her lifetime.

T team confirmed that of the seven tanks, four were captured and two destroyed. One was missing. Let Mishka have it, they thought. Let her pack her dead kin into the back trunk. S team had utterly destroyed the remaining carrier's weaponry, so the prisoners were set free on its hull and left to gather their belongings for the long walk to wherever. H team gave them a few med kits and survival gear and lifted off for home. Balder took off to escort H with his battle pogo and to hide or dismantle the generator once home.

T team headed back north in their new tanks, and the remaining teams hopped into the transports. Violet took one last look at her day's work. A giant mass of twisted metal and flame, too many dead to count, an organization destroyed, and her suit so covered with blood that not a spot of white showed through. Surely the common world would have thought she was a monster for taking pleasure in the horrors she had wrought, for smiling so broadly at this atrocity she'd committed. But there was no regret, not in the least. *If I am a monster*, she thought, *I'm a really fucking great one*. After all, her mother had once suggested she get into demolitions.

Something had snapped in her head. She had changed from the day's events. She wasn't sure exactly what she was becoming, but she knew exactly what she was leaving behind. Somewhere buried under the rubble of that carrier was the shame and repression she had always felt for who she was. All that waited for her back in Valhalla were pride and strength, and most importantly—her friends.

The last pogos left the site and flew north at a leisurely pace. Alopex broadcast to its occupants a transmission to Balder from Alföðr. "Having persuaded twelve tribal leaders, three military dictators, six CEOs, and several scattered mobs across the continent to abandon

Sasha's reign, we're about to return to the north. We haven't annihilated Sasha's mark, but we did decimate it, and according to the laws of psychohistory, our enlightened tenth will bring an end to the other nine parts. C team sends its regards to V for the capture of Marduk, who they look forward to interrogating in the new brig."

A second voice chimed in, the only one that might have brought Violet's spirits down, "Cato here, this is Cato. Hi, Violet? Is Violet there?"

"Yes," she grumbled, ready to shoot the antenna if he said anything she disliked.

"I just reviewed and analyzed your trip to the second carrier. Did you embellish that memory at all? Any alterations?"

"No," she said sharply, taking aim at the ceiling link. Varg grinned, waiting for her to blast the thing.

"Well, it was a beaut, Vi. Made it look like a piece o' piss! You really bottled your blood's worth!"

Despite herself, she blushed and lowered her microwave. Vibs giggled. "Yeah, Vi, you're really bottling piss now."

Violet gave her a light slap on the butt. People stared. She didn't give a shit. She leaned back against the wall and smiled, then closed her eyes and replayed the memory of her phenomenally skilled rampage.

Vibeke stared at her, thinking about how Violet had said, "Like a sister?" back before the mission. Vibeke realized she really didn't love Violet like a sister. Her thoughts for Violet were at that moment most unsisterly. Varg and Veikko laughed and mimicked Violet's balletic assault. Spirits were very high and very relaxed. That's why nobody noticed Mishka's Tikari hiding on the roof of their pogo.

Varg insisted that they swing by SchweizCo for some of his favorite chocolates, so V's pogo would arrive a bit later than the others. Violet liked the idea because they would not only make a more dramatic entrance but they would do so bearing what Varg called, "Chocolate so creamy your teeth will squeal."

They landed to find T team using their microwaves to scrape the old white paint off their new tanks. Veikko saw that they had also stolen some spare tank legs and jogged over to join them. "I've got something in mind for Alf, for when he gets back." The rest of V team didn't dare guess what joke he had in store. Varg headed for the cafeteria to transmogrify the ten kilos of chocolate into some sort of diabetes-inducing confection for the ravine to share. He left Violet and Vibeke alone. A crowd would soon form around them, but nobody was close just yet. Violet was high enough on endorphins that she thought to ask Vibeke if she wanted to hide from the oncoming crowd. They might head to one of the industrial sonic showers and clean off the thickly caked blood that covered them.

Violet walked up close to Vibeke to suggest just that. Vibs was suddenly easy to talk to, approachable, seemingly robbed of the tension that had surrounded her when Violet wanted her most.

The sudden shift in Violet's personality also meant that Vibeke found the feelings reversed. Violet was suddenly a powerful figure, one that reminded her at that moment too much of someone else. "Oh!" said Vibeke, "I need to get Alf's books back to him! I should do that before he gets back."

Before Violet could say anything, Vibeke was off. Jogging away, looking back at Violet with a look so subtly flirtatious that it made Violet slightly delirious. She enjoyed that look enough that she didn't need to chase after her. She told herself that Vibs might be under the impression that Violet had something else to do.

Perhaps she did have something. She didn't feel like showering alone at that moment and she had some inkling that there was someone else to see while she was still covered in red. There was one man who might be beneficially unnerved by such a sight. She always felt better after talking to Wulfgar, and for the first time, she had an idea why. She wanted to see what might happen if she went to see him in a good mood to begin with. A good mood and soaked in blood. She walked to the brig and passed Marduk, unconscious in his cell. She found Wulfgar awake and unaffected by her red coating, only noticing her smile.

"And why are you so happy, my dear?"

"Oh, I just blew up a lot of shit today," she bragged.

"And now you've come to blow—"

She wasted no time on his innuendo. "I think I know why I keep coming back."

He sat up straight, smug and waiting to hurt her with a snide response. "Tell me."

"Well, I didn't want to admit it at first. I thought I was a nicer person than I really am. I wanted to think of myself as a woman who would never get her kicks from seeing a man hurt. But I'm not so mature. Not really. I'm just a girl who likes seeing her enemy in pain."

Wulfgar was not amused by this train of thought. "But I'm not the one in pain...," he began. A petty attempt to assert himself. It didn't work on her, not this time.

She cut him off. "You are in pain. All your talk, that's how you squirm. You fantasize and flirt because you're afraid to let me see you broken. And you are so broken. You have no more upper hand. You have nothing. And maybe it's the childish thug in me, maybe I'm a sadist or a bully, but you know, I really like watching you squirm. If you were dead, I'd have taken no pleasure from it, but now I see you, head of the most feared gang, killer of the innocent, king of the bastards, now beaten down and sobbing in his cell. I've done so much worse than kill you. I've made you pathetic. And for a hundred years you'll live in here, pathetic. My taunts will be the closest to living you get. And when you die, it will be as an old man gone insane and weak. And call me a bad little girl for loving it, but damn, Wulfgar... I love it." She paused and leaned in closer. "Come on, call me a bad little girl."

He said nothing. He had lost his kind façade. He was angry, hurt, and he knew it was showing. And unlike the face he'd put on as he tortured her, his expression held no animalistic pleasure nor sadism anymore. He looked old and sad. Just a bitter, defeated old man. That's not to suggest she pitied him. Violet knew she was right about everything she had just said. She was the sadist, and he was in pain. She was in heaven, and he was in hell. She had won and he had lost. And she felt as she did when she'd returned from the second carrier, so good it was obscene, close to erotic bliss. And she had sucked it complctely out of the man before her. She was going off the deep end that day. She knew she wasn't her old self. She had been reborn as a warrior with a blade, and finally she felt truly victorious over Wulfgar.

She walked out of the brig with a bounce in her step as he raked his fingernails against the back of his neck.

Violet was hungry, so she ran to the industrial-sized shower and let it deblood her suit and skin. She found Vibeke again, joining Varg and Balder as they drank great amounts of beer. They had turned off their absorption implants and were acting very strangely as a result. Vibs handed her a slice of something brown and unhealthy, which tasted as sweet and piquant as Violet felt.

"Were you talking to Wulfgar again?" Vibs asked. Those around her turned their heads, surprised at the notion.

"Yeah," Violet answered, then explained, "I talk to him from time to time." She grabbed one of the pitchers from the table and drank. She was quickly reminded that she hated beer, the bubbly sting of it, the doughy taste as well. She set the pitcher down and reached for more chocolate.

"Why?" spat Varg from behind his own pitcher. Veikko was also eager to hear.

Violet thought for a second of how best to put it. She took a bite of flavorful goo and savored it, then said, "Cuz it's better than chocolate, and half as fattening."

TEN DAYS later it was the year 2231, and the polar night was at its deepest. Valhalla was at rest. No major projects were starting up. No urgent duties were called out over the loudspeakers. The biggest change in the whole ravine was a new bench in the communications room. It was like hibernation after the Congo affair, a time of rest and relaxation. The real fires in the lounges never felt warmer. On January 3, Violet tried to dwell on the fact that her family had died one year before. She found she couldn't dwell on it at all, firstly because 365 days seemed like a lifetime ago, secondly because her family, her real family, was not dead at all. They were alive in the bunks where she slept, alive around the ravine in the gym and cafeteria, all around her. Those who were dead, she felt, were as avenged as people can be. To some extent, she thought the rest of her life would be anticlimactic, because no mission, however important, could compare to what she had done in her first year.

Veikko was putting the finishing touches on the tank Balder had stolen. With four spare legs, Veikko had led Wart and Weather in adapting the tank to run on all eight, a gift of sorts for Alf. His new personal transport was now the fastest land vehicle in Valhalla, and if not for their shuttle it would be the fastest of all, able to outrun pogos across land and to travel at exceptional speed over the most rugged, terrain, even up cliffs and under water. Alf was very happy with his new steed and started riding the thing all around the ravine where he might once have walked. Veikko also supervised its adaptation to YGDR S/L quark power, giving it a fuel advantage over the other tanks, namely that it no longer needed fuel.

Varg continued his sexual odyssey through the female half of the base, as well as Vadsø and the rest of northern Norge. While Veikko was content as the mother of Alf's new tank, Varg also spent time with H team and Valfar, learning the technological secrets he had to offer and even going so far as to challenge Valfar's simple theories of strong nuclear force in favor of an encompassing particle that he dubbed the "scroton." Violet no longer minded being left out of the technological loop. She came to regard herself as the brute force of V team, the brawn to complement the others' brains.

As for Vibeke, she had plans forming within plans. She intended to return to the hot Congo jungle and find either an ant-cleaned skeleton or a clue. The project might have earned a plain Greek name, but Greek lacked a C, and V team had resolved to be more creative. They weren't really all that creative, so the project had yet to be named. That and other delaying factors kept them all at home, and home was comfortable enough that they didn't mind. Vibeke continued her plans despite all delays by heading to see Marduk in the brig, hoping he might have ideas about where Mishka would go after losing everything.

When Vibs entered the brig, she heard Marduk speaking. Wulfgar was asleep. He was talking to something in the corner of his cell. Vibs sent out an alert signal to Alopex and stepped up to demand that Marduk tell her who he was talking to. She stepped forward and saw, for just an instant, a recognizable razor-blade butterfly. The butterfly saw and recognized her, then executed its last standing order to detonate like a mine in her proximity. The synapses grown for Tikari were ever so slightly slower than those in humans, so Vibs had just enough time to turn her head before the blast hit. Fire broke through the brig ceiling and echoed loudly through the ravine.

Violet heard it from beside Alf's tank, where Veikko was showing her his additions. Alf started up the machine and extended its legs to give him a higher view. From there he could see the brig collapsed and expelling smoke. He lowered himself and said to Violet. "You asked why I didn't want a brig?" He rode off toward the ruin. Violet and Veikko ran behind him. Varg was already on the scene, holding Vibeke.

She was alive but half of her skin was burned off. Varg ran her to the med bay. Veikko followed, pushing away the crowd that was forming, their microwaves drawn to suffocate the fires. As soon as the flames were suppressed, Violet ran into the mess. She recognized Marduk's remains. He had taken most of the blast and was unsalvageable. But he was not in poor enough shape to have been the source of the explosion. Marrow bombs looked different. Svetlana recognized the pattern. It was a Tikari blast. Everyone around deduced instantly whose it must have been. But that wasn't what Violet was worried about. She prodded around the rubble of Wulfgar's cell. There were no remains. There was no prisoner. She doubled the alert sent out across the populace.

Launching bays sealed themselves, air ducts too. Alföðr rode past the nearby structures cursing the day he'd allowed a brig in his hall. Balder linked out to all the teams to assemble hunting parties. V team was listed on Alopex as a three-person team as soon as Vibs was injured, so the only job the system would list them for was walrus detail. Violet linked to Varg, who told her Vibeke was okay. The med team was going to use her brief unconsciousness to give her a new Tikari they had assembled. Vibs wasn't going to dispute it when she woke up. She would have work for it to do.

There was no clear sign of Wulfgar, nothing to suggest where he had gone. He couldn't have escaped. The HMDLR detectors around the top of the ravine would have spotted him. He was still there, somewhere. Balder's hunting parties linked to each other as they systematically checked around the remains of the brig in a growing perimeter. Violet had to do something. She couldn't just wait as her nemesis escaped. She looked to Veikko, but he was also at a loss for what to do. She linked to Varg, "How is she?"

"She looks like a Gotham DA, but she's fine. They're about to wake her."

Violet felt substantial relief and was again surprised at Dr. Niide's speed. Varg continued, "Two minutes medical, one minute Tikari activation. We'll be there soon. Anything from the hunt?"

"We're not on the hunt. Balder wants full teams for it."

"Violet, have any of us ever waited for an invitation?"

A damn obvious point. They weren't on Balder's controlled task force. They wouldn't want to disrupt it by trying to cover their territory, but there were other things to be done. Violet and Veikko came to the same conclusion at the same time: If the hunt was taken care of, someone had to be ready to gut the catch. They headed for the special arsenal to prepare something nastier than microwaves. It was past the search perimeter, so they wouldn't bother the hunters. As they ran, the wide variety of killing devices ran through her head.

"Gatlings?" Veikko suggested.

"Flame throwers," she replied.

"Drill-shot!"

"Flesh-eating bacteria injectors?"

"Too slow. Now, the grinding needle disks...."

"Calcium desiccation rays...." They turned off the main walk. The arsenal was only meters away.

"Not painful enough. Where do we keep the deep-organ-spaz razors?"

"SA9, other end of the pit." They came to the nearest special arsenal. Violet grinned at Veikko, then spoke aloud. "But this one has the chainsaw launchers."

He nodded back and reached to open the door. The arsenals had all locked when the alert went out, so they had to perform the intricate ceremony of unlocking the thing. As Veikko linked down the security measures, he found measures in place that shouldn't have been started: The arsenal was locked from inside. Violet linked to Balder's teams.

She and Veikko were knocked off their feet when the door burst outward. Violet caught her breath and sent her Tikari into the air. As Veikko shook off the concussion, she linked fully in to her Tikari and flew around the other side of the arsenal. She flipped through its available vision settings until she could see through the smoke. There was one body on the ground. Not Wulfgar's. Nergal. A civilian in the wrong place at the wrong time. She could never have left the team after Jylland. Civilians were no more than victims in waiting. She was a predator. She flew on to find her prey. She felt heat rising in her chest.

Veikko headed into the arsenal to collect the weapons they'd come for. Wulfgar couldn't have carried them all. Violet let her Tikari search on AI and returned to her body. Veikko came out of the arsenal without any weapons. "He blew up the launchers. Blew out the arsenal alongside the ravine wall. He'll be heading up and out."

Violet sent her Tikari to look along the spiral catwalk. She linked to Varg, "ETA?"

"On my way, fifty seconds."

"Forty-five for me," linked Vibs. "My new… Tikari… is exploring the catwalks."

Vibeke had run from med bay before they could even log her recovered. There was a tricky tone to her words, angry that they'd made a new bug against her wishes as well as thankful that they'd done it. For the instant she let herself consider it, Violet thought she understood. But there was no more time to think. There were two Tiks looking for Wulfgar. Alopex listed Balder's men as securing the ravine floor. Violet was about to link and ask why they weren't on the walls where he was likelier to be, but even she could figure that one out. The walls were best searched by a small contingent, only one team. Balder knew V team was back. He was letting Violet catch her man.

A brief link darted between the Vs, only fragments of thoughts. Veikko would take a lift to the top level, then head downward. Varg and Vibeke would start upward from the base of the spiral. Violet would follow her Tikari straight up the wall—hard work but likeliest to meet Wulfgar first. She pulled out her microwave and began pulling herself up the steepest parts of the wall.

Veikko linked to them, "On my way up, lift seven."

A rocket blast hit lift seven, destroying it completely.

"Did I say seven? Six. Sorry, lift six, on my way."

His second link was on high encryption. Was Wulfgar listening somehow? They looked up and tracked the rocket-propelled grenade's vapor trail back to Wulfgar, only one level ahead of Varg and Vibeke. They kept running. Violet sent her Tikari ahead across the ravine. She could see him better as it approached, still heading upward. But they knew the lay of the land better than he did. It was all one spiral, so at the first junction, Vibs and Varg climbed up to the next level. They would be only meters behind him.

From her Tikari, Violet could see him clearly, still running. The Tikari kept an eye on him as Violet fired upward to the catwalk above his level. She tractored up, painfully fast and a long distance, landing fifty meters ahead of where Wulfgar was heading. She could see him, running around the curve of the wall, right for her. She could see Varg and Vibeke, still half-burnt, coming up behind him. Now she needed her Tikari as a knife. She called it back, and it rocketed across the ravine to her hand.

She hid in an alcove where Wulfgar wouldn't see her waiting to spring. The anticipation was like fire in her veins, circulating through her. It was devoid of fear or nervous chill. It was pure heat, pleasure of the cruelest sort. She breathed calmly, waiting silently, counting, and calculating his speed until he would run past. She could feel him coming, smell him in the wind. And at the perfect moment, mind burning, she sprang to find nothing. Nothing but some of his weapons lying on the ground. The heat within her didn't subside.

Varg linked to her to tell her where he was. "He had a microwave rifle, tractored himself straight up. He's in the air."

Violet bit her lip and linked to Balder, "On the walls. Take the shot!"

Balder's reply shocked her. "Capture Ops are over. We've got link activity from him. He heard one of yours, and he's sending his own. Let him go."

Violet took a second to try to comprehend. It wasn't long enough to comprehend, so she requested an explanation. "What the fuck!"

"He's calling help, Violet. Wouldn't you like to see who comes?" She didn't. She really, really didn't. She wanted to kill. Veikko ran up behind her and spoke, out of breath.

"I heard. Do we stop?"

Violet only glanced back. It must have been an angry glance, given Veikko's startled recoil. She caught a link from Vibs.

"Well, if he's calling someone, let's go meet them."

Violet smiled. Veikko nodded to her. If Wulfgar could make the ascent, so could they. Varg and Vibeke were in. All four found load-bearing beams on the top level and fired. They shot up slowly to the highest level of the catwalk.

Wulfgar opened fire with wide stunning beams as soon as they were up. The beam was so wide it was weak and glanced off their armor. As soon as they were on solid metal, they opened fire and forced Wulfgar to use his last grenade to break open a door, storage room 1. *Oh shit,* thought Violet. She heard Varg link, "Alf! Did the alarm seal off our walrus trap?"

"Positive," Alf responded on high encryption, "but it reads as jammed. You might consider letting him go, V. We're monitoring his links. We'll find him *and* whoever he's speaking to in time.... And no, I don't really expect you to stop. But do be careful."

Wulfgar had sent a link—how could he with his antenna broken? They'd figure it out later. With the trap door closed, Wulfgar was cornered in that room. He probably wouldn't even guess that a cave leading out was hidden just over his head. They had him. V team gathered at the door. Violet could see Vibeke's face, burnt but sectioned and patched by the medical team. She could see into her cheek where they hadn't had time to grow new skin. But despite it, she could see that Vibs was grinning with anticipation. They were about to move in.

Violet went in first, microwave drawn to repel anything Wulfgar might fire, ready to fire herself if she saw him. Varg followed with his Tikari drawn as a sword. Then Veikko and Vibeke entered. Their own Tikaris set to detect motion. And they did detect it. Five meters. Four meters. Three meters as they walked in. They saw nothing on the floor but crates. Violet lunged around each to find what lay behind it, but there was nothing. Veikko pointed upward.

The motion was coming from the walrus trap itself. The ceiling panel was moving, jammed open. That made their directive clear. Violet linked to Alf to open the trap, then kept a suppression beam on the area. The panel fell open, offering a ramp up into the cave. Varg was closest so he walked up first, sword at the ready, Violet and Vibeke by his sides with microwaves set to deflect. Veikko's Tikari detected motion, coming toward Varg. Varg held out a hand—he could see something. Violet held her breath. Varg took a wide stance on the floor. Veikko's Tikari linked that the motion was inching closer. Violet tried to peer into the cave. Varg linked on high crypto, "Wait, I think I see him…. He's coming!" Varg punched into the darkness with his bare hand, hitting meat. Violet ran up to see.

Varg had knocked Umberto out cold.

"Varg!" Violet whispered. Varg shrugged his silly shrug and backed off. Alopex linked in to their heads, "Veikko, Violet, Varg, Sector 1F. Walrus detail."

Umberto groaned a half-conscious groan and rolled off the side of the panel, crushing one of the old crates. Then Violet heard something, a human something from below. If Umberto was obstructing the trap, Wulfgar was still in the room. And she had heard him. Somewhere. She gave a hand signal to the team, who were back on high alert. Varg and Veikko had the door covered. Wulfgar couldn't have gone out. She heard him again: a faint moan.

He was close, but something was muffling his voice. But why was he groaning? Violet didn't figure it out until Vibeke pointed to the crate next to the trap door—a crate smashed under the unconscious behemoth. Then it hit Violet with a degree of disgust. She held her microwave at the crate's remains as Varg and Veikko hopped onto the trapdoor to tractor Umberto off of the crate. She held her weapon on target as the great heap rolled and revealed the flattened mess underneath. Violet just stared at Wulfgar's remains, not knowing what to make of it all.

When Death had told her she might not be the one to kill her worst enemy, she really didn't expect Umberto would be the one. She was struck by the horrid anticlimax to their hunt, their rapid ascent, their skilled chase of a desperate man. And here it ended, with Wulfgar dead, crushed to death by three tons of fat. His last groans had been postmortem, mere gas escaping as the blubber pressed his ribs to a pancake.

Violet sat down by his side, speechless. She looked at his ear, still intact on his fairly intact head. The link under it was broken. She poked at the broken head with her foot and spotted the second link antenna, an ugly thorn sticking out from the back of his neck, now broken as well. It was her mistake not to have given him a thorough check when they caught him. But then, like Veikko said, training lasts until you're dead. She wouldn't forget it the next time. In any case he was dead now, smashed by a damn walrus.

No sooner had she accepted the sad facts of her enemy's death than Umberto came to and flopped his way to a corner near the door, glancing a look of betrayal at Varg, who in turn mumbled a useless apology to the monster. Umberto headed out to the ravine as V team began thinking up what to do with the man's flat corpse. They didn't have to think long because someone else had plans for it. Alf linked in, "Incoming! Two black pogos landing on your position!"

Violet jumped up before she fully registered what he meant. All four of the team fell into position around the walrus trap. Alf linked again, "Six men, in the cave. Repeat, incoming!"

Varg saw one of the first and fired. His wide stun beam did nothing. The men had armor. Not orange armor but black powered armor. They didn't look like any of the Orange Gang men they had seen before. This was a force they hadn't encountered, a part of the gang Wulfgar had kept secret—one of those loose ends they had kept Wulfgar alive to account for.

The men had massive wraparound microwave rifles hooked onto their armor. Varg hit the deck. Vibs and Veikko took cover. Violet, too, registered the threat and ran behind a crate. The intruders let loose with beams so powerful they set fire to the air, causing a backdraft when the door swung open again. Vibs leapt out first, knowing that such huge microwaves had to recharge. She aimed carefully and burned through the unarmored joints of one man's outfit. The other Vs fell into position and began to fire with less success.

The armored men were picking up Wulfgar's floppy corpse, scanning his head. Violet realized it was intact, the skull broken but not smashed. They could still fix him. She ran forward and sprang her Tikari, rocketing it into their microwaves to disable them. The others followed in kind and destroyed the heavy weapons before they could be used again. That sent the black guards into retreat, but they had made their objective—they had Wulfgar's body. Violet ran forward and grabbed her Tikari from the air. She wasn't going to give the corpse up.

She stabbed through Wulfgar's shin, trying to hook into the bone and get a strong hold. The men pulled with their machine-assisted armor and his damaged leg fell apart, her Tikari ripping through his shin as if peeling a zucchini. Vibs and Varg joined in the gruesome game of tug-of-Wulfgar, but whatever they grabbed was crushed and weak. They both got hold of his feet, and both sets of tarsals pulled free of his joints with a sickening sound. Violet leapt forward to grab at his head, the least crushed part of him.

She grabbed firmly onto his jaw. The team covered her with microwaves. She had a strong grip; they wouldn't get his head. No head, no brain, no resuscitation. She had him. Until one of the men took out a knife, a plain old blade, and began cutting through his cheeks. They made a disgusting mess of his face, but the bone gave way, and Violet fell back with the jaw in her hand. The intruders got the rest of his body, and they had the part with his brain, the only part that mattered. Veikko and Vibeke ran after them. Varg helped her up, and then she ran too, angry as hell that they'd gotten their target, that she was losing Wulfgar.

They climbed up through the cave, firing when they got a shot, flying through the hole in the rock to the outside with speed that should have caught up, but the enemy pogos had been right on top of them. The men were inside, safe with Wulfgar's remains. The pogos shot up into the sky, into a strange green glow that writhed around Kvitøya. Violet slipped down on the rock and caught her breath. She had nothing that could tractor them back or shoot them down. Valhalla's defenses were all grounded and would take too long to go airborne and active. Not that Alf even wanted to send them. He would be content to track them as they left. But tracking failed.

"We've lost them. They left through the electrical disturbance. A hazard of our location, I'm afraid. Sometimes it's to our advantage, sometimes to theirs. Don't worry, Violet, you'll find him again."

The last four words struck Violet in a way she hadn't expected. All the anger and fury that had grown in her on the hunt were extinguished, not in a bad way but as a true relief. She suddenly understood why Vibs wasn't screaming at the loss of Mishka and understood what was to come. Wulfgar was gone, and he would live again. He was out there, but that was why Violet was here, at Valhalla. As long as she lived, Wulfgar would never be safe. She could hunt him again, feel that same fury, and someday, end him forever.

There was nothing to be done for it now. Valhalla was there to find Wulfgar and Mishka, however long it took. They had losses and gains, and that's how it was. That was their work. Violet and her team sat down to catch their breath on the rock and snow. Varg thought about the annoyance of cleaning up Wulfgar's mess. Veikko thought of where first to track Wulfgar down. Vibeke thought of Mishka, another one still on the loose.

Violet looked up at the electrical disturbance that had hid the pogos in their escape. It wasn't a field made by Wulfgar's men. It wasn't a Valhalla defense. It was just a glowing green wave hovering over them. Her tactical eye gave way, and she remembered what natural phenomena lived in the northern skies. As a kid she'd wanted to see the aurora someday, and there it was, bathing them in light. It was pretty, she thought, but nothing special. She had seen far more amazing things in the last year. She was sure to see more.

ARI BACH's art can be found online at http://aribach.deviantart.com/.

Ari also runs a webcomic at http://www.twistedjenius.com/Snail-Factory/ and has a Tarot deck at http://surrealist.tarotsmith.net/.

But Ari is probably best known for the humor blog "Facts-I-Just-Made-Up" at http://facts-i-just-made-up.tumblr.com/.

Also from HARMONY INK PRESS

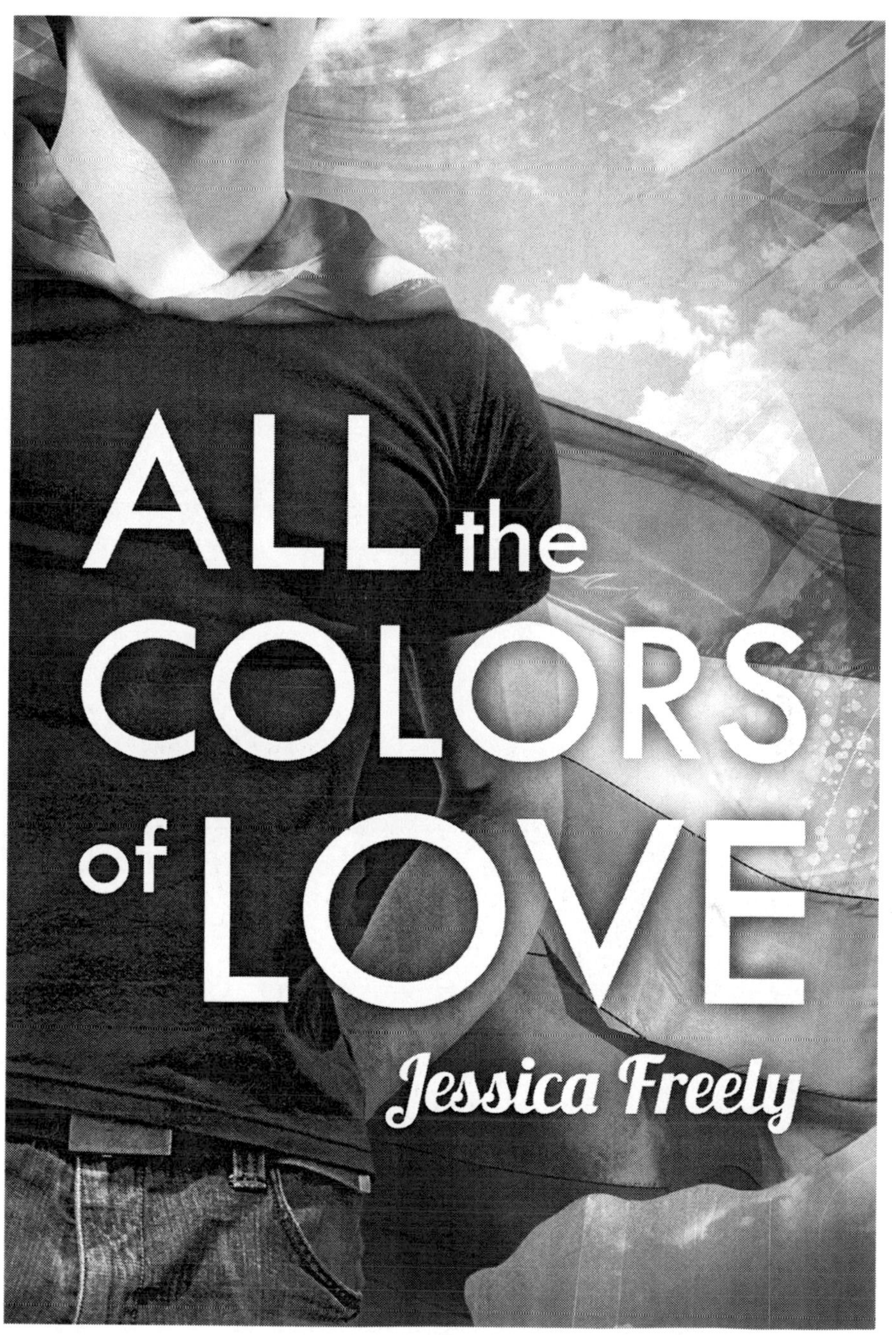

http://www.harmonyinkpress.com

Harmony Ink

CPSIA information can be obtained at www.ICGtesting.com
Printed in the USA
BVOW05s1652180515

400671BV00011B/55/P